Katharine McMahon is the author of six novels, including the Richard & Judy Book Club selected *The Rose of Sebastopol*. She lives with her family in Hertfordshire. Visit her website at www.katharinemcmahon.com

*By Katharine McMahon*

The Rose of Sebastopol
The Alchemist's Daughter
A Way Through the Woods
Footsteps
Confinement
After Mary

# FOOTSTEPS

## KATHARINE MCMAHON

PHOENIX

A PHOENIX PAPERBACK

First published in Great Britain in 1997
by Flamingo
This paperback edition published in 2009
by Phoenix,
an imprint of Orion Books Ltd,
Orion House, 5 Upper St Martin's Lane,
London WC2H 9EA

An Hachette UK company

Typeset by Input Data Services Ltd, Bridgwater, Somerset

Printed in Great Britain by
Clays Ltd, St Ives plc

The Orion Publishing Group's policy is to use papers
that are natural, renewable and recyclable products and
made from wood grown in sustainable forests. The logging
and manufacturing processes are expected to conform to
the environmental regulations of the country of origin.

www.orionbooks.co.uk

My thanks to Charonne Boulton,
Elizabeth McMahon and Lyn Trodd
for their help, and especially
Mark Lucas for his unfailingly
excellent advice.

# THE MAIN CHARACTERS

---

## PAST

---

*In The Rush House, Westwich*

**Ruth Styles**
Alan and Julia Styles, *Ruth's parents*
Harry Styles, *Ruth's brother*
Mr and Mrs Millerchip, *handyman and housekeeper*

*At Overstrands, Westwich*

Robert and Esther Mayrick, *parents of:*
Simon, Mark, Giles and **Clara Mayrick** (see following page)

*In Westwich*

Maud Waterford, *Julia Styles' friend*
Mrs Spendmore, *shopkeeper*

*Also:*

Hubert Donaldson, *photographer*
Alec McGrew, *Harry Styles' friend*
Miss Lily, *Ruth's companion and governess*
Margaret Shaw, *Julia Styles' mother; who walked into the sea*
Dr. Philip Shaw, *Margaret's husband*

## PRESENT

**Helena Mayrick**

Michael Mayrick, *Helena's husband, grandson to Simon Mayrick (see previous page)*

Nina Mayrick, *Helena and Michael's daughter*

Joanna and Robin, *Helena's parents*

Caroline Mayrick, *Michael's mother*

Elizabeth, *Michael's sister*

James Mayrick, *Michael's uncle*

**Clara Mayrick,** *Michael's great-aunt (see previous page)*

Myra Finny, *Mayrick family friend, housekeeper at Overstrands*

Nick Broadbent, *a photographer*

Victoria, *Helena's friend*

# Chapter One

I

On the morning of that day Helena received a letter from a stranger.

> *Flat 3, 27 Greville Rd,*
> *Putney SW15*
> *25th March 1992*

*Dear Helena Mayrick,*

> *I am writing to you because you are a researcher and the granddaughter of Hubert Donaldson, the photographer.*
> *My interest in Donaldson is twofold. In the first place I am a photographer myself and have always been a great admirer of his work. Secondly, I have been commissioned to compile a retrospective of his life and photographs, and thought you might like to collaborate, or at least advise on the project.*
> *If you are at all interested, perhaps you would get in touch.*
> *Yours sincerely,*
> *Nick Broadbent*

Helena read the letter twice and then put it aside, taken aback by so abrupt and unexpected an approach. You can have no idea, Nick Broadbent, she thought, of the distress such an undertaking will cause my family.

She was aware that the mention of Donaldson's name had already aroused in her a familiar sense of oppression.

In the afternoon she and Nina walked into Shrewsbury to go swimming. Afterwards Helena was to wonder that she had felt no pang or jolt at the moment of Michael's accident. Probably it happened while they were crammed into one of the cold-floored changing cubicles. Nina's voice was high-pitched in the echoing, watery warmth of the pool. On the way home the dying sun cast long shadows among the trees in the Quarry Park. There were rowers out on the river, their noses and elbows red with exertion. Nina raced along beside them, and then stood on the bridge, panting, and peered down into the slick, chilly water.

They ate supper in the kitchen where late sunlight lit up Nina's gallery of paintings on the larder door. Every so often Nina paused between mouthfuls to ask: 'Is it nearly time for Daddy to ring now?'

Helena looked at her daughter's tangled brown hair and anxious face with exasperation. 'I've told you, Nina, he said he might not phone tonight as he's coming home tomorrow.'

'What will he be doing now?'

'He'll be having his supper, probably.'

'I expect he'll be tired after climbing the mountain.'

'You know Daddy, he never gets tired. But with any luck all the children who are with him will be worn out. Some of them have never done any climbing, you see, and I expect Daddy will make them go right to the very top, however much they complain.'

After coaxing the child into bed, Helena at last returned to the letter which had been an unfocused but nagging intrusion into her activities all day.

Sighing, she unfolded the single page.

At that moment the doorbell rang.

From her place at the kitchen table, she could see along the narrow hall to the glass-paned front door. Two heads, one at shoulder height to the other, were dimly outlined. A little troubled, Helena tiptoed into the dark sitting room which overlooked the street and the porch. The taller figure was standing nearest the bay window. At once she noticed that he was in uniform.

As she walked to the door, Helena had time to register that she was moving from one phase of her life and into the next. Fear, like a cold sword, cut through her.

The woman had bleached hair and eyes harshly outlined by thick pencil. She smelt of cigarettes and crowded rooms. Helena heard her voice as if from the end of a long tunnel, and noted an attempt at softness. They were in the familiar kitchen again, at the table where the letter lay buckled on its fold-line.

The policewoman had hold of Helena's hand; her own was small and blunt with carefully manicured nails. Her words were thin, half-heard echoes in Helena's consciousness. 'He died instantly. No pain. So brave. A boy tumbled down a steep escarpment. Your husband went after him. Saved the boy's life. But then fell himself. A long way. Everyone else is all right. Have you someone we could telephone?'

Behind them the man moved about with the kettle and cups. A suffocating blanket seemed to press on Helena's lips and nose. Nauseous, she fixed her gaze on the woman's small mouth.

Wave after wave of black, comfortless silence blotted out the pictures on the cupboard door opposite, the white gleam of the letter and the empty doorway leading to the dark hall.

2

On the fourth night after Michael's accident Helena at last noticed Nina's pain. At tea that evening she saw the child's white face with a sprinkling of freckles frighteningly prominent on her small nose. Behind her glasses Nina's eyes were bleak with misery. Not even her grandmother could persuade her to eat. She merely turned her face into her grandfather's sweater, her unbrushed hair a tousled mop against his chest.

'Come on, Nina, and give me a hug,' Helena said, and they all looked at her with their habitual expressions of concerned alarm. But the little girl climbed onto her lap and Helena clasped the bony body and buried her nose in her daughter's hair, which smelt of plasticine.

Across the table Helena's mother Joanna coughed and then stood to clear the table.

'You'll be worn out, Mum,' Helena said.

'No, no. Good heavens, I can't do much but I can do this.' Joanna tied on her blue and turquoise floral apron – brought from home in her suitcase on the night of Michael's death – with the deft movements that were so typical of her.

'Then I'll put Nina to bed.'

'Let Dad do that.'

'I'm all right. What story shall we have, Nina?'

They did not waver from the familiar bed-time ritual. Undressed, Nina trotted along to the laundry basket in her parents' room with her discarded underwear. Then she and Helena went into the bathroom for a wash of face and hands and a clean of teeth. Back in the bedroom Nina chose *The Twelve Dancing Princesses* and both climbed beneath the duvet with the book, Nina tucked under Helena's arm, thumb in. For a while they were lulled into a false sense of normality. Michael was often out at parents' evenings or nights at the pub to plan the next expedition. Later he would be back with a clink of his key in the lock and a wolf whistle at the bottom of the stairs.

After the story Helena sat for a while with the child cuddled against her aching ribs. The gnawing pain in her chest and abdomen had been unremitting since the police arrived with news of Michael's death. She took a breath and said: 'You and I will be all right, Nina, you'll see,' and at once felt a surge of relief that she had made a commitment to her child, and even believed her own words. Until that moment she had struggled through a thick fog with only the thoughts: He's dead. I can't manage. He's dead. What will I do? whispering over and over again through her head.

'Shall I get Grandma to come up and say good night?'

'Yes please.' One last hug and Helena was released.

On the surge of energy created by her own optimistic words,

Helena went to her bedroom and closed the door. She sat on the green checked quilt, a wedding present from one of Michael's Mayrick cousins, and confronted the row of baggage lined up neatly along the wall. Michael's possessions had been brought to the house that morning by the same blonde policewoman who had delivered the news on the night of the accident. There was a plastic bag of clothes, his walking boots and his rucksack which looked even shabbier than usual propped against the shiny radiator. Michael had decorated the bedroom the previous summer and its paintwork had not yet lost its freshness.

Helena touched the hard nylon top of the rucksack.

'This rucksack's been the equivalent of several times round the world on my back,' Michael had protested when she offered to buy him a new one for Christmas. 'It wouldn't be right to abandon it.'

It had numerous bulging pockets. Occasionally Helena had felt irritated by the officiousness of that rucksack. 'Other people just go for walks,' she said. 'Why must you make every outing such a palaver?'

'I'm responsible. I take precautions.'

There were stains on the fabric from years of walking through rain and mud.

His boots, by comparison, were quite new. Helena found herself thinking: He only bought them last year. Ninety pounds, they cost.

She was afraid of the rucksack, the bag of clothes and the boots and wondered how his things could go on existing now that he was gone. And yet they already had the slightly decayed air of items put out for a jumble sale. We're used and discarded, they seemed to say, we shall never be important again.

Helena dealt first with the boots, which were clean. Even he would have let me put them away as they are, she thought. But the leather on the heel of the left boot was badly scuffed and, in a couple of places, torn back. The soles also had graze marks. She rested her palm on the roughened places as if they were sore but her mind shied away from picturing the force of impact

5

which had left such scars on the boots. She placed them carefully on Michael's side of the wardrobe.

The clothes in the carrier bag had been beautifully folded. Helena visualised the policewoman with her smooth, oval nails packing them away. The last time Helena had seen them was when Michael was tucking them in curved wads into the rucksack. He had summoned her to dig him out an extra pair of boxer shorts from the back of the airing cupboard. Now she could do no more than touch the soft cotton of his shirt inside the bag. She withdrew her hand as if burnt.

The contents of the rucksack were less intimate for in it were stored all the paraphernalia of climbing and survival. She arranged the things in a row under the radiator: Kendal mint cake, survival blanket, rope, pitons, hammer, first aid kit, compass, map, camera, water bottle, kagool, cartons of soft drink. In the side pockets were paper and pen, spare socks, chocolate, fruit sweets, tissues and a list of emergency phone numbers.

The last pouch was for rubbish. Helena used to jeer at Michael for such organization. 'Only you would have a designated rubbish pocket,' she said.

Nevertheless, she arranged each bit of litter as if it was of great value. She smoothed out the wrappers, made a pile of the balls of tissues and unfolded the papers: a shopping list and a couple of receipts.

Right at the bottom was a well-worn sheet of notepaper.

A letter.

The paper was of good quality and the note was handwritten.

*Can you feel me in your shadow? I could never be close enough to you.*

*I envy the mountains your footsteps.*

*Take care, precious man.*

*Love, and love, and love.*

Michael had been a committed atheist and Helena was only a nominal member of the Church of England, so the service at the crematorium was conducted by a stranger. Michael's head teacher gave a short, appreciative address and his sister Elizabeth read an extract from Wainwright, chosen to reflect her brother's love of the mountains. Helena had insisted only on the singing of 'Dear Lord and Father of Mankind' because it had been used during her marriage service. On that occasion Michael had submitted to her desire for a church wedding with an affectionate shrug.

The small chapel was packed to the doors, the balcony was crammed and there were still more mourners crushed into the waiting area outside. Colleagues from school, pupils past and present, friends and climbing partners were all there, as were many of Michael's numerous relations. It was, thought Helena, a macabre replay of their wedding, only better attended.

She would not turn round though she was conscious of a great wash of sympathy flowing about her bowed head. It seemed to her an intolerable weight.

Is she here? she thought. Are her eyes on me?

*Love, and love and love.*

At the wedding, nine years previously, both Michael's parents had been present. Now only his widowed mother, Caroline Mayrick, wearing a defiantly cheerful turquoise suit, sat beside his sister, Elizabeth, who was for once not cradling her latest infant to her breast.

Helena was supported by her father who had aged considerably over the last fortnight. He gripped her elbow throughout the service with a determination which caused her considerable irritation, as if by so doing he might transfer something of his grief and sympathy to her. On her right was Nina, a tense little figure with eyes fixed throughout on the long shiny box in which her big energetic Daddy was now encased.

Nina's presence at the cremation had been the subject of

argument between Helena and her mother. Joanna's view was that under no circumstances should a four-year-old child attend her father's funeral service.

'It's far too disturbing for a girl of that age. She won't understand.'

Joanna always avoided emotional language or behaviour. She could not bring herself to utter words such as 'coffin', 'cremation' or even 'death'. The days since Michael's accident had been a mine-field of potentially disastrous moments for her. When Helena cried, Joanna would rush away to make tea, bring tissues or run her a bath. Emotion, in her book, was dangerous and could easily run wild.

'I want her to be there. I want her to understand that Michael will never come back. It will give her a chance to grieve properly,' Helena insisted.

'But it's so terrible. The way they draw those curtains – you know, at the end.'

The entire conversation had been conducted by the two women in tight, subdued voices whilst they were making supper and Nina was in the living room playing Snakes and Ladders with her grandfather. Neither woman looked the other in the eye, a familiar pattern in all their struggles. Helena had been conscious of her mother's plump, expert fingers preparing a crumble mixture.

'If I don't let her go she will wonder forever what happened to him. She keeps asking to see him. And she'll have all the family there. I'm sure it's right.'

'What does Caroline think?'

It was rare indeed for Joanna to consult the opinion of Michael's mother.

'I haven't asked her and I'm not going to.'

'Dad thinks it's a big mistake.'

'Mum, Nina is going to the funeral and that's the end of the matter.'

But the result of this discussion was anguished self-doubt for Helena and hours of withdrawal by Joanna whose desire to assuage her daughter's grief was henceforth tempered by disapproval.

At the moment when the coffin began to glide forward towards the curtains Helena withdrew her elbow from her father's clasp, stooped down and lifted Nina into her arms.

'Will he be burnt now?' asked Nina in a loud whisper.

'He will. But he's not really there any more. He's looking after us in heaven.'

Nina thrust her thumb deep into her mouth and rested her head against her mother's shoulder. A tape was playing 'The Entry of the Queen of Sheba', a favourite of Michael's. The midnight blue velvet curtains swung shut with a practised flourish. Nina gave a deep sigh. Helena inhaled the salty perfume of her daughter's neck.

Afterwards, again in lonely imitation of their wedding, Helena shook hands with the throng of well-wishers. She viewed herself as if from a great distance, dressed in a navy jacket and red paisley skirt, her hair tamed by a blue ribbon, pale but dry-eyed, looking intently into a hundred concerned faces. Is it you? she asked inwardly of each youngish woman who came up to smile sympathetically and murmur words of comfort or explanation: 'I'm a colleague of Michael's from school …', 'I knew him from college …', 'Do you remember me? We met years ago …' Many were in tears, mascara smudged under the bottom lashes.

*I envy the mountains your footsteps.*

Helena shook hands with everyone and smiled restrainedly.

There were piles of flowers, although Helena had asked that donations be sent instead to a Mountain Rescue fund. Doggedly she walked among the wreaths and bouquets. What a waste, she thought, what a terrible waste of money. She read each message, all the tokens of love and regret. She was trying to identify the hand-writing in the note.

*Precious man …*

'Helena, are you ready to come back to the house now? The next people are coming out.' Through the glass doors could be seen a different group mourning another dead person.

Distracted at last from her search for Michael's lover, Helena thought wildly: I'm not ready to leave.

Even the typed name on the card by his flowers, *MICHAEL GILES MAYRICK*, seemed much too significant to abandon.

'Just a few more minutes, I won't be long,' and she crouched over a bouquet of freesia and late narcissi.

Michael, stay with me, she thought. Don't leave me. Don't let them take you away.

Joanna had accepted Caroline Mayrick's offer of help in preparing a buffet. When Helena arrived home people had already filed into the dining room. Nina, pleased with the presence in her house of two beloved grandmothers, was gravely passing round a plate of savouries.

Bewildered by the spirit of celebration, Helena made for the stairs but Caroline darted forward and took her hand. 'No. Don't run away. You'll regret it. You must drink lots of wine and listen to all the lovely things people will say about Michael. That's what I'm going to do. Come on.'

Looking into Caroline's face, Helena saw a glimmer of Michael, who had inherited his mother's steady grey eyes and wide mouth. Helena had never warmed to Caroline particularly, finding her detached and breezy. She wondered at her apparent calm. The loss of a child must be quite as unendurable as the loss of a husband. And now Caroline had suffered both.

'Come,' urged Caroline.

'No. I'll circulate. Don't worry. I won't disappear.' Helena had a perverse desire not to make things easy for Caroline. She's his mother, she thought. And look what he's done to me. Maybe she even knows about this other woman.

All afternoon she was talked at as people told her of their encounters with Michael. He was so reliable, they said, so funny, so good with his pupils, so dedicated, so kind.

'Yes, I know. I was very lucky to have had even a few years with him,' she said.

But she was burning with rage. He was not faithful, he was not loyal, he was not kind to me, she thought. I trusted him, but all the time he loved someone else.

In the right pocket of her jacket she carried the note.

Occasionally she turned it over and over in her hand.

Later, when she at last flopped into an armchair, she found Caroline beside her again.

'What are your plans now, Helena?'

'I don't know. I can't think at present.'

'Are you working at all?'

'No. I've done nothing since Michael's accident. In any case I'm between projects.'

Caroline leaned across to her. 'I'm taking Aunt Clara to Westwich. Will you come with us? For a couple of weeks. Please. We could talk about Michael. And I'm sure Nina would like to be by the sea.'

Westwich. Suddenly Helena was overwhelmed by a host of remembered impressions; The Rush House, Maud Waterford's cottage, the sea breaking on a million pebbles, a bright, bracing wind across the dunes, Michael in the garden at Overstrands and herself climbing the stile and seeing him there.

'I'm not sure,' she told Caroline. 'You know that's where I met Michael.'

'Yes. I remember.' All at once Caroline seemed much smaller and older, as if Helena's hostility had crushed her determination to be a source of strength.

Ashamed, Helena kissed her cheek. 'My own family has all sorts of convoluted connections with Westwich. It's where my mother was brought up, which is why I came to be there that summer. Has anyone told you about my grandfather, the photographer, Donaldson? There's the possibility that I might get involved in a book about him. Perhaps going back to Westwich will help me decide.'

'Oh, I hope you'll come. Please.'

Joanna, bearing a tray of cups, crossed the room towards them. 'I've made tea,' she said. 'I thought everyone must be terribly thirsty after all that alcohol.'

'Let me help,' exclaimed Caroline, rising to her feet.

Helena lay back in her chair, balancing her glass on the arm. Westwich. Donaldson.

Caroline Mayrick had thrown her a life-line, a pin-point of meaning.

There were very few people left in the room now. Helena looked down at the crumbs and discarded paper napkins on the rug she and Michael had chosen in the January sales. Debris.

Falling off a mountain is easy, she thought wearily.

# Chapter Two

I

'I spy with my little eye something beginning with "M".'

'No more, Harry, please.'

'Just one.'

'Go away and annoy someone else. Millerchip, for instance.'

'You've got to be quick.'

'Oh, for heaven's sake!' Harry had leapt across the room, seized her book and snapped it shut. 'Give that to me.'

'Guess first.'

'No.'

'Guess.'

'Oh. All right then. The mantelpiece.'

'No.'

'Mat.'

'No.'

'I give up.'

'I won't let you.'

'Can I see it from where I'm sitting?'

'Almost.'

'A mote of dust?'

'No. But it is a moving object and if you don't hurry it'll be out of sight.'

'I don't care. Give me my book.'

The doorbell rang.

'Too late. I won. The answer's Maud Waterford and she's at the door.'

'Oh no. Is there to be no peace? She surely doesn't want me

13

to go out with her today. Have you seen the sky? You go, Harry.'

'Sorry. Can't. I've far too much work.'

'You've done nothing all afternoon.'

'That's why I've so much now.'

There was a step in the hall and then came their mother's light voice: 'Ruth. Aunt Maud is here. She wonders if you'd take a walk with her.'

On her way to collect her hat and coat Ruth aimed an accurate kick at her brother's ankle. His only response was to stretch his legs lazily to the fire, lean his fair head back and close his eyes so that his features relapsed into serene repose.

Downstairs in the parlour sat two women. Ruth's mother, Julia Styles, was in her usual chair of patterned chintz, her hands resting on the piece of embroidery she'd brought from London. She looked harassed and exhausted, her delicate features obscured by irritability. Maud Waterford, her iron-grey overcoat fastened uncompromisingly across her bosom, sat bolt upright in a hard-back chair next to the door as if poised for instant departure. Ruth sensed animosity between the two. Maud never could accept the change in her friend. Instead she bullied her in an attempt to brace her into action.

Ruth's voice was low and placatory. 'Hello, Aunt Maud. How kind of you to call.'

'I thought you'd probably like some air.'

'Air, yes. But are you sure the wind won't blow us away entirely? Can't I persuade you to stay inside and have tea?'

Certainly the drawing room with its fire and lamp-light seemed very cosy compared to the lowering skies outside.

'No. No. Let's get out. Besides, I have an assignation.'

'Oh, my word. Did you hear that, Mother?' Ruth kissed her mother's smooth cheek and squeezed her cold hand. 'We shan't be long. Keep Harry's nose to the grindstone. I'm afraid he's been slacking as usual.' She gave her mother another encouraging smile, then closed the door softly behind her. A keen draught blew along the stone flags of the hallway as the women pulled on layers of jackets and shawls.

As soon as the front door was open the wind took hold of their skirts. 'My hat!' cried Ruth and dragged out the pin to thrust it more fiercely into place. 'Right, I'm fully armed. Where shall we go?'

'The cliff.'

'Oh well, goodbye world. We're sure to be blown to our deaths.'

'I've arranged to meet a man there.'

'A man?'

'Yes, but I'll say no more or you might refuse to come. I told him we'd be there at a quarter to four so we've plenty of time. I want to see if my lemon yarn's come. Do you remember I wrote that I was knitting for Josephine's baby? It's unlike me to miscalculate. I could have put in a white stripe but it's too late now and Mrs Spendmore said the wool might be in today.'

'How is Josephine?' asked Ruth mischievously. She knew how to embarrass Maud.

'Very well, considering.'

Considering she's about to produce a little bastard, thought Ruth.

Maud's gaze was now fixed firmly ahead. 'She's fortunate that her family has been prepared to take her in,' she said.

'Oh, surely most families would.'

'There are many, many who wouldn't. Certainly in my day most girls would have been cast out.'

There was something in Maud's tone that made Ruth quicken her pace in order to look more easily into her face. 'I know your own father was terribly strict,' she said.

'At least I had the advantage of not having the chance to get into Josephine's condition,' Maud said with some humour. 'I was never alone with a man in my life.'

At sixteen, Ruth thought of her own young womanhood spinning away into the distance, ripe with possibility. How terrible to be a spinster like Maud. 'You must regret that,' she said but her words were whipped away by the wind.

'Not that many young men ever come to Westwich,' Maud shouted.

By now they had reached the top of the village street. Here the wind was funnelled between low cottages. Further intimacies were impossible. Grit beat at their faces as they fought their way down to the shop where a lamp burned in the window despite the early hour. The stone step was long unwashed and the door stripped of paint by impatient village children kicking it open with their capped toes. The interior was dim and stuffy, quite chill despite an oil heater. An unpleasant smell of old cheese predominated.

The proprietor, Mrs Spendmore, lurked as usual on a high stool at one end of the counter, fat cheeks cushioned heavily on her three chins. 'I'm surprised to see anyone this afternoon,' she said, as if affronted either by the way the village neglected her in poor weather or that anyone should intrude in the deserted shop. She eyed Maud's stout boots and furled umbrella. 'You're surely not off on one of your walks, Miss Waterford. It's going to pour. If you're after the wool it's not in. I told you I'd send to let you know when it is. Deliveries, as you can imagine, are slow this time of year.'

Thus dismissed, Ruth and Maud retreated onto the street. 'She means she forgot to order,' Maud said loudly as she let the door slam behind her.

'Aunt Maud, why the cliff?' Ruth asked, trying to keep the reluctance from her voice. She was too lightly dressed for an afternoon such as this. As they neared the sea the wind redoubled its velocity and swept a blade-like chill from the water.

'You'll see. Only the cliff would do.' Maud tucked her arm through Ruth's. 'Hold tight, my love. You're young. Why are you complaining? Oh, you young people will never wear enough.'

The clouds to the south-east were a deep purply black. Distant rain sheeted across the sea. Ruth's cheeks and eyes smarted. Inwardly she cursed Maud and her friendly demands for companionship. 'She's been so good to us over the years,' Julia Styles always said, her long fingers stroking her daughter's arm placatingly, 'and she's so fond of you Ruth. You know how she looks forward to us coming down each year.' Certainly on Ruth's birthday came unquestionable proofs of Maud's affection; exquisitely embroidered petticoats or hand-painted miniatures parcelled in tissue and brown paper inscribed: *To dearest Ruth, from Maud, with love.*

Ruth clasped Maud's gloved hand. 'Shall we run then?'

'I'm far too old to run,' but Ruth knew her own power to enthuse and for a few steps they dashed forward and reached the cliff path.

A soaking drizzle was falling as they reached the stile. The cliff dropped steeply away to their left as soon as they began to climb. The sea sighed back and splintered on the shingle below – suck, sigh, shatter. Ruth's heart beat faster. The surface of the sea was so regular, so eternal. It gave no hint of what it had taken.

'I'm always afraid when I come here,' she confided to Maud.

'Why afraid?'

'It's so hard to imagine, isn't it, about this earth where we walk? It's hard to imagine that it won't be here soon, that this land will be gone.'

'Not gone, covered.'

'Crumbled. There'll be no sign of where we were.'

'But we shall still be alive. We're safe.'

'Nobody will be able to put their foot on this path and say: "That's where Maud and Ruth walked".'

'Would they want to in any case? Good heavens, Ruth, it's not like you to be so morbid.'

Ruth was aware of a more than customary briskness in Maud's tone. Both were conscious of the memory of Ruth's poor mad grandmother who had walked into the sea – an event that was always referred to locally in hushed tones. Such evocative observations from Ruth caused Maud some unease.

There was indeed a man standing at the head of the path, gazing out to sea. Behind him was the church, the sky cold in its empty windows, the nave torn jaggedly where the sea had taken the cliff from underneath.

'Who is he?' murmured Ruth.

'He's a photographer. He's making postcards of the area. I heard him talking in the shop yesterday. He said he wanted some human figures for his picture. So I asked: "Will I do? Shall I bring a friend?"'

'Goodness. Will we be famous?'

The photographer was very young, and even more inappropriately dressed than Ruth; like her he wore no overcoat but instead a long, flapping oilskin. There's no need for him to look quite so eccentric, Ruth thought indignantly. If he's a good enough photographer his work will speak for his art. Nonetheless she straightened her skirt and put her hand to her head to catch back a few stray locks.

'Mr Donaldson.' Maud had blown within shouting distance of the young man. 'What a day! Will the rain matter? Perhaps the photograph will come out wrong. This is my young friend, Ruth Styles.'

Young friend, thought Ruth indignantly. I'm not much younger than he is.

Mr Donaldson took her proffered hand distractedly in a cold, wet clasp. 'I want to work quickly before the light goes. It could be a wonderful picture – very dramatic with the clouds lowering over the ruin.'

'Why do you want us in it?' asked Ruth.

'To give perspective. The church's size will not register unless there are people in the foreground.'

'Now, where shall we stand? Shall I have my umbrella up or down?' cried Maud. Even her good nature was a little ruffled by the discomfort of the rain.

'Up, I think. Stand together here. As if you'd just met on the path.'

'This is hardly a place anyone would just happen to meet,' Ruth said.

She was ignored by the young photographer. 'That's it. Hold the umbrella a little further back. So.'

He retreated several yards from the path and began to struggle with a tripod, camera and case of equipment, considerably hampered by the need to protect the entire ensemble from the elements.

'I hope the rain doesn't get in his machine,' Maud whispered anxiously.

'I do wish he'd hurry, my hat will be ruined.'

'It'll dry out.'

'But the dyes may run.'

They were now instructed to shuffle back and forth across the path until their position exactly suited Mr Donaldson.

'Stand very still. Try to look more natural. No, don't speak. Now, very still. You have to be still for several moments as it's so dark. It will be a long exposure.'

They stood stiffly, gazing solemnly into each other's eyes. Then, as the seconds went by, Ruth began to giggle. Her grey gaze lost its solemnity and her eyes began to run with the effort of restraining laughter. When they were at last told it was over they collapsed with hilarity.

The young man was bemused by their behaviour. He tried to share in their laughter but succeeded only in looking somewhat baffled. 'Just a couple more!' he called. 'I have to be sure as I can't afford to come back.' His deft fingers eagerly exchanged the exposed plate for another.

'Why not try again when the sun's out?' Ruth said hopefully.

'Oh no. No. Not nearly so dramatic. Now then ladies …'

At last they were released. 'Please can we go?' Ruth pleaded, shaking with cold.

'Yes, we'll go. Will you come and have tea, Mr Donaldson?'

He would be pleased to have tea, he said, but could they wait while he dismantled his camera?

'We'll go ahead,' Ruth said firmly, 'and boil the kettle. I'll leave my glove on the door handle so you won't miss the cottage.'

Giggling and chattering like conspiratorial children they ran down the path away from the tardy Mr Donaldson and came at last to Maud's cottage where her warm kitchen provided a haven from the wind.

*

In ten minutes the table was set with Maud's best blue and white china, Maud had changed her dark brown skirt for one of navy blue and Ruth was wrapped in an old shawl, her hair drying in crisp tendrils on her shoulders.

Mr Donaldson emerged from the cold afternoon, clutching his camera. He propped his tripod and case in the hallway and came into the kitchen, smoothing down his shock of hair.

'You must be wet through,' exclaimed Maud. 'Ruth, you should have waited to help carry his things.'

'Where are you staying, Mr Donaldson?' Ruth asked, her voice gentle, as if to apologize for the turmoil and hilarity of their earlier meeting. He watched the pink glow of her cheek, the clarity of her bright eyes and her calm, slender hands as she made the tea.

'With Mrs Spendmore above the shop.'

'Oh dear. More scones, Aunt, the poor man must be starving.'

'Mrs Spendmore is not noted for her generous portions,' Maud explained.

'I'm only here a few days. I daresay I shall bear up.'

Ruth warmed to his attempt at gaiety and to the angular gaucheness of his body as he sat in the tiny kitchen, his knees bent up against the table edge. 'Aunt Maud makes the best scones in Suffolk.'

'Ah, but not London, I suppose. Miss Styles is a very smart young lady, Mr Donaldson. She lives most of the year in London and only graces our little backwater when her mama chooses to up sticks in the spring for a few months.'

'Oh yes, I'm very cosmopolitan,' Ruth agreed.

'I was born in London,' said Donaldson. 'Well, nearly London. Enfield.'

'We Londoners would say that was the country, I'm afraid.' Laughter bubbled in her eyes. Donaldson looked disconcerted, as if uncertain whether or not her mirth was directed at him. 'But I'm only half a Londoner myself,' she added. 'My mother's a native of Westwich. She has to come back every year. I tell her she misses the wind as if it were alcohol and she an addict. She must have her gasp of Suffolk or she pines.'

The two women exchanged glances.

Maud said: 'Mr Donaldson, will you be a very famous photographer one day?'

'I don't expect so,' he replied with an unconvincing attempt at modesty. But Maud had successfully diverted the conversation from the subject of Ruth's mother, Julia Styles. Donaldson was eager to speak at length about his apprenticeship and his good fortune at being commissioned so young to make a series of coastal postcards.

'Your picture of us is hardly going to lure people here,' Ruth said, 'a ruined church and wild sky.'

'But it's drama, mystery. The idea that in a few years nothing will remain of the church except my postcard is very intriguing.'

'Yes, I see.' Ruth recognized his vanity. 'Yes, that must feel quite grand – to capture something before it is lost for ever.'

He studied her carefully as if to assess whether or not she was laughing at him again but she had stood and was gathering the cups onto a tray. 'I must away. Harry will be driving Mother into a fizz without me to entertain him. Goodbye, Maud, thank you for the walk. Goodbye, Mr Donaldson, it has been a pleasure meeting you.'

Her hand was not released quite soon enough. 'Perhaps I shall see you again before I leave on Sunday,' he said and she was looking for the first time directly into his dark, eager eyes.

'Yes, perhaps.' She smiled and withdrew her hand. But the moment quickened her blood and was relived several times during the evening, and on waking the next day.

2

Shortly after Ruth's first encounter with Donaldson, Harry left Westwich and went back to school for the summer term. Mr Millerchip, who was employed as gardener and odd-job-man, borrowed the trap from Upstones Farm to take Harry to the station. The task of coachman was one of the few Millerchip relished, though from his air of long-suffering resentment his pleasure was difficult to detect. At eleven forty-five his doleful figure, draped in oilskins, could be seen perched level with the gate posts of The Rush House, the whip poised meanly in his hand.

In the hall Harry was creating a furore by not being nearly ready though he had begun packing his trunk two days earlier. 'Mrs Millerchip, have you seen my house-shoes?' he yelled. 'Ruth, go and look under my bed.'

Julia stood at the head of the stairs dressed in her favourite pale blue wrap, her hair tumbled and her hand fumbling restlessly with the banister. Her thin face with its fine, straight nose and delicate cheek-bones was contorted by ineffectual anxiety generated by her son's departure. 'Harry, Harry, you'll miss your train. Why didn't you get ready last night?'

Ruth flew about collecting garments and books and thrusting them into a large carpet bag. 'For goodness sake, Harry, you'll have to go. We'll send on anything you leave behind.'

Mrs Millerchip, the housekeeper, emerged from the kitchen holding a huge parcel. 'I've done you some nice pies and sandwiches for the journey. Make sure you don't crush them.'

'Oh, Mrs Millerchip, he'll never fit all that in,' exclaimed Ruth.

'Yes I will, here, give it to me.' The parcel was thrust into the carpet bag on top of the shirts carefully starched by Ruth the previous night. 'Thanks Mrs M. Thanks for keeping the wolf from the door. You're the only one who cares for the inner man. Goodbye Mother, stay warm and well.'

He picked up his bag, flung his muffler round his neck and permitted Ruth a fleeting hug.

She wrapped Mrs Millerchip's black shawl about her shoulders and followed him along the path. 'Write, Harry, promise you will. Just a few words occasionally.'

'I might, if I've time,' he responded grandly.

'Love to Father.'

'You'll see him soon.'

She held his hand for a moment, as if by so doing she might follow him into his life. But the trap lurched forwards and she was left with the fringes of the shawl tangling in the wind and her skirt already damp, listening to the receding rhythm of the horses' hooves and Harry's friendly goading of Millerchip.

'Come in, Ruth, come in! You're letting all the dirt blow into the house,' called Mrs Millerchip.

Ruth turned away from the lane with its puddled ruts and potholes and instead faced the straight brick path to The Rush House. Mrs Millerchip stood in the porch with her arms crossed across her full bosom. Behind her the hallway was dark.

With leaden limbs Ruth hung the shawl on its peg in the hall. A familiar pain caught at her breast-bone. Heartache, Ruth called it to herself.

She prepared a bright smile and went up to her mother's room. Julia had retreated back to bed and now lay crouched tautly against the white pillows, the floral eiderdown gripped to her chest. The curtains were drawn and the grey morning glowed dully behind the pink and green flowered material. Reflected in the oval mirror of the wardrobe opposite was the orange light of the bedside lamp. The perfumed fug of the room repelled Ruth, as did the clutter of books and papers which filled every surface. Julia was incurably untidy. Automatically Ruth began to pick up a discarded skirt and blouse, smooth them and hang them up.

'At least that's got rid of Harry,' she said brightly.

'You know you'll miss him.'

Ruth saw that her mother was clasping a hair brush with her free hand. 'Let me do your hair for you, Mother.'

'Oh I'm not ready to get up yet. I've a mountain of correspondence. I thought I'd deal with that first, if you wouldn't mind passing me my writing box.' This box, a present from her husband on their wedding day, was Julia's pride and joy. She spent hours reorganizing its contents, counting through sheets of paper, refilling the ink bottles and inserting mysterious little envelopes into its secret drawers. As Ruth knew well, a morning spent with the writing box on her knees was no guarantee that any useful work would be done by Julia.

'I'll put your clothes out for you, Mother. You'll need your warmest skirt.'

'No, no, I'll choose something myself later.'

'Shall I heat the water for a bath?'

'No, not this morning. It's far too cold to think of bathing.'

Ruth's small armoury of strategies to coax her mother out of bed had failed.

'Would you like help with your letters?' she asked, though the prospect of spending any longer in the warm, fussy room horrified her.

'No, no, you go now. You don't want to be shut up here with me.'

Ruth went to her own room where the fire was unlit. She was arrested by her reflection in the little mirror on the chest of drawers. It was as if Julia's features had been rubbed clear of all marks made by time, for here were the same wide-set eyes, the same square jaw and pointed chin. But Ruth's eyes were bright and questioning, her hair glossy and her complexion clear and pink. She gave herself a brief smirk and turned away.

The corner window which gave her a view both to the front and to the side admitted too many draughts for comfort. On the low chest by the bed were carefully arranged her books and sewing. She ought really to take her French grammar to the parlour and study, she thought. It would not do to have fallen behind the other girls if she returned to school in September. Or should she play the piano? Or offer to bake with Mrs Millerchip?

Instead she peered out at the still-wintry trees. The exuberance she had felt on the afternoon of her encounter with the photographer was forgotten. My life, she thought, my life. The sixteen and a half years of her past seemed to swoop away from her in rainbow colours. Ahead was a grey, grey wait. For what? For what?

She hurtled downstairs, clapped on her inadequate hat and allowed the wind to carry her through the garden and along the lane towards the beach. The melancholy would be beaten out of her, she decided. But the sight of the cluster of cottages which constituted the village did little to cheer her. Their paint-work seared by salt spray, windows tarnished by sandy rain, the little dwellings appeared to have shrunk into themselves. Nobody was about. Mrs Spendmore's shop lurked uninvitingly, its door

24

tightly closed, defying customers to enter. I wonder if that photographer's still there, Ruth thought, ducking her head lest he should be looking down on her solitary form from an upstairs window. She hurried past The Boat Inn with its flaky sign and then she was nearly at the sea.

As she reached the high pebble bank, rain drove into her face. Oh, it's so cold, so cold, was all she could now think. But she ran down to the water's edge and played her usual game of 'Dare' with the waves. Plant your boots firmly on the shining pebbles as a wave recedes, watch as the grey water somersaults forward, wait until the very last instant and then, when the water has dashed to within inches of your feet, run up the beach. Julia had taught her the game when they first visited Westwich. 'My mother used to play it with me,' she had cried. Ruth, then a young child, had not noted the significance of this remark. Julia's mother, Margaret, had played 'Dare' once too often.

Ruth's attitude to the sea at Westwich had always been ambivalent. It fascinated and intimidated her. She thought it grasping. It was never warm, rarely calm, and attractive only to a handful of stalwart holiday-makers. Once her father had taken them for a week to the south coast, insisting that the children needed some proper sea bathing. How different had been the sea there – blue, tolerably warm, a friend to the crowds on the sunny beaches.

Today there were little smooth shinings of sand left by the retreating tide, kinder to the feet than the pebbles. Ruth ran along these and turned to see that her footprints had disappeared instantly. For some reason this intensified her despair and she began to sob. The wind and waves drowned the sound of her tears and she became enchanted by the release of giving voice to her emotion. She flung back her head and howled at the turbulent sky.

It had not occurred to her that she might be watched but when she at last turned from the sea she saw that Donaldson was standing high up on the shingle bank with his tripod. Immediately Ruth began to laugh. Oh my, oh my, explain this away, Ruth-o, she said to herself. But she was also very angry with him. He had the whole coast of Suffolk on which to loiter with his wretched camera. How dare he come here and witness her crazed behaviour? Even at this distance she could see that he wore no hat and his wild hair was plastered unbecomingly about his ears. I hope he doesn't expect me to take him home and dry him off, she thought. Her heart began to pound with excitement and embarrassment. Dashing away her tears with her knuckles she wondered whether he would approach. He was standing stock still. Was he simply going to watch her?

After several moments during which Donaldson squinted down at Ruth and she stared back at him he left his camera and slid inelegantly down the shingle towards her.

'Good morning!' he shouted.

She found this hilarious. 'It's after twelve and it's certainly not good.' Had he not heard her wails after all? Of course if he had she preferred him to ignore them but he might show a little sympathy.

'Are you going to swim?' she enquired sweetly.

'It's far too cold.'

Marking him down as humourless she said: 'Oh, I would, only I haven't a bathing suit with me. Mind you, I could simply peel off here and now, nobody would mind.'

He gaped at her. He has nice teeth but a rather loose lower lip, she decided.

'Were you taking photographs or what?' she demanded.

'Yes. Of the beach. And the boats.' He waved ambivalently at the line of fishing boats pulled high on the shingle.

'There's not much to interest a photographer here, I would have thought.'

'That's why I was pleased to see you. Something alive.'

'Thank you very much. I'm so glad I have my uses. I shall have to start charging you a fee. But Mr Donaldson, I thought you'd be gone from Westwich by now.'

'I've extended my stay. There's so much more to photograph than I'd expected. My senior agrees that there might be much artistic possibility in the disappearing coastline.'

'Oh good. I'm so glad there may be profit for you in the tragedy of our poor cliffs.'

He would not be baited by her wit. He is stodgy, she thought, and vain. Well I'm fed up with asking him questions. 'I must get back,' she said briskly. 'It's almost lunch-time.'

'I'll walk with you, if I may.'

'I do know the way.'

This last remark was cruel, she realized, and he obviously felt the rebuff. In any case, she wanted him to stay with her. She imagined herself marching triumphantly along the village street, pursued by the young photographer. Such a conquest should set tongues wagging nicely. 'I'll be glad of your company, though,' she added more kindly.

He did not so much pursue as limp, burdened as usual by all the machinery of his craft.

'Do your boots hurt?' she demanded.

'They do seem to tighten when they're wet,' he answered humbly.

At her gate he asked: 'Is there anything else in the area I ought to see?'

'It depends what you mean by "ought".'

'For my photographs. The disappearing coastline. Lost communities.'

'I'm not sure I should encourage your desire to exploit my village.'

'Is it your village? I thought you were just a visitor. Mrs Spendmore says you've only been here a fortnight.'

Ruth was gratified that he must have made enquiries about her 'Have you seen the friary? I could take you there if you like'

'I have visited it. But the light was poor. I ought to go back.' He immediately made an arrangement for the afternoon.

Rather elated, Ruth stood watching his retreating form and listening to the clatter of his tripod as it caught against his legs.

From her bedroom window Ruth could watch for Donaldson's arrival. She expected him to be early and early he was – his head appeared level with the garden wall ten minutes before the agreed time of two-thirty. Ruth, who despite herself had let down her hair in order to dress it more becomingly, had to duck away from the glass in case he looked up and saw her.

He was not so bold, however, as to come early to the door. Standing well back in her room as she jabbed the long pins back into her hair, Ruth saw him hover at the gate for a while, glance at his watch, and then disappear along the lane.

By the time Ruth finally emerged at two-thirty-five poor Donaldson's carefully spruced appearance had been considerably dishevelled by wind and cold.

'I hope you haven't used your last clean shirt on a walk in muddy lanes,' Ruth said reprovingly.

'Mrs Spendmore does my laundry.'

'And how much does she charge per item?' But rather shocked by her own indelicacy Ruth waved aside this last question and turned her attention to his photographic equipment. 'Must you bring all that with you every time you set out?'

'I must, yes. I'm not a proponent of these little hand-held Kodaks. I like to take a perfectly composed picture, and for that I must have a tripod.'

Ruth was displeased by his pomposity. 'It slows you down so much,' she said, flouncing ahead, her skirts swaying with a forbidding momentum against her legs. They were walking away from the village past the little Victorian church with its high-walled graveyard. 'This church was built to replace the ruin on the cliff,' she told him curtly. She now wished that she had not agreed to meet him. Her clothes had not quite dried off since the morning.

'You could carry something if you like,' he said timidly.

She took his tripod grudgingly, feeling very disappointed in her companion. Donaldson was clearly no gentleman. The lane now twisted to the left, the fringe of trees disappeared and they were out in open country. Opposite was the gateway leading to Upstones. Thinking to amuse herself by shocking him she pointed to the row of cottages which stood near the gate. 'In that end house is brewing our latest scandal. One of the girls, Josephine, is in an unfortunate condition – it's thought the farmer's son has something to do with it.'

'Poor girl,' said Donaldson with real compassion.

Ruth was ashamed.

Presently they came to the high stone arch of the friary. She had regained her composure sufficiently to instruct Donaldson on its historical import. 'There were once several religious houses in Westwich but now there are only these ruins. Like everyone else, the monks and friars had to leave the town before the town left them, as it were. The friary is nothing now, but the leper chapel remains almost intact except for the roof. Odd, isn't it, that the place built for outcasts should survive and the rest perish.'

'You mean they ought to have put the lepers near the sea so that their chapel could be the first to go?'

'Well, the leper chapel is no good without the main church being there to exclude the lepers from.'

They were united momentarily in deciding on suitable angles for the photographs. Ruth posed obligingly by a pillar and on a crumbling wall but soon grew too cold to tolerate any further standing about.

'Do you want to walk on to warm up?' she asked hopefully.

'If you like.'

'Couldn't you leave that wretched stuff under a hedge for us to collect later?'

'It's much too valuable.'

'Nobody will take it from here. For heaven's sake.'

Without waiting for him she strode off to the stile and began walking towards the cliff path. Yet she rather despised herself for her anger. He was so well-meaning that it was unfair to bully him.

The sound of panting behind her warned that he was still on her trail. He had abandoned the tripod but not his heavy wooden case which he had strapped to his back, or his camera. Deciding that this was a fair compromise Ruth relented sufficiently to reply kindly to his next question. 'Do you regard yourself as a visitor here, as Mrs Spendmore insists you are, or a resident?'

'Half of each. The Rush House belongs to my family – well,

my mother. She was brought up in Westwich, as I told you. That's why she and Maud Waterford are so close. They were childhood friends. My father keeps the house up and each year we come down for the spring and summer. We have quite a big house in London though my mother is never really comfortable there.'

'I've not seen your mother out in the village.'

'No. She's something of an invalid. It's too cold for her.'

'Are you alone with your mother?'

'What a lot of questions, Mr Donaldson. No, I have an older brother, Harry, but he's gone back to school. Father comes at weekends when he can. He works in the City, dealing in stocks and shares. And we have the Millerchips to look after us. They live above the old stable block.'

'And what of your own education?'

'Oh, I've had enough of school for now. I may go back in the autumn. I don't know, I have so many plans.' She waved her hand as if to say his enquiries were too trivial to match her grand plans for the future. But she found his conversation peculiarly demanding, as if he had found her out, cut through the brightness of her skin and hair and discovered the grey deadness beneath.

She halted by the railings which marked an abrupt end to the sunken path from the friary. Far below the pale brown sea foamed on the pebbles. Ruth gazed at the breaking waves. 'The beach inclines so steeply that you get drawn down, don't you think? When Westwich was a thriving port the town would have extended for half a mile where the sea now is. You can't imagine it, can you? It looks as if there's been nothing but salt water for ever.'

'Mrs Spendmore claims that some villagers have heard the sound of church bells from beneath the waves.'

'That's just silly. The bells would have been taken from the churches long before they fell into ruins. And anyway it presupposes that the sea drowned the town. That's not right. It beat it into crumbs, pounded it into rubble. The old town is now washed up as shingle. It's no use trying to imagine homes and inns and shops intact on the sea-bed. Hardly material for a photographer, is it? All that sea.'

'So you don't believe any of the ghost stories.'

'No. No. I don't believe in ghost stories. Foolish nonsense – people who let their imagination run away with them.' Donaldson was staring at her. She tilted her chin and looked defiantly back at him, noting the pale, thick-textured skin of his forehead, the sprightly rise of his untameable hair and the unmistakable admiration in his dark eyes. She was conscious that strands of her own hair were clinging to her cheek and that her skirts were flying out behind her. The melancholy left her.

He had to wrench his gaze from her face. 'Is anything ever washed up?' he asked.

'Oh, for goodness sake. Haven't you been listening?' Suddenly tired of the bleakness and discomfort of the cliff-top she thought again of the delights of book and fire and of tea with her mother, who was always happier in the early evenings. 'Let's go back,' she said, 'the light is fading.'

With the wind behind them it was easier to talk. Ruth deigned to ask him questions and learnt that his father worked in a bank and his mother took in lodgers. He had an older brother who had followed his father's profession and Donaldson's first name was Hubert.

This last caused Ruth much amusement. 'What's your real name?'

He was very offended. 'I'm named after my grandfather. It's a perfectly normal name.'

'Oh no, please. Nobody could consider Hubert acceptable. Hubert Donaldson.'

They had by now collected the tripod and were approaching The Rush House. It was thus, with Ruth clinging to the arm of the over-burdened, ill-named photographer, that they met Alan Styles.

Ruth sobered at once, ran to him and gave him a self-conscious hug. 'Papa. What are you doing here?'

'I have taken a few days' leave of absence. I thought your mother might be missing Harry.'

'I'm sure she is. She'll be delighted to see you.'

Donaldson noted at once the change in her. She had become shuttered. He could not recognize the gleaming-eyed girl who had just laughed at him so remorselessly. He removed his cap from his untidy hair. 'Good afternoon, sir. Hubert Donaldson. Your daughter has been kind enough to show me the friary.'

Styles was a heavy, florid man, his complexion and girth bearing witness to a life of leisurely lunches and plenty of good wine. He had a ready, good-natured smile which was not quite in keeping with the look of keen appraisal in his eye. 'Has she indeed? I see you are a photographer.'

'Yes. I'm interested in this coastline. I want to try to capture as much as possible before more is taken by the sea.'

'Very ambitious. You suppose your pictures might replace the real thing I presume.'

'Not at all, sir. They will merely be a record.'

'Of no value though. Fruitless reminders of what was. I prefer to look ahead. I've always considered photography to be a rather stale science, merely reproducing in two dimensions what cannot be preserved in three.'

'But for the memories, sir. And as an educational tool – to reveal sights to those who will never otherwise see them. And … art.'

'Ah. Art. Now who, really, will be the better for your work, I wonder?'

'Father, you've always been fascinated by photographs,' Ruth said.

'You see, Mr Donaldson, my daughter tells me I am fascinated by photographs. I am not entitled to my own opinion. Well, it's very cold. I must get inside. Go and tell your mother I'm here, Ruth. Good afternoon, Mr Donaldson.'

'Good afternoon, sir.'

Donaldson caught a glimpse of a lamp burning in the hall as Ruth turned in the doorway to give him a fleeting, apologetic smile, and a slight flicker of her long fingers as she disappeared from view. Then he plodded back to his chill room over Mrs Spendmore's shop where he had an hour to wait for tea.

('Nothing hot on Sundays, Mr Donaldson. I never cook on Sundays for religious reasons.')

Alan Styles' arrival at The Rush House caused the women there great discomfort. Mrs Millerchip was not delicate in her house-keeping but she did not jar the atmosphere in the way of Harry or Alan Styles. None of the rooms was large, the ceilings were low and the furnishings old-fashioned and dainty. Styles imposed his over-bearing masculinity on every corner. After he had left a room an odour composed of cigar, alcohol and male-ness remained. He tried to tread softly but this only increased the tension. On every chair he left a deep indentation; his clothes, heavy jackets and shoes intruded in the hall and his laugh and voice were loud. In the London house Julia could sit apart from him, protected by the airy rooms and several floors. In The Rush House he was unavoidable. Yet he meant so well. He tried to cherish and protect his wife and daughter, for their sake moderating his language and drinking, but this deliberate attempt to be other than he was caused only frustration and anxiety in his wife.

Ruth was agonized by him. He seemed so gauche, so ridicu-lously eager to please and yet such a bully. She preferred to see him in his office where he was master and in scale with his grand surroundings. In The Rush House she could not bear him to touch her but the dining room table was so narrow that her feet frequently nudged against his and the shared bathroom was so small and poorly ventilated that signs of his ablutions were unavoidable.

Recently Ruth had become aware of the unusual nature of his marriage. Hitherto she had taken for granted his role as her mother's protector. Of course he should ordain that Julia be kept quiet and shielded from any hint of household disruption, should creep up to bed at eight o'clock – if she had risen at all that day – and should not have her fragile sleep disturbed by his presence in the bed beside her. In Westwich, Styles slept in a tiny box room and kept his clothes in his wife's wardrobe. Nowadays Ruth never heard his step on the landing late at night, followed by the closing of Julia's bedroom door and the murmur of voices. She watched with pain her father's clumsy efforts to be nursemaid to her mother, half recognizing that behind the patient smile and gentle hands lay a mind and body deeply uncomprehending of the neurotic shadow that his wife had become.

And Ruth found that her own relations with her father were clouded. He loved her so. But far from basking in his affection as formerly, she found it stifling. She could not meet his look of blazing love when she appeared in a new frock or had played successfully a difficult piece on the piano. Her flesh quivered with distaste when he lifted a lock of her hair, wound it round his fingers, raised it to his lips and gave it a light kiss. He teased her when she began to wear it piled on top of her head. 'Where's your hair gone, Ruth-o? Goodness me, what a lady. Let your hair down, girl, there's plenty of time to be grown up.'

When he embraced her he held her so tightly that her breasts crushed against his waistcoat. His kiss was too near the mouth. She hated the way he reached out sometimes and gave her waist a rough tickle though a few years previously she would have found the same gesture delightful. She feared the unbounded energy in his frame which never seemed to abate however far he walked or however many rounds of golf he played. And she pitied him in the long, quiet Westwich evenings when he sat in the parlour rustling through *The Times* whilst Julia read or sewed, for the way he so courteously stood whenever his wife left or entered the room and how his big, hairy hands ineptly folded her embroidery or clasped a delicate shawl as he accompanied her to the bottom of the stairs.

At dinner on the evening after his first meeting with Donaldson, conversation seemed particularly difficult.

Ruth asked after his business with questions she had learnt long ago from her mother. 'How are the financial markets?'

'And Miss Bloom?' His secretary. 'Has she gone into her spring skirt yet?' Miss Bloom possessed three skirts, one each for winter and summer and another for the rest of the year.

Styles responded with his customary vigour, referring constantly to his wife for comment. But Julia sat languidly over her meal, prodding at her food with a fork and looking every few seconds towards the drawn curtains. The dining room was at the back of the house and had a wide latticed window overlooking the trees and shrubs in the garden. Even with the winter brocade curtains drawn close the wind could be heard soughing through branches. But the room was snug enough with its blazing fire, polished furniture and richly patterned rug.

Inevitably Styles quizzed Ruth about Donaldson. 'Where did you find your young man, Ruth? Did you know our daughter was cavorting about the lanes with a nefarious-looking youth, Julia?'

'Oh dear, didn't you like my Mr Donaldson, Father?'

'*Your* Mr Donaldson?'

'Well, he's Aunt Maud's really. He thinks he's going to be famous one day.'

'I suppose he was polite enough.'

'I enjoyed his company. It made a change to speak with anyone my age in Westwich.' Ruth spoke more petulantly than she had intended.

Styles looked at her for a moment. 'Well, let's hope he stays a little longer. I can see that it is very quiet for you here.'

After a few more minutes Julia announced that she was too tired to sit up any longer. Styles rose immediately and took her elbow to escort her solicitously to the door and along the hall. Ruth could hear the rustle of her mother's skirts on the stairs, her soft, 'Goodnight then, Alan. I expect I'll be better in the morning.'

There was a pause before Styles returned to the room. When he resumed his seat he made a great play of tucking his napkin into his waistcoat. 'She does not seem much improved,' he said heavily.

'No. I don't think she is. These grey, cold days do her no good. She hates them. Are you sure we were right to bring her here, Father?'

'She was so insistent. Perhaps when the sun comes she will

pick up.' And then with a tenderness that caused Ruth much distress when she considered her own confused feelings for him, he asked; 'Shall you manage all right, Ruth-o? It is so very quiet for you. Do you miss school?'

'Oh, I think it was best that school and I should part company for a while, don't you?'

Her father smiled. 'My Ruth-o. I told you women weren't destined to flourish in large institutions. But what is there for you here?'

'Oh, I shall survive. As a matter of fact I've found Mr Donaldson's interest in this area quite inspiring. He's made me look about me with fresh eyes. Perhaps I shall do some sketching. Did you know the church has had another column bitten away since last year?'

'Is there anything I can send down for you? Or would you like to have a friend to stay?'

'I think Mother would hate that.' Ruth could not imagine friends relishing the extreme isolation of Westwich and the strained atmosphere of The Rush House.

'I thought of asking your mother whether she'd like to go for a drive tomorrow. What do you think?'

'You could always ask,' Ruth suggested gently.

Later she lay in her bed listening for her father's step in the passage and a knock on her mother's door but none came. Outside the wind performed its customary wake. Oh, leave us alone, Ruth cried inwardly, just for one night.

She thought of the three of them lying within feet of each other, separated by thin interior walls. Julia would be propped against piled pillows and her lamp would burn throughout the night. Every now and again she would sit up and read another few pages from one of her treasured girlhood books before trying to fight her way back into sleep. In the next room Styles would be uncomfortable in the small bed. Ruth imagined that his disappointment at finding his wife in such poor spirits must be as huge and all-enveloping as the rest of him. And last of all there was Ruth in her white nightdress embroidered by

Maud, physically tired after her walk with Donaldson, but sleepless.

She considered the young photographer once more. Now that they were distanced by time and space she could forget her irritation with his faults and bask afresh in his admiration. His gaze when focused on her held a similar expression to that of her father's. It was as if he were taking long sips at her. Ruth suddenly left her bed, relit the lamp and went to study her reflection in the small swing mirror which stood on the chest of drawers. Her eyes looked flirtatiously back, pleased with the thick cloud of hair and the mischievous curve of her lips. Not bad, Ruth-o, she told herself, it's no wonder he finds you so alluring. A little comforted she returned to the warmth of her sheets.

It was with a mixture of regret and triumph that the next morning she passed Donaldson in the lane. She was seated in the trap from Upstones Farm, flanked by both parents, whilst Donaldson was on foot and obviously heading for The Rush House.

Ruth gave him a carefree wave and called: 'Good morning, Mr Donaldson.' Glancing back she saw that he was standing stock still, staring at his feet.

She had cause to regret this missed opportunity when, the following day, after her father had returned to London, she ventured into the village with an errand at the shop. As soon as she opened the door and stepped into the gloomy interior, she knew instinctively that Donaldson had gone.

Mrs Spendmore volunteered nothing. It was her habit to serve all her customers as if she barely knew them. Every request for assistance was greeted by a heavy sigh and a long stare as if with amazement that anyone could possibly require such an item. Her several chins and sullen mouth had long settled into an immovable expression of discontentment.

'How are you, Mrs Spendmore?' Ruth asked brightly.

'Not so bad.'

'Busy?'

'Rushed off my feet.'

'My mother sent me for some crimson embroidery silk.'

After a painstaking rummage behind the counter a box was produced and banged down in front of Ruth. Inside was a multitude of tangled colours, but not crimson.

'We must be out of red,' announced Mrs Spendmore.

'Could you order it?'

Further heavy movement found a scrap of paper on which was written the order. 'I suppose your paying guests must keep you even busier,' Ruth suggested, swallowing her pride.

'Naturally.'

By now Ruth's face was hot. 'But Mr Donaldson seemed a very easy-going type.'

'In my experience no boarder is easy-going. They all eat, and dirty sheets.'

Ruth fixed her eyes on Mrs Spendmore's whiskery chin. 'Well, thank you for ordering my mother's silk,' she said smoothly and turned to go.

She could feel the tension behind her as Mrs Spendmore tussled with the opposing desires to withhold and disclose information. The latter urge won. 'Of course, I'm not quite so pushed now that the young photographer has gone.'

Ruth experienced a sharp pang of disappointment but not for an instant did her expression change. 'Yes, it must be a relief. I believe he stayed longer than expected, didn't he?'

She stepped out of the shop and stood for a moment breathing deeply in the salt air. Then she turned back towards The Rush House. She would not after all be going to the beach that morning.

# Chapter Three

*Present*

I

Helena's mother, Joanna, daughter of the photographer Donaldson, had also received a letter from the purposeful Nick Broadbent asking her to help with his research. But when Helena broached the subject with her, Joanna shut up drum tight, thin-lipped and cold-eyed.

'I have no information on Donaldson that would be of interest,' she said.

Joanna was always so busy that she never seemed able to give her undivided attention to a conversation. On this occasion she was in the dining room of the thirties semi to the west of Shrewsbury where she and her husband, Robin, had lived since their marriage. Joanna had set up her sewing machine on the varnished beech table and was making Nina a pair of harlequin-patterned dungarees.

'But you'd have no objection if I decided to work on the book,' Helena persisted. When there was no response she added: 'I wondered if we could get that box of papers down from the loft.'

The old-fashioned machine whirred into action. As a child Helena had been allowed to work the foot pedal, always pressing too hard so that stitching ripped along a seam at a terrifying rate. Her mother, by contrast, had everything well under control.

'What do you think, Mum?' Helena asked at last.

'About what?' Joanna raised bland blue eyes to Helena. She had an oddly expressionless face, plumper now, so that the once-strong lines of cheek and jaw were blurred.

There are times when I want to break her open, Helena thought furiously. She can just disappear. Even her skin seems to become more opaque. 'In any case,' Helena added, 'I'm going to Westwich with Caroline. So it would be interesting to take another look at Donaldson's photos of the area.'

'Where will you stay in Westwich?'

'Overstrands. The house owned by Michael's great-aunt, Clara. She's coming too.'

'I thought Clara Mayrick had been put into a home.'

'She wasn't "put" into one. She wanted to go. Overstrands was much too big for her.'

'So why ever has the family kept on that great white elephant of a house?'

'I think she couldn't bear to sell it. She makes a little money from summer lets. And the family uses it quite often.'

'Can Clara see at all now?'

'A little, I think. As much as ever.'

The presser foot was lifted with a subdued click, pins whisked from the fabric, thread snipped.

'Anyway,' Helena said, 'I'll ask Dad to get that box down from the loft, if that's all right.'

'Oh, I'm not sure I didn't throw it out.'

'You couldn't have done.'

'There's not a great deal of point keeping all that stuff. It doesn't mean anything to anyone now.'

'Surely it means a lot to you.'

'No. I don't think so.'

A long silence unfurled as Joanna fastened the waistband to the bib. The subject was closed. But still Helena sought her mother's blessing so that she could go to Westwich with a quiet mind, at least on Joanna's account. 'It will give you and Dad a break to have us away,' she said. 'Unless you want to come too … You could, you know.'

'Oh no. I'll never go back to Westwich. It's far too chilly.'

Helena drove east with a yawning space beside her where Michael should have been. She had no eyes for the way that even the dustiest verges had been beautified by the succulent greens of early May. Across a widening sky high clouds plumed. Nina, strapped into her chair in the back, munched her way through grapes and biscuits, dozed or listened to her selection of nursery rhyme tapes. Neither of them spoke much.

For Helena, driving a long distance whilst following a carefully annotated route required intense concentration. As both her parents had warned repeatedly, the journey across the Midlands seemed interminable. Not for the first time was Helena's dominant feeling one of resentment at Michael for leaving her to cope alone. She stopped frequently, though gripped by anxiety that they might somehow never arrive. But by late afternoon she saw the name Westwich on a signpost for the first time and began the last lap across the wide, softly sloping fields towards the sea.

Although she had not been back since meeting Michael eleven years previously, Helena found the house, Overstrands, without difficulty. The five-barred gate giving access to the garden was swung wide open, exactly as she remembered it.

Her mother-in-law, Caroline, came to the door at once, alerted by the sound of tyres on gravel. Her smile was as brisk as ever. 'Ah, look at Nina, is she asleep? Try not to wake her.'

The house smelt neglected, Helena noticed immediately. It had assumed its status of holiday home with resigned ease. The paint-work was chipped, the old carpets threadbare, and the furniture an unloved hotchpotch peculiar to seasonally let houses. All Clara's more valuable possessions had been moved with her or divided among the family so that the house could be hired out without fear of damage being done to precious things.

Helena had met Clara Mayrick only once at a family gathering. The old lady had attended neither Michael's wedding nor his funeral. Helena knew Clara to be something of an institution, part of the web of jokes and anecdotes that Michael had shared with his sister and cousins and which Helena, an only child, had found so alarming.

Clara was the last of her generation, the unmarried younger sister of three now long-dead, brothers. She was fiercely loyal to the Mayrick clan, devoted to her brothers' offspring and their descendants, although circumstances and ill-health had prevented her from visiting Michael and Helena in Shrewsbury. Clara was now in her late eighties and almost blind. With her advancing years she had also become very deaf and had shrunk to bird-like proportions. Her wrists and ankles were so frail-looking that it seemed one might snap them in a careless moment, and her angular shoulder blades thrust out the collar of her tiny shirt-waisted dress. Helena could tell that Nina, whose head had previously been lolling sleepily against her grandmother's shoulder, was now wide awake, riveted by the sight of Clara's thick stockings concertinaed at the ankle, and by her glasses with their translucent whorled lenses. Fortunately Clara's sight was so poor that she was unlikely to be offended by the child's stare.

'Please, don't get up,' Helena exclaimed as Clara levered herself out of a low armchair.

'Of course I'll get up.'

Helena's hand was clasped by dry, cool fingers and Clara's face was thrust upwards to study hers. The old woman's grey eyes were distorted by the thick lenses. It was clear that Clara had never been pretty, for her nose was very pronounced in her small face, her mouth obstinate. One of the Mayrick myths about her was that she hadn't a single filling and that all her teeth were her own.

'It was very kind of you to invite us,' Helena told her, and then had to repeat the feeble words much more loudly.

'Will you come and help me with supper, Nina?' asked Caroline. 'I expect your mummy could do with a cup of tea.'

'She certainly could,' Helena agreed.

'You sit there and rest. It's not easy driving so far alone, as I know only too well.'

Yes, thought Helena, returning Caroline's sympathetic smile, yes, I'm aware that you are a widow too. But you are able to grieve for your men with a purity of sorrow that is denied me.

The chair was by a popping gas fire, lit despite the warmth of the evening outside. Helena pushed her shoulders back against the old cushions and closed her eyes for a moment. Only now did she become fully aware of the tension created by the drive. Here, with her legs scorched by the fierce blaze, soothed by the distant clatter of activity in the kitchen and, nearer at hand, a persistent, metallic ticking from an old clock, she felt suddenly peaceful.

When she opened her eyes she realized that Clara had not moved but was standing with her hand on the arm of her chair, as if for support, and was gazing down at her. Helena smiled confusedly and murmured: 'I'm sorry, you must think me terribly rude. It's just so lovely to be here.'

It was apparent that Clara could neither see her smile nor hear her apology. 'Michael was always my favourite,' she said suddenly. Her voice, made harsh by her deafness, was so lacking in musicality that her words sounded shockingly deliberate. 'But I knew he would end like this.'

Helena almost leapt from her chair in surprise. 'Why?' she cried.

'He always took chances. He did not court danger, but he liked it. Risk. That's what I loved in him. And always for someone else. He put himself out for people. I wasn't surprised when he married you. But in the end you can give too much of yourself. I think so.'

Helena was too startled to untangle this. She had been used, of late, to people talking in hushed, careful words. 'It wasn't a risk marrying me, I hope,' she said, again having to repeat her words when Clara plunged her head forward with a blind, ducking movement.

'Oh yes. It was a risk him marrying you. All marriage is risky. I never tried it.'

Helena suddenly laughed. 'Yes, all marriage is.' And then she remembered the note. 'All marriage is a risk.'

Clara turned away abruptly and moved about the room, fetching first a little table, then a cloth and placing them carefully by Helena's chair. 'Let me!' Helena cried.

'No, no. You're tired.' She was surprisingly deft, presumably made confident by the familiarity of her surroundings.

'Is this house much changed from when you used to live here all the time?' Helena shouted.

'The furniture is. Not the rooms.'

'No. I suppose not.' The drawing room in which she sat was beautifully proportioned, large and light with its huge bay and glass doors opening onto the lawn.

'When I was a child I remember the floors were always gritty with sand. They still are because we let the house to families, and children find sand even on pebbly beaches. But then we had small rugs and polished floors, and of course I was close to them as a tiny child and I remember the textures.' She laughed, a somewhat uncomfortable, rasping chuckle. 'I loved the house because for me it meant holiday.'

In came Caroline and Nina, who was pushing an old-fashioned oak trolley, its wheels clunking agreeably over the bumps in the floor. Helena could tell that the child's spirits had lifted already. Caroline fetched the little girl a low footstool and gave her a special serviette embroidered with flowers. 'Aunty Clara did that lovely sewing when she was small,' she informed her. And Nina, enchanted by the delicate china plate on which was served her chocolate cake, favoured Helena with the conspiratorial grin of pleasure last seen at the swimming pool on the afternoon of the accident.

There were six bedrooms at Overstrands which was why it was so rarely let off-season. To heat so large and airy a house on that coast was very costly. Caroline had given Helena and Nina the main bedroom and its tiny adjoining dressing room where Nina had a bed adorned with a smart pink and grey duvet cover and matching pillow case. There was even a cut-glass vase containing cherry blossom on the bedside table. At bed-time Nina sat like a princess against a pile of pillows whilst her grandmother read her a story.

Helena escaped into the garden to breathe deeply the cold evening air, its aroma a heady mix of sappy grass and salt from the sea. She had found since Michael's death that she could never inhale sufficiently and that her breath came in shallow

44

gasps. She walked down the drive to the gate and looked out across the lane to the stile opposite.

Yes, it was exactly as she remembered it, although the foot-path sign had been changed to a modern, foreshortened variety. The sky above the fields was still luminous with daylight but distant trees were silhouettes.

How far I am, Helena thought, from that girl who sat on the stile eleven years ago and saw Michael for the first time. Yet the stile is only a few feet from me.

2

On the afternoon of her first meeting with Michael, Helena had been in Westwich alone.

After her finals she and two friends hired a tent near Southwold and for the first time Helena found herself within reach of her mother's childhood home. One morning she asked to be dropped off in Westwich. There she examined the small village and especially the churchyard, and then embarked on a circular walk.

Her head, as she set out along the lane leading inland from the village, was full of family history for she had discovered without difficulty the graves of her great-grandmother, Julia Styles, and of Maud Waterford who had been her mother's guardian for eleven years. For a while Helena followed almost blindly a path through a copse and across broad, flat fields.

But then she came to a stile and was confronted, across a narrow lane, by a wide opening in a neat hedge. A five-barred gate was flung back against the edge of a gravel drive and nearby was a little shed with one small window and a steeply pitched roof which was being creosoted by a tall, bearded man in a red and blue checked shirt. Behind him was the façade of a large house, curious both for its disproportionate number of windows and for its having been set slap in the middle of a great expanse of lawn, like a ship on the ocean. The sun was reflected slant-wise at a number of levels in panes of glass and burnished the man's dark hair. Helena thought his features too beautiful to be obscured by a beard.

He turned and noticed her perched on the stile, staring at him.

'Sorry,' was the first thing she said to him. 'I'm sorry. I was just surprised to see a house here. I hadn't noticed it on the map.'

'It is rather in the middle of nowhere,' he agreed, holding his brush still so that creosote dripped onto the gravel.

Helena was hot after her walk. She was glad to rest for a moment on the stile and smile back at this friendly man. His smile was unforgettable, she later realized. It caught her up and made her glad.

'Are you staying locally?' he asked.

'I am, yes. Well, in Southwold actually. But my mother grew up in Westwich.' She felt the need to be more than just an ordinary tripper to him. 'What about you, have you always lived here?'

'Good Lord, no. I'm just here helping out a great-aunt.'

'I see.'

There followed a moment when she might have moved on. The conversation had concluded its first formal exchange and there was nothing more for strangers to say. But Helena stayed on her perch, conscious of the sun-warmed wood beneath her hand, and he stood with one shoulder against the uncreosoted wall of the shed, his paint brush forgotten.

Then he asked: 'Where are you walking to?'

'I'm meeting some friends by the church in Westwich. I thought I'd go back along the cliffs.'

After a moment he said: 'Actually I was just going to the village – we're out of tea bags – would you mind if I came with you?'

'No. No, that's fine.'

'I won't be a second.'

He dropped his brush into the can of creosote and walked rapidly away into the house. She watched his broad shoulders and his rapid, easy stride and a little tremor stirred in her throat. And yet she was also conscious that his perfect absorption in his task, the self-possession which had at once attracted her, had been marred by her arrival.

46

She lowered herself off the stile and hovered outside the gate until he re-emerged, and then together they set off along the field-path which led to the cliff, her head bobbing along level with his upper arm, the sun hot on her hair.

## 3

As soon as she was up and dressed on her first morning Nina insisted that she be taken down to the sea. 'Yes,' Caroline said at once, 'I'll come with you. There'll be someone here to keep Clara company. I'd love a morning on the beach.'

By ten o'clock a little heap of bags and buckets had been collected in a corner of the hall. Nina hopped about on the black and white tiles asking every minute: 'Can we go now? Please.'

But then Caroline registered what her granddaughter was wearing. 'Nina, you can't go on the beach in shorts. It'll be very cold. It always is.' She took the protesting child upstairs for more wind-proof garments.

At that moment there was a tap on the kitchen door. 'Unlock it, will you, Helena,' Caroline called.

Helena dragged back the two old bolts and let in a stocky, competent-looking woman wearing a shell suit and holding a plastic carrier bag. 'You must be Myra,' Helena said, smiling. 'How nice of you to come.' In fact she was aware that Myra had looked after Overstrands for years. She cleaned between lets and babysat for the family when they were staying. 'I'm Caroline's daughter-in-law, Helena.'

'Yes.' Myra had an alarmingly cool, judgemental gaze and a severe mouth. She did not smile.

'Anyway, I'll go and get ready, if you'll excuse me.' Helena retreated hastily from the kitchen. She was accustomed to kid-glove treatment these days and Myra's apparent hostility was unnerving.

Caroline, by contrast, seemed eager to spend a few minutes gossiping with Myra before they left, and Helena and Nina kicked gravel in the front garden, waiting for her to emerge from the house. She might apologize for keeping us waiting,

Helena thought childishly when at last Caroline appeared. Her mother-in-law's determination to be cheerful and her brisk energy had an enervating effect on Helena. Besides, she dreaded the coming walk through the fields to Westwich which would be so steeped in the memory of those first minutes with Michael.

Yet she found there was comfort after all in the blowing May morning. Nina tugged and pulled at her hand, ran ahead, then hopped about, waiting impatiently for Caroline and Helena to catch up. They followed the path along the edge of the field opposite Overstrands, through a little copse afloat with bluebells, and out into the darkly hedged lane which led to Westwich.

Helena's memory had compacted the village. She had forgotten the long curve of the lane after the church and she did not expect to see a line of parked cars pressed against the hedge. Feeling suddenly proprietorial she stopped opposite the gates of The Rush House and told Nina: 'This is where your other gran's mother used to live. She was called Ruth.'

Caroline exclaimed, 'I don't think I'd ever realized that your family actually belonged here.'

'Yes. For a while. The house was sold in the twenties.'

'I know the current owners a little,' Caroline said eagerly. 'I'm sure they'd let you go in if you wanted.'

Helena resisted this idea at once. 'I wouldn't wish to intrude,' she said.

The house was set behind a high brick wall, broken only by a wide gateway flanked on either side by unpretentious square pillars. Ruthless modernisations to the Victorian structure had been inflicted by recent owners. Helena had difficulty seeing past the maroon BMW, white mock-Georgian front door and double glazing to the house which had once belonged to her mother's family. Each window was draped with heavy lace curtaining; hanging baskets adorned the porch, and the garden at the front had been crazy-paved to allow extra parking. A summerhouse and various children's toys could be glimpsed in the back.

'Let's go to the beach before Nina explodes with impatience,' Helena suggested.

But she could not resist stopping once more, this time at the cottage which she had identified on her last visit as Maud Waterford's. 'When your gran was a little girl,' she told Nina, 'a very kind lady lived here called Maud. She looked after Gran all the time.'

Nina stopped dead. The cottage had untidy thatch and in the tiny garden to the side was a rusty whirligig washing line strewn with old vests and greying shirts. 'It's like Milly Molly Mandy's house,' she said and turned away.

'You must ask Clara if she remembers your mother or grand-mother,' Caroline said. 'I told her about your grandfather, Donaldson, and she says she actually met him a couple of times. But the trouble is, her memory is patchy. It's worth asking her though.'

Helena responded wearily. 'Oh, I don't think I'll bother with Donaldson after all. He was rather an obscure photographer, and I really don't want to go burrowing about in family history, some of which is rather sad and painful to my mother. They can get someone else to do it.'

'But it's all here,' said Caroline. 'How can you resist it?'

Access to the beach was gained by following the single street away from the little row of cottages which constituted all that remained of Westwich Town, down to an untidy track which led past a small car park and onto the shore. The beach consist-ed of long, high banks of pebbles and was consequently not a favourite spot for most holiday-makers. Even though it was unusually fine for early May a stiff breeze blew in from the sea. A few stalwarts walked their dogs or marched briskly along by the water's edge, but this was not Nina's idea of how to spend a morning on the beach. A picnic blanket must be unfolded, towels and buckets unpacked and shoes and socks discarded.

The trek down to the water was arduous as Nina had to be lifted across stones strewn with various unpleasant jetsam to where stretches of coarse sand had been left by the low tide.

Nina then stated that if there was sea she must be allowed to swim. 'It's far too cold,' Helena said at once.

'It's not, it's boiling.' So, despite the bracing wind and the patchy clouds which frequently obscured the sun, she had to be dressed in her little swimming costume and escorted down to the water again. Helena stood shivering with irritation and cold while her daughter pranced in the waves. 'Hurry up, Nina. It's freezing…' Had Michael been there he could have scooped Nina up and whirled her about in the water. He would have had endless stamina and in any case never seemed to feel the cold.

'I'm not cold, I'm too hot!' shrieked Nina though her lips were pale and goose pimples roughened her arms. She became like a malevolent sprite in the water – her eyes darting with excitement, her wet hair clinging to her shoulders.

Once Nina had allowed herself to be dried, she and Caroline set off in search of unusual pebbles and shells. Caroline, dressed in a tracksuit and soft shoes, moved with a cheerful, determined stride, her features set in an expression of unquenchable hopefulness. Meanwhile Helena lay back on the stones and felt the sun warm on her face. There was almost a pleasure in grieving on a day such as this. Her suffering gave her purpose and identity. It filled her up.

But at her hip, tucked into the pocket of her jeans, was the letter.

For a moment she thought of taking the crumpled sheet of paper and tearing it up in a dramatic sacrificial gesture. She would cast the little scraps onto the waves and let go the anger and jealousy incited by that letter.

She stood up and thrust her hand into the pocket in readiness. But it was hopeless. She could not discard the one link she had with this other woman.

All of a sudden there was a surprising interruption to the tranquillity of Westwich beach. At the end of a forlorn row of deserted huts was a wooden shed from which hung an aged *Walls Ice Cream* sign which even Nina could tell offered no hope to holiday-makers in search of refreshment. But at half past eleven precisely the hatch of this shed was flung open and a pimply face emerged to peer gloomily out over the sparsely populated strand. With white, slow hands the youth arranged a few polystyrene beakers on the counter, a number of which were immediately seized by the breeze and whooshed smartly off along the beach. Undeterred, the youth boiled a kettle on a small gas ring and then cried in a thin, high voice: 'Teas, coffees, sundries.'

Nina, fascinated, came running back to Helena. 'Please can I have a sundry?' she asked and was disappointed when the sundry turned out to be a choice between a Wagon Wheel or a Kitkat.

Caroline was eager to talk of Michael. Memories, anecdotes and observations spilled out of her all the time. She and Helena sat side by side, sipping coffee from a thermos. Close by, but out of earshot, Nina was making a burrow with her metal spade. She had organized her best pebbles into a family, and was intent on constructing a home for them. She seemed not to mind that the stones kept falling in on themselves but with endless patience began again on building a little walled fort.

'Michael adored this beach,' Caroline said. 'Well, both the children did when they were small. They were the envy of all their friends, having a relative by the sea. We used to come here most summers to stay with Clara.'

'It's not a very hospitable coast,' Helena said.

'The children never seemed to mind about the weather. They were like Nina. The sea was enough for them. And Michael was always making friends, always picking up other children and involving them in elaborate games down by the water.'

'I would have thought he found this area very dull. He loved mountains so much.'

'He liked the openness of this landscape, I suppose.' Caroline sat with her knees drawn up, her gaze on Nina's small, absorbed form. 'I must buy Nina a hair-band,' she said suddenly. 'All that hair must irritate her.'

'Michael always said that about my hair. He thought it too intrusive and floppy.' Helena spoke in a clenched, hard voice which reflected the enraged irritation she was beginning to feel with Caroline, who sat so strong and noble in her grief.

'He was dreadfully conventional in some ways, I'm afraid. And terribly tidy. Did you find that? He liked everything in place. I can imagine him going on about your hair. He used to brush mine for me when he was a boy. He loved that. And then he'd clip it back severely in place. You could tell he was destined to teach.' Caroline put her hand to her short grey hair, as if to relive the touch of her son's hand.

'His mania for order was one of his least endearing qualities,' Helena said savagely.

Caroline seemed oblivious to her hostility. 'You could forgive him almost anything because he was so kind. He would do anything for anyone. Even people here, who haven't seen him for years, remember that in him. The number who've come up to me and spoken of him with fondness! Unstinting, he was.'

'Would you mind,' Helena said, her face turned away so that all she could see was the long sweep of beach stretching away to the distant, low headland, 'if we didn't talk about Michael?'

She sensed Caroline's startled hurt and experienced a thrill of triumph. Hadn't she intended to interrupt the woman's smug eulogy? But quickly following came a desire to weep at her own cruelty, a sensation familiar from those times with Michael when his blithe good nature had led her to wound, simply to make some impact. To soften her words she added: 'How terrible for you to have lost a husband and a son. You bear it so well.'

Caroline now sat with her head bent, dropping pebbles one on another through her finger and thumb. 'I try simply to be glad that I had those years with Simon and Michael,' she said. 'I try to thank God for their lives, but it is hard. And I was fortunate that I married into a large family like the Mayricks. I think you'll find them a source of strength too.'

Most days, after lunch, Caroline would take everyone for a drive. Clara, it seemed, loved car journeys. In preparation for an outing she would dress in her minute beige raincoat, leaf-patterned scarf, brown mohair hat and cotton gloves. Lastly she picked up the large, cream handbag without which she never moved. She was so small that the seat belt in the car cut across her throat when she was strapped in. She plucked at the tight band in annoyance. 'I'm sure they wouldn't arrest an old woman like me if I left it off,' she muttered.

'No. It's me they would throw into prison,' said Caroline, and became involved in a long conversation with Nina about this interesting possibility.

One afternoon Caroline suggested that they should go boating on the lake at Thorpeness. They parked near the water and sat for a while watching the bright-painted boats, all freshly decked out for the new season.

'Actually,' said Helena suddenly, 'if you don't mind I'll stay in the car with Clara. I don't feel up to a rowing boat.'

She knew it was mean to expect Caroline to take Nina out on the water alone but she could not bear to accompany them. They walked off together towards the jetty, Nina skipping along but turning occasionally to wave at her mother. Caroline's posture suggested her habitual good cheer.

Clara did not speak for several minutes after they had gone, and Helena suddenly realized that the old woman had fallen asleep, her head flopped against the warm upholstery, her mouth slightly open. Helena sighed with relief. She had not relished the prospect of half an hour's strained conversation with Clara.

4

By the end of her week's camping holiday Helena had met with Michael on three successive evenings. On the last day she and her friends planned to go boating at Thorpeness and she suggested to Michael the evening before that he might like to go with them.

He refused. 'I have to help my great-aunt Clara. There's still so much to do and she's moving in a fortnight,' he explained, 'and besides, you'll want your friends to yourself on the last day.'

Helena was offended by what she took to be a rejection of her company. We might never see each other again, she thought, and he can't even give me one afternoon. Or perhaps he's not interested in me enough to meet my friends. So when they parted she was huffy and offhand. 'I don't expect I'll see you tomorrow night,' she told him. 'I expect the others will want to have a special meal. But I may be in touch when I get home – if I've time.' She didn't kiss him, but walked away with a carefree wave of her hand.

But the next day, which was cold and blowy, not at all suitable for spending a couple of hours in a rowing boat, was miserable for her. Like all last days it suffered from too much pressure to be joyous, and already preoccupations about the future had taken over from undiluted pleasure in the holiday. Rachel was going immediately to a law firm in Manchester, and Victoria was embarking on a career in retailing and had a room in Putney. Only Helena had not yet found a place and would be returning home whilst she waited to hear from the numerous publishing and broadcasting companies to which she had applied. And her cold parting from Michael haunted the day. She had never before experienced such longing to be with a man but had not expected falling in love to be so complex. Why could she not be whole-hearted? she wondered. Why did she resent the hold he already had over her?

By the end of an interminable afternoon she was in a state of agonized self-reproach, terrified that he would refuse to see her again. Immediately they reached the shore she called him from a phone box and asked if he would meet her in the evening. He seemed unsurprised to hear from her and agreed at once to come to Southwold.

She expected him to be offended and difficult, but found that he had not even noticed her ill humour of the day before. It was a very chill evening but he suggested they walk rather than sit in a stuffy pub. He was wearing a huge, fleece-lined jacket, but she was inadequately dressed in a thin waterproof. After a while he tucked her playfully under his arm and wrapped his jacket about them both. She savoured the warmth of his body and was so consumed by the desire to make love to him that she could scarcely breathe.

He seemed happy simply to stride along by the sea and talk to her about his family in Birmingham and his job as a teacher there. His life to her seemed wonderfully settled, his pleasures uncomplicated. When he told her of his enthusiasm for mountaineering she regretted that her own life had been so unadventurous.

Eventually, though, she could not suppress her shivers for as the last light died from the sea the wind grew stronger. He made her run back along the sand beneath the dunes, stumbling and laughing as the wind buffeted them. She was terrified that they would return with nothing said, no commitments made.

'Let me buy you a drink,' she offered.

'No, I don't want to go inside. I love the night air.'

Panic rose in her. Did he not want to be with her then? But she had begun to realize that despite being several years older he was intensely shy. 'If only there was bit of shelter I would be fine,' she said.

He pulled her close and buried his nose in her hair. 'I'll give you shelter, any time you like.'

When she raised her face to his he was waiting for her. That kiss was the first she had ever returned without feeling a tremor of reluctance. They tumbled down into the cool, fine sand among the dunes, laughing and kissing and edging their bodies closer and closer together.

At three in the morning he delivered her back to the tent dizzy and stupid with love. She lay awake in her sleeping bag until six, listening to the calm breathing of her companions, her mind crammed full of the memory of him.

5

'Of course, I knew your grandmother, Ruth Styles, very well.'

Clara, it seemed, had woken up.

Helena opened her eyes and saw the brilliance of the afternoon. In the distance was the little yellow paddle boat making a slow circle near the edge of the lake. Nina's short legs were finding the pedals hard going. 'Yes, I suppose you must have met her if you came to Westwich when you were a girl,' she replied at last.

Clara gave no indication that she had heard. She was sitting forward in her seat, catching at the metal clasp of her handbag with eager, restless fingers. 'Yes. My brothers and I thought her the most beautiful and exotic creature that ever lived.'

'Did you?'

'You see, she was a very young woman when I first knew her. She had wonderful shiny hair, like yours, and brilliant eyes. She was so lively. She could make us laugh and laugh. And as I just had brothers, this girl in her light dresses seemed terribly glamorous to me.'

'And my grandfather, Donaldson?' asked Helena, her heart leaping with interest.

'We came down every summer, right up until the war, and after that Overstrands was used as a convalescent home. And anyway we wouldn't have a holiday there without the boys. But your grandmother Ruth came to stay with us in Oxford several times. And then no more.'

There was a long silence while Helena watched the little yellow boat move hesitantly back to the jetty. 'How did Ruth come to be acquainted with your family?' she asked.

For once her question was accurately heard. Clara cocked her head and listened attentively. 'Oh, you could not miss in a village the size of Westwich.'

Helena tried again. 'Did you ever meet my grandfather, Hubert Donaldson? He was in Westwich too, you know. It's where the two of them met.'

'Donaldson.' The name was spoken deliberately, as if it were answer enough. Clara's small, knotted fingers with their ridged nails plucked at the wool blanket. 'Donaldson came to our house in Oxford once. Yes.'

'What was he like?'

Clara rested her head back against the seat and closed her eyes. 'I could see much better in those days. I saw them together. And I knew that Donaldson did not wear a ring.'

'What do you mean?'

Caroline and Nina had by this time disembarked and were approaching the car carrying large, dripping ice creams and grinning triumphantly.

'I don't understand,' Helena said, leaning forward and speaking loudly into Clara's ear.

'No. No. That's all right. My mother, in particular, was very fond of Ruth, you see. Very fond of her. It was a blow when she disappeared so suddenly. Without a word.'

Helena's door was flung open to reveal Nina's beaming face. 'Gran's bought us ice cream with flakes. Did you see us? Did you see me on the boat?'

'Oh yes,' said Clara. 'We saw. You were splendid.'

# Chapter Four

*Past*

The Westwich summer was crowded with new faces. At the beginning of his long holidays Harry was accompanied to Westwich by a silent friend named Alec McGrew. Abnormally tall for his age, Alec was so thin that his head seemed too heavy to be supported by his reedy torso so that he resembled a drooping tulip. His expression was amiable enough but he never spoke and his only impact on The Rush House was the flapping of his huge feet on the stairs and the disappearance of vast plate-fuls of Mrs Millerchip's cooking. Alec was fascinated by birds and this obsession made him an ideal companion for lazy Harry who lay dozing idly whilst his friend sat silent among the reed-beds, watching.

Maud was exasperated by Alec. One morning she came bustling up to The Rush House to find Ruth sprawled face down on a rug under a rowan tree revealing her ankles and calves to Millerchip who shuffled about in the nearby vegetable patch. 'Ruth. Those boys really are the limit. Can't they see that you're alone all day? Surely they could offer to take you out with them?'

Ruth rolled over onto her back, the flounces of her petticoats askew, her eyes dazzled as she gazed up at Maud. She laughed. 'I have absolutely no desire to go with them anywhere. I'm just relieved that Alec keeps Harry blamelessly occupied.'

Maud plumped down beside her, smoothed her skirt careful-ly over her knees and glowered forbiddingly at Millerchip's stooping form. 'How's Julia?'

'Tired, she says. I can't persuade her to come out.'

For once Maud did not comment further but said 'Well you won't be lonely any more. I've found you an entire houseful of interest and purpose. You're needed.' Maud pronounced this last word with such an air of triumph that Ruth could not help laughing.

'That sounds ominous. I'm not sure I want to be needed.'

When she had a mission Maud was very difficult to deflect. 'I was in the shop this morning and I met the solicitor who's taken Overstrands for the summer. He has three young sons and his wife's... There will be a baby very soon. The poor man had the boys with him and looked very harassed. Mrs Spendmore did not make them welcome, I'm afraid.'

'I should think not.'

'Well, I waited outside and said: "I expect you're the family staying at Overstrands." He was delighted that I had troubled to introduce myself and he admitted that the boys were rather a handful. And then I thought of you. "I know someone who's excellent with children," I said, "and I'm sure she would be glad to lend a hand."'

'Maud! I know nothing about children.'

'Oh, of course you do. He is such a nice man and seemed very pleased that I should take such an interest. So we're going up to tea tomorrow.'

Ruth wondered what else had been said during that conversation and how much of her own predicament had been explained. But she took Maud's hand and gave it a squeeze. 'Three boys. Maud, I had been anticipating a peaceful summer.'

The next day Ruth and Maud crossed the fields to Overstrands, a large, modern house built by the Moores at Upstones to replace their ancient farmhouse. But having spent two winters in the new building the family had decided that Overstrands was too cold and too exposed to the elements compared to their snug, low-ceilinged old house. So, much to the entertainment of their fellow villagers, back the family had moved, leaving Overstrands unloved and empty amidst its wide lawns.

Ruth thought the exterior of the house beautiful and had always been curious to know what it would be like inside. She and Maud scrunched up the short gravel drive and climbed three semi-circular steps to the porch. The door was opened by a boy of about nine who shook hands solemnly with them. 'Good afternoon. I'm Simon Mayrick.' They followed his slender form with its wonderful head of thick wavy brown hair across a light hall to the drawing room. Glancing through open doorways Ruth saw that the rooms were spacious, and innocent of heavy furniture and ornaments. It was as if a great sandstorm had scoured the walls, curtains, wooden floors and chair coverings and left them faded but bleached clean. And through the large, sunny rooms were strewn the Mayrick family belongings: children's toys, buckets and spades, fishing nets, towels and bathing suits.

Mrs Mayrick was seated in a low chair by glass doors opening onto the garden. Her bulky figure was swathed in loose cotton, her neck was slender and her smile bright. She had the same clear, alert eyes as her son.

Ruth and Maud sat with her at the window while tea was brought by a procession of little boys. The middle son, Mark, was the quietest and, once released from his duties as waiter, disappeared into the garden with a book tucked under his arm. Giles, the youngest, had enchanting blue eyes and a mop of fair curls. He was obviously used to charming his mother's friends for he pressed confidingly close to Ruth and offered to show her his drawings.

'Take no notice of Giles,' exclaimed Esther Mayrick. 'He will get you in a corner and claim all your attention for hours at a time.'

'That's all right, I don't mind.' Ruth rested her hand on the child's warm hair and returned his smile. How lovely, she thought, to be Giles Mayrick, in this affectionate, joyful family.

Afterwards Maud remarked to Ruth that she could not imagine Robert Mayrick writing wills or advising on law suits, he was so frivolous and engaged in such noisy rough and tumble with his children after tea. 'A great deal of me hopes that this child will be another boy,' Esther said, tapping her swollen abdomen and watching her husband gallop across the grass with one son clinging monkey-fashion to his neck. 'Just imagine a girl in the midst of these idiotic males.'

'She would certainly be spoilt,' said Maud.

'I would fear for her. I think it is hard to be a girl in a family of boys. She would have the burden of the house and the care of Robert and myself on her conscience. I would wish my girl to be independent, a scholar perhaps, not a servant to these boys.'

Ruth leaned forward in her chair. 'I should love to be an independent woman. I want to do something with my life.'

'Oh dear,' cried Maud, 'don't go filling this child's head with radical ideas. She reads enough as it is.'

But in Esther's smile Ruth saw sympathy and affection. Esther will be my friend, she realized with mounting excitement. She understands me.

2

Hardly a day went by without Ruth going to Overstrands. Much of her time there was spent with the boys, particularly the two youngest. Mark was a collector and he and Ruth scoured the beach for shells that he later classified and displayed. Giles, the golden-haired rip of a child, was a natural comedian, wild and tough but requiring an audience to admire his every exploit. For him Ruth was an ideal companion. He loved her to chase him along the lanes, to applaud his somersaults and to listen to the ridiculous stories of villains and heroes he invented for her amusement. She was very touched by his affection for her, but his boundless energy exhausted her so that it was a relief when the boys were whisked away by their father or by bosomy Meg, the maid they'd brought with them from Oxford.

Ruth's greatest pleasure was to be left alone in the sunny drawing room with Esther Mayrick, to be quiet in her calm presence and to listen to her views on literature and politics. She was the first university-educated woman Ruth had met.

On the night before the Mayricks were due to leave Maud

offered to keep Julia company until supper so that Ruth might have a farewell tea with the Mayricks.

Ruth had never known a family so lacking in constraint. She watched fascinated as the parents embraced their children, or teased them, or chivvied them upstairs to bed. The Rush House, where Julia lay in her hot, dim room, occupied only a distant corner of Ruth's consciousness as she observed Esther Mayrick, a child tucked under each arm, lean against the headboard of her oldest son's bed to read Giles the story of 'The Little Red Hen'.

Afterwards Ruth and Esther sat in the garden, warmed by the last of the sunshine. It had been a jewel of a day, the air heavily scented with ripe vegetation, the sea a distant sigh and the sky a rich, still-blue.

With Esther Mayrick, Ruth was always thoughtful and diffident. Esther made Ruth feel like a child on the cusp of adulthood instead of an adult pretending to be a child, as was more customary.

'So, Ruth, we all know what the months ahead hold for me. What shall you do?'

'We return to London next week. There'll be masses of work to get everything straight, and then the usual callers. And I have my piano and my books.'

'I hope you will read. I'll send you anything worth while I discover. But I suppose there's no question of your continuing a formal education?'

'I could, of course. But I was glad to leave school last March. The discipline seemed to me petty. And they worked us very hard. We had to be good at everything, sport, languages, music, the lot.'

'Of course. Girls must excel. It's the only way for them to get on. I can't understand you, Ruth.'

Ruth remembered the bustle of the cloakrooms, the delicious hours spent poring over history text books, and the rush and shout on the lacrosse field. But such delights had been tempered by the acute apprehension that she had experienced, not because she had been unable to flourish in such an environment, but because she had succeeded too well. So much was expected of her. Too much. And then Julia had become ill. 'It was my mother. She was desperate to come to Westwich. And I couldn't allow her to be alone here. She won't have a paid companion. So I gave up school, willingly as it happens. But you've made me want to go on learning. I feel so ignorant when I talk to you.'

'Your mother sounds a little selfish.' Esther spoke mildly, kindly.

'Oh no. She can't help the way she is. She's ill. She never used to be like it. Please don't think I suffer. Not at all. I'm spoilt. I have these wonderful summers by the sea – and a splendid home in London. But you make me feel ... hungry. Excited. Bold. Do you understand?'

'Yes. Oh Ruth. You have no idea of the possibilities before you. You almost make me envious to see you so young with so much to discover. Look at me.' She lifted her hand in mock despair at her heavy body.

Ruth saw only Esther's composure and her joyful motherhood. 'I think your boys are very lucky,' she said, drawing a deep breath.

Esther reached out her hand to squeeze Ruth's. 'Write to me. Be strong.'

It was a moment that Ruth wished she could hold for ever. She smiled at Esther who sat warm and rosy in her pregnancy, serene and purposeful. Ruth did not want her to go away into the future.


Back at The Rush House Harry was at his most obstructive. Since Alec's departure he had chosen to loll about the garden or the small parlour. He had become awkward and morose so that mealtimes were a trial. Only when Alan Styles arrived did he mend his ways a little.

Alan was inclined to sympathize with his son. 'I was the same at his age. A household of women. What do you expect?'

And then came the flurry of packing for the return to London. The Rush House cringed. Harry blamed Ruth for misplacing his books, his grey pullover, his rugby stockings. Alan

Styles sat helplessly in the drawing room, leaping to his feet and collecting papers together in an attempt to look busy should anyone enter. Ruth and Mrs Millerchip washed, ironed, folded and labelled. Julia lay in her bed.

At first no notice was taken of her mood. After all, it was quite normal for her not to emerge from her room for days on end. But on the morning that the family was due to depart, Maud, arriving with a package of flapjacks she'd baked for their journey, found Harry in the lane teasing the horses Millerchip had hired from the farm. Inside, Ruth was collapsed in a despairing heap in the drawing room and from Julia's bedroom came the sound of Alan Styles's raised voice. The kitchen door was ajar to allow Mrs Millerchip full enjoyment of the drama.

'She won't go, Aunt Maud,' Ruth wailed. 'She says she's never going to leave, that she'll die if we take her back to London.'

'What nonsense. Whatever brought this on?'

'I don't know. But I'm afraid Father is only making matters worse.'

At that moment the door above slammed and Alan Styles's heavy tread could be heard descending the stairs. His bewildered face appeared in the doorway. 'Should I call the doctor, do you think?'

'Would you like me to have a word?' asked Maud.

As she climbed the steps to Julia's room Maud reflected how little the house had changed since she and Julia had played dressing-up games here when they were girls. Amidst squeals of delight they had encased themselves in a crinoline long since discarded by Julia's mother. Each was allowed a turn at playing the queen, flouncing up and down the hall with the glorious folds of skirt rustling and swaying. Here were the same, familiar oak boards in the passage, the same print of a woman with a dog above the banister, the same little table holding the same jug decorated with forget-me-nots. But the crinoline, like every other vestige of Julia's childhood, had been swept irrecoverably away one March morning. And now Julia lay wanly against the pillows, her hair a wild tangle, her enormous eyes staring fearfully at the door in anticipation of her next supplicant.

At sight of her friend Julia pleaded: 'Let me stay, Maud. Don't allow them to take me away. Let me stay.'

Maud at once realized that the situation was hopeless although she replied calmly: 'Of course you must go. You are needed in London. Alan cannot manage without you, and Ruth has been isolated here long enough.'

But Julia was far beyond being swayed by her responsibilities. She began to cry weakly. 'I can't go away. It will all be gone when I come back.'

'Whatever can you mean? Everything will be as you left it. It always is. I shall be here waiting for you, and Mrs Spendmore, the fat spider, will be sitting behind her counter in the shop. You need not fear that anything will change.'

'No. No. The sea will take it all. The church on the cliffs is already almost gone, Ruth says.'

'This house will not be taken by the sea in your life-time, Julia. Nor in Ruth's.'

'But I must stay here. It's safe here.'

Maud laid her hand on Julia's forehead, but despite the greyish pallor of the cheeks and the dilated pupils her friend showed no sign of fever.

For a moment Maud wondered about the practicalities of forcing Julia into her clothes and ushering her downstairs. But it was unthinkable that Julia should be subjected to such indignity. Ruth was hovering at the door. 'Stay with her a moment. I'll speak to your father,' Maud told her.

### 3

At Maud's insistence Julia was consigned to her care. Alan could not neglect his business any longer and Harry must be sent back to school. Ruth was too young to take on this new phase of her mother's illness. The local doctor was trusted by the family and undertook to restore Julia to a condition in which she might be induced to return to London.

Amidst all the excitement and anxiety Ruth had no time for farewells. It was her custom, at the end of the summer in

Westwich, to run about the house and village crying inwardly: 'Goodbye bedroom, goodbye garden, goodbye lovely beach…' Even Mrs Millerchip usually received a hug. But this time Ruth climbed numbly into the carriage and passed the first miles of her journey home in miserable contemplation of her mother's plight.

It was not until she was on the train that she began to consider her own predicament. Her father was seated opposite, his eyes closed in exhaustion. She gazed at him fearfully. Now he would be her only companion in the London house. Suddenly her yearning for the long summer days spent with the Mayrick family was so strong that she almost wept.

# Chapter Five

*Present*

I

Helena's father, Robin, was a tall man with a slightly military bearing. His face was deeply lined by worries about the small details of life for he attempted to protect his little family by being ever on the alert for possible mishap.

Robin was a man of simple tastes. After a conscientious career with the Inland Revenue he had found in retirement much pleasure in the golf course, his garden and his granddaughter. He had been passionately fond of Helena when she was a child but his love for Nina was unalloyed by the demands of work, or by the weight of parental responsibility. In the years since he had been a father of a young child domestic politics had changed, and now he would put on a pinafore to give Nina a bath or to cook dainty meals for her in the kitchen. He bought her wholesome little treats, planned expeditions to amuse her and loved to sit in his armchair with the child curled on his lap. For her painstaking attempts to read and her long, stumbling accounts of days at nursery he had endless patience.

His horror at Michael's death seemed to Helena to be more for the psychological damage such a blow might do Nina than for even his daughter's suffering. It was as if he regarded it as a personal failure that he had been unable to guard against the tragedy.

When Helena and Nina returned home to Shrewsbury after the holiday in Westwich, Robin was waiting for them in their front room, peering anxiously out of the window while his wife fussed in the kitchen. Helena, seeing him in his tie and neat sleeveless pullover, and with his rare smile of pure pleasure, had a sense of displacement. He was the wrong man in the wrong house. And she felt suddenly as she had when bringing home a disappointing report. Her father's faith in her ought not to be dented, and his present pain seemed to her almost as if she had failed him.

But Nina, feeling none of this, flew gladly into his arms.

Later, when his wife was bathing Nina, Robin said: 'A man rang today. I've written down his name. Nick Broadbent. It's about Donaldson.'

'Ah yes. I see. Was Mum here? Did she know?'

'Yes. I told her.'

'What did she say?'

'She said that if you were determined to work on a book about Donaldson she couldn't stop you.'

'Did this man explain his connection with Donaldson?'

'Oh yes. And in any case, your mother had a letter from him a couple of months ago herself. Of course, she wants nothing to do with any of it.'

There was a long pause. Helena continued piling washing into the machine while Robin made a pot of tea with the slow, deliberate movements which so infuriated his wife and had ensured his banishment from the kitchen for most of their married life.

'Dad. I really want to work on the Donaldson book now that I've been to Westwich. But do you think Mum would be upset?'

'She's bound to be.'

'I wish you'd explain why. I've never understood. Obviously the thought of her mother is painful to her. How could she forgive being abandoned like that? But it was hardly Donaldson's fault. He seems to have been such a good man...'

Robin was silent for a moment. 'Perhaps the fact that Donaldson never married your grandmother has something to do with it.'

'It must be more, surely.'

'Shall we have this tea here or in the living room? What do you think?' There it was, the deft change of subject.

68

'Anyway,' said Helena, 'at least I'll telephone Nick Broadbent. That can do no harm.'

On the day Helena climbed the mountain to see for herself where Michael had fallen, the sun baked hot on the heather, and light, high clouds cast fleeting shadows across the sweeping expanses of hills.

Michael had taught Helena to love the mountains. He had walked with her in all weathers, teased her for being unfit, taken her hand over streams and boulders, and once had tumbled to the earth with her in sweaty, unforgettable passion when they reached a deserted summit. So how could Michael be dead on a day such as this? How could she be mourning when the sun warmed her cheeks and the perfume from the new grass promised life and growth?

Helena carried nothing but a waterproof tied about her waist. Michael's friend Bill, who had offered to accompany her, was burdened with the weighty rucksack. The third member of the party was Sarah, one of the colleagues who had been with Michael on the mountain that day. Shirley, the other teacher, was still on sick-leave, suffering from shock.

Bill and Michael had been at school together. Although desperately shy of women, Bill had a fraternal affection for Helena which allowed him to be relatively easy in her presence. He was a huge man, bespectacled and sturdy, an academic of few words. His own grief was palpable for he bore his pain like a noble, wounded animal, and his efforts to comfort Helena were clumsy and therefore burdensome. He was too kind, too gentle, too deferential. And yet he was not able to anticipate her needs as Michael always had.

Sarah came because she knew where Michael had fallen.

Helena had met Sarah twice before: at a Christmas party and at Michael's funeral. During the party she had noted Sarah's lush figure and auburn, glossy hair. Sarah had worn a calf-length, button through black dress that would have made

Helena look wan and angular. The girl had seemed shy and rather over-awed by Michael.

At the funeral the pair had shaken hands. Sarah's clasp was tight with emotion, her eyes wet.

As they began the long climb up the mountain Helena was irritated by Sarah who seemed unnecessarily vague about what had happened, though it soon became apparent that the reason for her monosyllabic comments was that she was biting back tears. Ever on the alert for the author of Michael's love letter, Helena had hitherto considered Sarah far too young and naive to have written anything so confident but now, listening to her faltering account, it seemed entirely probable that Sarah was the unknown woman.

'Shirley and I were waiting down below by the lake with the group who didn't want to go all the way to the summit. Michael went off with the small party who wanted to climb right to the cairn, and that was the last we saw of him,' Sarah said. 'It was very peaceful by the lake and we had no idea anything had happened. And then two girls came pounding down the mountain, and I knew at once there was terrible trouble. But even when they said it was Michael who had fallen I didn't imagine he was dead…I mean…I'd just waved goodbye casually an hour before…' Her low, breathless voice became contorted by grief. 'Thank God this other party of hikers came, and I went up with one of them. The boys who had been with Michael were still there. They were shaking and silent. I began to grasp how bad it was. But I didn't register he was dead until I saw the helicopter. It was the way they heaved him onto a stretcher without proper care for an injured person that made me realize at last.' She raised her hand to her eyes. The breeze played in her bright hair.

Behind her the mountain beckoned invitingly, swathed in gorse, the path winding and well-trodden.

Helena was almost suffocated by rage and suspicion. What right had this woman to display such emotion? Had Sarah not been so weak and incompetent Michael would still be alive. He should never have gone alone to the summit with a party of inexperienced youngsters. Was it purely guilt at her professional neglect that was upsetting Sarah, or was she guilty on another count?

Unable to suppress her distrust and antagonism Helena walked on but called back in a light, high-pitched voice: 'Did you get on well with Michael while you were in his department?'

'Oh yes. I found him a marvellous teacher.'

'He always spoke very highly of you.'

'Did he? I'm so glad.'

'Yes. In a small department it's very important that people are friendly, I'm sure.'

'And then Michael gave us all a lot of support.'

Both women were panting with the exertion of climbing fast and steeply. Sarah added tremulously: 'I'm so glad I had the opportunity of working with Michael. I think it was a great privilege.'

A good many people had written to Helena expressing similar sentiments. '"Better to have loved and lost..." you mean,' she said with a harsh laugh.

'Something like that. Oh, I'm sorry to cry. You must think me terribly weak. You're the one that should be crying.'

Helena's thoughts at that moment were unspeakably violent. She gave another bark of laughter and with a sudden burst of speed caught up with Bill.

He too wanted to talk about Michael. He was, thought Helena, like some immense, loyal dog, untiring on the mountain but bereft of his chief companion. He recalled experiences shared with Michael, including other moments of danger. 'Remember when he and I spent a night in a bivouac on a mountainside in Ireland? We couldn't see a damn thing the rain fell so hard. And Michael had a mouth organ. I can still remember the sound of it, almost drowned by the drumming of the rain on the nylon of the bivouac. I have never been so wet in my life.' Helena thrust one hand through Bill's arm. His muscles tensed, though he endured her proximity with good grace. She had successfully excluded Sarah.

A soft voice from behind asked: 'Did you go climbing much with Michael, Helena?'

'A fair bit. Yes. Didn't Michael say? We walked a lot before we had Nina. It was always a shared interest.'

'I'm sure mountaineering must give one a great thrill, a huge sense of achievement. I mean, even in that one week with him he made me feel so different about the countryside. I'm a geographer but I'd never thought about the mountains in the same way – you know, almost as having personalities. He knew this area so well. It was like being introduced to friends he'd known for years.'

'I expect you feel terrible coming back like this,' Helena said, barely hiding the edge of dislike and sarcasm in her voice.

'The worst thing is that I can't help blaming myself all the time for not going with him to the top.'

'What could you have done to save him?'

'I don't know.'

'You can never guard against every possibility,' Bill said. 'You can be ninety-nine point nine per cent prepared and then something will happen: a rock fall, a storm, a flood. The weather is unpredictable. People think the mountains are eternal, but they change all the time.'

'Michael knew that,' Helena said defensively. The sun was too hot and her feet felt heavy.

'He did. And it's some comfort, isn't it, that he would have understood why he died? He would not have felt cheated. He knew the risk.'

'How can you say that? It was a gorgeous spring day apart from a bit of mist. He was on a simple geographical field trip with a bunch of school kids. Of course he should have been safe.' The word *cheated* had shaken her. She longed for her grief to be as simple as Bill's.

A sense of recrimination hung in the air. Sarah was silent. As well she might be, thought Helena. The mountain seemed to be listening to Helena's thoughts. The children had been in Michael's care. The boy should not have required rescuing. The newspapers had been generous, dubbing Michael a hero, but he should not have needed to display his courage. Perhaps his relationship with Sarah had proved too great a distraction even for him to think sanely.

'I hated the sun when it came out again later that afternoon,' Sarah said suddenly. 'I wanted it to be dark.'

After another pause Helena cried: 'What I keep thinking is: I hope the child that Michael saved is a good child. I hope he was worth it.'

'Michael would think any child worth saving,' Bill said at once.

Sarah added softly: 'And it's what I admired in him. He never considered his own needs.'

'Oh yes,' cried Helena. 'That's pretty admirable. To leave a four-year-old daughter and a wife and all your future simply to give yourself the satisfaction of knowing you have not been selfish.' She was remembering Clara's words about the risks Michael took. What right had he to take risks when ultimately she had to pay the price for his foolhardiness?

As she spoke she was overcome by such immense weariness that she could scarcely place one foot in front of the other. Everything was so wrong it could never be right again. How could she struggle on with such a sense of discord and misery? Her skin was moist and salty with sweat and her calf muscles ached as the ground climbed steeply, pitted by sheep shelters and criss-crossed by tiny paths, rabbit droppings and new heather. No one spoke for a very long time.

They ate the lunch provided by Helena's mother and walked on. Still the clouds scudded swiftly overhead and the skylarks sang. Other walkers greeted them. Helena wondered if they were aware of the recent tragedy, whether perhaps the mountain now had particular allure because someone had fallen to his death. Maybe the event was discussed in pubs and hostels: 'And he was an experienced walker. He fell whilst rescuing a pupil. Of course that scarp face has always been treacherous...But the weather was quite fine that day...'

Helena's heart was beating very fast in sick anticipation when they reached the summit. She tried to be calm. What are you expecting, she asked herself, blood-stained rocks? She knew that the mountain would be unmarked, for the wind had blown since that day, the rain had fallen, sheep had grazed. What she most feared was being left dissatisfied. She wanted Michael's death to be a certain, clean, inevitable event. She wanted to be sure that he'd had no alternative but to die.

Far below was the lake of deep, deep blue, reflecting the sky. On the other side of the horseshoe forming the edge of the plateau, scree slopes fell almost vertically. Sarah pointed to where she and the less adventurous members of the party had eaten lunch in ignorance of the drama above them.

'Do you want to visit the cairn, Helena?' Bill asked carefully.

'Did Michael, do you know?'

'Oh yes,' Sarah replied. 'One of the children had a photograph. Haven't you seen it?'

The wind was much stronger by the cairn, smelling sweetly of earth and heather, and even the sea. Helena picked up a tiny stone and added it to the pile of rocks. She felt that it should have been a holy moment, but she could only feel irritated that Bill and Sarah both copied her, and that the wind was ruffling Sarah's fine, glinting hair.

'It was over there,' Sarah said. 'I think the boys ran off, you know, too near the edge.'

They walked slowly across the boulders to where the cliff fell away.

'But how could anyone have fallen here?' Helena cried. 'There's so much space. I had imagined there must have been a narrow ridge to negotiate or something.'

'They were playing and fighting,' Sarah said miserably.

'Michael had far more sense than to let them do that.'

'I expect he couldn't reach them in time.'

Helena lay flat on the rocks and shuffled her body forwards to look over the edge. 'But it's so difficult to fall here. There's a ledge underneath. Are you sure this is the right place? How could he have fallen?'

'That's it. The child was caught on those rocks. He was safe. Michael went down and tied him to the rope. They pulled him up quite easily.'

'Then why did Michael fall?'

Helena noticed, in the intervening pause, that there were

picnickers far below on the shores of the lake. It must be very sheltered down there.

At last, brave Sarah said: 'He didn't use the rope. Only for the boy. Michael climbed up alone. The girls said he was managing easily until a handhold came away from his grasp.'

Helena rested her cheek on the rough stone and closed her eyes. No rope. He simply climbed. That was it. At last she knew. Of course. Michael must climb a slightly more difficult route than other people. He must go down a pothole that has claimed a life in a flash flood the year before. A ball is stuck in a tree? Very well, he must climb and climb until the treetop sways and shakes and he can reach out his hand with the thumb and index finger curled to a small O and shout: 'The branch is that thick, Helena.'

She thought: I was worth less than the thrill of the risk he took.

She looked down at the shining lake and thought of him tumbling. She remembered the scuffs on his boots.

And did you think of me as you fell, Michael? Did you?

The letter was a terrible burden.

She was conscious of Sarah, a crouched heap of misery, behind her.

Refusing supper, Bill and Sarah drove away immediately after returning Helena to her home. Joanna was very disappointed. The table in Helena's dining room had been carefully laid for three people and from the kitchen came the smell of casserole.

'I thought you'd all be so hungry,' Joanna exclaimed when she was alone with her daughter. As she filled the kettle she cast worried glances at Helena who was slumped on a stool.

'I think we are all too tired. And they wanted to get back.'

'You must eat, Helena. It's all ready.'

'It was terrible to see where he fell,' Helena murmured.

'Yes, well, I did say it was silly to go. But you'll feel much better with some food inside you.'

'I'm afraid I didn't find Sarah much of a comfort,' Helena added after a while. 'She seemed too upset herself.'

'Of course she would be. What did you expect?' Joanna moved deftly about the kitchen with utensils and pans.

'I thought she might perhaps have been too fond of Michael.'

'Now how could anyone possibly be too fond?' Joanna always excluded any mention of sexual relations from her conversation. For a moment she was engaged in taking the casserole from the oven and the pause enabled her to turn the subject to Nina.

But for once Helena would not be deflected. She did not want this particular brand of mothering, symbolized by hot food and an unwavering domestic routine. After one mouthful she pushed the plate away and said: 'I wish you would speak to me about Michael. I need to.'

'Of course. What do you want me to say?' Joanna's cheery tone was a clear indication that she was distressed.

'You never really liked him, did you? You were always suspicious of him.'

'Of course I liked Michael. Dad and I both did. We could tell you were very happy with him.'

'But you were never whole-hearted about him.'

'I don't think any girl's parent considers any man good enough for her.'

Joanna's little self-conscious laugh and her persistent, unnecessary activity caused Helena to cry: 'You just avoid everything, don't you? You disliked him, I know. You hated the fact that I'd met him in Westwich. You didn't like him being a Mayrick because his family might have known your mother when she was a girl there. Was that it?'

'You do talk nonsense, Helena. If I were you I'd eat up and then go and have a nice bath. If you like I'll stay until you get out, in case Nina wakes.'

'No. It's all right. I'll manage fine.'

Joanna gathered up her coat and handbag. At the door mother and daughter kissed each other dutifully on the cheek, though their hostility was almost tangible. 'Give me a ring in the morning if you want anything,' were Joanna's parting words.

'Thanks for all you've done,' Helena called back.

In the morning Helena took Nina to nursery as usual and went back fearfully to the empty house. Before Michael's death her days had been partitioned into comfortable segments of time with Nina, time alone to work, and time with Michael. Now, only her hours spent with Nina had any substance.

Helena had always considered that Michael brought her luck. After meeting him on the camping holiday in Suffolk, she returned home, exhilarated by her new love affair, to find a letter from the BBC inviting her to interview. The job proved to be ideal. For eight years she worked as a researcher specializing in the quirky, lighter side of English history. But after Nina was born she resigned and wrote freelance for a glossy monthly magazine called *Heritage*. Helena was a little ashamed to acknowledge her connection with this publication, which took a bland, orthodox view of the nation's past, but for her it was easy money as she was able to rework old material. Now that Michael was dead she wished she had a more absorbing job, perhaps in a busy institution which would take her away from the house.

After their marriage Michael obligingly found a teaching job in Shrewsbury and they bought a red-brick Victorian villa at an appropriate distance from Helena's parents, the deposit funded by money inherited by Michael from his father Simon Mayrick. They carefully restored all the period features, and Helena had always loved the high-ceilinged, old rooms. Now, though, she found the house dark and cold, crammed with memories of Michael. Despite the kindness of her family and friends she was always lonely.

The front door of the house was set in a stone porch littered with leaves and sycamore seeds from the tree in the road outside. When Joanna came she liked to sweep the porch – it was the kind of contained task she most enjoyed. Since Michael's death the porch had been kept scrupulously neat, a sign of Joanna's almost constant presence. That morning it contained a cardboard box. Pushed into the top was a torn-off sheet of notepaper on which Joanna had written *I found this after all. Hope all is well.*

Well, good heavens, thought Helena, whatever made her change her mind? Had the tortured little dispute of the previous evening disturbed her so much?

This was a peace offering of huge significance.

Although she'd been given access to the box only once before Helena was familiar with its contents and its history. It had been left to Joanna by her guardian, Maud Waterford, along with Maud's cottage and its other contents. Maud's other beneficiary had been another Jo, Josephine Tate, a fellow villager, to whom she had left two hundred pounds. In the box were the only keepsakes Maud had preserved of Joanna's mother, Ruth Styles, and of her family. If there had been other papers, Maud must have destroyed them. The family's history was a tragic one, and presumably she had not wished her ward to be haunted by unpleasant reminders of the past.

Helena well remembered her first touch of those old photographs and papers. She had returned from her visit to Westwich chock full of Michael Mayrick and eager to establish her own inherited connection with the village. She had not, at that time, disclosed to her mother anything about Michael except that she had met a fellow visitor to the area.

Joanna acknowledged with some reluctance Helena's right to see the family papers, which had been stored for so long in the loft that grit had blown in through gaps in the roof-tiles and permeated the careful packaging.

The box contained quite a substantial collection of Donaldson's photographs. There was also a letter written in a childish hand by Ruth, thanking Aunt Maud for a beautiful nightgown, and a couple of short, scrawled notes from Harry, Ruth's brother, addressed to his mother at The Rush House. The only other memento of Harry was a telegram. Two other items completed the collection. One was a tiny painting of a kitten wrapped in a sheet of wafer-thin writing paper and the other a china box.

The picture of the kitten had made even Joanna smile. 'Apparently that was done by a woman called Miss Lily who was my mother's governess for a while. I believe that everybody loathed her.'

Joanna had seemed pleased and startled as she withdrew the china trinket box painted with blue flowers. 'Ah, this belonged to my grandmother, Julia Styles. According to Maud it used to live on her dressing table at The Rush House. Here, I'll find you Donaldson's picture of Maud.' She pointed to a tall, unsmiling woman with heavily etched, vertical creases at the sides of her mouth and between her eyes. She was dressed in a serviceable skirt and jacket and, clamped onto her head as if with exasperated ferocity, was a black cloche hat. She was holding by the hand a stocky, smiling little girl. In the background was a low, white-washed cottage. 'That's me in the short dress and gappy grin,' explained Joanna. 'Maud never smiled for photographs but I remember her smiling a good deal at me.'

'Are there any photos of your mother?'

'I expect so.' Joanna spoke with much less enthusiasm. 'I believe she was considered very beautiful. Donaldson often photographed her. Yes, here she is. That sort of dress would flatter anyone, don't you think?'

Helena peered at the picture of a young woman standing by a gate, her light skirts blown backwards to reveal the shape of long, slender legs, one hand holding in place a wide straw hat. 'She was lovely, I think,' Helena exclaimed. 'Her bone structure is so clear. No wonder he loved to photograph her.'

Next Joanna produced a black and white postcard which showed two women facing each other across a wet path. Behind them, dark and uninviting, was a ruined church, its arched windows lit by a pale, lowering sky. 'This was Donaldson's picture of my mother and Maud in front of the church. That's how he and Mother met. He needed a couple of humans in the foreground.'

Helena was too clumsy, over-eager to discover more. She had found a very old portrait photograph of a woman with a long white neck and hair drawn smoothly back from her brow, her

79

large eyes revealing sensitivity and humour. 'Who's this?'

Joanna glanced at it and replied dismissively: 'That's Margaret Shaw, my great grandmother. I've told you about her.' Ah yes, thought Helena, the mad woman who walked into the sea.

Abruptly Joanna appeared to lose interest. 'We must clear this lot up. What a horrible mess they've made on the table. Look at all this dust.'

'We ought to find a better box,' Helena suggested. 'Everything will be ruined.'

'No no. That's all right.' And Joanna actually resealed the box with the same tape as before and bustled away with it under her arm.

Such was the only opportunity Helena had been given of exploring the pitifully inadequate records of her family's history in Westwich.

Like so many treasures glimpsed only once and then concealed for years, Helena found the contents of the box far less glamorous than she remembered. She had not recalled them to be so faded and insignificant. The telegram and the letters from Ruth's brother, Harry, she put firmly aside. Michael's death had made sight of these particular papers unbearable.

What struck her most when sifting through the photographs was that an odd selection had been preserved. There was a dull view of The Rush House, which in Donaldson's photograph had a straight brick path leading to a deep porch, and heavily latticed windows. A further print was of a town house with *Primrose Hill* scrawled on the back, but another city dwelling, much more lowly, was unidentified. A picture of a little terraced cottage in a narrow street was labelled: *Miss Lily. 1924.* Indeed there was a pale old face peering through an upstairs window.

With a pang of remembrance, Helena carefully unwrapped the delicate miniature of a kitten. Inked underneath was the name *Harry the Second*. This time Helena read the letter which formed the wrapping.

Written in a small, artistic hand, it was dated April 1912 and addressed Primrose Hill.

*My dear Ruth,*

*I have completed the study of a black kitten for your dear mother. Please find enclosed.*

*I write this in the drawing room into which I creep daily thinking it will do no harm as no one else uses it. Forgive me, my dear, am I trespassing? I'm sure Mrs Arthur doesn't like it but for your sake, dear Ruth, I put up with the opposition as I want to keep the room lived in and dear Cloud so enjoys the sunlight through the French windows.*

*Mrs Arthur will not buy the proper brand of tea. Hers is far too strong. I have told your father many times that it cannot be doing him any good. For myself I would not worry.*

*Your dear brother was here at the weekend, hale and strong as of course he should be. I forget he's a man now. I'm afraid Cloud was disturbed by his visit. Your brother will tease him and he tripped over him on the stairs. No apology but then neither Cloud nor I would expect it. I'm only a temporary visitor but someone has to hold the household together until your poor mama is quite well again. I'm glad to hear you're playing and painting.*

*Your brother said: 'Send her this bundle.' Why you want it, dear, I can't imagine. Affairs of the world. Women so unwomanly. Don't get involved. Of course if anyone asked me, and they don't, but I was brought here as your mentor, I like to think ... the reading I'd recommend. Well you can't go wrong with Ruskin and Arnold. Wonderful Wordsworth. Don't read modern novels, dear. Nobody asks me, I know and I'd hate to interfere. I'd come to you at once if you asked though what the journey would to do to poor Cloud ... Mrs Arthur calls him 'that animal'. You know how his poor little constitution is upset by travel and then the sea air. But we could manage somehow. I've offered to accompany your papa many times.*

*Your papa is well though often out. I insist on Mrs Arthur providing good meals. One cannot let things slip like at the galleries.*

*Well, my dear, so much to do, must dash. But just call on me. My rheumatism isn't so bad that I wouldn't be able to come. I'm used to pain and I think nothing of my own comfort, as you know. Don't consider the terrible bout of influenza I had last year when I was moved from my room when they spring-cleaned.*

> *Your affectionate servant,*
> *Florence Lily*

Miss Lily, thought Helena, must have been quite a character. I wonder how well Donaldson knew her? The face at the window was so pale and distant that it lacked features or identity.

As she sorted through the pile of photographs, looking for a pattern in Donaldson's choice of angle or pose, Helena was arrested by a portrait of Ruth on the beach near Westwich. Donaldson had captured perfectly the movement of nature on that bright day, the tossed grasses in the far distant sand-dunes and, near Ruth's feet, a wave's seething retreat. Ruth was looking away from the camera out to sea so that her face was almost in profile. A tendril of hair clung to her throat and it seemed to Helena that the photographer had noted every gracious curve of Ruth's body and how the material of her dress fell softly on the supple flesh.

But why is she looking away? Helena wondered. And why, despite her uplifted chin, is she so sad?

She took the photograph to bed with her that night, after calling in to kiss Nina on her way along the landing. In her own room the double bed was coldly awaiting her. She lay back against the pillows under the Art Deco lamp presented by her best friend, Victoria, as a wedding present, and gazed at her grandmother.

Ruth. You were so loved, Helena thought. I can see it even now. His love for you shines like a beacon through the eighty intervening years between us. He caught you, like a butterfly, and froze you in time.

She closed her eyes and thought of her own love affair, and of Michael's betrayal.

All I now ask, Michael, she told him, is that I be given peace of mind. I want to be reassured that you once loved me as Donaldson loved Ruth. You have been wrenched away from me, but you will not leave me free. By your betrayal, by this other love, you have taken away my peace of mind. Every memory I have of you is soiled by the question – why did you fall in love with someone else? What was so wrong? Were you lying every time you told me you loved me?

Now that Helena had been to the place where Michael fell from the mountain she could see him tumbling again and again in her mind's eye. She pictured him flying out into the air, as if momentarily buoyant, before crashing raggedly to the rocks below. And it occurred to her that his death might almost have been wilful. Was it that he had not loved her enough to preserve himself? Or that the terrible tension of being married to one woman and loving another had been too much for him to bear?

Helena realized now that Michael's love letter inspired in her not only anger and resentment, but envy. She could not have written those same words. Her love for Michael had not been whole-hearted. She had not thought of him much during the week he was away. Hers had been a critical, niggling affection so trammelled by domestic detail that she could not see through it to the pure strong thread of love and desire that she had first felt for him.

She looked again at Donaldson's photograph of Ruth. He had known his subject and all her passing moods so well that he had been able to capture a particular, fleeting expression. And despite the sorrow in Ruth's eyes there was a flirtatiousness in the way she held her body that signified an awareness of Donaldson's feeling for her.

And what did you give him in return, Ruth? Helena wondered. Why did you disappear so suddenly, leaving him and your child? Oh, please don't let it be that you wasted your love as I wasted mine.

# Chapter Six

*Past*

Maud had a friend who had a second cousin down on her luck but well connected, accomplished and artistic, who would therefore make the perfect companion for Ruth.

Spurred on by her conversations with Esther Mayrick, Ruth expressed a desire to return to school, but she was too late to apply for a place in the autumn term and in any case her father remained dismissive of the idea of educating wealthy girls beyond the rudiments of music, French and literature. So, as an interim measure, Miss Lily was installed, together with her cat, an evil-looking beast with long white fur and mean green eyes.

*They are alike*, wrote Ruth to Esther Mayrick. *They have the same expression and the same matted clumps of hair spurting from their foreheads. I swear Miss Lily even has a peculiar feline snuffle in her nose. The cat is dirty. One of the maids is supposed to make sure he is put out regularly, but you find droppings in any room where the door has been left open. As for Miss Lily…*

Miss Lily was restless, prejudiced and despotic. Intent on communicating her irrational obsessions to her pupil she would don a shapeless brown coat and hat and whisk Ruth out to the National Gallery. Although short-sighted, Miss Lily refused glasses on the grounds that her nose was so sensitive that the metal would affect her skin. Darting up to a painting she would scrutinize the plaque and study the small area of canvas she could see at close quarters before stepping back with the loud exclamation: 'Well, *he* couldn't paint.'

Ruth cringed self-consciously in her wake, aware of the

shocked hush in the galleries. Miss Lily liked anything English or Italian, the rest were liable to be dismissed as over-rated. English water colours were a favourite, foreign water colours, in Miss Lily's opinion, pale copies. Religious subjects were bad, nudes bad, the new Impressionists very bad, Turner good, Gainsborough good, Constable very good. At least, under Miss Lily's direction, Ruth was able to develop her own tastes, disliking instantly any painting admired by her tutor and expressing defiance by standing studiously for many minutes before the very masterpieces Miss Lily had rejected.

So with music. Miss Lily was a talented pianist, if rather unpredictable. She would play the opening bars of a piece, sing a few bars, play a few more, hum a little and then skip to the end. 'Well, it's not worth playing the whole thing!' she exclaimed. Beethoven she considered too passionate, Mozart acceptable. Schubert was too romantic, Chopin tolerable. Above all she loved showy pieces by Rachmaninov or Tchaikovsky and could play extraordinarily complex works in her bizarre, leapfrogging style. Ruth's observation that both Miss Lily's favourite composers were foreign without being Italian was ignored.

Drawing lessons were Ruth's worst torture. These took place in Miss Lily's room. She had been allocated a large, airy bedroom on the second floor, decorated in a fine white and blue print and furnished with a delicate walnut suite inherited by Alan Styles from his mother. Miss Lily lost no time in transforming the room. To protect her pigeon-chested modesty thick lace curtains were brought from her 'humble cottage' in Cheltenham. She also accumulated chenille table covers, piles of lace mats and a black screen lacquered with birds over which were hung an assortment of straggly crocheted shawls.

Cloud had his own paraphernalia in the form of china feeding bowls and a basket with lace cushions. The room smelt of cat, chopped liver and Miss Lily's unwashed body. She did not hold with too many baths and insisted that frequent cleansing was detrimental to her hair. 'You'll never have really long hair like mine if you wash it too often,' she instructed Ruth. 'A

85

vinegar rinse once a fortnight is best.' And indeed her hair fell in yellowish strands to her hips.

The easel was placed near the shrouded window and a subject selected. Miss Lily favoured plants, preferably dried or wax. Ruth painted with sulky, clumsy slashes of colour which when completed were angry, awkward reproductions. But Miss Lily had the knack of instilling life into the dead or artificial foliage. She loved bright colours and her paintings were endowed with supernatural radiance.

By Miss Lily's brush the hideous Cloud was likewise transformed. She had a miniature in which he was portrayed as an alert, silken-haired little puss with winsome, wide-awake eyes. 'I got him to the life,' she told Ruth proudly.

Only the news of Esther Mayrick's safe delivery of a daughter, named Clara, cheered Ruth that autumn but her dragging, irritable days with Miss Lily were brought to an abrupt end in late November.

Miss Lily breakfasted alone in her room, spent from ten until four-thirty with the unhappy Ruth and then retired to pursue her lace-making and her avid consumption of racy novels. She did not use Boots' library whose books she considered too dull. Instead the novels arrived weekly in brown paper packages.

Ruth dined alone with her father.

At first it was a thrill to eat with him in the long dining room with only one silent servant standing by to serve. The clock ticked softly and on the quarter struck a delicate chime. Alan Styles could be excellent company. He loved to tell stories against himself and would describe colleagues and minions with affectionate derision. Intrigued by Miss Lily's eccentricities he encouraged Ruth to mimic her appraisal of fine art.

In the absence of Julia Styles, Ruth had moved along the table so that she sat at her father's right hand. Occasionally their knees touched. When news of his wife came, Styles would pat Ruth's arm reassuringly or stroke her shoulder.

*No improvement yet*, wrote Maud in October. *She cries a good deal and the wind depresses her but she will not think of moving from here.*

At bedtime Styles always kissed Ruth on the cheek. One evening his heavy lips landed full on her mouth. The next night, arriving home very late, he stumbled up to her room. 'Come to tuck you in, Ruth-o,' he whispered and buried his face in the hair at her neck. Half asleep, she turned her head away, but afterwards lay wide awake for many hours.

She wrote to Esther: *I am worried about my father. I'm afraid he misses mother very much. I understand so little. It is his — appetites. Do you understand? He frightens me sometimes ...*

By return of post she received an invitation to stay with the Mayricks in Oxford. Her father refused permission saying that he did not know the family and could not think of letting her go to strangers. That night, after the maid had removed the dishes, Ruth distinctly felt his knee rub against her thigh.

She loved her father and, pitying his bewildered, wifeless solitude, knew that she must put them both out of danger.

The next morning after he'd left she packed her bags and announced her intention of travelling to Suffolk to see her mother. Miss Lily made no objection save that it was a shame to interrupt her studies.

Ruth took a cab to her father's office and was received by him with delighted surprise which turned to dismay when he heard of her intention. Realizing that she would not be dissuaded, however, he gave her money and appointed his secretary as her companion to the station. A telegram was sent to The Rush House.

Finally Ruth embraced him warmly and sensed in him a reluctant relief. 'I don't know what you're going to do about Miss Lily, Father.'

'I'll deal with Miss Lily.'

And so ended Ruth's brief sojourn in London.

2

Ruth returned to The Rush House on a wet, blowing evening in late November. Millerchip came in the trap to collect her from the station at Saxmundham.

London, in Ruth's imagination, now seemed to represent brightness and throngs of people. It had also seemed to her, even under Miss Lily's fusty guardianship, a city alive with promise. She had begun to understand that Esther Mayrick was right and that she had been a fool to give up school out of fear for the possible future it held out to her; a future of work beyond the confines of her home, or a world of ideas that would take her far from her mother's restricted domestic environment of bedroom and drawing room.

The trap, Ruth knew, as she sat bolt upright within it, was pulling her in quite the wrong direction, back to her mother, back to the hypnotic surge of the sea. Bumping between black Suffolk fields as if through a fallen sky, The Rush House, Westwich, was to Ruth a prison of darkness, silence and secrets.

But the door of The Rush House was thrown open by Maud Waterford to reveal the amber glow of the lamp on the hall table and a richer light from the open drawing room door. Maud exclaimed at the damp chill exuded by Ruth's coat and shawl and ushered her into the cosy drawing room where Julia sat beside a blazing fire, dressed in a woollen gown of rich blue, her delicate features aglow in the warmth and her hair carefully arranged at her nape. On her lap, in readiness, were Ruth's old crimson slippers. All was so ordered, feminine and familiar that with a sob of relief Ruth leapt across the room, fell to her knees and buried her face in her mother's skirts.

At once she smelt Julia's faint, familiar perfume – the rose-water that she used for her complexion. But then Julia laid a tentative hand on her hair and with a sickening sensation of disappointment Ruth recognized at once her mother's absence.

While the women watched and sipped tea Ruth ate the meal Mrs Millerchip brought in on a tray. The housekeeper made a great commotion as she moved tables about: 'We ate at six,' Ruth was informed pointedly.

Knowing that she could not easily explain why she had returned so suddenly to The Rush House, Ruth adopted a bright, strong voice and proceeded to give Maud and Julia an hilarious account of Miss Lily's activities. She was aware of

Maud's keen interest and of her mother's frequent, anxious glances at the door.

Afterwards Maud gave Ruth the local gossip. 'The baby at the farm cottage flourishes. Josephine called him Lawrence. I think something plainer might have been more appropriate. Thomas. Or William, I like. The poor child.'

'Lawrence is a fine name, full of character,' Ruth rejoined.

'It's not character that the child will be lacking. I take them along a few bits and pieces. Raspberry jam or a bowl of stewed lamb. She needs feeding up, poor girl. She's getting nothing from the farm. *He* won't go near her. She's asked me for a reference. Of course her previous employers, the Morgan-Freechilds, won't give her one after what happened.'

'And the baby?'

'The mother, Mrs Tate, will care for it, and spoil it as she did Josephine, I don't doubt. It's a lot of work with her legs, but Josephine must earn.'

'Will you give her a reference?'

'What could I say?'

'That she's a generous, friendly girl.'

'Ruth!'

'And what about you, Mother?' Ruth asked gently. 'It's lovely to see you looking so well.'

Julia's eyes would not focus on Ruth's. Her hands fluttered to her tea-cup and away, and her wavy, pale hair, caught back in heavy coils, shifted against her cheek. 'Oh my dear, there's so much to do. We may never rest. We are never still.'

Maud murmured, 'If you're tired, Julia, I should go to bed.'

As Julia made her quavering retreat Maud assembled the tea things. Ruth sat very still and raised her hand to her forehead in an attempt to ward off the sensation that the walls of The Rush House were closing in on her, and that she would suffocate in this atmosphere dense with voluminous skirts and too many fussy, feminine possessions.

'My dear,' said Maud tenderly, 'you must be very tired.'

Ruth could scarcely speak. 'She is no better, is she?' she murmured in a low, despairing voice. She was now quite certain that her mother would never be persuaded to return to London, however great her daughter's need.

'No. I fear not. And the winter is worse still. She hates the wind. It terrifies her. She will not normally leave her bed.'

'We should get her away.'

'I keep hoping that she will tire of it herself. There are times when I look at her that I think she is watching me, as if to calculate whether I really believe that she is sick and helpless. And then I think that if I could only catch her I might find the old Julia and help her break free. But she eludes me each time. The shutters come down and Julia is gone.' Maud paused, and Ruth was conscious of her friend's gaze upon her. 'Why did you come, Ruth? I can manage. I am used to Julia. And to Westwich. There is nothing for you here.'

For an instant Ruth thought it possible that she might confide in Maud. Yet her fears now seemed so inappropriate. Had she perhaps imagined those too intimate touches, too fierce embraces? She looked away, to the fire. 'It seemed so awkward, Aunt Maud. To be just me, and my father.'

'But you have a companion.'

'Oh. Miss Lily!'

'Ruth. I hope you have not become so wild and independent that you can no longer tolerate people's weaknesses. I hope you do not despise Miss Lily because she is old and a little ridiculous, as you described her at length in your letters to me.'

There was enough truth in Maud's accusation to make Ruth blush, but she persisted. 'It didn't feel right at home. I don't seem to belong there any more, in that great house with my father. I was too much alone with him. It soured our relationship. Do you understand?'

'I understand,' said Maud, 'that relations between father and daughter can be strained. But heaven knows, Ruth, enough of us have endured such troubles.' And again Ruth felt reproached, for Maud had lived with her own clergyman father through forty-three years of her life, watching her young womanhood ebb away in his service, and ending at last in her little cottage, a spinster of precarious means.

'I'm not as strong as you, Aunt,' she muttered.

'Nonsense.'

'And I thought of the sea. I missed the sound of it at night. And The Rush House, and you and Mother. And there seemed no reason to stay away if I wasn't happy in London.'

'You were afraid,' Maud exclaimed triumphantly. 'I know you, Ruth. You could not face the choices you had in town, so you came scuttling back to Westwich. Well, you be careful, or you'll end up like your mother.'

The conversation had been a failure. Ruth had returned to The Rush House hoping for comfort but instead her mother was obviously disturbed by her arrival, and Maud decidedly unsympathetic. She asked wearily: 'Why is Mother so sad? I don't understand. She used to be happy.'

'No. I think she appeared to be happy but she always had her darker side. You know of course what happened to her mother, Margaret Shaw. I think a child never forgets the horrors of a morning such as that. Julia was ten when it happened. Quite old enough to spend the rest of her life wondering how she had meant so little to her mother that she should take her own life. I remember, you see. I was in Westwich. I saw what it did to her. That's why I can't get too irritated with her.'

'We should never, never have let her return here,' Ruth said vehemently. 'I can't understand Father. Surely he must realize that Westwich can only awaken all the old fears and memories.'

'Perhaps he thought it would make her face her fear. Perhaps this would have happened anyway. You should talk to him, Ruth. Everything should be open in families. I think so. It is what I most dislike in myself, this reluctance to speak of distasteful or uncomfortable things. My parents, again, you see. They would never drop their guard.'

At that moment Mrs Millerchip reappeared in a flurry of self-righteous indignation. 'I'm going to bed,' she said, sweeping up the tea tray. 'Don't expect your room to be aired, Ruth. There hasn't been time.'

'Thank you, Mrs Millerchip, I'm so sorry you didn't have more notice.'

'Of course, I don't usually work here at all in the winter.'

'No.'

Perhaps Ruth's listless, weary responses awoke some tremor of sympathy in Mrs Millerchip for she added a little more gently: 'Well, I dare say you'll give me a hand in the morning. You were always very good at that.'

## 3

Ruth had never before spent a winter in Suffolk. She had not heard the wind come from the north and keen through the birch trees which sheltered the most exposed side of the house. She was not used to waking in the dark to hear the dry rattle of twig on twig or the long, wintry cry of a bird as it was whisked from branch to branch on the breast of the wind. On rare days the air was dry and still and only a faint breeze cut across from the sea. Then it seemed to Ruth that her eyes filled with sky and she would return from her walks with her skin aflame with the frosty air.

The question of Julia went entirely unresolved. Ruth could tell that the signs of improvement on her first arrival had been an illusion – indeed she subsequently wondered how much of Maud's considerable fund of will-power had been spent in arranging such a welcome for her. Julia had *slipped*, as Maud put it. She would not engage in conversation or undertake any task or recreational pursuit. She never left the house. The doctor came weekly, patted her hand and shook his head at Maud. 'Of course I could get a specialist to take a look at her, but she's quite fit in herself.'

'Don't you think we should have another opinion?' Ruth asked.

'We'll wait until your father comes at Christmas.'

Julia required little nursing and was restless if Ruth was with her, as if tormented by a vague recollection that she was responsible for her daughter. She was happiest lying in bed, her head turned towards the window, her gaze on the shifting clouds.

'What does she think about all day?' Ruth asked Maud.

'Heaven knows, dear.'

Ruth saw that she must survive by finding herself purpose. It occurred to her that she might apply for a place as a boarder after Christmas, perhaps at Cheltenham, a place much disparaged by Miss Lily and therefore boundlessly attractive to Ruth. So she devised a daily programme of self-improvement: an hour at the piano, an hour sketching, an hour reading, an hour studying French. In the afternoon, be the weather fair or foul, she walked, sometimes alone, sometimes with Maud.

The evenings were spent on correspondence. She wrote letters to Harry, a thankless task for he never replied; to her father who always included a note for her in messages to his wife; to Esther Mayrick, who responded with long, rushed missives and piles of books, and to her old school-friends whose communications were of dubious benefit for most of them were poised for their first London season, or were kept busy by large families of sisters, cousins and brothers and therefore emphasized Ruth's comparative isolation. Ruth even wrote to Miss Lily who was still installed in Primrose Hill, and whose replies provided a rare source of hilarity.

The Millerchips were in surly mood. Mrs Millerchip pointed out that she was not employed as a full-time housekeeper and had agreed to work only during the summer months. Mr Millerchip, hovering near the stove, cap twirling purposefully in his big hands, nodded in agreement.

'Very well,' answered Maud tartly. 'We'll put up a notice in Mrs Spendmore's shop and see if we can get someone in from the village.'

'Oh, I dare say I can manage for now,' sighed Mrs Millerchip, swiping at the table with a wet dishcloth. 'It would only cause more work in the long run to have strangers make a mess of things.'

Maud's own position in The Rush House was made awkward by Ruth's return. The house was too small to accommodate two females as independent as Ruth and Maud, and both knew that Maud longed to return to her own cottage. But Ruth was terrified of being left alone with her mother.

At Christmas Harry came for a few days and with him Alec McGrew, several inches taller but no broader, and no more eloquent. Their arrival improved matters at The Rush House considerably. It was as if Julia was forced to draw on some ancient internal code which insisted that for visitors an effort must be made. During Alec McGrew's visit she dressed after lunch and appeared at tea-time in a trail of shawls and draperies, gave him her hand and subsided into her chair with a carefully prepared question or two for her son and his friend. 'And what have you boys been up to today?'

'We've been on the beach, looking out for Alec's infernal birds,' said Harry, his cheerful face ruddied by the open air. 'You should come with us tomorrow, Mother, you could perch in Alec's knapsack to keep warm.'

He was rewarded by Julia's vague smile. She was aware that he had been witty but could not quite engage enough with his conversation to make a suitable response. 'I hope your clothes are dry, Alec.'

'Oh, Millerchip put them up in the kitchen. So if the dinner tastes of wet socks, that'll be why,' said Harry.

Had Alec been less benign Ruth would have relished the idea of tormenting him into speech, but his brown eyes were so warm and understanding that she hadn't the heart to distress him. When he did utter, everyone was stilled, as if waiting for a pearl to fall from the lip of a god. But usually he simply grunted: 'I wonder if you could pass the salt.'

He left three days before Christmas, on a clear, watery morning with the air still awash with last night's rain. Ruth shook hands with him at the door and turned back to the kitchen where she and Mrs Millerchip were baking. But she was at once aware that she had moved too swiftly and that Alec had been on the brink of speech. She paused a moment and looked back at him. Indeed he was tensed, his bags gripped in his hands, his whole being caught up in the ordeal of saying: 'I hope you have a good Christmas.' It was, Ruth knew, a considerable gift from him and she was touched. Impulsively she reached up and kissed him on his high, boyish cheek. 'And you, Alec,' she said, and skipped away to the kitchen, breathless and smiling.

Mrs Millerchip was elbow deep in flour. 'I don't suppose there'll be time now to get the pies done before lunch,' she said pointedly.

The next day Alan Styles arrived, took one look at his wife and sent for a specialist.

That afternoon Maud left The Rush House and travelled up the coast to spend the festival with an elderly cousin. She had seen Alan Styles greeted with pleasure by his children and noted that the Millerchips had drawn themselves together and were bustling about carrying bags and lighting fires as a result of the master's advent. Even Mr Millerchip moved relatively swiftly as he lumbered up the back stairs with pails of coal and then took a hammer and nail to fix a loose rail on the banister that had long been adrift.

The doctor was brought from Great Yarmouth. On the day of his visit, Ruth and Harry borrowed the trap from Upstones and rode to Saxmundham to buy Christmas presents. The little town was unusually bustling, the streets aglow with seasonal cheer. They drove home in high spirits through a countryside made luminous by a light powdering of snow.

At The Rush House Ruth met the doctor in the drawing room and conceived an instant dislike for his heavy-set, florid face and self-satisfied manner. She withdrew her hand quickly from his fulsome grasp.

'So you, Miss Styles, are the little nurse I've been hearing so much about.'

'Hardly that, sir.'

'I'm told you came back here specially to care for your mama.'

'Yes.'

'I think that's highly commendable. So many modern young ladies would shun such a duty.'

He refused dinner as he was expected at his brother's house

in Southwold. His boy was summoned from the kitchen and the horses redeemed from Millerchip's care. The doctor then walked to the door with Alan Styles and was gone.

Afterwards Ruth saw that her father's eyes were bloodshot and that as he stood over the fireplace with stooped shoulders he was holding a large tumbler.

'Well, Father?'

He clasped her in his arms. Her face was pressed to the thick tweed of his jacket which smelt of soap and male flesh. She withdrew.

'It's no good, Ruth-o. He says we must consider an asylum of some kind.'

'Father!'

He rubbed his forehead with the palm of his hand. 'She will deteriorate, Ruth-o. It's a nervous disorder, a sickness of the mind for which there is no cure. Your mother is adamant that she will not be moved from here but Doctor Russell says she must be got away and that she will soon require proper nursing care.'

'Did you tell the doctor about my grandmother?'

'I mentioned that she was drowned, of course. He said that must have had some effect, but in itself would not cause such mental disturbance as your mother suffers. He thinks it best that she be got away from here as soon as possible but that she will never be free of her sickness.'

5

When Maud returned from her brief holiday she agreed with Alan that an attempt must be made to move Julia to London. If the alternative was an asylum drastic measures must be taken. They would simply suggest that Julia should drive with her family to the station in order to say goodbye to them. Harry was to be the lure. It was thought that she would consent to the expedition if he implored her.

Ruth could not regard the plan with anything but horror. She had begun to realize that Julia's will could be formidable. Her withdrawal from normal intercourse and her desire to be absent was so forceful that any companion felt helpless and unwanted. Julia had not left the house for months. How would they even persuade her beyond the front door?

But Julia walked into the snare with little fuss. She agreed to accompany the family to the station with such alacrity that Ruth could only suspect that she wanted to be sure of getting rid of them.

The sun seemed almost to give off a little heat that morning, certainly through the thick hood of the carriage. Frost glimmered on the ploughed fields. Maud sat beside Julia, her arm firmly linked through that of her friend. Ruth was opposite. Harry and Alan Styles had gone ahead. Ruth could not keep her gaze from her mother's face. She wondered what was going on behind those downcast eyes and thought that if she could only make Julia look out at the bright day she might be brought back to life.

Maud said: 'Don't you wish you were returning to London too, Julia?'

Not by a flicker did Julia give any sign that she had heard.

'Do you remember how you and I used to love train journeys? What about that time when we were invited to stay with my Aunt Elsie? My mother fell asleep and you and I pretended that we were travelling alone when a gentleman came into the carriage. He was very shocked. I remember saying loudly: "Oh Julia, I hope by the time we reach Paris our guardian will be there to meet us."' She laughed in an attempt at gaiety. 'We were so naughty in those days. And then there was the time when I came with you up to town to choose your trousseau. Oh, that was exciting. We thought ourselves such fine young ladies.'

But suddenly Julia cut through her speech and said in a low, fierce voice. 'You cannot make me go back to London.'

The horses' hooves clip-clopped over the stones in the lane. Ruth's gaze was still riveted on her mother's face. Neither she nor Maud spoke for a moment. Maud patted Julia's hand. 'We will never do anything to harm you, Julia.'

With a startling motion of her eyelids Julia stared suddenly at

Ruth, her expression not pleading, but compelling. 'Don't let them take me away.'

Ruth turned to look out at the hedgerow.

At the station everyone dismounted except Julia. Alan came up and held out his hand to her. He spoke firmly. 'Come along, my dear. Come with us. We want you home.'

Julia would neither speak nor look at him.

Maud added coaxingly. 'It'll only be for a few weeks. In April you will come back as usual. It's too cold for you here. It does you no good to be cooped up in The Rush House.'

Again Julia looked directly at Ruth who was standing at her father's shoulder.

Ruth picked up her bag and walked into the station but at the door she turned. Her father had stepped up into the trap and was offering to lift his wife. Maud was urging Julia to move forwards. But Julia had braced every muscle rigid. Her elbows were pressed into the cushions, her ankles thrust against the opposite seat, her face upturned so that her hat twisted askew. Eyes tightly shut, she made no sound.

Less gently, Alan pulled at his wife's arm. His voice was commanding. 'Come along now, Julia, don't make a scene.'

Ruth slowly retraced her steps to the carriage. 'It's no use, Father. Don't make her. I'll stay with her. It's all right.'

For a moment Alan looked at her in fury. She could tell that he thought her treacherous but, disregarding him, she jumped up into the carriage. 'I'll take you back to The Rush House, Mother. We thought you might like to leave if we made it easy for you. But I'll take you home.'

She and Maud drove back in silence. Ruth was weeping, but not for her parents, now split apart so hopelessly, nor for herself, but for Maud who had invested her considerable portion of integrity and loyalty to Julia in this little act of deception. Their defeat made her appear diminished, less sure.

'I'll care for her, Maud,' Ruth said. 'She's my responsibility now.'

Mrs Millerchip seemed unsurprised to see them. 'She wouldn't go then,' she stated with some satisfaction.

Julia undressed slowly and deliberately, apparently oblivious to the activity around her as the fire was rekindled in the grate, her shawls and nightdress laid on the bed and tea and toast brought up.

A couple of hours later Ruth looked in and found her sleeping peacefully. All the anxiety had been smoothed from her face and she looked youthful and serene, like a young girl.

Ruth retreated to her own little room and sat at the window, her warm forehead pressed to the icy glass. She could hear the sea sucking at the pebbles, quite calm tonight. She imagined its inky, eternal blackness.

With a kind of thrill Ruth understood that she had arrived in her own future.

6

For weeks after this incident Julia would speak to no one except Mrs Millerchip whom she seemed to regard as the only member of the household not implicated in the plot to get her to London.

Ruth considered this treatment very unjust. 'For heaven's sake, Mother, I brought you back here,' she cried one morning, gazing furiously at the set, white face framed by a tangle of soft hair. But her mother's expression was unrelenting.

Ruth tried to re-establish the balance and sense of purpose she had achieved during the weeks before Christmas, but she had lost heart. She could not stay in The Rush House for long without the presence of her mother in the stuffy first floor bedroom, idle, wasting and unforgiving, provoking in her a great rage. So out she went into the vicious January mornings to return at lunch-time shaken from head to toe by the wind from the sea. There had been a tacit agreement that Mrs Millerchip would cook and clean the kitchen, but that Ruth should keep the rest of the house in order, so her afternoons were spent sweeping and polishing.

Day in, day out, in a tightly controlled voice she made offers to her mother. 'Shall I read for you? Shall I help you dress? Shall we write to Harry?' She brought Julia books, papers and little pieces of embroidery. Julia would not respond by look, word or movement.

Ruth took to walking always alone. She shopped at Mrs Spendmore's early in the morning, skipped out of sight if she saw anyone likely to speak to her and hurried away from the village. 'I don't think we should both be out of reach at the same time,' she explained to Maud. 'There must be someone within calling distance.'

Choked with hopelessness she did not wish to talk to anyone. She wanted only the sea, the clouds and the shut-up face of nature.

7

One weekend she travelled to Oxford to stay with the Mayricks. Her system responded with a jolt of amazement to the sudden change of atmosphere from the tense solitude of her days at The Rush House to the wild, haphazard regime of the Mayrick household.

Their home was large and shabby, maintained by a couple of cheerful servants overworked by the incessant demands of four children and the unwieldy, old-fashioned accommodation. Esther Mayrick had lost none of her serenity but was constantly busy, not only with caring for the baby but with a stream of demanding visitors. The baby Clara was a fragile, pale child with huge blue eyes and downy fair hair. Ruth, with no experience of babies, made Esther laugh at her tentative handling.

The boys were delighted to see their former playmate again. Simon and Giles had changed considerably in the intervening months, only Mark seemed the same quiet, composed little self. It was, confided Esther, Giles who had suffered most as a result of the new baby Clara. The other boys doted on the child but Giles, the spoilt younger son, had been known to show little acts of jealousy. He confiscated her presents and had even once locked the yowling baby, cradle and all, into a dark cupboard. He was particularly glad to see Ruth and lost no time in clasping her hand and carrying her off to the nursery where he surrounded her with books and games and insisted she work her way through each of them. She, used to Julia's icy detachment, revelled in the boy's affection, invited him onto her knee and was happy to sit for an hour at a time with his soft head beneath her chin, inhaling the innocent aroma of his warm, vital body and delighting in his sly kisses.

Esther had much advice for Ruth. 'You must find a companion for your mother,' she insisted. 'You cannot possibly give your life to her like this. You look exhausted.'

'I'm not sure anyone would take her on,' Ruth said, 'except Maud Waterford and I can't ask her to make so great a sacrifice. And I love my mother, and Westwich, and the sea. It's not so terrible.'

But Esther was impatient, more managing than Ruth remembered. Perhaps her pregnancy and the heat of the summer had softened her in August. Now her hectoring tone caused Ruth some resentment. 'You must be careful, Ruth, that you don't lose all sense of purpose. It's an age-old trap for women. Of course in the past we had no choice. There was no future for women beyond hearth and home. But you, you have a choice. Society will understand if you choose education and a career over the care of an invalid parent.'

'Esther, my place is with my sick mother. And you need have no worry. I am seventeen years old. I have plenty of time. I'm full of ideas for the future.'

'Such as?'

'Oh well, I think I might like to teach – music or history. And I'll travel with Harry one day. He's written to me about it.'

'Have you done anything definite about these schemes? Do you know what examinations a teacher must pass?'

'I'll find out soon.'

'Make sure you do.'

When she was with Esther amidst the friendly chaos of her Oxford drawing room, the baby Clara asleep in her arms, nothing seemed so bad to Ruth. She felt strong and calm, and could contemplate a further spring in Westwich with some equanimity. Still, Esther made her determined to pursue her studies, so that when the moment of release did come she would be ready to take on the world.

The woman's suffrage movement occupied much of Esther's limited free time. A meeting was to be held in the drawing room. 'I'm glad you'll be able to attend,' said Esther. 'I think it will do you so much good.'

Ruth could not help but be amused by Esther's pioneering spirit. She is like a child with a new craze, she thought, determined that everyone should feel as enthusiastic about it as she does.

The following day she sat next to Esther and thought how much Maud Waterford would have enjoyed such a gathering, even though Maud professed to be hotly opposed to the suffragette cause. The curtains in the dining room were undrawn and the trees in the garden were chilly onlookers to the seven ladies clustered at the table, hats cast aside, elaborately dressed heads and white hands constantly moving as they gestured and exclaimed.

The meeting was witty and good-humoured, but the topic was a serious one: *Marriage, Motherhood and the Suffrage*. The other participants were predominantly married women of Esther's class, and there seemed little disagreement among them.

'We must,' stated Esther in her cool, sure voice, 'counter the argument that the homes of women who fight for the suffrage have become battlegrounds and that family life cannot sustain the concept of equality for women.' Here she smiled calmly at her friends, and Ruth was conscious of the large Mayrick house humming with activity, Esther at its centre.

The women agreed eventually to write and circulate a pamphlet stating that in the modern age it was perfectly possible for a wife and mother to ensure the smooth running of her household and maintain political and educational interests. Further, that a woman, who bore a great responsibility for the moral and spiritual development of her children, had a duty to encourage them, by example, to play a useful part in society.

Tea was brought on large trays and the women passed cups and plates with deft quiet movements which did not interrupt the flow of conversation.

'And what about you, Ruth,' Esther invited, resting her hand on Ruth's arm, 'what do you think of all this?' The ladies waited politely for her answer. Earlier she had been introduced by Esther as 'My dear young friend from Suffolk'.

'I think... You have servants. I think that you should bear that in mind. The women at home...' and here, with a rush of homesickness Ruth thought of the women who lived in the farm cottages at Upstones, the fishermen's wives in the cluster of dwellings nearest the shore and the coarse-handed landlady of The Boat Inn, 'poor country women, don't have time. They just work. They have no leisure to think about anything else.'

'And, my dear Ruth, that is why we must have the vote, to alleviate such suffering. Men don't see the plight of such women. They have no vision.'

The meeting moved on but at least Ruth had felt the thrill of having made a contribution.

'It's such a shame you can't stay longer,' Esther exclaimed afterwards. 'I think you could be a great asset to our movement. And you are precisely the sort of woman who most needs our help. There are so many like you who have their own lives eaten away by the demands of others.'

Ruth was stung to reply. 'But look at you. You do nothing but care for your family. You do not study or work outside the home.'

'It's my choice,' said Esther softly. 'For most girls expectations are made of them, and they are imprisoned by the demands of parents, husbands and children. I have chosen freely.'

8

Things did seem better on Ruth's return to The Rush House. Julia had not cared for the less sympathetic ministrations of Mrs Millerchip and Maud, and appeared actually to have missed her daughter. And Ruth was armed with a large portmanteau of books and a programme of reading supplied by Esther. Besides holding subscriptions to *Votes for Women* and *The Labour Record*, Ruth's world was now enriched by the works of E. M. Forster, Galsworthy and H. G. Wells.

But more to her taste were the darkly romantic writings of the Brontës, Hardy, Byron and Tennyson. She needed no companion on her walks but the characters of fiction whose futures beyond the novels and poetry she pursued in her imagination. Gradually all were discarded save two, Jane Eyre and Rochester, whom she took in fantasy far into their married life. And then these two disappeared as well and in their place was another pair, bred entirely in Ruth's dream world. The woman was young, beautiful, witty and clever, a countess, confined in a dark and gloomy house by a mad great-aunt. Her hero was a powerful, fearless adventurer and politician who came one day to beg access to the aunt's extensive and priceless library of charts and books of exploration. He fell in love with the beautiful countess and pledged to rescue her.

With gaze turned inward, blood pulsing, Ruth followed this pair through secret encounters on the beach at night. She tasted their first kiss and felt a thrill as his strong hand fell on her back, his warm breath touched her neck. In bed she no longer heard the wind or the creak of the bed-springs as her mother turned restlessly. Instead, Ruth plunged herself into sleep at the side of her countess, who stood on the shore and watched the waves pounding, pounding, knowing that her adventurer had been called to London, where he was being asked to journey to a far country on a dangerous mission...

9

On the morning that the first daffodil opened its tender petals to the bracing air of the Westwich churchyard, Donaldson re-materialized into Ruth's life.

She had dreamed her way through communion, mesmerized by a quivering reflection of jewel-like stained glass on the whitewashed wall of the chancel, and now stepped out into a surprisingly bright morning. There at the church gate was Donaldson, camera at the ready. Ruth halted in disbelief as Donaldson submerged himself beneath the black cloth, the shutter clicked, and his face reappeared wearing an expression of combined triumph and anxiety. He bustled up and took her hand. 'Good morning, Miss Styles.'

'Good morning, Mr Donaldson.' Suddenly, as if it had been reserving strength for this moment, the sun sailed from behind a cloud and shone full and hot on Ruth's face, dazzling her and casting Donaldson's pale, clumsy features into shadow. Ruth lifted her chin and prepared to move away, but Maud was upon them.

'Mr Donaldson. Well I never. No need to ask what you're up to. Surely you've taken enough pictures of our little village.'

'I'm on holiday. I wanted to come back. I'm working on an album of photographs about this coast, you see.' He looked significantly at Ruth. 'I did not expect to find you here, Miss Styles.' His eyes were guileless with innocent enquiry but Ruth was sure at that moment that he had known she was in Westwich, and that it was for her sake he had come back.

'I did not expect to be here,' she said tartly.

'Mr Donaldson,' exclaimed Maud hurriedly, 'your project sounds so interesting. I should like to hear about it. Why not come to tea this afternoon? You too, Ruth.'

'I cannot leave my mother. I'm sorry.'

'Nonsense, of course you can. She must come, mustn't she, Mr Donaldson?'

But Ruth was not to be persuaded.

Donaldson's arrival marked an end to Ruth's solitary walks. She had only to take a few paces down the lane beyond The Rush House for his willowy, ill-clad figure to detach itself from the hedgerow and hover at her side.

'Where are you off to today, Miss Styles?'

'I have to buy groceries in the village.'

'May I come and help you carry them?'

'Certainly not. I can manage perfectly well.'

'May I keep you company? I have an errand there myself.'

'Mr Donaldson, you are staying over the shop. What can you possibly need to buy?'

But he scurried along beside her, undaunted even by the prospect of a confrontation with Mrs Spendmore who was far from pleasant in the spring when her arthritis troubled her most. Her customers had a limited diet during the early months of the year for they dared not ask for anything which required a climb to reach a high shelf or a stoop to a lower. If someone proffered sympathy for her condition the response would be: 'Yes, this shop will be the death of me.'

If help was suggested she retorted sharply: 'I trust *no one*.'

For taking the room above the shop and requiring breakfast and dinner Donaldson was her arch-enemy. At sight of him her eyebrows shot up into her sparse hair-line. 'Yes?'

After their trip to the shop he joined Ruth on her walk. At first she was quite civil and made conversation.

'Well Mr Donaldson, has your career made giant strides since last spring?'

He had an annoying habit of scuttling crab-like a little ahead of her so that he might peer into her face as they walked. 'I would say so, yes,' he replied eagerly. 'I have been given a rise. I think soon I may be able to afford my own studio. And I'm beginning to be noticed by newspapers and journals. I sell a lot of my work. I'm known for catching the mood of an occasion rather well.'

'But Mr Donaldson,' Ruth could not help exclaiming, 'surely it requires much sensitivity to understand mood?'

If he was stung he did not show it. 'And you, Miss Styles?' he asked, opening a gate for her with fumbling haste.

'And I, Mr Donaldson?' she mocked.

'I understand you have been an attentive nurse to your mother this winter. I'm sorry that her health has not improved.'

But Ruth would not be pitied. 'I have all this,' she said, and with a sweep of her hand took in the brightness of the morning with the white, lit clouds flowing swiftly across a bright sky and the field dewy and brilliantly green.

After a couple of days Ruth became annoyed by Donaldson's persistence and one morning exclaimed: 'Mr Donaldson, I do wish you'd leave me alone.' She thought the turmoil of her dream-world preferable to the spiky discussions she had with Donaldson. But when the next day he did not appear, she missed him on her walk along the beach. She could not retrieve the haven she had found in her imagination. The sight of the lively waves and shining pebbles held no charm for her so she returned early and rather to her chagrin passed Donaldson at the gate of Maud Waterford's cottage.

'If you come with me tomorrow I shan't mind,' she told him grudgingly.

After that they walked together every day. She even put up with his requests that she should provide a human model for his photographs. He was surprisingly well read and they became entangled in fierce arguments about the merits of their favourite books. And she questioned him fiercely about the events he had attended in his professional capacity. What did everyone wear, she wanted to know, what were they talking about, what did they eat?

One day, towards the end of his visit, when the air was balmier and the hedgerows beginning to green he snatched at and caught her hand.

'You've changed,' he said. 'Did you know?'

She looked coldly into his eager eyes, conscious of irritation that his brush-like head of hair, white skin and prominent chin should be so unprepossessing. Oh, why can't you be beautiful, Donaldson? she thought. 'I don't believe I've changed,' she said.

'You have. Sometimes you seem to lose all heart. Last year I had only to stand near you and I could feel warm waves of vitality, fine and glorious life in you. You're often like that still, but underneath it I feel emptiness. Is it only your mother's illness that troubles you?'

She thought of saying: 'Not my mother. Everything. Don't you see? I'm adrift. I'm terribly afraid.' But his concern irritated her, as did his assumption of superiority and his success.

She turned abruptly away. 'I'm going on one of my favourite walks today. Last summer I used to visit a holiday house taken by a family called the Mayricks. I helped with the children. I like to remember what a happy time I had there. It was the best part of the summer.' She had meant to be cruel but he seemed indifferent to her intention.

They found the house shut up and uncared for, the uncurtained windows blindly reflecting the sun. Ruth went boldly up to the drawing room window and peered in. The furniture was shrouded in sheets and there was little to remind her of the warm days spent with the Mayricks.

'Don't be sad,' Donaldson pleaded, looking into her face. 'Don't be sad.' And he took her hand again and led her swiftly away along the field-path to the dunes. The sea was alive with light, the waves small, tossing flashes of sunshine. 'Don't be sad,' he repeated and looking again into his eyes she experienced a flood of sorrow that he should be so ineffectual and pleading.

Suddenly he darted his head towards her and kissed her.

The gesture was entirely unexpected. She was conscious of the impact of warm flesh on her lips and the sky being momentarily blotted out by his face.

She was furious. 'How dare you!'

He turned away.

My first kiss, she raged to herself. It should have been magical. Not a peck from a mad photographer who does nothing but irritate me.

She saw that his shoulders were shaking. He was laughing at her. 'For ten days I've been plucking up the courage to do that. I couldn't decide how you'd respond. I never thought that you'd be so cross.'

She wanted to hit him. He danced a little jig among the dunes. 'I'm sorry, I'm sorry.'

She would not listen to him. Clasping her hat, plucking up her skirts, she marched home.

At the gate of The Rush House she turned. There was no sign of him.

# Chapter Seven

*Present*

I

The phone rang. 'Helena Mayrick?' An unknown, male voice, rapid and cultured.

'Yes.'

'My name is Nick Broadbent. I rang a few days ago.'

'Yes. I received the message.'

'I wrote to you about the possibility of a book on Donaldson. You didn't reply. Does that mean you're not interested?'

'I'm sorry. I didn't realize there was a rush.'

'No rush. It's just I'm keen to get on. Look, I happen to be staying with my brother in Malvern at present, so perhaps we could meet to discuss the project.'

Helena was not used to being confronted by such decisiveness. She had found that her bereavement protected her from the world so that for the past months she had inhabited a small, sad cocoon.

'I'm afraid it's not terribly convenient just now.'

'I see. I'm sorry.'

He sounded so disappointed that she wavered. 'Well, how flexible are you? I suppose you might come in the morning, though I won't be able to concentrate much as my daughter will be around.'

'That will be fine.'

'Look, Mr Broadbent, what exactly do you need from me? Do you really want my help with the book, or are you after information on Donaldson, because I actually have very little.'

'To be absolutely honest what I want is your family

connection. It would double sales. Donaldson fans, and there are many in the world of photography, are always very intrigued by his private life because so little is known of it, particularly his relationship with Ruth Styles.'

After he had rung off Helena smiled ruefully. At least this unknown Nick Broadbent possessed the virtue of honesty.

Nicholas Broadbent arrived at eleven o'clock the next morning. Not anticipating such punctuality Helena was upstairs nervously arranging her hair, so Nina answered the door. As usual when confronted by a stranger her courage failed her, and leaving the man on the doorstep she ran to the bottom of the stairs and yelled for her mother.

Never had Helena met anyone whose appearance was so at odds with his voice. She had expected him to be youthful, well groomed and alarmingly self-assured. Instead Broadbent was very thin and tall with over-large hands. He wore a creased, well-washed business shirt open at the neck, and ancient jeans. Though he could not have been more than forty his face was scored by creases which ran even down his thin cheeks. The length of his face was accentuated by an extraordinary hair-cut, heavily gelled into a spiky, iron-grey quiff, like a tooth brush. He was pale and looked as if he might recently have been ill but his gaze was piercingly direct as he took her hand and scrutinized her face. 'You are not at all like him,' he said at once.

'I'm only his granddaughter. And they always say that the female line is very strong in our family. Apparently I resemble my grandmother, Ruth Styles.'

'You do. Yes. You do. I've studied many photographs of her.'

She led him through to the kitchen, conscious of the intimate details of her domestic world: a pile of feminine undergarments in the washing basket, a small vase of fading roses cut by her father the previous week, and a scruffy engagement calendar on which were scrawled such items as: *Nina opt. 10.45.* It struck her that Michael's death had somehow robbed her of social veneer. She had lost the ability to be casual, to put strangers at their ease. Neither she nor the house had taken

Broadbent's visit into account. 'We could go into the garden if you like. I expect you're hot. Would you like coffee, or a cold drink?' Nina had shuffled close against her leg. Helena touched the child's hair, lifting and stroking the soft curls.

'Yes. Thanks. A cold drink.'

Broadbent crossed to the door on which Nina's pictures were Blu-Tacked. On one she had copied the words: *mummy. daddy. nina.* None of the three figures illustrated had necks or shoulders and all wore garments heavily patterned in Nina's favourite fluorescent felt tips.

'You're good at drawing,' Broadbent told Nina, and he seemed sincere in his praise as he studied each picture carefully. Nina, who never smiled at unknown people, peered at him suspiciously, her thumb wedged tightly into her mouth.

In the garden Helena placed the tray of drinks on the long grass and went to the shed for chairs.

'It's a nice garden,' Broadbent said. He stood awkwardly under the apple tree with the air of one who had once known how to handle a situation such as this but had forgotten. But he did seem to appreciate the breezy garden with its lawn carpeted by daisies and the trail of purple clematis so heavy that it bowed the fence. Helena's father, Robin, had made some attempt to tame the grass but the beds were very overgrown already. Pansies and dandelions bloomed in equal profusion.

'I've let everything grow very wild this year,' Helena told him apologetically, unfolding old canvas chairs. When she sat down Nina leant against her knees sucking at her beaker and dropping biscuit crumbs. 'Nina, go and get something to play with.'

'I don't know what to do.'

'Bring out a jigsaw or a game. What about your colouring?'

'I don't want to do anything.'

Helena could not be bothered to press her further. 'Anyway. Where shall we start?' she asked Broadbent who was leaning slightly forward in his chair, watching them intently.

'I thought we could exchange what we know of Donaldson. I won't disguise how eager I was to meet you. There are gaps in our collection.'

'Collection?'

'The Donaldson Collection. In Bury St Edmunds. You must know of it. It's been open for five years now. I'm a trustee,' he added. 'We definitely contacted your mother.'

'I see.'

'Donaldson's liaison with your grandmother makes research into his private life tricky. Your family – your mother – has been decidedly unforthcoming, and it seems that Donaldson's only brother also disapproved of the love affair. So there are no family records to go on.'

'I don't really see how I can help. I know less than you.' Helena was a little ashamed of her obstructiveness. She was aware that Nina sensed her hostility to the photographer. The little girl was not usually so clingy. 'My mother won't speak of him,' Helena added, 'although she had no real cause to dislike him. We have a few photographs but nothing much. And I have only just begun to realize how prestigious he was. So you see, I am hardly qualified to write a book on him. Apart from because I'm family.'

Broadbent favoured her with a rather cheeky, lop-sided grin that revealed neat white teeth. 'I have also seen your other work.'

Helena felt a hot flush seep upwards from neck to forehead. 'I suppose you mean the pieces in *Heritage*. Oh dear.'

'Don't apologize. I've read worse.'

Helena gave a little gasp of amazement at his condescension. 'Why, thank you!'

He was oblivious to the fact that he had offended her. 'Donaldson's intention in his pictures was usually so clear that they won't need that much explanation. And I can do the technical bit about his craft, if you like.'

'I don't think you need me at all,' Helena said huffily, clasping Nina tightly to her.

'Oh, I'm not much of a poet. Someone needs to wax lyrical over his great contribution to the war and his compassionate portrayal of refugees in the twenties. You can do that.'

Helena was suddenly laughing at him. 'You said you were a

photographer yourself, Mr Broadbent. What sort? I can't imagine you doing portraits. You don't have the patter.'

He shielded his eyes from the sun with one of his long-fingered hands. 'How did you guess? No, I'm a news photographer. I'm sorry, I should have explained. I've been put out to grass for a while because I'm a bit of a nutter. I went off my head. This Donaldson thing is the first paid work I've felt like doing in ages. I couldn't resist. Donaldson has always been a guru to me. I latched onto his work when I was a student.'

'I see.' Helena sat for a moment watching him. 'I'll go and get the Donaldson photographs I have, shall I? I've put them in order for you.' She pushed Nina away from her lap and got up. 'Come on, Nina, we'll find you something to do.' But rather to her surprise Nina did not follow her back into the house.

Helena ran upstairs and stood at her bedroom window, taking deep breaths and laughing again. How was she to work with such a maverick? His appearance was so strange and his history so unusual. The room overlooked the garden, and she saw that Nina had crept nearer to him and was scrutinizing him closely with her formidable, bespectacled stare, her thumb still deep in her mouth.

Broadbent said something and then, gaining no response, closed his eyes and rested his head against the chair-back, his thin body sprawled unbecomingly on the awkward seat. Helena opened the window to call Nina away, worried that the child might suddenly take fright.

Then she heard Nina say in her clear, high voice, 'My daddy died.'

The visitor's eyes opened abruptly. 'What?'

'He fell off a mountain. I've got a picture. I'll go and get it.'

He sat motionless, hands folded in his lap, staring after the child.

Nina returned with her picture clasped against her T-shirt. Helena knew the painting well for despite its morbid connotations Nina had insisted on keeping it in her nursery folder. She had used a piece of computer paper which still had a perforated strip hanging from the edge. In one corner of the painting was a bright yellow sun beneath which was a wobbly, pointed triangle representing the mountain. An upside-down, neckless figure had been placed mid-air. Written underneath were the words *for daddy*.

Helena took pity on the unfortunate visitor who was studying the picture with unnecessary diligence, lost for words. She scooped up the box of photographs and hurried downstairs. Nina now rested confidently against Broadbent's chair-back and was relating all her memories of the morning she had learnt of her father's death.

'I'm sorry,' Nicholas said, at sight of Helena. 'I should not have come.'

'It's OK. Please don't speak of it.' But his eyes were so sympathetic that she had to speak more briskly than she'd intended to stifle her tears. 'You can borrow these if you like. I'll fetch you a bag and you can take the photographs.' She was conscious of the sun's warmth and the buzzing of insects on the clematis. There had been an exchange of kindnesses and her sore heart was a little soothed.

But he would not take the photographs. 'You must keep them safe. They may be very precious. Why don't you come to the gallery some time and view the collection? Bring these with you and we can compare them.' He rose, ducking his head a little to avoid a low branch. 'When did your husband die?'

'A couple of months ago.'

'Please forgive me. Please forgive me for intruding like this. I had no idea. You should have said.'

Helena shook her head, moved by his confusion. She understood his desire to leave and followed him to the front door. 'Thank you for coming, Mr Broadbent.'

'You could call me Nick. You sound like my bank manager otherwise.'

He drove off in a flashy white soft-topped BMW, a strange contrast to his shabby appearance.

'He was nice,' Nina commented after he'd gone.

Helena's friend, Victoria, rang to announce that she would take an afternoon off work and drive up on Friday to stay the weekend. She arrived at supper-time wafting Armani perfume, her weekend luggage packed into one brown leather hold-all, her hair cut into a new urchin style. Nina, who doted upon her exotic godmother, had begged to be allowed to stay up and was rewarded by a bear hug amidst the soft billows of Victoria's silk blouse. She was then swept upstairs and given a prolonged reading of her current favourite, *Hansel and Gretel*, which culminated in an orgy of tickles and convulsive laughter and the presentation of a quiveringly soft panda. From the kitchen below Helena could hear Nina's delighted squeals and infectious, throaty chuckle, an unusual sound these days.

Later that evening Victoria, who had not seen Helena since the funeral, informed her that she looked terrible. 'What have you been doing to yourself? Do you still feel dreadful?'

Indeed, for the first time since Michael's death, Helena had felt a glimmer of dismay at the sight of her own jaded complexion and untamed hair in the glass, even more disturbing beside Victoria's vibrancy. Victoria was not noted for compassion or patience, and on this occasion Helena found her efforts to be tactful and sympathetic both touching and amusing.

However, half an hour of unnaturally polite dialogue was enough. 'It's all right,' Helena said at last, 'I'd much rather you treated me normally. I'm sick of sympathy.'

'Well, that's nice. You might have told me before and spared me all this effort.'

'I wanted to make the most of it.' She went over to a drawer in the oak sideboard which had once been in her mother-in-law's house and produced a photograph. 'Look, this came today. It was taken half an hour before he died.'

The print had been sent by one of Michael's pupils with a little tear-stained note stating that it was of Michael and the rest of the party at the cairn. The group looked damp and windswept, wild-haired and triumphant. Michael stood at the back, one arm up as if he were ducking away from the photographer. 'Doesn't it seem terrible that you can capture someone like that with a camera, and the next moment they are dead?' said Helena.

'I'm sure that's why we find old photographs so poignant.' Victoria held the picture for some moments, smiling with rare tenderness at Michael's bearded countenance. 'It doesn't seem possible that he's gone. Oh, Helena, you must feel so appalling.'

'Do you know what I felt when I saw that photo this morning? Rage. That he should be so oblivious to what was about to happen, that he dared to joke like that a few minutes before he fell. I know it's irrational, but I can't help it. Sometimes, do you know, I loathe Michael. I don't grieve for him. I hate him for being so careless with his life. And nobody allows me to say so.'

Victoria lifted her legs onto the sofa and lay back against the arm. 'I'm not stopping you. Say what you like.'

'I've just said it. Do you think I'm terrible?'

'No. I understand totally.'

Helena continued more calmly. 'It's as if the circumstances in which he died were so stupid, so much the matter of an instant's misjudgement, that if only I could find the right switch I could undo it all and have him back. I think: If I'd phoned him the night before, if Nina had spoken to him, he might have been a tiny bit more careful. It ought to be easy to put right, the way most mistakes can be. I torture myself.'

'I expect you're right. One alteration in circumstances would have prevented it. I expect we've all felt that.' Victoria's refusal to mince words had always been disconcerting.

'We? What do you mean?' Helena stared across at her friend who was unusually still save for her thumbs with their glossy nails which passed lightly one over the other.

'I'm sure all his friends must think the same. If only we'd taken a little more care of him. Or at least made more of what we had of him.'

Helena had never considered Victoria to be a friend of

Michael's. Victoria was her own friend. And surely it was most unlike Victoria to waste her highly paid time on such speculations? 'Is that what you've thought?'

'Of course. Well, don't be surprised. Why are you? I'd known Michael almost as long as you, remember. I loved him too.'

No. No. Not Victoria. It had not been Victoria's bold handwriting on the note. And it was not like her to attempt disguise. Was it? Or was her normal hand-writing a disguise? 'Of course I know you've been friendly with him through me for years,' Helena said slowly.

'Yes, that's typical of you, isn't it?' Victoria's quick temper had been roused. 'You are so busy wallowing you hardly give thought to how the rest of his friends might be suffering. I have reason to grieve for him too you know. Don't you remember how he helped decorate my flat when I moved into my own place? And that he spent ages sorting out that financial mess when Jack left me? Or how he escorted me to that retailer's ball when I had no one else? He was lovely, Helena. You were so, so lucky. Do you realize that? You don't find many men like Michael – generous and thoughtful and just so kind. Has it not occurred to you that such a person might be very badly missed by other people and not just you?'

As usual Victoria's eloquent directness shamed Helena. 'I'm sorry. But I do blame myself in particular. You know. For somehow letting him do it.'

'But you would blame yourself however he died. You'd try and find a reason that came from your own guilt. Or it would be the fault of your wretched mother or grandmother.'

Helena smiled. 'I really can't blame my errant grandmother for this.'

'You do surprise me. All your other faults are attributed to her.'

'I'm not that bad.'

'Oh, come on. You're always going on about how restrained your mother is and how she repressed you in case you became reckless like your gran.'

'My mother thinks that all the women in our family are

doomed. That's why she's always been so careful with her own life. She's the only one who's stayed on the rails. She keeps watching me in case I do something desperate.' But as she spoke, Helena was thinking: I must make her prove that she wasn't the one. I don't want to suspect Victoria. I must put it out of my head. After a moment she asked softly: 'Victoria. Did you know Michael was having an affair?'

Victoria swung one long, black-clad leg against the side of the sofa. Not by the flicker of an eyelid did she show surprise. But she spoke very clearly. 'Don't be so bloody ridiculous.'

'I'm not. It's true.'

'What possible reason do you have for saying that?'

'I found a letter.' Helena produced the crumpled page she carried with her night and day. 'It was in his rucksack.'

Victoria read it. Her hands did not shake, nor her face betray agitation. 'Was this the only letter? It could be ancient. From before you were married.'

'Even if it is, it doesn't account for its being in his bag. Finding this letter was almost worse than hearing that Michael was dead. I can't be free to be sad. I think about this woman all the time. I can't be simple about his death. People say how sorry they are and how dreadful I must be feeling and I hate the fact that I do feel dreadful – but because of resentment and loathing. And I think: Why did he need someone else? I thought we were happy. Wasn't I good enough for him?'

'Maybe it was completely one-sided. Perhaps he was pursued. He's the type who might not even notice that someone was after him. He had you and Nina, and everyone could see how he loved you both.'

'He carried her letter with him. He had nothing of me.'

'You were his wife. He didn't need love letters from you.'

'He cared so little for me that he couldn't be bothered to keep himself safe. Maybe he loved her so much it was tearing him apart and he wanted to die.'

'It doesn't work like that. Why do you have to read all this crap into it? Michael was his own person. You fell for him because of who he was. On the mountains he was completely absorbed by his surroundings and by his charges. I doubt he gave anything else a thought. He probably didn't even know the note was in his bag. And whatever the reason it was there, surely you know that Michael was far too honest to have had an affair?'

Helena bowed her head. She could not be comforted.

Victoria lost patience. 'Find the woman then, and set your mind at rest. It shouldn't be difficult. His circle wasn't that wide.'

Helena gazed bleakly at Victoria. 'How would I know who she was even if I were to look her in the eye?'

'You'd know. Of course you would. If she cared for him that much she'll emerge in the end.'

### 3

Helena and Nicholas Broadbent arranged to meet outside the grandly named Hubert Donaldson Gallery in Bury St Edmunds at two o'clock one Saturday afternoon. It was not an easy place to find, being tucked away in a back street, situated in the unpretentious, Georgian terraced house where Donaldson had spent the last twenty-five years of his life. A dark green plaque, etched in white, proclaimed the opening hours of the gallery and declared that besides a unique collection of Donaldson's work, there was also a display of his photographic equipment.

Although it was late June the day was very cold. Helena had left Shrewsbury in bright sunshine and wore only a light cotton blouse and skirt, so after waiting for a quarter of an hour in the draughty little street she ventured inside where a superior-looking girl with a mass of dark hair was arranging postcards. 'Excuse me,' murmured Helena, aware that the girl must have observed her waiting outside.

'Yes?' The twist of her head sent a wave of patchouli scent from her heavy locks. Long amber earrings glimmered against her white neck.

'Do you know if Nicholas Broadbent is around?'

The girl blinked heavily mascaraed eyes. 'He's not. He never comes at weekends.'

'Oh. Only I'd arranged to meet him.'

'Really?'

Helena was still so emotionally fragile that the girl's aloof attitude threatened to reduce her to tears. Lifting her chin she said in a clear, loud voice: 'Well. I'll have a look round. Perhaps you'll tell him I'm here when he turns up.'

'That'll be three pounds fifty. Four pounds if you want a brochure.' She pronounced the word 'broshooer'.

'Thank you.' Helena humbly produced a five-pound note but inwardly cursed Nicholas Broadbent.

At first she was too flustered to take in much of the collection, but after a while she was soothed by the quiet of the little rooms, and by the knowledge that here her grandfather had lived alone for many years.

The house had been left by Donaldson to his brother, according to the brochure, who had in turn donated it to the town as a gallery for Donaldson's work. The rooms were very small, but brightly lit by institutional striplights that robbed them of atmosphere. The photographs were all carefully labelled with neat, typed explanatory notes supplemented in the brochure by more detailed explanations of Donaldson's technique.

The earliest prints had the slightly dream-like quality of black and white photographs taken early in the century and the subjects were frozen and distant. Those preserved from Donaldson's youth were, however, touching in their pretension. One, entitled *Her Letter*, showed a small mail box besides which stood a woman in a long pale skirt, caught, so the viewer was intended to believe, in the very act of posting a letter. For a family portrait, Donaldson's parents and brother had been arranged stiffly in the back garden, their distant faces grim, the small boy in particular wearing a look of bored resignation. Helena was rather surprised that she felt no pang of recognition – after all she was looking into the eyes of her own blood relatives. But they seemed so far away.

Next were the east coast photographs. A typed note disclosed that Donaldson's favourite human subject had been a girl named Ruth Styles who had lived in Westwich, a village which was to hold particular emotional significance for Donaldson. Above was a photograph of Ruth with her hand on a gate, behind her an expanse of reed-beds and a high, bright sky. The expression on her face was affectionate but pensive.

Displayed in a nearby glass case were Donaldson's camera, exposure meters and shutters of this time. Helena peered past her own reflection into the case, and imagined her grandfather's skilled fingers making these complex pieces of wood and metal work small artistic miracles.

Another room was devoted to Donaldson's war photographs. *Donaldson had a distinguished war record* stated the typed notes pompously. *The audacity and vividness of his shots reveal his refusal to be daunted by fear of personal danger.*

Then came photographs taken at the height of Donaldson's career when he had been invited to attend the most important public events. He had travelled so widely that the type-written notes sprouted thick and fast, extolling his career with various prestigious publications.

And then in 1927 he had journeyed to India.

By this time Helena had reached the tiny staircase which led from the inner ground floor room to the upper floor. The photographs of India were tucked away in an awkward corner of the landing.

A note related that in 1927 Donaldson had travelled through-out India but for once had kept a very limited photographic record. It was obvious that the pictures he had taken were displayed in an obscure corner because they were unusually dull; a mountain, an anonymous temple, a colonial-looking mansion and a graveyard. Or rather a single grave bedecked with white flowers and marked by a plain cross. This photograph pierced Helena's heart. How could Donaldson have understood light and shadow so perfectly that he was able to infuse so simple an image with so much yearning sorrow? She remembered the wreaths piled round the pathetic little ticket bearing Michael's name at the crematorium. Print and petals replacing flesh and blood.

'Can you shed any light on that one?'

Nicholas Broadbent was standing at the bottom of the stairs.

Had he not been so late Helena might have been more forthcoming. 'None at all,' she said.

'Have you been here long?'

'About an hour. We said two o'clock.'

'Yes. Sorry. I'm no good at time-keeping.' But his appearance belied his casual apology. His clothes were rumpled, his eyes exhausted.

Helena was brimful of information and questions but she moved away and walked in silence to the next room.

'Any surprises yet?' he asked.

'Oh, I don't think so. I obviously knew all the public details of his life.'

The little gallery was suddenly crowded by three students who moved solemnly through the rooms murmuring about focal length. Helena walked self-consciously towards the last room, aware that she was behaving badly by not accepting Nicholas's apology, but still angry with him for subjecting her to the torture of an encounter with the girl at the cash desk.

'What do you think made Donaldson such an exceptional photographer, Nicholas?' she asked.

'His affection for his subjects. You can tell. Especially in photos of Ruth. He protected her from any rough angle or crude light.'

'Isn't that what any skilled photographer would do?'

He shrugged. 'You can see it's more than that. It's in his landscapes too. He tended to photograph subjects he cherished. See the church here. He knows that church. He's made himself familiar with all its dimensions. And so he finds the right moment to capture it.'

Broadbent led her to the corner of what must have been Donaldson's bedroom. 'Do you know this picture? It's my favourite. It's him, a self-portrait, done a year or so before he died.' Donaldson had taken himself full face, gazing impersonally at the camera as if to say: 'Here I am. No frills.' He had gaunt features and owlish, short-sighted eyes. His hair was white but still unruly and strong, cut very short, the mouth was wide and unsmiling.

'He looks so solemn,' Helena said. 'And he's not exactly a Lothario in that prim suit, is he, or with his strange face? The way my mother speaks of him you'd think he had lured Ruth to a life of complete immorality by his evil charm.'

In the last ten years of his life Donaldson had resumed his photography of the east coast. The typed notes were reproachful. *In his later years Donaldson chose to ignore stirring world events and returned instead to familiar, best-loved subjects.* He had taken the beach at Westwich, waves churning on shingle, desolate fields, flat, rippling reed-beds, and lonely churches. His favourite location was the cliff-top where he'd first met Ruth. *His love affair with Ruth Styles ended tragically when she abandoned their child and went to live abroad,* another of the notes said. *But Donaldson returned again and again to the places where they had been together.*

'Who wrote all this?' demanded Helena.

'Some old trout on the board of trustees. Why, aren't they accurate?'

'There's a lot missing, I would say. I thought it might have been the girl at the door.'

'You mean our Sally? We're lucky to have her. She's here all day on Saturdays and we can't afford to pay her much. She's got a bit of a thing about Donaldson.'

Helena stood at the window and looked down at the narrow, treeless street. Opposite was a shop selling electrical goods. 'You'd think Donaldson would feel very stifled here after all that travel.'

'I suppose it was a kind of retreat. He was quite a lonely man, you know. Though the town adored him because he was a great benefactor. Eccentric, but full of largesse. He loved children.'

Helena thought of Donaldson's own child, Joanna, who from the age of fifteen had refused contact with him, believing him responsible for the way she had been abandoned by Ruth when a baby.

The rest of the room was occupied by photographic

instruments. Helena approached a case containing two twin lens reflex cameras. 'Were these Donaldson's?'

'They were. He was a modest man, very loyal to his cameras. He didn't go for swanky equipment. But the one on the right is a beauty, incredibly sophisticated for its time, built-in exposure meter, the lot. A Contaflex. And well worn, see? Every photographer has a camera that's special to him or her. It becomes like a third eye. I can imagine how he would have loved the weight and substance of that camera.' How close we are brought to people by their possessions, Helena thought, looking down at the little machine. She thought its modest, workmanlike appearance exactly suited the Donaldson of the self-portrait.

Nicholas produced a key and unlocked a small door which led to some steep, attic stairs. 'Now, through here are the pictures I want you to look at. We don't display them because they seem to have very little meaning and Donaldson didn't choose to label or date them. That wasn't like him. He was normally extremely punctilious.' In the little room at the top, light from a gabled window illuminated neat cabinets and boxes. It was warm under the roof. Helena sat on a stool and thought of Donaldson living alone in this modest house after a life of public work and undying affection for one woman.

'I wonder why Ruth left him?' she said. 'He seems to have been a good man.'

'Don't expect me to explain any woman's motives,' Nicholas said wearily.

Helena smiled at him. 'I suppose you're implying that men are simple, straightforward souls without a single fault or complexity.'

'Plenty of fault, not much complication.' He favoured her with his waggish grin. 'Now take a look at this pile. I'm pretty sure from the camera he used that this little group were all taken around the same time – about 1923 or 1924 I suppose. We know that Ruth disappeared in 1925 – there are no photographs of her after that. I'll show you the last one he took of her. We don't display it because it's bloody awful. And these are the puzzling ones.'

The first three were all of a large house isolated amidst flat fields. Helena recognized Overstrands at once and saw that it had been taken from different angles; one photograph was of the back of the house with its little porch and wide bays, but for another Donaldson must have sat on the stile across the lane. 'I know this house very well,' she exclaimed. 'I was staying in it only a few weeks ago. It belongs to a great-aunt of my husband's, you see. Michael and I first met in Westwich. He was helping his Aunt Clara decorate this house at the time. But why on earth should Donaldson have been so interested in Overstrands?'

Broadbent was gazing at Helena with considerable interest.

'Perhaps he thought it atmospheric. It does look grand among the fields. It's unusual for a house of that size to be so exposed.'

'It was well-cared for, though, wasn't it? Look at the flower beds and the shining windows. It's not like that now. I'd love to show these to Michael's Aunt Clara. She'd certainly be able to say when they were taken. Except that she's almost blind.'

He laughed. 'That'll be an unusual credit in the book – *Photograph identified by kind help of blind aunt*…Now what about these others?'

'Oh, that's Westwich village street, looking down towards the sea – you can just make out what were probably fishing huts. They would be right at the top of the beach. And this is the lane just outside The Rush House, where Ruth lived. See how the lane bends – well, that bend is at the top of the village street. You could put the photos together and it would show you the way to the sea from The Rush House. Oh my goodness, these gates in this one, they belong to The Rush House, but he's taken them from within the garden, see, there's the lane outside, and the little brick path. I have a photograph looking the opposite way, up to the front door. Look, it's among this pile I brought with me to show you. But why did he bother with this view, I wonder?'

'Unless he was simply showing the route to the sea. He must have associated it with Ruth. Anyway, these were all together in an envelope and with them was this other one, probably Donaldson's least inspired.' The offending photograph was simply of a plaque in the wall of a tall, Victorian town-house which read *Philip Shaw MD*. Even the age of the photograph could not disguise that the plaque was decidedly tarnished.

'Well, I know who this was,' Helena said. 'Philip Shaw was my great-great-grandfather. His wife walked into the sea one morning and died.'

'Suicide?' She sensed the acuteness of his interest.

'I think so. Yes.' The little attic room was silent except for a fly tapping lightly against the window and, below, the soft tread of feet in Donaldson's bedroom. 'Yes, my mother told me the story. Philip Shaw was the village doctor at Westwich. I think his family had been there for generations. Anyway he met his wife, Margaret, when he was a student. She was from Manchester, so Westwich, being so quiet and isolated, was a bit of a shock to her system. Nevertheless she was quite happily married and had a daughter. But gradually Margaret became a bit strange. My mother said she was obsessed by the sea and by the way it was eroding the land. As you know, one of the fascinations of Westwich, certainly for Donaldson, is that it is gradually disappearing into the sea. Like a lot of that coast. One morning, after a bad storm, Margaret simply put on her bonnet, walked out of the house, down the village street and into the sea. Her husband was just too late to save her. He and his daughter moved to London to get away from the tragedy. But the daughter, Julia, who was Ruth's mother, was left The Rush House and she returned there. That's how Ruth came to be brought up at Westwich.'

'And why do you suppose that Donaldson took this photograph of Shaw's plaque? Presumably he set up as a doctor in London – but he must have been dead by the time Donaldson came on the scene.'

'Perhaps he was just intrigued. Everyone in Westwich would have known the story. I believe it's one of the reasons my mother will never speak of the place. She doesn't like emotion – or family scandal.'

'And your Margaret killed herself because she was afraid of the encroaching sea?'

'I believe so.'

Nicholas touched the little pile of photographs Helena had identified. 'The way to the sea. Margaret Shaw's last walk.'

'But why should Donaldson have bothered? By 1924 Margaret had been dead for about fifty years.'

'I don't know. Perhaps as a photographer he was trying to re-create her mood. It happens, you know. You try to get inside people's heads. You have to know what you want to reveal in the picture.'

'Is that how you work?' She looked up at him, conscious that she had not previously given thought to his professional life.

'Used to.' He tapped the little pile of prints into order and replaced them in their envelope. 'It seems odd to walk into the sea when you're afraid of it. I'd go the other way, inland.'

'The women in our family have a reputation for being odd.'

'Well, it can't have done Margaret Shaw's little girl much good to have her mother drown like that. How old was she?'

'I'm not sure. Ten or eleven. And no, it didn't. As I say, she was Ruth's mother, Julia Styles. She went mad and would never leave The Rush House. Ruth had to care for her.'

'Ah yes, look. Here's Donaldson's last photo of Ruth, taken at about the same time as these others.' Ruth stood leaning against the gate-post of The Rush House. She was dressed in a calf-length dark garment that accentuated her thin body. Her face was pale but excited and she was smiling directly at the camera.

'It's a dead smile,' Nicholas said. 'That's why I don't show it. It exposes Donaldson too much. I can feel his hurt.'

'Goodness me. You read a lot into photographs.'

'Yes. Yes I do. Because there's a lot there.'

He carefully filed everything away and led Helena back through the gallery to the little entrance hall where the dark-haired Sally was counting the day's takings. This time she looked at Helena with considerable interest. 'You found him then,' she said.

'Thank you. Yes.'

In the street outside where a light drizzle was now falling Helena said, 'I didn't know whether to introduce myself as Donaldson's granddaughter or not. After all, she'll have to get used to having me around.'

'No, I wouldn't tell her you're his granddaughter, there'd be too many questions. His biographer will do.'

# Chapter Eight

*Past*

After the abortive attempt to take Julia to London Alan Styles gave up on his wife. He was generous with money, wrote frequently to his daughter and visited The Rush House twice a year but it was clear that his concern for Julia was now solely as a dependant who must he supported.

His daughter's situation gave him some cause for unease, but she was obdurate in her refusal to have her mother cared for by strangers and the solution she offered was too convenient for him to refuse. Every time he went to The Rush House a similar discussion took place. He stood in the little parlour, on each visit more florid in complexion, his belly more pronounced, his great hands clasping the back of one of the fragile, delicately carved upright chairs Julia had inherited from her mother. Ruth sat in her low chair by the fire, her forehead supported by one hand, a book open on her lap. Her features were illuminated by the warm light which played across her delicate cheekbones and her fine, glinting hair. She was, he thought, very like her mother at that age, though her mouth was firmer and her posture more confident.

'You're looking well,' he told Ruth, 'the country air does you good.' And indeed she always did look in the pink of health for the sea air brought a bloom to her cheeks and a brightness to her eyes that the occasional sleepless night could not remove. 'But you must get terribly low watching your mother go downhill like this. Why won't you let me get someone in?'

'She'd hate it. It would be too disturbing.'

'I could have Miss Lily come down here. She'd be company of sorts.'

'Father, how can you suggest it? You know I can't stand Miss Lily.'

'She's an obliging enough soul.'

'Father, please. I can just about manage Mother – but Miss Lily as well...'

Then he looked helplessly out of the little window at the enclosed garden and said: 'I can't imagine why she's like this. She was so full of life when I married her. I blame myself.' And for a moment a tear glistened at the corner of one eye.

'The doctor said she must have been very disturbed by her mother dying so suddenly. You could do nothing to cure that. You mustn't blame yourself.'

Gradually he became more remote from Ruth. Far from troubling her, his embraces were now so perfunctory that she longed for him to show more warmth. It was as if he were given totally to his London life and had no emotional tie with his wife and daughter. His eyes, at meal-times, had a vague, disinterested expression, as if he were inwardly far away.

Harry, who had become an indolent, good-natured young man, graduated from school to Cambridge and divided his vacations between London and other pursuits. If he came to Westwich it was for a day at a time. Ruth understood his horror of the cramped, feminine rooms and his mother's painful attempts to be gay and girlish for him.

But despite his distaste for her condition, with Julia, Harry was unfailingly gentle and patient. He sat at her bedroom window talking or reading until she grew restless and begged to be allowed to sleep. Any guilt he felt for the rarity of his visits was assuaged by the numerous gifts he brought; a gossamer bed-jacket, chocolates and journals. Julia took no more than a passing interest in anything. His most successful present was a kitten – he was blithely unaware of the dislike Ruth had conceived for anything feline since her acquaintance with Miss Lily's Cloud. The kitten, christened Harry Two, was a sensible creature and recognized a good home in the folds of Julia's coverlet where it spent most of its time, a round, black bundle on her bed.

But aside from these fleeting visits by father and brother Ruth was left to care for her mother unsupported by anyone except Maud Waterford and the kind offices of other Westwich neighbours. Once a year the Mayricks came to Overstrands and Ruth had a fortnight running wild with the boys, nursing little Clara and listening to Esther Mayrick. After they'd gone she'd walk along the path to Overstrands, sit on the stile and stare at the blank windows of the deserted house, listening for echoes of the days past.

2

In Westwich time passed softly. One Sunday, walking slowly out of church with a neighbour, a woman might suddenly notice that the skin beneath her friend's eyes was a little puffier and criss-crossed with lines like fine threads, and on returning home would realize that her own face too had aged. And in the same discreet, insidious way, a few more stones from the ruined church on the cliff fell into the sea. Mrs Spendmore stocked a new brand of biscuits and the pattern books for the summer season pictured a different cut of skirt. And each moment of the passing years was marked by the sea, by water falling on shingle, waves overlapping, breaking, retreating, on and on, without faltering.

Westwich was a very long way from the centre of things. Nobody ever went there as a route to anywhere else but even in Westwich the present could not be avoided, although a villager might well hear of an event and wonder: what has that to do with me? There were always visitors and newspapers to force a confrontation with the present. And the telephone of course. The Rush House was late in installing the telephone and when on rare occasions it rang, a quarter of an hour afterwards Julia might be found huddled under her quilt, trembling with fright.

Everything Ruth did was by proxy. In her head she was wild. Her great source of information was Harry who gladly had all the latest radical publications sent to her. She knew more than anyone else locally about the great happenings of those years; the building of the *Titanic*; Scott's expeditions; the strikes on the railways and the troubling fermentation of events in Europe. But her greatest passion was still the suffrage movement. She was always writing letters and sending donations. Westwich thought her very fast. What did women want with the vote? But Ruth was allowed and forgiven any eccentricity by Westwich. Nobody underestimated the sacrifice she had made.

She would never accept that her youth was sifting through her fingers. She survived by convincing herself that her bondage was only temporary and that any day her mother would recover and they would return to London and take up the old life. And so she had to keep herself ready. She persevered with her music and reading, keeping a carefully annotated bibliography and detailed commentary on all she studied. She had graduated now to drama and European literature, and exchanged vigorous letters with Harry on the rival merits of Racine and Shakespeare.

Ruth never let anything slide. When she emerged from The Rush House she was always carefully and modishly dressed. Here she had Miss Lily to thank. Miss Lily herself looked a fright, as anyone who saw her on her one visit to Westwich could have testified. She made a point of dressing badly to emphasize her inferior status, but she had an artist's eye for quality and made it her business to go to the most fashionable areas of town to observe the ladies and their clothes so that she might advise Ruth. Specifications for Ruth's and Julia's clothes were then sent to London and Miss Lily considered it her duty to plague the unfortunate dressmaker until each garment was finished and packed to her satisfaction.

So Ruth would appear in Mrs Spendmore's shop on a May morning in a tucked lawn blouse and fine blue wool skirt, her hair carefully pinned in the latest elaborate style, her wonderful clear skin aglow with health from all her walking. Only her eyes gave her away. Her eyes betrayed her craving for life. And they were haunted by too many stormy nights at The Rush House.

In the day during a storm, doors banged and the curtains

lifted at the windows of The Rush House. Outside, the garden was a tossing chaos of dancing branches and old leaves rattling along the paths. The clouds were so low that they met the sea and even, for tantalizing moments, broke apart in their tearing hurry.

The sea hurled shingle against the soft cliffs, waves exploding so fiercely and so far that each retreating wave was swallowed up by the onslaught of the next.

And at night the sea became a wicked black broth, and the familiar lanes and trees around The Rush House teemed with secret demons which waited, taut and menacing, to be unleashed.

At night the Millerchips retreated to their cottage in the stable block. This was a condition under which they agreed to work at The Rush House. 'I must have my privacy,' Mrs Millerchip had informed Alan Styles. 'It's enough that I should be rushed off my feet all day without giving up my own place. They'll have to fend for themselves at night.'

The Millerchips left at about seven-thirty. Two hours later Ruth extinguished the lamps in the drawing room and hall, tucked her latest book under her arm and climbed the stairs, her feet heavy with dread of what was in store.

She always called into her mother's room. Julia never slept in the dark. She had one lamp by the bed and another close by in case of emergencies. She lay against the pillows, her eyes clenched shut, every nerve sewn into the wind. Ruth kept her mother's room tidy and comfortable and Maud Waterford's gifts of bright cushions and hangings were supplemented by Alan Styles's abundant supply of expensive ornaments and pictures, but for all the notice Julia took of her surroundings she might have been inhabiting a cell. With her whole being she followed each gust as it circled the house. Ruth's dutiful bedtime kiss was an intrusion, for Julia was afraid to lose her grip on the wind.

Nevertheless, Ruth approached the bed and kissed her mother's tense brow. 'Goodnight, Mother. Call me if you need me.'

The only response was a flicker of Julia's moist, translucent eyelids and the lifting of a limp hand to push her daughter away.

Ruth took comfort from the familiarity of her own room where thick curtains were drawn snugly against the night. She undressed with slow, deliberate movements as if by so doing she might keep control of the night. The wind throbbed and buffeted and when for a moment it was silent, a wave, like a giant hand tossing a million stones, turned on the shore.

From the next room came a low sighing and gasping. Ruth ran along the short, lit passage to where Julia lay back on the pillows, hands to her throat, face contorted. 'Mother, Mother. You're dreaming again.'

But Julia could not struggle out of the nightmare.

She lunged from the bed, stumbling on the hem of her voluminous nightgown, pushed past Ruth and hurtled along the landing and down the stairs. At the closed door of the dining room she halted and laid her hand on the smooth wood. She seemed calmer now but cried softly and whispered: 'No more, please. No more. Please stop.'

Ruth flung open the door and lit the lamps, crying: 'Mother, there's no one here. You see... What is it? Mother.' The room flickered into normality. Ruth went to the table and perched on its cold, polished surface. 'You see. It's just you and me. In The Rush House.' Slowly the dream faded. 'You see.' She placed her arm round Julia's shoulders. 'Silly old Mother. There's no one here. Let's go up to bed now, shall we? Let's have some tea.'

Companionably, they returned to Julia's bedroom. Ruth drew a couple of chairs to the fire and tucked her mother up with rugs and pillows. Julia watched the bright flames leap in the hearth as Ruth heated warm milk on a little spirit stove. Together they sat out the night until a chill grey light at the window signified the approach of dawn.

After a storm Julia was at her most lucid, as if the drama had wiped clean her troubled mind. She even, occasionally, talked to her daughter of the past.

'Stormy nights always remind me of my mother,' she said. 'I dream of her.'

'Bad dreams?'

'Always bad dreams. But not because of her.'

'What was she like?'

'Quite shy. She had very few friends here. She was not used to the sea and did not understand it. I remember her young, soft hair. I remember holding the folds of her skirts and touching the tiny buttons at her cuffs. I remember her face was cold and wet when she kissed me that day. Afterwards he brought her home and the runnels of water from her dress and hair made a trail all the way up the stairs.'

'Why do you stay here with these terrible memories?'

Julia lay back in her chair and closed her eyes. 'The sea took her. She walked into the sea and it never gave her a chance. I can only be close to her here.'

So clear was the still early morning that Ruth ventured one step further. 'I should like to go back to London.'

'Ruth, I have never prevented you.'

Afterwards they both slept and when she woke, Julia was as usual; limp, exhausted, silent. Ruth crept to the kitchen.

'We're very late up this morning, Mrs Millerchip.'

In Mrs Millerchip's hard, suspicious glare flickered a hint of compassion. 'Had one of her nights, has she? I don't wonder. Poor little soul.' She banged the kettle onto the stove. 'It was always said to be worse on stormy nights.'

Sick and weary, Ruth said: 'I wish I understood.'

But Mrs Millerchip turned away, heaving a great pail into the sink. 'Oh, you wouldn't want to know what happens behind closed doors. You'd be surprised.'

3

Ruth's saviour was Donaldson. Whenever he was free he came to Westwich where he stayed with Mrs Spendmore, which to most men would have been torture enough. Donaldson said that he had grown used to his room above the shop and that he had even come to regard it as a second home.

He could have afforded much better for he had become a

successful man. His motor cars were frequently updated and his clothes well-cut, though he was of the figure and features destined always to look untidy. His hair grew far back on his forehead straight upwards and outwards. His skin was of a fine, pale texture and his eyes large and clear but he had bought himself a pair of thick spectacles which obscured both. His mouth was over-large but generously curved and he had a ready, diffident smile.

The villagers loved him. 'I see Mr Donaldson's back,' people would remark to Mrs Spendmore, who would sniff and complain about the trouble he caused. But even she grew to like him. There were little signs of favour. She'd sugar her apple pies more liberally for him and order better cuts of meat. If his visits were more widely spaced than usual she'd be heard to remark: 'Of course that young man's got too good for the likes of us. It's very inconvenient to have to keep that room nice when it's never used.' As the years went by and her arthritis worsened she never rented the room except to him.

Donaldson came to Westwich for Ruth's sake. His devotion to her was a by-word in the village. People assumed that the pair were courting though Ruth would have none of it and always denied that she had any special feeling for him. 'If he's got nothing better to do than follow me around then that's up to him,' she told Maud Waterford tartly. She certainly gave him no encouragement. It was one of the sights of the village to watch them: Ruth very upright, carrying the long umbrella she used as a walking stick, her hat clamped firmly onto her thick hair as she walked very fast with brisk little steps, and Donaldson scuttling along beside her, always encumbered by his camera.

Both seemed quite happy with their peculiar friendship. It was said in the village that neither could entertain a formal engagement, Ruth because she would not leave her mother and Donaldson because he must be based in London. But Maud Waterford often wondered about Donaldson. She would study his intelligent brown eyes and comical, wide mouth and wonder how much heartache was hidden beneath his habitually benign expression. She believed that he would have done anything for Ruth, even thrown his precious camera far into the depths of the ocean for her. And unusual though he was in his looks, she thought that there was little doubt that with his great talent and his qualities of kindness and loyalty he might have found any number of women willing to marry him. Only Ruth, proud and isolated, refused to love him.

Late one July evening, serving over-cooked potatoes onto a delicate, floral plate for Julia's tray, Mrs Millerchip said: 'That young photographer is back in Westwich, I see.'

'Goodness. We're never safe from him and his camera!' Ruth replied, but with a lightening of her heart.

Mrs Millerchip sniffed. 'He seems a decent enough young man.'

Ruth smiled, wondering whether Mrs Millerchip had ever considered her own spouse a decent young man. Had Millerchip ever been without his shifty expression or salacious leer?

The next morning, aware that Donaldson was in Westwich, Ruth patted the shining coils of her hair before shouting up the stairs, 'I'm going for my walk now, Mother. I'll see you at lunch-time.'

When closing the door of The Rush House behind her, Ruth always felt a lifting of her spirits because she was in the open. On that breezy July morning the tufted clouds scudded joyously overhead and the leaves in the hedgerow danced. Ruth's wits were a-twitch for the opportunity to sharpen themselves on Donaldson. She opened the gate, and there he was.

'Oh, it's you, is it?'

'Well, it's very nice to see you too,' he said, giving her a deep bow and removing his straw hat which, being a size too big to accommodate his wayward hair, looked clownish rather than debonair on his high head. He took in every detail of her dress and scrutinized her face for signs of anxiety.

She gave him a carefree smile. 'I was about to walk along the beach, as it's such a glorious day. What a pity you have to work,

Mr Donaldson. I see you've got your camera.' He had graduated after all to a natty little hand-held machine which left him less encumbered.

'But by chance I was heading for the beach. Might I accompany you, Miss Styles?'

'You might, Sir, as I've not seen you for a while.'

They chose not to go through the village, where there were too many interested spectators, but went instead along the lanes to the field-path that led down to the sea. Ruth cast her usual, nostalgic glance at Overstrands, but not even the ambivalence of her feelings about the Mayricks could dampen her spirits that day. The breeze made sheeting sweeps at the pale corn and a couple of skylarks shot high up into the blue.

Ruth loved to live vicariously through Donaldson but would not stoop to question him too directly – she could not bear to reveal her interest.

'Well, Mr Donaldson, I suppose you're going to bore me with all your latest achievements?'

'Well, Miss Styles, ships and strikes this month sum it all up.' And there followed a heated debate on the rival causes of government and miners. Ruth, despite her affiliation to the cause of women's rights, was considerably less liberal in her views on workers' direct action than Donaldson, and became tighter and tighter lipped as he answered each argument with a measured response.

They came to the gate which led onto the high, banked-up path above the flat reed-beds behind the sea. Donaldson watched Ruth carefully latch the gate behind her.

'I'd like to photograph you here,' he said.

'For goodness sake, Donaldson. There is nothing of interest.' But she could not resist him. His admiration was a balm to her lonely soul.

He took her hand and rested it on the smooth, old wood. The day was so warm that she had removed her gloves. 'You have musician's fingers,' he told her.

'A pity I haven't a musician's talent, then.'

'You would if you didn't keep trying pieces which were far

too difficult for you.' At Maud Waterford's recently he had heard her battle through a Beethoven sonata.

'I think Miss Lily has put me off the piano for life.'

'By the way,' his hand was still touching hers, 'I brought with me details of a correspondence course in literature and history. I thought you might be interested.'

'Why Donaldson, do you think I am getting dull?'

'Not dull. But you must find it hard to maintain your studies on your own.'

'I prefer my independence. I know all about these stuffy correspondence courses. I'd rather allow myself a free rein.'

'Maud worries about you. I do. You have so many talents. You should try to make something of them.'

'Oh, for heaven's sake. There are plenty of young women in the world who take correspondence courses. And they end up typists or telephonists. I don't want to be ordinary, Donaldson. Do you understand? I want my life to be special, not humdrum.' She thought of herself in her room, ploughing through pages of close print.

'You could never be humdrum.'

But her annoyance with him for challenging her caused her brow to crumple into three fine lines and the ends of her mouth to twitch downwards so that the tiniest dimple appeared in her left cheek. Then, as he ducked behind the camera, she became absorbed in the familiar landscape; the soft grasses speckled with harebells playing along the path, the blue rim of sea in the distance and the ripple of reeds in the marshes. Unaware for the moment that the camera's eye was Donaldson's eye her body tilted forward, yearning towards the sea. Only the click of the camera aroused her.

A little dazed she asked, 'Why are you forever taking photos of me?'

'You are interesting because though you're always complaining how dull this coast is, you love it. It shows. I have never seen a woman more wedded to her landscape.'

Rather pleased with this image of herself, Ruth marched on, not waiting for him to cover his camera and hook it over his shoulder. She was wearing a filmy summer frock that fell in delicate folds to just above her ankles. As she walked Donaldson was treated to glimpses of her slender lower calves above the sturdy heel of her cream summer shoes.

'Race you to the beach,' she shouted and set off at such a pace that her hat blew sideways so she removed it completely. Then, abruptly, as she went careering over the pebble bank, she crumpled into a tumbled heap on the stones 'Oh,' she exclaimed, rubbing her ankle and gulping back tears of pain.

'You shouldn't be so unladylike,' Donaldson said reprovingly, dropping down beside her.

'Who cares whether I'm ladylike or not?' She looked up at him defiantly with her hair a tousled golden cobweb against the sun and her eyes bright with shock.

'Certainly not I,' he told her, laughing. 'Let me see the damage.'

She rested back on her elbows while he gently took her foot into his lap and undid the strap of her shoe. She was conscious of his hands cupping her heel and his thumbs firmly stroking the sore ankle. Studying the top of his hat, aware of his absorbed caress of her foot she gazed at him with pitying tenderness. He glanced up at her, his face suffused with love, and for a moment they exchanged a look of complete understanding.

He replaced her shoe, stood and extended his hand to her. 'I'll support you, Miss Styles,' he said. 'Just lean on me.'

She tucked her hand through his arm and limped beside him down to the water. There they stood side by side and watched the long waves break at their feet in white, leisurely pools of lacy froth.

4

In the winter of 1913 Ruth made her final visit to the Mayricks in Oxford.

There was a conspiracy to get her there in which both Harry and Alan Styles co-operated. Harry, in his final year at Cambridge, had at last become alert to his sister's predicament and persuaded his father that Ruth must have a holiday, whatever her objections. Accordingly, both he and Styles declared their intention of spending the festival at The Rush House. A nurse was to be hired to care for Julia. The idea of importing Miss Lily had been mooted and as rapidly rejected. Even Alan Styles could not pretend confidence in the nursing skills of that lady.

On the morning of her departure Ruth went up to see her mother who lay in the dim room, eyes closed, hands clutching the sheets.

'Goodbye, Mother.'

Julia could not or would not attend to her though she was quite capable of understanding all that was said. But poor Ruth was not given the comfort of knowing whether her mother would miss her. There were no affectionate kisses, no pleas that she might stay, only a tortured silence loaded with whatever emotion Ruth might choose to interpret; reproach, fear, dislike or endurance.

Harry, aglow with self-sacrifice, drove his sister to the station, tucked her into her carriage with exaggerated fraternal concern and stood waving until she was out of sight, doing his best to blot from his mind the expression he had glimpsed on her face as the train jolted away.

Things improved at The Rush House during Ruth's absence. In the first place the Millerchips were far more obliging because the master was in the house. Mrs Millerchip considered it a waste of her culinary skills to cook for women, although Ruth had a healthy appetite and Julia, despite her inactivity, was not an especially dainty eater. But for 'the men-folk' as she called them, especially one who paid such generous wages as Alan Styles, Mrs Millerchip was prepared to produce meals of miraculous quality and abundance. And she bullied her husband into carrying quantities of fuel, polishing windows and tidying the gardens. One of the Tate girls was brought in from the farm cottage to take over Ruth's numerous domestic tasks, and Mrs Millerchip had a wonderful time berating the hapless child into an efficiency never displayed by her mistress.

And then Christmas brightened the rooms. A tree was bought and decorated by Harry, and Mrs Millerchip was urged to order supplies of dates and raisins from the village shop in an attempt to mollify Mrs Spendmore, who had learnt that Styles had imported his wine and oranges from town. Everyone who had been kind to the ladies of The Rush House was presented with generous gifts; even the postman and the surly Farmer Nichols at Upstones who supplied the milk. Mrs Millerchip was given a white cashmere shawl chosen by Miss Lily who never stinted when spending other people's money. Her taste was impeccable. Maud Waterford's gift was a little silver brooch fashioned into a pair of dolphins and Ruth had painted a view of the old church for her, almost as Donaldson had once photographed it. Inscribed on the back were the words: 'The scene of our glory, Maud.'

The nurse from Norwich had at first sight seemed an unfortunate mistake, a heavy-chested, tall woman who announced on arrival that she could eat neither meat, cheese nor bread. Looking into the room appointed to her she stated that she did not hold with fires in bedrooms and requested that damp cloths be brought so that she might clean thoroughly as she was sensitive to dust. Mrs Millerchip, who had spent the morning polishing the room and laying the fire, was deeply offended, and the two immediately became implacable enemies.

When introduced to her patient, however, Nurse Goode proved her worth.

She took one look at Julia, who at midday was still in bed, and exclaimed: 'Mrs Styles, we must get you up this moment. Why have they let you stay in bed? What are they thinking of?'

Nothing on earth normally would get Julia up if she had a mind to remain in bed, but in Nurse Goode she had met her match. By one o'clock she was seated at the dining room table eating a slice of lean gammon and enjoying half a glass of red wine. Afterwards Nurse Goode accompanied her to the drawing room where the nurse stabbed at a cross-stitch cover destined for a kneeler in her local church and Julia read one of her daughter's fashion books and fingered the Christmas cards: 'I must write more next year,' she was heard to murmur although she had not inscribed a card for six years. Nor did she have the opportunity to grow tired and restless. At three o'clock the needle was laid down and Nurse Goode announced that it was time for Julia to go to bed. 'We cannot have you overdoing it, can we?'

Julia, who had been quite contented in her chair by the fire, was rather taken aback and perhaps reluctant to return to her familiar bedroom. After all, she was used to deciding her own times for rising and sleeping. Nevertheless she found herself being hustled between the sheets.

'I was going to stay up and have dinner with Alan,' was her only protest.

'Maybe tomorrow, dear. I must be the judge of whether you're well enough.'

For the first time in years Julia looked forward to the next day when she might or might not be allowed to stay up for dinner.

Perhaps Nurse Goode could have worked miracles at The Rush House with her prosaic and infuriatingly faddy approach to her task, but there was no time for the experiment to take effect. Two days after her arrival, on Christmas Eve, a slim figure appeared in the porch.

Tired and chilled, for she had walked from Blythburgh, she stood weeping until at last she summoned the courage to ring the bell.

Harry answered. 'Ruth!'

He pulled her into the small entrance hall and she fell on his neck. The only words he could make out were: 'It was terrible to be away.'

Alan Styles telephoned the Mayricks who had been frantic over Ruth's disappearance. To Ruth, Mrs Mayrick wrote a kind, reassuring letter, begging her to come again, perhaps in the summer. To Maud Waterford, Esther communicated at greater length, describing in full Ruth's disastrous visit to Oxford.

*I drove Clara to the station to meet her. Unfortunately, we were a little late, five minutes, perhaps, and when we arrived Ruth was* standing in the forecourt with her bags tucked close to her skirts, extremely agitated. At first she could scarcely speak, and then her tone was accusing. 'What would I have done if you'd not come?'

'My dear Ruth, I am here. There is nothing to alarm you.'

'But what would I have done?' she insisted.

'I am here. Of course I would be here.'

She relented sufficiently to follow me to the automobile, but already I was alarmed. She seemed so different to the buoyant Ruth I had known previously. Fortunately Clara's long speech about the preparations we had been making for Ruth's visit and for Christmas proved a distraction.

Our house is large, set back from the road in a street of similar houses. Ruth seemed intimidated, despite her familiarity with it in previous years. Giles came galloping down the stairs to welcome her but she held him at arm's length, and seemed unable to respond to his excited questions. She followed me up to her room which overlooks the garden. She said she wanted to rest so I left her. Giles was hovering outside, ready to pour all his latest treasures into her lap. He was of course greatly disappointed by her desire to be alone.

Three quarters of an hour later she had still not emerged. I knocked and entered. She had not moved from the window and simply stood gazing at the garden. She turned and said: 'I cannot hear the sea.'

I laughed. 'Ruth, you could scarcely be much further from the sea.' But Maud, those eyes. They made my heart beat faster with despair for her.

I persuaded her downstairs. She had brought us gifts which she placed at the base of the tree. We had one of our usual noisy suppers. Robert came in and gave her a mighty hug which was not returned. Occasionally, she glanced anxiously at her watch or the door and once she raised her hand to Giles as if to hush him that she might listen for something. But she seemed bright enough and had not lost her ability to make us laugh at Miss Lily and some of the Westwich folk. She is such a mimic.

The boys went to bed and I thought we might talk but she would not be open with me. I asked if she were not terribly sick of her Westwich life and she was angry. 'My mother needs me. I never complain of being useful.'

145

She seemed tired and went early to bed. Robert said he thought she may be homesick having been so long in one place, but that she might settle soon. Late at night I heard her pacing. I went to her and she said she was worried about her mother. I promised that we would telephone The Rush House in the morning but she would not hear of it as the shock of the bell terrified Julia. I don't know if she slept. The next day she was pale, her eyes shadowed and over-bright.

She would not be still. I took her shopping, thinking she would love the bustle of the city at Christmas, but she was frightened of the crowds. She bought nothing though she had a full purse. I had seen some silk scarves and asked her to choose one for herself. She selected grey saying that it reminded her of the sea.

She scarcely ate at dinner. I asked her again if she'd like to telephone, but she refused.

By now the children were uneasy. Clara would not go near her, and Giles, after two days of being rebuffed, took to his room. I asked Robert to speak with her. He too was disturbed by her behaviour. 'Acute homesickness,' was the verdict. 'She must be given time.'

I heard her pacing again in the night.

In the morning when I went to call her for breakfast she and all her things had gone. She'd left no note.

I gather she walked to the station and took the first train – not the right one.

Thank goodness she found her way safely home at last.

Maud, I am dreadfully afraid for her. I blame myself. I should have invited her sooner. She must be got away from that house.

What can we do?

The instant she was home Ruth began to recover. By the next morning she had regained her composure. Her curtailed holiday was explained to the village by the words: 'I could not leave my mother for so long.'

But Julia showed no pleasure in her daughter's return. Instead she set her daughter's more gentle rule against Nurse Goode's dictatorial regime. When the nurse insisted Julia get up and take a bath, Julia cried for Ruth, and Ruth, who had traded her freedom for her mother's dependency, could not resist. The result was Nurse Goode's hasty and incensed departure and the rapid resumption of what passed for normality at The Rush House.

Alan Styles left the day after Ruth came back. To have lost his wife had almost broken him and to witness his once head-strong, independent daughter so tied made him run away completely. He was seen only once more in Westwich.

Harry made all kind of resolutions. He would motor down more often and take Ruth out. Gradually he would wean her away from The Rush House.

Very little came of this. Events overtook poor Harry.

# Chapter Nine

*Present*

Donaldson had been a prolific photographer. By August Helena's study was so strewn with documents, journals and prints that only stepping stones of carpet were visible.

This was the one room Michael had not decorated and it was still papered in dingy brown and cream vinyl and furnished sparsely with an old divan and an ungainly wardrobe. Against one wall was a large oak desk bought by Michael from a junk shop when he was a student and used by him for his school work. Its deep drawers were still filled with relics of his academic past: O and A level certificates, files of notes from university and travel documents from his climbing expeditions. In the desk were also stored receipts, paid bills, guarantees and all the paraphernalia of running a household. Since his death, Helena had been very thankful to him for his systematic approach to their financial responsibilities.

Now that Michael was gone Helena had appropriated the room for her own use. She kept a pile of jigsaws and toys on the divan in the hope that these would occupy Nina for an hour or two a day while the book progressed.

Donaldson's career had been very complex. When Helena applied to the National Photographic Society she was swamped by information, and the Newspaper Library and the Imperial War Museum were even more forthcoming. To her astonishment she discovered that Donaldson had been decorated during the First World War when he abandoned his freelance work and received a commission as an official photographer.

Thinking that Nicholas Broadbent might be able to shed some light on this unexpected development she telephoned him at his London home and left several messages on his answering machine. He did not reply.

In any case, Helena had little time for piecing together the details of Donaldson's career in the employ of His Majesty's Government. Nina was not an easy child to amuse that summer and Helena's fond hopes that she might work while Nina played contentedly were rudely smashed.

One afternoon only five minutes had elapsed before Nina grew bored. She lay on the bed with her thumb in her mouth and her feet in the air and proclaimed loudly and repeatedly that she wanted a drink. Inwardly, and for the thousandth time, Helena cursed Michael for not being there to entertain his daughter.

'Go and get some water from the bathroom,' she snapped. 'You can reach the tooth mug. And don't talk with your thumb in.'

'I want orange juice not water.'

'Wait a minute.' She was studying a photograph of a cemetery in Arras. In the centre foreground was one cross, but behind were many more. The inscriptions on the foremost crosses were clearly visible: *KILLED IN ACTION 2nd Lt P. B. Bloodmore. 2nd Lt A. D. McGrew. 9.4.17.* Remembering Nicholas Broadbent's comment about how Donaldson had cherished his subjects, Helena noted that, above the weedy graveyard, sunlight was breaking through high clouds. She pondered the significance of the luminous sky in Donaldson's photograph.

The doorbell rang.

'I'll go!' shrieked Nina. In her eagerness she skated across the room on piles of papers, creasing a photocopy of a seventy-year-old *Times* newspaper under her heel.

'Nina! For goodness sake!'

Helena replaced the photograph of the cemetery in the *War 1917* folder. Downstairs she heard the door open and the low murmur of a woman's voice. 'Who is it, Nina?' she yelled, and then staggered to her feet, her knees cramped from so much kneeling.

'It's a lady.'

The woman on the doorstep looked familiar but for a moment Helena could not identify her. She was perhaps a couple of years older than Helena and plainly dressed, with a face devoid of make-up and her short, mousy hair cut in an unprepossessingly practical style. But by the time Helena reached the bottom stair and came face to face with the visitor she had recognized her. That cold, uninterested gaze was unforgettable.

'I hope you don't mind me calling so unexpectedly.' If the woman was nervous she covered her feelings by a slightly aggressive directness. She did not smile.

'No. Of course not. I'm sorry. I couldn't place you for a moment. You know what it's like when you see people out of context. Weren't you at Overstrands?'

'That's right. Myra Finny. I look after the house for the Mayricks.'

Helena remembered her first morning in Westwich a few weeks after Michael's death. She and Nina had stood outside on the gravel while this woman and Caroline Mayrick talked on and on in the kitchen. And with the memory, like a sharp stab of pain, came the same rawness of grief that she had been experiencing then. 'Well,' she murmured after a moment, 'it's very nice to see you.'

'I brought this. You left it behind. I was passing.'

Myra gave a small plastic bag to Nina who loved packages and opened it at once. 'Oh Mummy, it's my blue hair-slide. We were wondering where that was.'

'Good heavens, I hope you didn't come all this way for a hair-slide,' Helena exclaimed, laughing.

'No, that's all right.' Still Myra did not smile.

'Would you like some tea or coffee?'

'Yes. Thank you.'

Helena had been sure that Myra would refuse the invitation but the woman actually entered the hall and waited expectantly to be shown to another room.

'Come through,' Helena called with false cheer. 'Though I'm afraid it's awfully messy.'

'I don't mind.'

In fact the kitchen looked very neat. Since Michael's death it had acquired an under-used aspect, as if it too yearned for the old days when he would load the table with spices, vegetables and beans for one of his notorious vegetarian stews.

'Please sit down,' urged Helena, indicating one of the pine chairs.

Myra made no effort to ease the situation. She did not offer any conversation but sat in the proffered chair and gazed about her, making no comment and giving no indication whether or not the room pleased her. Nina posted herself in the corner between a cupboard and the washing machine.

'So, what are you doing in this area?' Helena asked, leaning her back on the sink and smiling at the visitor. Although she was wearing only jeans and an old white T-shirt the other woman contrived to make her feel over-dressed. Myra's clothes were entirely neutral, consisting of a beige skirt and chambray blouse. She wore no jewellery.

Myra replied, as if with some effort. 'I'm going to visit a friend in Wales. My husband has the boys.'

'I didn't realize you were married,' cried Helena effusively, delighted to exploit the conversational possibilities of this information.

'I'm not,' Myra said. 'We separated five years ago.'

'Oh. I'm sorry.'

Again Myra's lack of reaction killed the exchange. Helena willed the kettle to boil faster and made a great fuss with mugs and milk bottle to take up a little more time.

'We did enjoy being in Westwich, didn't we, Nina?' she said next. 'Have you lived there long, Myra?'

'All my life.'

'Goodness, you must know the village well.'

Since this was not a question, Myra made no reply.

A few more minutes were filled with the intricacies of pouring the coffee and handing round biscuits, which Myra refused. Then Helena bustled about finding a peg board and mosaic shapes to occupy Nina. 'Come on, Nina, I'll help you make a lovely picture of a train,' she said.

Nina hurried to her side, amazed by such an unexpected offer.

'And how old are your children, Myra?' Helena asked.

'Twelve, ten and seven.'

'All boys?'

'Yes.'

'Gracious, what a handful!' For a moment Helena was tempted to giggle. Her own voice sounded so false and bright, like a character in a sit-com.

The skin above Myra's upper lip, she noted, was darkened by fawn hairs, but her wide mouth with its disappointed, down-turned corners, was not unattractive.

Helena took a large gulp of her own coffee in the hope that it would encourage Myra to drink hers faster. 'Now then, Nina, red wheels?' she muttered encouragingly, conscious that the other woman's stern gaze was now fixed on Nina's bent head. 'I think you're marvellous the way you look after Overstrands,' she added effusively to Myra. 'I know Clara Mayrick thinks terribly highly of you.'

Such a patronizing comment, she thought, deserved no reply. It received none.

'Oh Nina, that's lovely!' she enthused. 'Now what about black smoke? How long have you worked for Clara?' she asked Myra.

'Years and years. And my mother before me. We're glad of any opportunity of steady work in Westwich.'

'So you must know the Mayricks quite well then. My husband used to go there a lot for holidays when he was a boy. His grandfather was Simon, Clara's oldest brother.'

'That's right.'

'Do you remember Michael?'

'Of course.' Her keen, grey stare met Helena's. 'We used to look forward to the family coming to stay.'

'Oh. Well. You probably know them better than I do. I never met Michael's father. He'd died before Michael and I got together.'

But it was no good expecting Myra to follow such an obvious invitation for comment. Painstakingly, Helena added: 'What was he like?'

'Very pleasant.'

I give up, thought Helena in exasperation, immersing herself in Nina's train. She hoped that next time if something was left at Overstrands Myra would think to use the pillar box.

At last Myra drained her coffee mug. She stood, but apparently not with the intention of departing. Instead she crossed to the door where Nina's pictures were displayed. They had not been changed for months, and the painting Nicholas Broadbent had admired of *mummy daddy nina* was still there. Myra peered at it closely. Then, with her back to Helena she said: 'I understand from Caroline you're writing a book about Donaldson.'

'Yes. Have you heard of him?'

'Oh yes. My mother used to talk about him a lot. Everyone in Westwich knows about him. They think of him as their photographer.'

'Well, I suppose he was in a way. Did you know that I am related to the Styles family who used to live at The Rush House? He was especially fond of Ruth Styles, my grandmother.'

'That's right.'

It was as if, all of a sudden, a series of doors were opening, letting light into a dark corridor. 'Oh Myra,' cried Helena, addressing her in a natural voice for the first time. 'You could be a great help. I'm trying to gather any information I can about Donaldson. What do you know about his time in Westwich?'

'Not much. Only that my mother remembered him as being always alone. She said he would just turn up in the village and you'd find him in the graveyard, or on the beach with his camera. And he was very kind. And friendly. He loved the village. But it made him sad.'

'Perhaps because of Ruth Styles having died so young,' suggested Helena gently.

'Yes. Perhaps that.' Myra suddenly cast Helena another searching glance.

'Did she say anything else about him?'

'Not really. Only the usual.'

'What was the usual?'

'You know. That he was so self-effacing no one would have guessed he was a spy.'

'I beg your pardon?'

'And that he was keen on the village history. He loved to talk to people about what the village must have been like in the old days, before most of it fell into the sea.'

'What did you say about Donaldson being a spy?'

'You know. In the First World War.'

'I thought he was an official photographer.'

'He was. But a few years back it came out that he'd done a lot of intelligence work. Didn't you know?'

'No. I had no idea.' What about Broadbent, did he know this? Or her mother? Helena's mental picture of her gauche, self-effacing grandfather had to be abruptly readjusted 'It doesn't sound like him,' she said feebly.

Myra shrugged. 'You can never take people at face value.'

The comment hung in the air for a while. Outside the sun had broken through and the kitchen suddenly felt very warm. Helena opened the back door to admit a waft of balmy August air. She was again acutely conscious of Myra's scrutiny. Nina abandoned her picture, ducked under Helena's arm and ran out into the garden to find her bike.

'She's like you,' Myra said.

'She is, poor soul. If she'd taken after Michael she'd have been better looking and had a nicer temperament.' But this self-deprecation, though inviting a shared laugh, reminiscence or reassurance, was greeted only by a long silence.

'Caroline always says Michael was a sweet-natured boy,' Helena said, abruptly, confronting Myra's unfaltering gaze. 'Was he?'

'He was fun.' Myra answered fiercely, as if Helena's comment had been critical and must be refuted.

'And what are your own boys like?' Helena asked.

'Hard work.'

'They must find it pretty quiet in Westwich.'

'They have each other,' said Myra and the other part of that sentence, which might have spoken of her own isolation, went unsaid. She had now turned her attention back to Nina who was wobbling across the grass, brakes full on despite the minute size of her bicycle and the fact that it had stabilizers.

'She has no physical courage,' said Helena. 'In that I'm afraid she takes after me too.'

At last Myra moved to the table and picked up her bag. 'You do yourself down all the time,' she said. 'You shouldn't. It sounds as if you're always waiting for compliments. There are a lot of people who would love to be you.'

With that she marched down the hall, said goodbye, and drove away in a shabby blue Escort.

Afterwards Helena stood in the hall with her hand up to her mouth caught between laughter and tears, guilt and amazement.

Myra had said: 'There are a lot of people who would love to be you.'

2

'Did you know,' demanded Victoria over the telephone, 'that your Nick Broadbent is *the* Nick Broadbent?'

'What on earth do you mean?'

'Only you could not have heard of him. I thought when you mentioned him you must have got the name wrong but you hadn't. He's a brilliant photographer. He's done stuff for all the supplements and held exhibitions all over the place.'

'Gracious.'

'A mate of mine works with a friend of his ex-girlfriend and she says he had a nervous breakdown and was sent home from Bosnia. He would speak to no one, not even the girlfriend with whom he'd been living for six years, and he refused to contact his family. Eventually he went to hospital.'

'Oh my word. He said he'd been put out to grass. Poor bloke.'

'You're bloody lucky to be working with him. I hope you

know that. He must be ill to have agreed to collaborate with you.'

'Why thank you, Victoria.'

'He could work for anyone, do anything in the world. I rang a friend who's with *The Sunday Times*. Nick Broadbent's work is just the best, according to Ted. When he's on form. But he took to doing really odd stuff – bits of litter instead of a shot of a street battle, or a tree instead of a military camp. All the people who'd commissioned him were tearing their hair out. In the profession they think he may never go back.'

Although Joanna could not bear a display of emotion in her own family, she relished the discussion of trouble in other people's domestic worlds. Perhaps this also explained her love of television soaps. Through their characters she could explore vicariously passions which were never given expression in her own life. When Helena repeated the gist of her conversation with Victoria about Nicholas Broadbent, Joanna was full of sympathy and eager questions.

'The poor man. But I'm not surprised he had a breakdown. It must be terrible to have to photograph all those wars.'

'Certainly he looks battered.'

'It's fashionable to be messy these days. Especially if you're artistic.'

Helena laughed at her. 'Mother, what do you know about what's fashionable?'

'Don't be cheeky.' They were friends again. During the summer months a new stage in their relationship had been established with Helena once more dependent on her mother, and Joanna's life being given renewed purpose in the care of her daughter and Nina. Today they were walking in the grounds of Attingham Park, a favourite picnic spot. Nina danced along beside her grandfather or darted behind a tree trunk to leap out on him, unfailingly rewarded by his feigned surprise.

'Anyway, it makes me more determined than ever to write this book well. If Broadbent is such a star it will do my reputation no end of good to share the credits with him.'

'I'm glad you're enjoying the work,' said Joanna, and Helena knew that she had been forgiven.

She said: 'Actually, I think Nicholas Broadbent probably feels considerable affinity with Donaldson. After all, they share a war record. I hadn't at all realized that Donaldson was a spy. I mean, I knew he was decorated for bravery, but I thought it was just for his work as a photographer.'

'Who told you he was a spy?' Joanna sounded genuinely amused. She was marching along with her hands in her pockets, her face upturned to the warm shafts of sunlight piercing the canopy of leaves.

'That woman Myra who came. She said the whole of Westwich knew.'

'Donaldson never said anything about it to me.'

'What did he talk about when you were with him?'

'Oh, his work a bit. Of course by the 1930s he was doing all state occasions and public events. I used to think him terribly glamorous. But he never volunteered much about himself. He was always more interested in me.'

'Could you, do you think, give me your impressions of him? It would be such a help.'

'Tall. Very tall. Smiley. His clothes smelt of the outside. I mean, of places beyond Westwich. He spoilt me dreadfully. Presents, outings, treats. He was always wanting to take Maud and me on holiday, but she would never let him.'

'But why not?'

'She didn't think it would look right. And of course when Maud died I was sent to school and I used to look forward to his visits so much. All the other girls thought him wonderful. He was quite famous. And then I found out... Anyway, he became a stranger.'

'But why? Please, Mother.'

There was a long pause. 'I hope Nina isn't tiring Dad out,' Joanna said, moving forwards, 'she can be a bit wilful.' Robin and Nina had reached a clearing where trees had been felled. Nina was pretending to be a high-wire artist along the broad length of an old trunk.

'Mother, what happened between you and Donaldson? Why won't you speak of him?'

Nina had reached the far end of the trunk where it had fallen against an oak tree. She hooked her leg over a branch and hoisted herself well out of reach. 'Should she climb so high?' asked Joanna.

'Oh dear!' Helena exclaimed, running forward. 'Nina. Do be careful. Come down.'

Robin stood at the bottom of the tree. 'I couldn't stop her. She insisted on going up.'

'She's all right, don't worry. Nina, come down!'

'I'm going higher,' Nina shouted.

'No. You'll get stuck. Come back at once.'

But already the little girl had climbed onto yet another branch and was reaching up for a further handhold.

'Nina.' Robin rarely raised his voice to her but now he spoke very sternly. 'Don't be a silly girl. Come down.'

'I've got some sweets in my pocket,' added Joanna in a more conciliatory tone. 'Would you like to come and pass them round?'

'Daddy would let me climb it,' Nina yelled, hauling herself upwards.

Helena was waiting for this. Nina had taken to using her father's absence as an excuse for bad behaviour. In this case she was quite right. If Michael had been there he would have encouraged her to climb the tree with him. He was always a little derisive about her lack of courage. 'You take after your mum,' he teased her.

'But we can't get you down,' Helena called helplessly, by now close to tears.

'Daddy would have helped me,' called Nina.

'Daddy would have been very cross with you for being such a bad girl.'

'Don't, Helena, you mustn't say that,' Joanna said. 'Nina. You've done very well to get so high. Come down, my love.'

All that was now visible of Nina was the odd flash of her pink dungarees – the rest was obscured by the thick mass of leaves.

'I'm nearly at the top,' she shouted, and Helena could hear by her voice that she had frightened herself. 'Daddy would have helped me,' she added.

Almost sobbing with frustration Helena yelled, 'But Daddy's not here, Nina. Come down.'

'I can't.' And then after a moment came the inevitable: 'I'm stuck.'

Bloody, bloody Michael, thought Helena. Who's going to rescue her now?

Robin, grey-faced with anxiety, took off his jacket and gripped the lowest branch. Helena's heart contracted with love for him that he should venture his thin, unathletic frame for the sake of his granddaughter. Regaining her own presence of mind she said laughingly: 'Father, you're not going up there. I'll get her down in no time. Don't worry.' She removed her sandals and, hooking the back of her skirt between her legs, began to climb.

They went camping in Italy and France for their honeymoon. Helena's salary was very low and Michael's, as a teacher, was not much better. And they were saving to buy a house. So they took Michael's little two-man tent, bought a rail card and headed for Europe. Helena, whose travels hitherto had been strictly limited either to sedate seaside holidays with her parents or carefully plotted expeditions with girlfriends, was light-headed and nervous because of Michael's refusal to plan. 'We'll just take off,' he said. 'We'll be fine.'

But Helena could not stop worrying. She feared that they would lose their money; that she would not be able to sleep on the foreign trains; that they would get tummy upsets and that they wouldn't be able to find a camp site. Twenty-three years of Robin's painstaking attempts to foresee every possible eventuality could not be shed by a couple of years' acquaintance with Michael whose breezy approach was an anathema.

By the end of the holiday they reached Carnac and at last Helena felt safe. She was near home again, there were lots of English people about and it was not too hot. Michael, who agreed to stay there because he wanted to view the menhir, took one look at the hordes of fellow countrymen and said: 'Two days and off. Next stop Normandy.'

Helena lay on the hot sand and felt truly happy for the first time since their wedding. She was soothed by the familiar cries of holiday-makers and by the rhythm of the breaking waves. Occasionally she lifted her head and looked out at the undulating sea, brightly dotted by dinghies and swimmers. Straight ahead was a diving tower upon which boys were clambering, anticipating a higher tide. 'We'll have a go on that later,' said Michael.

He lay beside her with his head pillowed on a towel, eyes closed, one arm across her back so that his fingers could stroke discreetly the side of her breast. Helena eased herself closer and pushed her face against his side, dropping light kisses onto his damp, hot skin.

Later, as the breaking waves reached nearer and nearer, they moved up the beach. Disliking cold water, Helena had swum once and considered her duty done. But Michael was constantly in and out of the waves, returning to her glistening and salty.

The diving tower, which was little more than a high scaffold, was now half submerged, and the youths were swarming up onto its various levels and plunging down into the water. Michael could not resist the challenge for long. He ran across the short expanse of dry sand to the water's edge and dived into a wave. Helena watched his strong, efficient crawl across to the diving tower, and his tanned, long legs as they climbed rapidly up the ladder. He had to stand for a while waiting on the top while other people crept to the edge of the board and then dithered before taking the plunge. Some jumped inelegantly, holding their noses, while others performed slick, effortless dives. To Helena's surprise, when it was his turn, Michael seemed to falter a little. She sat up and yelled at him. 'Go on Michael. It's not far.'

Suddenly he shot his hands above his head and did a tentative, awkward pitch into the water, emerged almost at once, cleared his face with his hand, and swam rapidly back to the diving tower. In all he dived three times before returning to Helena who by then had lost interest and transferred her attention to her book.

Michael scooped up his towel and began drying his neck and ears. 'You get up there and it suddenly looks a long way down,' he exclaimed.

Helena rolled over on her back, shielded her eyes and smiled up at him. 'I was wondering why you hesitated.'

'And then you think, I wonder if it's deep enough? Though I'd watched other people do it. And I had checked the depth under the diving board. But still it crosses your mind that it might be too shallow.'

'You were very brave,' she soothed mockingly, as if to a child. 'After all, the other divers must have been at least nine years old.'

'You ought to try.' He knelt above her and kissed her, his mouth cold and briny.

She put her hand up to his neck and pulled him close. 'I knew that was coming.'

'You should. It feels great. It's better than diving into a swimming pool. It's the quality of the unknown – and then the sea is so much bigger.'

'I've got too much sense,' she said firmly.

'No, come on.'

'Michael, as you well know, nothing on earth will induce me to go on that diving board.'

'Oh, come on. Then you can say you've done it.'

'Who cares whether I do it or not?'

'You'll love it.'

'I won't. I won't.'

He ducked his head to kiss her in between each of her refusals, and she was laughing up into his grey, teasing eyes. Then he took her hand. 'You're a lazy bones. I dare you.'

'I really don't want to.' But his persistence had awoken in her a nervous excitement. He actually did believe she would go up onto the diving board and his certainty had infected her.

Half dragged by Michael, laughing and pulling back, she was edged towards the water. 'I won't even be able to reach the bottom of the ladder,' she cried, hopping about as the waves closed over her feet. 'It's much colder than this morning.' But at last she was in the water, her shoulders flinching and then relishing the cold, her body lifted by the swell. 'Oh, it is lovely,' she cried, 'just lie back and gaze at that beautiful sky.'

'You'll be even closer to the sky if you climb the diving board.'

She knew she would do it now. It was not in her nature to commit herself to something and then change her mind. A group of youths splashed noisily ahead of her and she doggy-paddled to let them climb the ladder first. Then she began her own ascent. Michael was behind her, reassuring and kind now he had persuaded her to dive. 'You know I can't stand heights,' she called down to him.

'It's all in the mind,' he told her.

'Precisely.'

The ladder was very firm, the steel rungs warmed by the sun. She was comforted by the steady climb but did not look down. 'Perhaps I could try from half way first,' she suggested.

Michael would have none of it. 'It would be far more difficult, because there isn't a proper diving board half way.'

So up she went, conscious that there were a couple of children behind Michael who were jostling him in their haste. All too soon she was on the small flat platform at the top of the ladder. She sat down abruptly and let the two boys get ahead of her to join the little crowd hovering beside the springboard.

'If you think I'm diving from here you must be out of your mind,' she told Michael, her voice thin with fright and exertion. The sea was a distant, shining floor, the beach peopled by little puppets darting about, miraculously safe from this insane perch above the waves. 'I've only ever dived from about six feet before.' She was actually shaking as the breeze hit her wet costume.

'Well, you can't go down the ladder without causing a major traffic jam. I'm afraid it's a one-way system.' He was delighted by her squeals of fear. 'Brave girl. I'll go first so I can catch you at the bottom if need be.'

The platform was quite crowded with shouting youngsters who one after another ran to the edge of the board and sprang off. Michael walked calmly along the narrow, springy plank, stooped over and disappeared. Helena was alone with the two boys who had come up behind her. They grinned and then scooted along the board and made wild, delighted leaps into the blue. For a moment the platform was empty. In the distance Helena could hear Michael calling her. She edged to the side of the tower and looked down. The perpendicular plunge to the water was sickening.

Behind her others were climbing the ladder. Her mind was black and empty. 'You don't have to do it,' said a small, sane voice in her head.

But she edged forward, shivering despite the hot sun. She hated to dive from a sitting position so she stood, her toes clenched on the edge of the flimsy board. Tilting her body forward, she almost lost balance and tumbled feet first into the water. The other divers were behind her now, chattering excitedly, unaware of her fear. She raised her arms, inclined her body, and dived.

She hit the water in a second and the shocking cold flashed up her arms and along her chest and stomach. Her mouth and eyes were stung by the surprise of salt and her fingertips skimmed the sand at the bottom of the sea. Then her body began its automatic reach for the air. And suddenly she was up, gasping in the bright afternoon light, greeted by the shouts of swimmers who had not even noticed her dive and by Michael who was waiting and reached out loving arms to her.

'You were brilliant. What a dive. What a girl.'

Helena laughed too, and was pleased and relieved though she slapped at him and shouted: 'Don't you ever make me do anything like that again.'

'I'm so proud of my brave girl,' he teased, and chased her up the beach to where she flung herself down panting on the towel. She could not stop smiling as she gazed up at the diving tower, which she had conquered.

*

The tree, an oak, was wonderfully solid, but the branches were quite far apart and at awkward angles. Nina, with her neat little limbs and smaller size had ducked and clawed herself a route that Helena, with her greater caution and less supple body could not easily copy. But hearing the child whimpering above, she called out in a low calm voice: 'Don't worry, Nina, this is quite fun. We'll have you down in no time.'

'Oh, do watch that branch, Helena. Robin, go and find a man to help!' urged Joanna.

'I'm quite all right, Mum,' shouted Helena, exasperated. 'For goodness sake, it's not that high.' Nina was just above, straddling a branch and looking more afraid of her mother's wrath than of the tree.

'My goodness me,' exclaimed Helena, 'fancy meeting you up here.'

Nina managed a smile.

'Isn't it lovely among these shiny leaves, and being up with the squirrels,' Helena said, taking Nina's hand. And indeed, if she didn't look down, it was wonderful to be knit into the heart of the tree. 'Still, we'll go down, shall we? I'll guide your feet.'

With plenty of reassurance, and with Helena gripping tight hold of Nina's ankles from branch to branch, they were soon within reach of Robin's waiting arms.

We should be cross with her for such disobedience, Helena decided, but we can't be because of Michael. She's learning all the wrong lessons.

As she sat half asleep in her father's car on the drive home, Helena thought: I was very afraid that day when I dived from the tower at Carnac. I would rather have stayed on the beach where I was so happy. Why was I so sure afterwards that I had achieved something wonderful? Was it because I had become for a moment the sort of woman I thought Michael wanted?

3

A more detailed investigation into Donaldson's work during the First World War led to a web of piecemeal references and cross-references. Donaldson had been employed ostensibly as an official photographer to take propaganda photographs for use at home and in Allied countries but his activities had extended far beyond this innocent brief. Many of his photographs were certainly stirring tributes to the British war effort. In particular he seemed to have sympathized with the new army of women labourers, and had taken pictures of munition workers, a coke heaver and a female grave digger. Helena wondered whether, when photographing the robust forms of these women, Donaldson had thought of Ruth in her fragile, pre-war frocks.

In France Donaldson had been at the front line for a while, photographing men in the trenches and the field hospitals. He had then gone freelance again and travelled as a journalist. But, noted the Public Records Office, whilst in the guise of a cheeky, ambitious photographer, Donaldson had been busily gathering more sensitive information.

When Nicholas Broadbent rang for an update of her work Helena smugly related these findings.

'Oh yes,' he replied, 'I knew all that. We've got the archives in the museum.'

'Oh really? But I've spent weeks on it. Where have you been? Why didn't you listen to the messages on your answer-phone?'

'I've been away,' he said airily. 'But what are you up to now?'

'On Thursday I'm going to Cheltenham. I thought I'd chase up this woman Florence Lily. I've got an appointment with the library, and another with the chair of an art society she used to belong to. Donaldson had a photograph of her at home in Cheltenham and I'm interested to know why he bothered.'

'I'll come with you if you like.'

'There's no need. I don't even know what street she lived in. I've only got the photograph to go by. It's probably a wild goose chase.'

'I'll pick you up. I'm staying with my brother again so it's not far out of my way.'

There was no arguing with him.

Nina did not wish to be left with her grandparents while Helena went to Cheltenham. She refused breakfast and hid behind a chair in the living room, hugged her knees to her chest, stuck in her thumb and refused to speak or move. By the time Nicholas arrived Nina had still not relented and Helena left in the miserable knowledge that her daughter was still behind the chair, a stubborn, unhappy heap of little girl.

As Nicholas drove off at great speed Helena shut her eyes and unclenched her jaw in an effort to rid herself of the tension of the last hour. 'Nina's being very difficult at the moment,' she told him. 'Very clingy.'

'You should have brought her with us,' he said abruptly.

The day was very close. Moving from house to car Helena had felt a hot, humid blanket close round her, though the BMW that Nicholas had once again borrowed was equipped with air conditioning. He played Schubert at full volume. Helena waited for a conversation to begin but he drove in silence, and with a furious disregard for Give Way signs or speeding restrictions.

Helena tried a few questions. 'Have you had a good summer?'

'Not really.'

'Why's that?'

'I don't know what a "good summer" means.'

'Nice people. A holiday. Sunshine.'

'None of that.'

'I'm sorry. Have you got anywhere with Donaldson?'

'No.'

Helena gave up. She was not in the mood to humour him but wondered why he had offered to accompany her if he was not going to speak. She felt like shouting: 'It was your idea to come! I would have been quite happy on my own. Happier in fact.' She thought of how, a year ago, Michael would have been beside her in the car, unfailingly good-humoured.

Beyond the car the countryside looked arid and tired as the hot weather burnt the last of the sap from the fading leaves. Already Helena dreaded the winter: Bonfire Night, which Michael had loved, and Christmas.

She glanced for comfort at Nicholas's unpromising features. He must have been aware of her deliberate scrutiny of his profile. She decided that his only attractive point was that he had long, strong fingers, although the nails were bitten.

'What's the matter?' she demanded resentfully. I'm the one who needs sympathy, she thought. But she remembered Victoria's revelations about him and felt a little sorry for his bleak concentration on the road.

'Nothing.'

'There must be some reason why you refuse to speak.'

He turned on her. 'I have nothing to say.'

She almost wept with the surprise and loneliness of rejection. The rest of the journey proceeded in tense, bitter silence. Never, never had she been treated like this. It's more how I used to behave with Michael, she thought ruefully, in my worse moments. Their rows had always come about because of the differences in their priorities. If Michael said he'd be in by eleven, Helena was furious if he returned at midnight after an enthralling conversation in the pub about the next mountaineering trip. If they were going out for the day Helena thought he should help her pack up the lunch and Nina's equipment, not spend half an hour in the shower and another twenty minutes in a rough and tumble with Nina before arriving in the kitchen to ask blithely: 'What can I do?' Such infuriating disregard for her desire to be punctual and organized resulted in many arguments, all one-sided, for he responded to her accusations with bemusement. Usually the result was that Helena relapsed into a sullen silence only broken when Michael at last realized how badly he had upset her.

Once in Cheltenham Helena said: 'What do you want to do? Stay with me or go off on your own?'

Nicholas shrugged. 'You might need me for some photographs.'

'Right. Well, here is the only picture I have to go by.' She presented him with Donaldson's photograph of Miss Lily's house, with its owner peering eerily through the curtains. 'The house was called The Bower in 1926. I'm just curious to know why he took it, and if I can find out anything else about Miss Lily. She seemed such a head-case.'

Nicholas displayed no real interest in the photograph, or in Miss Lily, so Helena tucked the picture back in her bag and stalked off, aware that his tall, lolloping figure followed in her wake.

And so began a long, frustrating day. It felt, thought Helena, like wading through old porridge as she pursued her own indefinite idea of what she was searching for. Beside her loped the depressed, silent Nicholas Broadbent. Helena somehow had to maintain the energy for both of them as she made fruitless enquiries at Tourist Information and embarked on a hike around the older streets of the town looking for a cottage called The Bower.

By three o'clock, when they had found nothing, Nicholas suddenly volunteered to go to the library to peruse the local papers of the time of Miss Lily's death. Meanwhile, Helena had to keep her appointment with Mr Stephens, the chairman of the Cheltenham Art Society. He lived in Cedarvale, a mock Tudor, detached house in a leafy lane on the outskirts of the town. Nicholas dropped Helena at the gate.

'I expect I'll be about an hour,' she told him, but he didn't reply.

Mr Stephens was white-haired, soft-chinned and dressed in a spotless short-sleeved shirt and linen slacks. In his manner he was painstakingly correct. He had retained a precise, clipped, public-school accent and sat with Helena on the patio overlooking a beautifully maintained lawn while his wife, a fragile but cold-mannered lady in a Jaeger two-piece, served them tea in eggshell-thin china.

'I have done my best for your research into Florence Lily,' Mr Stephens told Helena who was wishing that she had tidied herself up a little for this unexpectedly ceremonious occasion. As she hungrily took a piece of wafery shortbread she noticed that her fingernails were grubby after a morning tramping the hot streets of Cheltenham.

'I do remember Miss Lily,' continued Mr Stephens,

'although as you know it's forty years since she died. You're not related, are you, so you won't mind if I tell you I remember her chiefly for her obsession with cats. I'm afraid she was probably a little eccentric by the time I met her. She always submitted pictures to our biannual shows, and was actually quite successful in selling her work. Her paintings wouldn't be fashionable now – she was rather a sentimentalist and, I think, idealized things. And she was not much liked by other members because she was terribly critical. I remember her castigating one of my own paintings – deservedly I expect.' Even his teeth were neat and trim, Helena thought, returning his modest smile.

'Anyway, when she died she left us – the society – all her paintings. It was a shame, and much talked about, that she probably had no other beneficiary. We sold most of them over the years – we have little room for storage. But I have dug you out a catalogue from that year when we actually did photographs of the pictures displayed and I have found a miniature which we kept in her memory.'

While he fetched these items, Helena sat on her cushioned patio chair, gazing out over the immaculate garden where blackbirds sang and all was manicured and verdant, despite the lateness of the season. She thought reluctantly of the return journey in company with the taciturn Nicholas and wondered whether Nina would be satisfied with the stickers she had bought as a present. How marvellous, thought Helena, to be cared for like Mr Stephens: tea on the lawn at three-thirty and no doubt a daintily cooked supper at seven. The source of these services, Mrs Stephens, could now be seen at the end of the lawn, snipping away at a rose bush with a pair of secateurs.

The miniature was of a cat, of course, and in the same style as the picture of Harry Two. But the photograph in the catalogue made Helena lean forward with sudden interest. Miss Lily had painted a house with her usual attention to detail overlaid with whimsy. Despite its rustic charm, and picturesque gardens, the house was unmistakable. In any case the picture was called *Overstrands. A house in Suffolk.*

At the end of three quarters of an hour Mrs Stephens

returned and gathered up the tea things onto a wide, lacquered tray. She gave a pointed glance at her small gold wrist watch as she reached across Helena for the plate of shortbread. Helena revised her favourable opinion of Mr Stephens's life.

'Thank you so much for the tea, Mrs Stephens, and the delicious shortbread,' she exclaimed in what Michael had dubbed her: 'I've been to an all-girls' grammar school voice'.

'That's all right, I hope your conversation with my husband has been of some use,' replied Mrs Stephens, in tones as reserved as her gaze.

'Oh yes, it's been invaluable. I don't know whether he told you I'm researching a book on a photographer called Donaldson...'

'He did mention it. You wanted to know about Florence Lily. A secretive little woman. Untrustworthy.' So saying, Mrs Stephens took up the tray and with careful, over-precise movements stepped across the threshold of the patio and into an inner room.

Helena hastily gathered up her things. 'Thank you so much, Mr Stephens.'

'Oh, there's no need to dash off.' He regarded her with a rather wistful expression in his faded grey eyes.

'Yes. I'm with a friend. He'll be waiting.'

Mr Stephens accompanied her round the side of the house along smooth paving stones to the gravel drive. Helena shook his hand and scrunched away, aware of his gaze on her departing back.

In fact she was ten minutes early for Nicholas and her brief acquaintance with him had not given her any cause to believe he would be punctual. She walked down the lane a little while until she came to a broad verge where she could wait without being spotted by the Stephenses. Exhausted by a day in which all her companions had been decidedly uncongenial and the weather oppressively sultry, she subsided onto the dry grass, leaned back on her hands and closed her eyes.

'Can I photograph you there? I've never seen you look so abandoned.'

She had not heard him approach but he was standing beside

her, looking down at her reclining form as if already measuring angle and focus. She jolted upright. 'No.'

'Go on. Be a sport. I'll let you have the print. It'll be a souvenir of your quest for Miss Lily.'

He was a different man. She did not dare ask what had transformed him, but accepted the change with some relief. The drive back to Shrewsbury was very convivial, accompanied by REM and a long and speculative discussion between them as to why Miss Lily had chosen to paint Overstrands, especially since Helena had no reason to think that she had ever been to Westwich.

Joanna had invited Nicholas for supper. She told Helena the night before that they could not send 'that poor man' all the way back to Malvern without a meal inside him. Helena hoped that his genial mood would withstand a dose of her mother's conversation and Nina's unpredictable behaviour. I am surrounded by mavericks, she thought wearily, why can't anyone behave normally? Certainly she resolved never to allow Nicholas to accompany her on further research expeditions. One day in his company was quite enough. As it was she must face the prospect of his long, shabbily clad legs folded against her mother's pale green dralon sofa and his casual but undoubtedly polished bearing in the little dining room. If, as Victoria had suggested, he was used to rubbing shoulders with the great and the good, and of photographing far-flung places and famous people, he would find the small semi in Shrewsbury a little suffocating.

But her reservations were unfounded. Nicholas proved to be a thoughtful conversationalist and took a genuine interest in how Robin, Joanna and Nina had spent the day. Robin would not normally have taken to a man with an earring and a provocative haircut, but within minutes he was talking readily with Nicholas.

Nina was a nuisance. She was very tired and should really have been taken home rather than sat at the table eating chicken casserole.

'I don't like potatoes.'
'I don't like carrots.'

'I don't like apple juice.'

Helena snapped at her, Robin spoiled her, Joanna cajoled her, Nicholas ignored her unpleasantness and encouraged her more sociable moments.

Helena told Joanna about Miss Lily's picture of Overstrands. 'I hadn't realized she'd even known the house,' she remarked.

Joanna's lips tightened. 'It's an interesting house to an artist, perhaps.'

Nina knocked over a glass of Ribena on the best table cloth. Helena shouted: 'I told you not to give her blackcurrant, Mum. Nina, what do you say?'

Nina cried. Joanna urged: 'Don't worry. Don't make a fuss,' and proceeded to cause chaos by fetching dish-cloths, tea towels and more mats and cutlery. 'I'm sure it won't mark the table,' she said doubtfully.

4

A few days later Helena received a bundle of photographs from Nicholas Broadbent. Included were a couple of Nina and Robin in the garden. In one photo Nina bent over a late snapdragon, intrigued by its gaping mouth. In another she clutched at Robin's leg, her face turned up to his with a delighted smile while he gazed tenderly down at her.

Helena, studying her daughter's wide-set eyes and angular jaw, thought her remarkably like Joanna. The similarity had not struck her quite so forcibly before. It occurred to her then that her mother might be beautiful if she would only discard her terrible clothes – knee-length, A-line skirts and beige cardigans. And she still set her hair as in the sixties.

There were a couple of photographs of Cheltenham. One, amazingly, was of The Bower. *Found the address in the Obit. in the library*, Nicholas had scribbled on the back.

And lastly was the picture of Helena, sitting on the grass verge with one hand behind for support, the other resting on her thigh, her skirt tucked round her knees and her hair a tangle. Her expression was distinctly unencouraging – she had not realized herself capable of such a glare. Yet Helena rather liked the photograph. At least I look full of life, she thought.

Broadbent had made a note on this photograph too: *You're the only person I know who calls me Nicholas.*

# Chapter Ten

*Past*

The sight of Harry Styles strolling along Westwich High Street in his officer's uniform made even Mrs Spendmore's embittered heart flutter beneath its hefty bosom. Cutting a less romantic figure but taller by a head was Alec McGrew, also in military garb which, like all his clothes, hung forlornly on his thin frame. The two had roared up unannounced to the gates of The Rush House in Harry's latest monstrous motor car, causing Julia to huddle beneath the bed-clothes in terror and Mrs Millerchip to summon her spouse from his noisome lair in the old tack room so that he might hurry over to Upstones for meat and butter. She then embarked on an extravagant baking session.

There was no sign of Ruth at The Rush House, so the two fledgling officers set off to find her, the leather of their boots and belts gleaming in the autumnal sunshine. Harry was certain that she would be by the shore, but could not at first bring himself to follow her there. 'I can't go on those pebbles in these boots. Any contact with salt water will be the ruin of them.'

Alec McGrew was not so easily deterred, but strode off along the expanse of empty beach, eyes straining for a sight of Ruth. Grumbling and tentative, Harry followed, the sea breeze ruffling his immaculately cut hair.

And sure enough, there in the distance was a slim figure walking rapidly towards them, the skirt of her blue dress blown sideways. From quite far away she must have identified them for her pace quickened, so that within a few minutes they came face to face. Her cheeks were flushed and her eyes bright. Her hand clasped the lapels of her jacket to prevent them flying out. A pulse in her throat was clearly visible as she fought for breath.

Alec, as usual, was rendered speechless by her vivid presence, and could only twirl his cap round and round in his fingers and gaze past her left ear to the distant headland. But Harry, burdened by no such inhibitions, swept her up in an exuberant fraternal embrace: 'Well, well, Ruth-o. What do you think of your little brother now?'

'I think he looks like a little boy playing soldiers,' she said reprovingly. Having regained her composure she made a slow circumference of the pair.

'Outclassed as usual,' said Harry. 'I told you she'd be jealous, Alec.'

'Nonsense, how could I possibly be jealous of children dressed up?' But she could not resist casting admiring glances at their tailored lapels and collars. Nor, as they turned from the beach, could she suppress a sigh as her eyes fell on the familiar dwellings of the village; Maud Waterford's cottage set low behind its stone wall, the ragged line of terraced houses constituting the main street, and beyond, just visible, the roof of The Rush House. The uncertainty and drama of the men's lives made her own seem doubly drab and futile.

But for the time being she was caught up by Harry's eagerness. Lunch was the most lively event The Rush House had witnessed for years, with Mrs Millerchip gruesomely flirtatious as she handed the peas and Harry ruthless in his satirical commentary on his first encounters with the military. Alec McGrew ate with silent intensity, pausing only occasionally to glance at Ruth, who sat between them at the end of the table, eating little but laughing obligingly at Harry's jokes and smiling with fond condescension on them both.

Afterwards Harry went upstairs to pay a dutiful visit to his mother while Ruth, having helped Mrs Millerchip with the dishes, came upon Alec McGrew loitering, cap in hand, in the hall. Taking pity on his embarrassment, she invited kindly: 'Perhaps you'd come up the lane with me and help me pick blackberries. Mrs Millerchip and I have been making bramble jelly.' She lifted her battered straw hat from its hook, ducked into the kitchen for a couple of bowls and marched from the house, not waiting to see whether he followed.

The hedgerows hummed with late bees and all the tired flowers and leaves were burnished with a honeyed haze from the warm, low sun. Alec was too meticulous to be a successful black-berrier. He lifted each fruit with almost tender care, examined it for flaws and then, if it passed muster, dropped it with a mellow thud into his bowl. Ruth was conscious that his attention was more often on her own quick, slim hand as it darted among the leaves. Her method was much more wholesale. She plucked the berries into her palm until she had gathered a handful and then released the soft, pulpy bundle into her dish. She was aware too that Alec McGrew was in a state of anguished tension. There was about him that same desperate yearning for expression that she had noted before when he was leaving The Rush House.

At first she talked all the time, asking him questions about his posting and his ambitions as an officer, for form's sake pausing for a few seconds in case he should manage a reply, and then moving to another topic. But at last, after ten minutes or so, she fell silent, and they picked at the hedgerow with only the bright calls of blackbirds for accompaniment.

They came to a gap in the hedge where a gate admitted the farmer to his field of best milkers. The cows were spread across the rich, flat pasture, heads down, knee deep in the same dusting of gold haze which covered the hedgerow. Alec rested his hip against the gate and lifted a long, loose arm. 'Pied wagtail,' he said.

Following the direction of his pointing finger Ruth saw two little birds flitting among the cows. 'Goodness, how can you tell from this distance?'

'Distinctive black and white markings. Long tail. See?'

'Yes. I see.' They stood at the gate looking across the field to the cows and the birds. For a moment, Ruth saw as Alec McGrew saw, not a familiar field with its herd of cows browsing amidst luxuriant grasses, but a canvas across which darted a host of fast-moving creatures, each one of them carefully identified, observed and memorised. 'I wish I knew more about birds,' she said. 'I pass here every day and it's never occurred to me really to look before.'

They heard a shout that was Harry summoning them back. 'I know you've a long drive ahead,' said Ruth, 'I mustn't keep you any longer.'

She picked up their bowls of blackberries and gave him one of her rapid smiles. His eyes, with their clear, liquid gaze, were fixed on her face. And for the first time the significance of his ill-fitting uniform dawned upon her.

She said softly, 'I expect you would give all you have to be left in peace so at you might spend weeks and weeks here, watching the birds. I can tell you love them.' And you ought to be able to have that, Alec McGrew, she thought. Is it asking too much for a man to be allowed to stand at the gate of a field and watch the birds? 'And here's me,' she continued, with her usual jesting tone, 'always complaining that I get no excitement because this is where I am all the time. You and I were born in the wrong skins, Alec McGrew.'

They had reached The Rush House, where Harry stood at the door with Mrs Millerchip, who was loading paper bags of fruit and cakes into his arms.

Alec stood still and said: 'I could send you a book if you like. On birds.'

She rested her head on the high stone gate-post and smiled up at him. 'I should like that very much, Alec McGrew. And you take care of yourself in this rotten old war.'

He lifted his hand, as if perhaps to touch her cheek, but at that moment Harry bounded up. After half an hour with Julia he was yearning to be gone.

'Goodbye, little sister, mind you sit up late and make some nice scarves for the troops. Though with your knitting, I hope none comes my way. Right-o, Alec. Goodbye Mrs Millerchip. Goodbye, Ruth.' And with a clanking and winding of the starter and much revving and chuntering of the engine they were gone, leaving an aroma of petrol and the sound of the motor hanging amidst the quiet afternoon somnolence of Westwich.

Westwich men, the few there were of them, began to disappear. The village became the haunt of women and old men. But even the females were busy. One of the Tate daughters enlisted as a nurse and other strapping girls arrived to work on the land. Mercifully two of the most lascivious Nichols sons of Upstones Farm had signed up, but the girls still had to endure the farmer's over-enthusiastic attempts to 'jolly them along'.

Maud Waterford spoke with effusive admiration of the girls' courage. 'What I would have given for the chance to serve,' she cried. But Ruth viewed all these developments with envious, frustrated eyes. She thought: It should have been me. I should be there.

She had to content herself with helping out at Overstrands, which had been requisitioned for use as a convalescent home. The women of the village spent many a morning up at the house preparing for imagined, romantically wounded soldiery. The real invalids, when they at last came, were in a state which gave even the most hardened Westwich farmer's wife enduring nightmares.

For once Ruth might have found purpose in Westwich, but more than usual, Julia needed almost constant attention. Her night fears were now increased by the spectre of invading armies. The idea of an airship, which she had seen pictured in a magazine, haunted her. Before, destruction had always threatened from the sea. Now she anxiously searched the skies for those ominous parcels of gas. So troubled were her nights that even during the day she was fretful and fevered if Ruth was absent from the house for long.

If possible, Ruth's glimpses into the outside world became even more restricted as the war progressed. Esther Mayrick's second son, Mark, was killed in 1915 and for a while her letters stopped completely. When she wrote again it was with the news that Giles, the most madcap of the boys, intended to enlist himself well before he was eligible, but that she thought he would survive. He had, she said, a charmed life. The oldest, Simon, fortunately had been wounded in the shoulder early on and was unfit to fight.

Even Donaldson no longer came often to Westwich. He was, by that time, an honorary son of the village and people had at last begun to realize that he was really famous as a photographer. His work was seen in newspapers and someone's niece had been to London where she had noticed his pictures in an exhibition. It was murmured that he was engaged in 'special war-work'. But perhaps one of the reasons his visits were so scarce was that he invariably found Ruth to be in a state of cold fury when she greeted him. Not only did she resent his involvement in the war, but she despised what she called his 'safe cushion of art'. 'You get all the glory and none of the danger,' she told him. Maud had presented her with a newspaper picture of a munitions factory attributed to H. Donaldson, and this she now brandished accusingly. 'What right have you to come and tell me about the horrors of war when you don't have to fight in it?'

He accepted her hostility with his usual good natured acquiescence. 'Perhaps if I go and get myself shot you'd at last be impressed,' he said.

'Don't bother, nobody would waste a bullet on you,' and then, ashamed, she grasped his arm, and begged to know more of where he'd been and what he'd seen.

He protected her from knowledge of the worst atrocities.

2

One day, in the June of 1917, after an eight-month absence he was waiting for her at the gate of The Rush House when she emerged for her walk. She gave him a nod of acknowledgement, but did not deign to notice how weary his eyes were behind his glasses or how thin he had become. All the life in him now seemed to be concentrated in his shock of thick, springy hair.

Neither spoke a word of greeting but he said: 'Get your coat, Ruth.'

'Don't be ridiculous. It's June and quite warm.' She was wearing a calf-length dress of her favourite deep blue.

'Get your coat, Ruth.'

For once she did not argue. Every nerve in her body was instantly alert to the significance of his arrival. She knew at once what message he had brought, but she did not force questions upon him. He took her elbow as they walked through the village and up along the cliff path, past the two remaining pillars of the ruined church, on and on until they came to the long stretch of beach backed by sand-dunes which lay to the north. They spoke of Ruth's work at Overstrands, of the Mayrick news and a little of Donaldson's work. He said he'd been in the West Country for a while taking photographs for a series entitled *A Country Knuckles Down to War*, which was to be used to convince the enemy that the British spirit would not easily be vanquished.

The sky was dove grey and the sea fell quietly on the long stretch of coarse sand. Ruth stood with her face to the water and waited.

'Your brother's dead, Ruth.'

She became glass. The blood drained from her face so that he thought her skin would bleed transparent. He tucked her coat about her shoulders but she twitched away and turned on him. 'Tell me how he died. I want the truth, Donaldson.' Their ability to read each other had not diminished over the years and she knew that he had been intending to hold back a good deal from her. But she fixed him with her unfaltering, most fearsome gaze until he told her everything.

It had taken four days for Harry to die of a wound in his side which would not have killed him in other circumstances, but he was left in the sun for eight hours while a battle raged and he was half dead of thirst when they finally picked him up. The wound was infected. Donaldson had somehow gleaned the information that Harry Styles was injured and found him festering in a field hospital, crying piteously for his mother.

At the conclusion of this account they stood for a moment side by side. Then Ruth turned away from him to the sea. 'We will tell my mother only that he died quickly and bravely,' she said at last.

He nodded, glanced again at her fixed profile and walked away to the top of the beach. There he lay down in the warm sand among the dunes and closed his eyes. He had not rested properly for many days. For too long his senses had been assaulted and abused. Now he could hear only the call of sea-birds and the hushing of the sea.

Ruth stood by the water's edge and looked towards a blank horizon. Not a boat, not a buoy disturbed the relentless, rhythmic swell of waves. She stooped down and snatched up a handful of sand which she flung into the water, making a weak splutter of spray. Watching the feeble peppering of the sand in the water she felt as though she were bound by an invisible skin, like the liquid, ungraspable surface of a bubble, only hers was impenetrable. She could not reach through this skin and make an impact on anything. She spent her days nudging through air, forcing a path for herself despite the suffocating bubble, and all her impressions, all her actions, were limp and futile. And Harry had been a free spirit, bounding through his life, thoughtless, impulsive and casual. Now he was dead. But he had felt, he had seen, he had breathed foreign air. Even his pain seemed to her enviable, in that it must have been sharp and cruel and bitter, not deadening, heavy and unwaveringly dull. She remembered how she had stood on the doorstep of The Rush House after her frantic journey home from the Mayrick house in Oxford. How could she have been so desperate for readmittance to her prison? Harry had held her face against his neck and she had smelt the scent of another world to which she had no access; male, sensual, highly coloured. But she had shunned that world because she was too afraid, too safe in her bubble.

Her lips contorted and she began to speak his name over and over again. 'Harry. Harry. Harry,' until the sound of the name and the sight of the wet, brownish sand, became inextricably merged in her mind. Harry. Harry.

All at once she turned, lifted her restricting skirt from about her knees and ran up the beach. Her feet slid on the finer sand of the dunes but she clambered on until she found Donaldson lying flat on his back in a little hollow, one arm shielding his face.

She stood above him. 'I want to live, Donaldson.'

For a moment she gazed down, willing him to understand, then she crouched beside him and rested one hand on his chest. 'Donaldson.' Under her hand she felt his heart beat strong and fast. She moved her fingers until they lay beneath his jacket against the smooth, warm fabric of his shirt.

He said: 'Ruth. Let it not be out of grief, but out of love.'

She went on gazing down at him, the breeze straying through her hair. One long strand fell briefly across his nose and he brushed it away. Her eyes pleaded with him. She whispered: 'Donaldson. You know. You know how I love you.'

Yes, he knew.

My friend. My companion. My laughing stock. My rock solid Donaldson.

'Donaldson.' The sky was blotted out as she kissed him. At first his lips made no answering move and for a moment her courage failed her. But his resistance ebbed away. She had known that in this, as in all else, he would not refuse her.

Afterwards, in the hours when she was free to contemplate that time, it struck her that he had been gentle and accomplished, and she wondered how he had gained such knowledge. He had taken charge. She had been afraid that he would fumble, but when he touched her it was with a hand that for years had cherished every inch of her. He held her in the crook of his arm and stroked the fine glossy hair at her crown and the rougher hair where it fell on her shoulder. He touched the mole on her left cheek and the tip of her nose. He kissed her lips and teeth and eyebrows and the two creases at her neck and the hollow in the centre of her collarbone. She closed her eyes and felt his hand on her shoulder and breast and curled herself into him, like a child.

He did not confuse her with speech. He broke through her ugly, stale sense of stifled ambition and waste, and woke her up. His hands and lips spoke to her. Beautiful, beautiful woman. Here is your soft flesh and here the clear, pure air of Westwich. You will not be hidden and unused any more. My love will restore you, and burn in you, and give you life.

She gazed up at him with trusting, absorbed eyes, listening to his touch. And she took him like a warm, shining glove. She was not afraid.

They lay for many minutes until the clouds thickened and her skin contracted with the sudden chill. She stirred, sleepy as a cat, turned on her side and whispered: 'I will always love you, Donaldson.'

He picked up her clothes for her and helped her dress, carefully buttoning her frock, watching her pale flesh disappear under the blue fabric.

When they were both dressed Ruth reached forward to kiss him again. She kissed him like a lover. The tearing of their mouths away was the most terrible of partings.

They walked slowly back along the beach, not speaking, while behind them the sea turned dark beneath a purple sky. Ahead a flash of light, which was the orange sun reflected in a cottage window, was all that could be seen of Westwich. Love and Death. Harry was cold flesh in a foreign field and Ruth had felt the blood pulsing through her veins, Donaldson's warm breath in her hair. What could that impulse of love and joy mean that had sprung from Harry's death? She had cast her body on the warm Suffolk sand and forgotten Harry's pain and her own disappointments. She had simply loved. She had been awash with hope.

Ahead a fisherman pulled his boat high on the shingle and bent to secure the oars. Ruth withdrew her hand from Donaldson's. There was no hope. Donaldson was a weak, love-sick photographer; Westwich a forgotten village tumbling off the edge of a country mired in a filthy war. Ruth was a woman who refused to face up to the sad truth that she had done nothing with her life and was too ensnared by her feeble nature to make life happen for more than a brief wild moment behind a sand-dune. The summer day held no promise but of heavy rain. Sand had become shingle underfoot. Her feet dragged. Donaldson, beside her, was weary, elated, afraid to speak. Ruth looked away, to where the beach fell sharply downwards, into the sea.

And then she knew that Harry was dead.

One consequence of this news was that Westwich was given its first and last dose of Miss Lily.

Alan Styles, who had received the official telegram, journeyed to visit his wife and daughter, and with him he brought Miss Lily. Whether as a kind of chaperone, or because he thought the women at The Rush House needed further female succour, or at Miss Lily's behest, was never discovered, but come she did, with the deceased Cloud's replacement, Cirrus, protesting loudly in a basket beside her.

Alan Styles had a peculiar disregard for, or tolerance of Miss Lily's eccentricities. He emerged from the motor looking not a bit dismayed by six hours in the sole company of a lady who had Mrs Millerchip handing in her notice within twenty-four hours and Mrs Spendmore turning the sign on the shop door to *closed* at any intimation that Miss Lily was in sight.

Miss Lily wore the coat and hat in which she had first arrived at the house in Primrose Hill, nine years previously. Her hair had faded in the intervening time and the cat had changed but otherwise she was unaltered.

She had brought an immense trunk which had to be carried up to her room by Millerchip and Alan Styles. In it was all the bric-a-brac required to make her feel at home.

Minutes after her arrival, Miss Lily carried Cirrus into the kitchen. She prefaced nearly every remark she made at The Rush House with the words: 'I don't want to be any trouble but...' Mrs Millerchip was told: 'I took the precaution of bringing some fresh cod for poor Cirrus to help her settle. Perhaps when you cook it you could ensure you remove all the bones.'

'I've no saucepans free. They're eating chicken tonight,' said Mrs Millerchip.

'That little one on the hook will be fine.'

'I never use that saucepan for fish.'

'Very well. The large one with the wooden handle.'

No one else would have attempted to outface Mrs Millerchip in her own kitchen. The housekeeper's normal tactic for removing unwanted visitors was to splash hot dishes near the skirts of the intruder in order to hustle her from the room. Miss Lily was not so easy to displace as she was a moving target. She had begun to explore Mrs Millerchip's culinary arrangements with her singular myopic snufflings. As she thrust her face up to shelves and sink, racks and stove, she talked: 'Of course I'm here, in this time of great distress, in my capacity as acting head of the family on the female side. I have troubles of my own, but I am never one to put myself first. So I have come, and I shall be unstinting in the carrying out of my duties. I make it my business to look into the diet of the family. Ruth, I think, looks thin. When you have boiled Cirrus's cod, Mrs Millerchip, perhaps you could bring me the menus for the week. I assume you have plenty of eggs here in the country?'

She retired to her room with the yowling cat under her arm, to find Millerchip still engaged in lighting the fire. Despite the heat of the day Miss Lily had announced that she could not possibly manage without a fire. 'I suffer so badly from my joints. It wouldn't do to have two invalids in the house, would it?'

Meanwhile Alan Styles trod heavily up to his wife's room and placed his weighty figure at the window where it blotted out most of the light. Julia lay against her mound of pillows, exhausted and frightened. Ruth stood at the door looking from one to another, hoping for one small crumb of comfort to fall from this rare encounter.

'Well, Julia,' said Alan. 'This is a terrible thing. To have lost our son.'

Julia shrank back.

'We must all pull together now,' added Alan, lifting his hand to his eyes. Ruth saw that he was lost in a fog of emotions, some arising from a desire to say and feel what was right, others unexpectedly raw and distressing. She crossed to him and tucked her hand in his arm.

'We are not alone in suffering like this,' she said softly.

'My family. Harry.' He waved his hand in a helpless, all-embracing gesture which took in the two women confined in the little bedroom, and his son lying under the soil far away. He looked to his wife, but her face was shuttered, her lips compressed.

'I do not know what she thinks,' Ruth said in a low voice. 'She has not once reacted to the news. When I told her, she just nodded and said she was cold.'

At that moment Miss Lily made her entrance with Cirrus still in her arms. Julia's eyes jerked open as a bundle of fat, long-haired animal flesh landed on her bed and spat furiously at the black cat, Harry Two, which lay as usual against the warm mound of Julia's thighs. The battle of wills was won easily by Cirrus and the black cat retreated hastily to the kitchen where it was fed on its rival's cod by Mrs Millerchip.

Miss Lily, meanwhile, installed herself on a chair beside Julia's bed, took Julia's hand and introduced herself: 'My dear Mrs Styles, I cannot tell you how much I have looked forward to meeting you. We have so much in common. We both have so much to bear.' She turned confidingly to Alan. 'I'll keep her company. I can tell we'll understand each other. You go and rest. It's what I'm here for.'

Half an hour later Ruth returned to find her mother in a tight little huddle, gazing open-mouthed at Miss Lily who was explaining her plans for a series of miniatures entitled *War. A Woman's View*.

After lunch Miss Lily set forth to inspect the village. For this expedition she donned a long, shapeless cardigan, the coat, the hat and a cream crocheted shawl. 'I'm not used to the sea air,' she murmured, piling Cirrus into Ruth's arms. 'Could you look after Puss? I'm so afraid of her being kicked by that Mrs Millerchip if she strays into the kitchen. She's such a confiding little soul.' And out sallied Miss Lily, sniffing at the sweet air but ducking her head as if to avoid inhaling too much of the heady stuff.

The shop was open. Miss Lily stepped inside to ask for a tube of ochre paint. Addressing Mrs Spendmore as 'my dear' she announced that she had come from town to care for the folks at The Rush House but had unfortunately forgotten some of her paints. 'I cannot let my art suffer, my dear,' she confided. 'It would be allowing the Germans to get the upper hand if art were to decline.'

'I don't stock paints,' said Mrs Spendmore, her face nesting motionlessly among her chins, her gaze hostile.

'No paint?' Miss Lily snuffed dubiously in the direction of a particularly gloomy corner. 'Perhaps old stock? In my little corner of Cheltenham there is a shop just like yours and the proprietor keeps all my colours, just for me.'

'No paint,' affirmed Mrs Spendmore.

'Ah.' The inflection given to this sigh intimated deep sorrow that Mrs Spendmore had been found so grievously wanting. 'Then,' added Miss Lily, as if conferring on Mrs Spendmore a great favour, 'I'll have a quarter of humbugs.'

The jar of humbugs was not quite obscured from Miss Lily's view by Mrs Spendmore's broad shoulders. 'I don't stock humbugs,' said Mrs Spendmore.

For a moment the two eyed each other.

The shop bell rang and admitted a small boy. Mrs Spendmore looked past Miss Lily to the child. 'Yes?'

The following morning, which was showery, Ruth retreated to her room after breakfast to fetch her walking shoes in the hope of escaping unnoticed. But no sooner had she shut the door behind her than there came a tentative knock, repeated more commandingly after a few moments.

'Ruth, dear, it's only me, can I come in?'

Ruth hastened to the door lest Miss Lily should indeed enter and ever afterwards pollute the atmosphere of the room with the memory of her presence. 'Yes?'

'I understand you walk every morning. Today I shall join you. I want you to find me some subjects for my art, and you and I have so much to say to each other. I'll just fetch my things.'

For one who aimed to present to the world a figure of down-trodden humility Miss Lily was remarkably proficient at getting her own way. Short of running down the back stairs and escaping through the garden, there was nothing Ruth could do but plan the shortest of walks and aim to say nothing. Accordingly, she waited for Miss Lily by the gate, and when she emerged set off at a brisk pace along the lane. But Miss Lily was encumbered by voluminous, pre-war skirts and her clumsy shawl, so Ruth found herself dragging her feet, whilst making monosyllabic responses to Miss Lily who scurried along behind.

'I said to your father of course I would come, it is my duty to come. Only the need to make sure he is untroubled by domestic affairs in London has kept me there, otherwise I would have hastened to your side long before this. My poor Ruth, don't you find it terribly quiet here? That dreadful woman in the kitchen. And no art, and no music. My dear, how do you stand it? Your mother looks so ill. It's bound to be a blow to her, poor dear, losing her son. There's no doubt in my mind that she must be got away.'

Ruth had led Miss Lily along the field-path towards Overstrands so that they could return by the lane – a round trip of perhaps thirty minutes and therefore respectable enough to satisfy her companion. At mention of her mother, Ruth quickened her pace.

'And so, my dear Ruth, how do you spend your time? Your father tells me you have many friends in the village, but are they suitable? And I see some charming water colours that must be yours, but they could be so much more developed. And now your dear brother is gone, who will help you understand the world? I know you relied on him for information. I know he sent you periodicals. Not always the most appropriate for a young lady. And of course you confided in him much more than in your father. Poor Ruth, so isolated, without a mother's loving solace. Poor Ruth, dreaming your dreams in this sad little place. Such wild, unfinished ideas you have.'

With sickening clarity, Ruth remembered the letters she had sent to her father, and to Harry on the rare occasions that he had stayed at the London house. She thought of them lying on the tray in the hall, waiting to be collected, and without a shadow of doubt she knew that Miss Lily must have read every one.

'Let's sit here for a while,' suggested Miss Lily, patting the broad wooden step of the stile opposite Overstrands and settling her plump frame like a large, untidy fledgling. She half closed her eyes as the breeze played across the wispy hair on her forehead. 'I shall get a chill but never mind. Goodness, what an ugly house. Whose is that?'

From the open windows of Overstrands came the soft sounds of institutional routine, a tray being set down, a door closing. With rising anger Ruth thought of the men inside and their hideous wounds of body and soul, and of smug Miss Lily and her parasitic, self-satisfied existence. 'It's a convalescent home,' said Ruth. 'For wounded soldiers. I expect you'd like to look in there too.'

Miss Lily was oblivious to the bitterness of Ruth's tone. 'I think not. Let them heal. Let them heal. We'll tiptoe away.' She never showed interest in the sickness of others, which was why Ruth's suspicions were aroused when, as they walked away down the lane, she next said: 'Your poor mother. One never recovers from the loss of a son.'

Miss Lily was now panting and wheezing to keep up with her companion. Suddenly she shot out a yellowish hand and grasped Ruth's arm. 'You know dear, I took one look at her and I thought: That woman needs proper care. This is no place for her.'

Ruth twitched her arm away.

'Your father worries himself sick, you know. He wants you to have a proper life. So I said: "I'll sort it out, Mr Styles. Leave it to me." I knew, you see, that it needed a woman's gentle persuasion. Ruth, dear, you come back to London. Your mother is past your help now.'

Had she been less angry, Ruth might have paused to wonder what could have been Miss Lily's motive in making this request. But she cried: 'How dare you? How dare you come here and disturb us all and say such things about my mother? Leave us alone.'

Miss Lily looked frightened. 'My dear, it is for you … I spoke from the best possible motives. For you.'

'I never wish to talk of it again. My mother is my affair, not yours. You have no right even to speak her name. Or enter our house. We don't want you here.'

So saying she lifted her skirt and began to run, on and on until she came to The Rush House. There she let herself into the hall and pounded upstairs to her mother's room where Julia lay sleeping. Ruth knelt by the bed and buried her face.

That afternoon Maud Waterford walked up to The Rush House to invite Miss Lily to tea. After all, as she reminded Ruth, she had been responsible for introducing Miss Lily to the family in the first place.

'I should think you do feel responsible,' Ruth told Maud. 'Perhaps you can now suggest how we shall ever be rid of her.'

She need not have worried. After two more days Miss Lily had wished on herself a streaming cold. She deposited crumpled handkerchiefs in every corner of the house and in her wake came a flood of camphor. Mrs Millerchip was plagued for basins and cloths so that Miss Lily might indulge in hourly inhalations to prevent the infection from getting to her chest.

But despite her ailment, Miss Lily still insisted on sitting with 'poor Mrs Styles', coughing and sniffing dolefully in a chair beside the bed. Even Alan Styles could not ignore his wife's distress at Miss Lily's proximity.

The next day he returned to London, and Westwich saw neither him nor Miss Lily again.

# Chapter Eleven

*Present*

November, the bleakest of months, was brightened for Helena by three invitations.

The first she received with mixed feelings as it was to attend Clara's birthday party. Such an event was bound to be an ordeal and had it not been for Nina, Helena would not have agreed to go. Even when she had been able to lurk in Michael's shadow she found the Mayrick family formidable. However, she took Nina shopping and felt better able to face the occasion once they'd both been equipped with new dresses. Nina was so pleased with her turquoise, full-skirted frock that she paraded it nightly before Helena's bedroom mirror, preening and twirling until she made herself dizzy.

The second invitation came from Victoria who rang to ask Helena and Nina to stay for a few days after Christmas. 'It'll be no trouble,' she announced. 'We'll live on yoghurt and lettuce to get all that pudding and turkey off our hips. Seriously, you must come. You need a break. And so does Nina. With a manic depressive like you for a parent she needs someone to show her a bit of life.'

And finally Nick Broadbent telephoned. 'Can we meet? I've found something out about those Donaldson photos you showed me of London houses. You must come and see for yourself.'

'I don't expect I'll bother,' Helena said loftily. Nick was so elusive himself that she didn't see why she should leap immediately to his beck and call.

'You should bother. It's about your family. Really, come. I even know what happened to Ruth's father.'

2

There had been much debate among Clara Mayrick's great-nephews and their wives as to where her party should be held and whether or not to include the clutch of infants which now constituted the newest generation of Mayricks. Belatedly they decided to consult Clara, who loved family gatherings, and who said at once that a lunch with all the children present would be her preferred option. As one of the wives commented, this was the typical choice of a woman who had no children herself, and therefore no idea of the difficulty of keeping several under-six-year-olds quiet and civilized in the middle of the day. But James Mayrick, the oldest great-nephew, offered the large family home in Oxford, all the wives contributed salads and puddings, and by twelve-thirty on the Saturday after Bonfire Night, everyone was assembled.

Most of the Mayricks belonged to one branch of the family. Clara was the youngest child of Esther and Robert Mayrick. She had three older brothers. The second boy, Mark, had been killed during the 1914–18 war. Michael, Helena's husband, was the grandson of the oldest brother, Simon. But most of the family was descended from the third boy, Giles, who had three sons, each of whom in turn had produced two or three children, mostly boys.

This prolific 'Giles Mayrick' branch of the Mayrick family was very close. The cousins met often and their small children were dressed in each other's hand-me-downs. Families frequently combined for joint holidays and Christmases. There was even a very distinct family likeness. The children were fair, brown skinned and sturdy. They tended to have engaging blue eyes and wide grins. Nina, with her lighter, unruly hair and slight frame, was quite an oddity, though sometimes Helena saw an uncanny look of the 'Giles Mayricks' in the way she smiled or when a certain expression of mischief came to her eyes.

It was apparent that on the occasion of Clara's birthday the children had been primed to treat Nina nicely because her daddy, who had been their Uncle Michael, was now dead. As soon as they arrived, Nina was taken by the hand and led away to have her lap filled with toys and her mouth with Twiglets.

Helena too was given the kid-glove Mayrick treatment. She was greeted by May, whom she and Michael had always considered the most stodgy Mayrick wife. May was plump and benign and ran a play-group in addition to having two toddlers of her own. Her purple and pink Viyella best dress had a smear of some food substance on the shoulder and she was wearing a pair of orange rubber gloves. 'There's just been a little accident in the bathroom,' she confided. 'I told Kirsty I'd clear it up.'

Kirsty, married to James and therefore the hostess on this occasion, was formidably assured and had an air of wonderfully polished serenity. Motherhood had not marred the slender perfection of her figure and she outclassed her less stylish relatives by dressing in the plainest of fabrics and designs. She kissed Helena and clasped her hands in sympathy. 'Let me take you through to the conservatory. Clara keeps asking for you.'

Clara was enthroned amidst lilies and ferns in the damp warmth of the conservatory. Wicker and glass tables, arranged to receive her gifts, were already covered by an assortment of ornaments and jewellery. She was merry and smiling as she clutched a glass of sherry, and engaged in a shouted conversation with her nephew, James.

Of all the Mayricks, James the elder, Giles's oldest boy, was the least pleasant, thought Helena. It was said in the family that Giles had had the Midas touch, and James had certainly inherited his father's ability to make money. After leaving the army Giles had been a diplomat, with postings at a number of exotic locations, but then he resigned from the Civil Service and was made the director of a company of silk importers. He had also opened a successful travel company which his oldest son had inherited, as well as the Oxford house which Giles had long since bought from his parents.

Michael had been fond of the older James and as ideological

opposites they enjoyed the odd sparring match together. But Helena found him remote. She felt that he had never given her a chance to show him her worth. With his sons' wives he was debonair and flirtatious but to Helena he was painstakingly, almost offensively polite. He was tall and lean, with a high forehead and very white hair. All his life he had been an energetic amateur sailor, an activity which had given him a deep tan and strong, muscular hands.

When he saw Helena he smiled, but without warmth. 'Well, Clara, here's someone much more interesting than me. Come and sit here, Helena.'

Despite her protests he vacated his chair and went away to fetch her a drink.

Helena leant forward to kiss Clara's cheek. The old lady smelt of talcum and sherry and did not immediately release Helena's hand from her claw-like fingers. 'Sit. Sit,' she ordered in her loud, rasping voice. Helena sat down obediently and Clara nudged a bowl of peanuts towards her after raking up a few for herself. 'It's good of you to come all this way.'

'Nonsense. I wouldn't miss it for the world. And look, here comes Nina to give you a present.'

Caroline, in her best red frock and a hint of lipstick, had approached, clasping Nina by the hand. She stooped to kiss Helena: 'My dear, you look so much better. I'm very glad to see you. Thank you for coming. I think all the family appreciates it. Now see, Clara, what Nina has brought you.'

Nina had been awaiting this moment for hours. She and Helena had chosen a brilliant crimson and blue silk scarf. Nina loved the texture of the fabric and the gorgeous dyes. She waited breathlessly while Clara fumbled with the paper and could scarcely resist reaching out to help her.

Clara's response was gratifying. 'Oh, isn't that beautiful. What lovely colours. I'm going to wear it now.'

'Oh, it's so bright, Aunty. Aren't you lucky?' gushed a passing Mayrick wife. 'But I don't think it goes with your frock.' Clara was decked out in a tiny dress with a gold and brown print.

'It will go with everything,' Clara said firmly. 'I shall wear it.

Help me tie it, Nina.' Nina stood at her side and carefully folded the scarf into a crooked knot. On Clara's little throat the scarf did look strangely at home, as if her age and her minute stature had given her the ability to wear anything with dignity, like a child.

Seated next to Clara, Helena felt at a considerable disadvantage. Any conversation had to be conducted at such a volume that she was bound to be overheard, though there was plenty she wished to ask about Overstrands and why it figured in pictures by both Miss Lily and Donaldson. Furthermore, people kept coming up to greet 'The Birthday Girl', and to ply her with presents.

Helena was treated rather as a sick relative. After greeting Clara effusively they would rumple their brows and turn on Helena with softened voices: 'And how are you?' They might touch her hand or her knee and then add: 'You're looking very well, so much better than last time we saw you.' Most people at the party had been present at Michael's funeral. Helena thought that, despite Caroline's assurances, they probably resented her presence. They could hardly indulge in a full-blown Mayrick fling, she told herself sourly, with the poor widow-woman in their midst.

By the time lunch was served, however, they had lost their restraint and with it their desire to put Helena at ease. She managed to escape her prominent position beside Clara, and went in search of Elizabeth, Michael's sister, whom she found in a small downstairs study, breastfeeding her youngest child. Elizabeth had been close to her brother, although they were wholly different in temperament. She was like a large, exotic bird, dressed in floating skirts, surrounded by a clutch of children, married to a dentist and herself a successful GP. Her breezy competence usually made Helena feel incomplete and faded. But Helena was comfortable enough with Elizabeth to sit with her for a while, talk to her about her book and share memories of Michael.

'And I had a very strange visit a few weeks ago from Myra Finny – you know, the woman who cleans at Overstrands,' she told Elizabeth, as if as an after-thought.

'Good Lord. Yes. I know Myra. We used to have a riotous time when we were kids.'

'I couldn't work out why she called. She's quite difficult to talk to.'

'She's had a bloody hard time. Her husband was a right old weirdo. A musician of some kind. Left her for one of his students. The poor soul has no money and those huge boys to keep.' Elizabeth let the baby's head fall away from her breast and lifted him against her shoulder. Now that he was sated, his head lolled sideways. Helena was fixed by Elizabeth's wide, lustrous gaze. 'I think it's brilliant that you have come to Clara's party. You must still feel terrible. I do. Limbless. As if someone has cut away my hip or half my lung. He was the other half of my childhood. He was part of the buffer that was between me and the rest of the world. Our relationship gave me strength and sometimes without him I feel terribly helpless.'

'But you always seem so self-sufficient. I imagine that you, as the eldest, were an inspiration to him.'

'Perhaps I was. I hope so. But no. He was the self-reliant one. Until he met you. I don't think he was ever vulnerable until he met you.'

The two women sat in silence in the plush, dim room, with the baby's quick breath huffing into Elizabeth's hair while Helena considered the implications of this remark. 'Was that a good thing, that I made him vulnerable?' she asked at length.

'Of course. It makes you more human, don't you think, if you've really loved, or suffered for someone else?'

'I hope I didn't make him suffer.'

'Of course you did. How could you not when he loved you so?'

The letter. The letter.

'Oh, Elizabeth. I wish he had loved me and I him a little more. I hate to think that if we'd only known how short time was we could have made a better job of our marriage.'

With one broad hand supporting the baby against her chest, Elizabeth stood up. 'Let's go and get some lunch. Those gannets will consume the lot if we're not quick.' She gave Helena a brisk peck on the cheek. 'Never doubt that Michael loved you. Take it from me. You turned his world upside-down.'

After lunch the children were collected together and sent out into the large, well-tended garden for a run, supervised by the men. There was a wonderful tree-house tucked amidst the branches of an old beech tree to which they all made a bee-line, oblivious to the fast-fading light and damp, chilly air. Standing dutifully by the sink in the kitchen, Helena polished glasses and watched Nina haul herself up the ladder into the tree.

May was cheerily rinsing crystal glasses in a froth of washing-up liquid and extolling the merits of a dishwasher to Helena, who didn't have one.

'Forgive me asking,' said May, 'but was Michael properly insured? I mean – are you financially secure, at least?'

Helena doubted that concern was the only motive behind this question. 'Oh yes,' she said coldly. 'I'm fine.'

'Oh well, that's something – to be free from money worries.' May's plump hand carefully placed the next glass on the draining board. 'Now, Helena, what will you do for Christmas? We've been talking it over and we thought you might like to come to Kirsty on Christmas Eve and...'

But at that moment the back door burst open and in came three children, one howling, and three men who made soothing noises and looked sheepishly at the women.

'Whatever's the matter? And do mind your boots on this nice floor!' cried May.

The injured child was her own portly five-year-old, Georgina. The little girl's shoulders heaved with grief as she thrust a pink, quivering hand towards her mother and yowled: 'She bit me.'

'Who did? Who bit you?'

'It was Nina. She bit me.' There was a very nasty red mark near the child's knuckles.

A split second of silence. May was in a difficult position. The fatherless Nina was the only child who could not be castigated for so terrible a crime. But she could scarcely explain this to her affronted offspring in front of Helena.

But Helena, aware of the silence, and suddenly feeling unbearably isolated in that brightly lit kitchen, went to the door and yelled: 'Nina!'

Nina was standing under the huge, leafless tree, awaiting retribution. She came slowly and sullenly across the lawn.

'Nina!' shouted Helena, grasping the child's arm. 'Did you bite Georgina?'

'Yes.'

'You must never, never bite. Naughty girl. Say sorry.'

Nina said nothing.

'Say sorry.'

Nina's brow was stormy, her lips tight in an expression which reminded Helena with awful clarity of her own mother. 'Nina!'

'It doesn't matter,' soothed May. 'Poor little girl. She probably doesn't understand.'

Helena rounded on her. 'Of course she understands. I bring her up to understand she mustn't bite. Of course I do.' She could feel, with rising panic, that a great welter of uncontrollable emotion was swelling within her. 'Nina. Say sorry to Georgina.'

But Nina was like a leaden, intransigent puppet. She would not speak.

'Right Nina. That's it. We're going straight home.' Helena took the child by the shoulder and shook her violently. She heard her own voice break as she shouted. She was crying herself now, shrieking and looking wildly about. 'Where are our coats, does anyone know?'

Kirsty was at her side. 'Helena. It's all right. Don't worry. Nobody blames you or Nina. I expect she was upset.'

In a sudden, spitting explosion of rage Nina cried: 'She said she was better than me because she had a daddy.'

Consternation caused the Mayrick men to disappear in search of stiff drinks, and the women and children to flutter and cluster about Helena and Nina. The hapless Georgina, finding herself ostracised without further sympathy for her throbbing hand, began to wail.

Caroline flew to Nina's side and gathered her against her

friendly bosom. 'Come on, Nina, let's go and find a nice book. Perhaps you'd like to come too, Georgina. I expect Helena could do with a rest, Kirsty, if there's a room free.' Helena found herself being escorted up wide, powder-blue carpeted stairs to a white bedroom with a vast double bed and acres of fleecy carpeting.

'Would you like me to stay?' asked Kirsty.

'No. No. I'm so sorry. I'll be all right.' She could scarcely speak for gasps and residual sobs. 'I'm so sorry. I've ruined your party.'

Kirsty found her a box of tissues. 'The bathroom's through there. Have a bath if you like. Anything. You won't be disturbed. But Helena. Please. Don't think of us. Don't worry about what's happened. We just don't know how to say how terribly sorry we are about Michael. Please. We're family. We want to help.'

She retreated, closing the white door softly behind her.

Helena stood in the ocean of carpet and felt the blessed peace of the room seep into her clenched muscles. Rather to her own surprise she then kicked off her shoes and climbed onto the white brocade bedspread. Lying flat on her back she stared up at the ceiling and noted that the immaculate plastering was uninterrupted by a light-fitting. All the lamps were on the walls or tables. Outside the window she saw a heavy grey sky and the top of the ill-fated beech swayed.

Helena's mind journeyed back over the last few hours. So the Mayricks did care. How odd it was, Helena thought, that she had not considered how bereft they too must feel without Michael. And to make matters more difficult for them, Helena had arrived dressed in her new navy silk frock, her hair tied severely back in a black velvet bow, and her make-up immaculate, determined not to reveal a weak chink to anyone. Perhaps inevitably, all her resolve had been undone.

I have failed my daughter, Helena told herself. I leave her alone to face a world without her father. Far from making allowances for her, I expect her to behave even better than before, to be even more self-sufficient than when he was alive because I want my own time to grieve. I don't want her with me. I push her away because it's too much trouble to take her feelings into account.

And then her mind drifted back again, this time to Clara who had been so joyous as she received her presents – a different woman from the Clara of Helena's memory who had sat in the car by the lake at Thorpeness, fragile and secretive.

She stopped crying. Her body sank gratefully into the soft covering of Kirsty's bed. Occasionally her chest still heaved but she felt deliciously sleepy. She closed her eyes and began to float a little, her thoughts skidding away. And into her head, as clear as if it were actually before her, came Donaldson's self-portrait, as it hung in his gallery at Bury St Edmunds. But this time when she considered his face she knew his expression to be not lonely, but composed and complete. As Helena lay with her hands clasped softly together, very still, very untouchable, she felt an immense affinity with the Donaldson of the portrait. It struck her now that he was a man who had reached a measure of acceptance with himself and his achievements. Sleepily she contemplated his life: the suburban family, the apprenticeship to a jobbing photographic studio, his war work, his society photographs and his protracted journeys abroad. And his emotional life which had left him solitary, estranged from his daughter Joanna.

For the last sixteen years of his life Joanna had refused to contact him. He had died abroad at the age of sixty-seven, whilst travelling alone.

Why?

Turning on her side, Helena began to doze, lapped by the white waves of the bed. Ruth Styles stood at the gate, her gaze to the sea, her hair blowing. Ruth Styles. Caught by a photographer with eyes which loved her.

Clara Mayrick had come in.

'They told me you weren't well.' She stood at the door, looking hesitantly about her, unable quite to tell where Helena was. The light had faded and the room was now very dim.

Helena propped herself on one elbow and wished the old woman would go away. But Clara was treading tentatively across the carpet. She reached the bed and felt along its length until she could perch beside Helena. She was so tiny her feet did not touch the ground.

Clara said: 'This is a huge house. It must be very expensive to heat. Yet it's very warm.'

'Yes. And so comfortable.'

'Everyone's been terribly good to me, considering I'm such an old encumbrance. It's more than I expect at my age.'

Helena realized that Clara was trying to put her at ease. The old lady jutted her chin from side to side in an effort to see Helena and details of the room. 'It's dark in here,' she said.

'Yes.' Helena sat up and swung her feet off the bed. 'I'm glad you woke me; I must go and find Nina.'

But Clara did not hear. 'Overstrands was never warm. That was its greatest failure as a house. Cold. I was always cold.'

'I'm surprised you lived in it for so long,' Helena shouted.

'There were lots of open fires, of course, and paraffin heaters, but you could never get rid of the cold in the winter months.'

'I went to Cheltenham to find the source of one of Donaldson's photographs,' Helena said, enunciating every word. 'My grandmother had a companion called Miss Lily.'

'Miss Lily.' Clara's mouth snapped shut on the name.

'She painted Overstrands,' prompted Helena. 'Isn't it amazing how fascinated everyone was by the house?'

'Donaldson took many photographs of Overstrands, of course. He would not leave the place alone. A terrible pity all that was.'

'What? What, Aunt Clara?'

Suddenly Clara focused on Helena. 'So how is the book going?'

'Very well. But there are gaps. Why did my grandfather photograph Overstrands?'

Clara reached forward and took Helena's hand in her little, clutching fingers. 'You are still very upset about losing your husband, I expect. They think I see nothing, but I have sense. I quite often know what's going on. The Mayricks have plenty of family traits in common. I can see Giles in so many of them here.'

'Did you get on specially well with Giles? He was closest to you in age, wasn't he?'

'We did get on. Yes. Until after he was married. I couldn't speak to him then.' She laughed, suddenly. 'Overstrands. No romance ever came into my life there. Except I could not be fooled. No one ever fooled me.'

# Chapter Twelve

*Past*

I

Harry's death and the end of the war brought two notable changes to life at The Rush House.

In the first place the money went. Nobody was quite sure what happened to Alan Styles's fortune, but it disappeared sooner than anyone else's. It was said that he had invested it unwisely in military equipment. In any event, the London house had to be sold in a great hurry.

The immediate consequence of this was that there was a brief exchange of letters between Ruth and Miss Lily.

*Primrose Hill*
*29th November 1918*

*Dear Ruth,*

*You cannot imagine the work. Even the furniture is to be sold from under me, though your father says I am to ask do you want anything from the house before auction? I do not think you could – there is so little space in your dear seaside house – and the little mahogany dressing table that used to be in your room is too old-fashioned for a modern young woman's taste. And if you don't want it, dear, perhaps you wouldn't mind a poor old woman using it for her few bits and pieces. It has little drawers and they suit me.*

*I have the job of dismissing the servants and writing them references. Mrs Arthur has not been gracious but fortunately has a sister in Leeds. The cook is to be kept on until the last moment though I need nothing but a crust and your father is never here. Poor man. Worn to a frazzle. The worry.*

*You know there is a porcelain shepherdess on the mantel in the drawing room. Of very little value. Her crook may even be chipped. She reminds me of all the happy days with my art. Might I keep it to treasure, do you think? It would fetch nothing at auction.*

*I never expected that my own welfare should be taken into account. But of course I now put myself entirely at your disposal and shall be arriving on the twelve-thirteen train next Saturday. Perhaps you could arrange for me to be met but don't put yourself to any trouble. I'm sure there will be transport of some kind and we can talk about the cost later. If I'm reimbursed on arrival that will be quite all right. I have few possessions and the room I was allocated before ought to be adequate. You may breathe again, Ruth, now that you know that the great burden of running the household in Westwich will be taken out of your hands.*

*You father sends his best wishes to you and your mother.*

*And I am keeping the crimson brocade footstool for Puss who has become so fond of it, though it's cumbersome and worn. It wouldn't do to take that from under him, like the rest of his roots.*

> *I am, ever, your obedient and affectionate servant,*
> *Florence Lily*

Ruth received this letter at breakfast, and without waiting to shake the crumbs from her skirt or put on her coat, ran pell-mell down the village street to Maud Waterford's cottage and arrived at the door in a state between hilarity and tears. 'Maud. She can't come here. But how can I stop her? I can't leave her destitute.'

Fortunately, when Maud wrote in desperation to the friend who had originally introduced Miss Lily to the Styles family, the friend stated unequivocally that Miss Lily had been letting The Bower, her own small house in Cheltenham, all these years and undoubtedly had sufficient means to support herself. Armed with this information, Ruth wrote back to Miss Lily:

*The Rush House*
*5th December 1918*

*Dear Miss Lily,*

*Thank you so much for your letter. I'm sorry you are forced to leave, and I would like to take this opportunity to thank you for all you have done to make my father comfortable during the past years.*

*Unfortunately, due to financial circumstances, I am unable to accept your offer and have you to live here at The Rush House. I'm sure you will, in any case, be only too glad to return to your own home in Cheltenham.*

*I am very happy for you to take the dressing table and the footstool, but please leave the china shepherdess which has sentimental value.*

*With very best wishes for the future,*
*Ruth Styles*

This, however, was not the end of the matter.

*7th December 1918*

*Dear Miss Styles,*

*At last the tears have dried, and I am able to put my shaking hand to the pen.*

*I shall be returning to my little cottage on Wednesday week. I have not seen your father for many days.*

*I always said: 'I will serve the Styles family to my dying hour. I have given them my all. And in return they have been loyal to me.'*

*Well, times change. I never thought to see you so hard, Ruth dear. When I remember the young, ardent girl...*

*I hope you never live to regret this.*

*My dear, I wish you and all your family well. If you ever need me, I shall be there. I shall never let my devotion be dimmed. Ingratitude cannot crush me.*

*I regret that in any case the shepherdess alluded to was broken by Mrs Arthur when cleaning.*

*I am ever your affectionate servant,*
*Florence Lily*

The Rush House was in Julia's name and therefore could not be touched by Alan Styles's creditors. But although the two women had the house, their income was tiny and consisted solely of the money Julia had been left by her father. The Millerchips were 'let go', but agreed to continue reduced services at The Rush House in exchange for their home in the stable block. Ruth's beautiful clothes now had to last and last. She became an excellent needle-woman and managed to retain her air of elegance. But many a small household item, including all that was salvaged from the London house in a foray by Maud just before the auction, was taken by Millerchip in the borrowed cart from Upstones for sale in Norwich. Ruth was too proud to ask for help elsewhere even though she was always disappointed by the pathetically small sum he pressed into her hand after his return.

She challenged him once. 'Are you sure my grandmother's ring fetched only five pounds?'

She sat at the dining room table with her account books at her elbow, her voice strained as she tried to catch his eye.

He was at the door, head down, the yellowish dome of his head gleaming in the lamp-light, his heavy shoulders bent. 'You should go yourself if you don't trust me.'

She was stung by so precise a hit. 'Thank you,' she said at last. 'Thank you for going.'

After he'd left she stayed at the table. The kitchen door closed and she imagined Millerchip ambling across the yard, entering the snug cottage in the stable block, hanging up his coat and emptying his pockets of the money she knew he had stolen from her during the sale. Yet she could not hate him. She clenched her thin hands against her upper arms so tightly that she winced. It was herself she loathed. You are so weak, she spat inwardly. You are such a fool. How can you sit here day after day and allow him to cheat you, and have all these people in Westwich laugh at your poverty?

The house was absolutely quiet save for a stirring of the bed in the room upstairs. The evening pressed against the window.

Ruth's self-disgust was like slow poison. It did not inspire her to action, but negated and devalued all she did, and made her bitter. Any compliment to herself she laughed harshly away. She was no longer comforted by the thought of her own nobility. She saw herself as a small, trapped creature, a mouse or a stoat maybe, made ugly by the way the cruel claws of the machine which held it contorted its whole being.

And day after day she pressed herself through the familiar routine. Long years of inactivity had now taken their toll on Julia's health so that she could no longer help herself much. The wasted, long body had to be washed and clothed and turned and fed. Her room had to be kept bright and fresh. Ruth's reward was Julia's silence. Only the eyes spoke in the sallow face. I see all you do, and all you think, they told her. I know that you are as afraid as I. Go, if you want to. I shan't mind. Don't expect me to be glad that you are here.

The other change was that there now emerged a rift between Ruth and Donaldson.

After his visit to tell Ruth about Harry's death, Donaldson disappeared for many months, and it was not until the spring of 1919 that she left the house one fine morning to find him by the gate. Behind him in the lane, nature had taken its first deep breath of the new season. He was dressed in a creased charcoal-grey jacket and heavy trousers. A battered hat was held to his chest. His wide mouth beamed a welcome, and his bright, all-seeing eyes took in every detail of her appearance. He reached out a hand to her.

She very nearly dropped her basket and took the three steps that would have propelled her into his arms. He had forgiven her, then, for not having written in reply to his ardent letters composed in the days and months following their last meeting. Not even her stony silence had crushed him.

The letters had appeared, almost daily at first, and then at more sober intervals and Ruth had read each one, but only once. Afterwards, every carefully penned page had been torn into tiny pieces and consigned to her bedroom fire. She stood with the flames scorching her skirts as she wept hot tears.

She was too honest to blame Donaldson for what had happened. Had she not begged him to love her? Very well then, but let that be an end to it. As day followed day, she forgot the joy of making love to Donaldson and thought only of the heartlessness of lying with him among the sand-dunes, moments after hearing news of her brother's death.

And the stormy nights when Julia was caught in a recurring nightmare of remembered suffering were a constant torture to Ruth.

Margaret Shaw. Harry. Donaldson. Harry. Torn flesh.

And now that Donaldson was here at last, what should she say? He was not, after all, a monster, he was Donaldson. Donaldson, whose love for her still shone like a beacon.

Well, a voice in her sighed inwardly, it's all right. Don't fight against him any more. He loves you despite your cruelty to him, and your weakness. Why not give in and let him love you? She thought of how it would be to rest her head on his shoulder and put her lips to his flesh.

But she resisted. Another voice argued fiercely: You'll never love him enough. Each time he comes to you a part of you will not want him, and you will have to go through this struggle over and over again. You will always be dissatisfied.

Wait.

Wait. There will be other chances.

Listening to this hard, clear voice in her head, his eagerness became irksome. To fend him off she extended her hand and took his in a brief, impersonal hand-shake. 'Why, Mr Donaldson. This is a surprise. You've been gone such a long time.'

It was, she saw at once, a terrible blow to him. All the expectation died from his eyes. His hand in hers went still. He had a speech prepared, but now fumbled for words: 'I tried to reach you. Events, you know.'

'Yes. I understand. You are a busy man. Not to worry. There has been so much to do.'

With every word she became more controlled. She felt the chill waters of her isolation close inexorably over her head. She could never let him near her now. Her pride was a shield between them, and once re-erected he could not beat it down. He was not equipped for such a battle, being armed only with his tenderness.

They walked, but every step they took pushed them further apart. His inability to break through her resolve infuriated her, and he was made more and more miserable by her monosyllabic answers and averted face. He was grieved too by her appearance. She was, at twenty-five a gaunt, severely dressed woman. Her slender body had lost its elasticity and the severely cut clothes she wore emphasized the tension in her neck and hips. The sides of her mouth were marked by deeply etched, vertical creases, and time had sharpened her cheek-bones. Only her hair was uncontrolled, still uncut, pulled back from her face into an uncompromising knot at the back of her head, but soft, floating tendrils would escape and play across her temples. He had revisited the memory of kissing her ear and temple a thousand times. Now that she was inches from him the memory seemed only a cruel dream.

They walked by the sea where business-like little waves frilled whitely against the pebbles, and excited birds whisked and swooped from shore to cloud. Ruth kept her gaze on her sturdily clad feet.

'Ruth.' He stood still and called her name. 'Ruth. You didn't answer my letters. I couldn't come before. Don't blame me for that, Ruth.'

But she walked away from him, on and on, as if she had not heard. He began to run until he had caught up with her and seized her elbow. She shook him away.

'Ruth.'

She turned on him. 'It meant nothing. Don't forget that. I have done nothing but regret it. Don't refer to it. Ever. I wish you had stayed away.'

Her angry eyes burned in her tense white face. She marched away again and the sunlit beach went black for him. But then he ran after her and turned her round to face him. 'I know what you are doing, and why. I know you. Never forget that. I have always known you inside and out.'

'I don't want you or your knowledge. Leave me alone, Donaldson. I don't want you.'

Never before had she spoken to him in this harsh, small voice. Still his love felt strong enough. 'I'll come back again. And again. There may come a time when you need me. And I will always be here.'

'No. No. I will never need you. Of all people.'

When she returned to The Rush House she found that her throat hurt from when these words had come rasping from her mouth. She thought that had he been ten times his size and twenty times as forceful he could not have filled the gaping wound that the years at The Rush House had opened in her. She hated him for his futile attempt to reach her.

The next day a small parcel arrived, and a note. Ruth received the package from Mrs Millerchip with a haughty toss of the head. All day she refused to open it. I will not give him even the satisfaction of my curiosity, she thought. But in the evening she saw it again on the window seat in her room and could no longer leave it alone.

The parcel contained a small, worn copy of a book entitled *Birds of Coastal Britain. A Pictorial Review.*

The note said: *Alec McGrew (d. April 1917) asked me to give you this. With best wishes, H. Donaldson.*

2

After that, Donaldson no longer came to stay with Mrs Spendmore above the shop. He called perhaps twice a year to take tea with Maud Waterford and to catch a glimpse of Ruth, but he never again waited for her outside the gates of The Rush House. He told Maud simply that he had bought a house in Bury St Edmunds but was travelling a good deal.

Only Mrs Spendmore ventured to broach the subject with Ruth.

One morning when Ruth came to the shop for flour and tea she noted that Mrs Spendmore was ensconced with more than customary heaviness behind the counter, her chins drooped over an unstarched collar.

'Good morning, Mrs Spendmore,' said Ruth brightly.

The ensuing silence was an indication that no further conversation with the shopkeeper should be attempted. Ruth scooped her flour into a brown paper bag and asked for the tea which was slapped down with such force that it was a wonder the package held together. With purse at the ready, Ruth waited to be asked for money. Mrs Spendmore still did not speak.

'Let's see,' exclaimed Ruth, 'how much is flour at the moment? I hope it hasn't gone up again.'

Mrs Spendmore brought both hands down on the counter and swung her enormous bosom forward to rest on them. Her eyes glared upwards into Ruth's. 'Your young man was here yesterday.'

Only by a slight lifting of her chin did Ruth register the remark. 'How much, did you say, Mrs Spendmore?'

'He always makes a point of calling in. And usually brings me something. But he doesn't stay here any more.'

'No.'

'You drove him away. Or perhaps the village became too small now he's got so grand.'

Ruth's hat was low on her brow so that her eyes, when cast down, were not visible. She waited.

'I thought of him as my son,' moaned the old woman. 'He was like a son. I kept his room so nice.'

'I'm sure Mr Donaldson was very fond of you, Mrs Spendmore. But I understand he has his own house now. Naturally he no longer needs to rent accommodation.'

'I hope you never come to realize what a fool you are,' was Mrs Spendmore's final remark. 'That'll be one and three.'

The pain Ruth suffered after this encounter was searing. For the next fortnight she bribed Mrs Millerchip to do her shopping for her.

# 3

Julia outlived her husband, who died at an unfamiliar address in East London. The women at The Rush House knew nothing of the event until they received a large parcel containing clothes, a wallet (empty), a couple of handkerchiefs and a small, crumpled photograph of Ruth. The only enclosure was a terse message, *Belongings of the late Alan Styles.*

By the afternoon Maud had heard the news and on walking up to The Rush House found Ruth in the drawing room taking tea with the vicar, a precisely spoken, pink-complexioned man, who loved to be in on the drama of a death. At sight of Maud he returned his tea-cup to the exact centre of the nearby table and stood with both hands clasped. 'My dear Miss Waterford. How wonderful it is to see how friends hurry to the aid of the bereaved.'

Ruth watched him with scarcely concealed distaste. 'I will fetch another cup,' she said.

'How odd this is,' exclaimed the vicar, shaking a cushion for Maud and indicating with a smooth hand that she should be seated. 'And how unnatural for the girl to be so unaffected by the death of her parent. I came to offer comfort but I find I am not needed.'

'I think Ruth owes her father little,' replied Maud tartly.

'Oh, filial responsibility is one of our first duties, Miss Waterford.'

Maud, remembering her own father, said bravely: 'You, Vicar, have never been the daughter of a despotic father.'

The vicar had inclined his head and prepared to embark on a little homily when Ruth reappeared with the words: 'I'm sure my mother would love to see you, Vicar, if you would go up,'

The vicar rose with appropriate goodwill. He had visited Julia on only two previous occasions, and found her as rigidly unyielding as had all her other visitors. It was cruel of Ruth to subject him to even ten minutes of her mother's company. When she returned from escorting him to the bedroom she could not resist grinning at Maud as if to say: I had to get rid of him somehow.

'What can it mean?' she cried, handing Maud the note and package of her father's things. 'We should have been told he was ill.'

They studied the address, Deptford, and looked it up in the gazetteer. 'You should go,' Maud told her severely. 'You should go to Deptford and find out what happened.'

At once a look of fear and defeat came into Ruth's eyes, all the more disturbing because it was so alien to her usual spirited expression. 'I cannot, Maud.'

Maud stared at her in exasperation. 'Ruth.'

'I cannot leave Westwich.'

'Not even to lay flowers on your father's grave?'

Ruth thought of the love burning for her in her father's eyes, of the pressure of his thigh on hers, of his huge frame blocking the light as he stood at her mother's bedroom window. And she imagined packing her bag, putting on her coat and hat and driving to the station. The train would carry her far away to a great, friendless city. And here, without her, the sea would lap the shore, the clouds would skim endlessly overhead and birds would flit and dive in the reed-beds oblivious to her absence. 'No. I cannot go.'

'Then I shall go. I shall make sure all is in order.'

'As you wish.' Ruth could not bring herself even to thank Maud.

So Maud went to London and returned a day later with the news that all was well. Alan Styles had died of heart disease, in cheap lodgings. His landlady had seemed respectable enough. Maud had seen the death certificate and placed a wreath on Styles's grave, on behalf of Ruth and Julia.

Shortly after the drama of Alan Styles's death, Mrs Spendmore was cutting cheese in the village shop when the door was flung open by a startlingly well-dressed young man who was so tall that he had to duck his head as he entered and who towered above the counter with a lazy, affectionate smile. Mrs

Spendmore put her hand to her throat to adjust her brooch and even managed a girlish simper.

Her customer placed one tanned hand on the counter and tapped a sixpence against the scratched wood. 'A quarter of toffees if you please. And am I right in thinking The Rush House is at the end of the street on the left?'

'You are, young man.'

He actually blew a kiss at her as he turned back to the door.

'Well!' she exclaimed, fanning herself. 'Of all the nerve.' But she sat quivering for some minutes, and inhaling the indefinably expensive aroma of masculinity and soap that he had left behind.

It was a blowzy September afternoon, with sunlight flashing across the ill-kept lawn on either side of the path to The Rush House. Ivy smothered the wall to the right of the porch and extended long, rusty-leaved tendrils into the gutter under the roof. The front door was flung wide open, giving access to a dark interior, and a woman was cleaning a downstairs window with brisk sweeps of her cloth.

'Excuse me,' called the young man, 'could you tell me, is Miss Styles at home?'

The woman turned and still he did not recognize her. She was dressed in a calf-length blue skirt and a cream blouse but both were almost obscured by a vast floral pinafore. Her hair was covered by a tightly knotted head-scarf thereby cruelly exposing the sharp angles of her face. The cloth dripped between hands swollen by too much immersion in soapy water.

'Yes?'

'Could you tell her that Giles Mayrick is here to see her.'

There was a pause. The cloth was then carefully and unnecessarily squeezed out and returned to the bucket, the hands wiped on the apron and the woman's face lifted towards him. 'Giles. How lovely to see you.'

Then he saw that it was indeed Ruth. To cover his embarrassment he removed his hat, laughed and leapt forward to take her hand. 'Ruth. My God, of course. How many years has it been?'

She smiled at last. 'About ten, I should say.' She withdrew her hand. 'Will you have tea?'

'Yes. Thank you.'

She led him to a neat drawing room with over-regimented furniture and few ornaments to clutter its polished surfaces. 'If you will excuse me.'

She disappeared and he heard her talking to someone in another room and then her quick step on the stairs. He stood at the window watching leaves skip and twirl across the lawn. Suddenly he clapped his hand to his forehead and gave a brief laugh. She was so changed. How could he have been expected to know her? He remembered a slender girl with unruly hair, glowing skin, and eyes which softened when she looked at him. On their last meeting, her disastrous Christmas visit just before the war, she had been tense and strange, but even then he had warmed to her familiar fragrance and to her clear voice.

Now she was almost middle-aged, her complexion weathered, her mouth disappointed. He awaited her reappearance with some trepidation.

She had worked miracles. The pinafore was gone to reveal a slender waist and trim hips. Highly polished shoes set off perfect ankles. And her hair was drawn softly back, though in her haste one long tendril dangled over her collar. This time her smile was unrestrained and revealed even teeth. With a flash of her long fingers she indicated the deepest armchair and seated herself near the hearth.

'Well, Giles, if it's any consolation I wouldn't have known you either. You have tripled in length and doubled in breadth. I'm only glad I haven't done the same.'

His relief to find her so humorous was palpable. He tossed his hat to a distant table and hooked one long leg over the other. 'I'm hoping to be a diplomat. What do you think my chances are?'

'Nil, Giles.' She smiled into his cornflower-blue eyes. He was the most beautiful creature to have sat in this little drawing room at The Rush House. He must be about twenty-one or two she estimated, just growing fully into his size. The furniture in the room seemed too spindly to withstand his repressed energy or to support his huge frame with its strong neck and great shoulders. Rather endearingly she saw that the shape of his head was still boyish with the steep diagonal from back of neck to crown and the dark blond hair cropped close.

Mrs Millerchip, who was no longer paid to wait on Ruth, barged in with a tray of tea things which she dumped on a table with the words: 'You'll have to fetch your own hot water if you want another cup.'

Ruth looked calmly at Giles. 'Sugar and milk, Mr Mayrick?' and he could not but admire the way she remained unruffled by the housekeeper's rudeness. She smiled and nodded as he laid his ambitions before her, as in the past she had listened patiently while he revealed his collections of birds' eggs and butterflies and had allowed herself to be led along winding paths to the sea. He had always been a little unrealistic in his plans, but undaunted by setbacks. He intended to stay a further few years in the army 'to squeeze all I can from the blighters', and then perhaps to get a posting with the Foreign Office. She enquired after his family. 'Pa' and 'Ma' were well, his oldest brother, Simon, married to some awful girl he had met at a dance, and little Clara, now fourteen, as ugly as ever. 'And did you know she's almost blind?'

'No. Oh no.'

'Her sight's been deteriorating practically from birth. She might be left with something, but not much.'

In a couple of mouthfuls Giles dispensed with his tea and clinked down his delicate cup and saucer, which in his hand looked dangerously doll-like. He then leaned forward, ready to leave. 'I almost forgot why I called,' he exclaimed. 'Mother heard I was coming by this way. I've been with friends up the coast. She asked me to bring our condolences, you know, for your father's death. Very sorry. You know.'

'Thank you, Giles.'

'Oh. Think nothing of it.' For a moment he tried to readjust his expression to something more appropriate to a discussion of the deceased. Then he leapt to his feet. 'Must dash. I'm expected for dinner in Cambridge.'

Ruth noted with some amusement that he had not thought to enquire after her own affairs. Or perhaps, knowing of Julia's condition, he was reluctant to speak of her.

She accompanied him to the door and he clasped her hand between his large, warm fingers. 'Please send my love to Mrs Mayrick,' she said. 'Tell her my mother and I are both in good health – if aged.' The light gleamed in her eye and impulsively he stooped to kiss her cheek.

At the gate he turned and called back: 'If you do see Ruth Styles tell her Giles Mayrick called. And that her servant is no good at cleaning windows.'

She darted down the path after him. 'I'll tell her she was fortunate to miss the rudest young man in Suffolk.'

But she did not go back to her work. Instead she went to the drawing room and sat in the chair he had left, his empty tea-cup in her lap. For a while she glowed in the aftermath of their shared laughter and the memory of his quick smile and the kiss he had left on her cheek. And then the solitude of the shabby little room returned to her. She heard the familiar creak from upstairs that signified her mother had woken and was raising herself in the bed.

Fortunately, after a brisk knock, Maud Waterford entered, her intelligent eyes alight with curiosity. 'Ruth. I hear you've had a visitor.'

Hastily Ruth replaced the cup on the tray and stood. 'Yes. And you'll never guess who. Giles Mayrick. Grown into a great, lanky man.'

She gathered up the tray and moved to the door. 'Are you going up to my mother? I'll bring you tea.' And she left Maud, who was chock-full of questions, to face an empty doorway.

# Chapter Thirteen

*Present*

I

During the Christmas period Helena and Nina were seldom alone. People, as Joanna rather gracelessly put it, rallied round. But despite lavish gifts, a constant flow of cards, a persistently ringing phone and countless invitations, the gaping hole left by Michael was more deeply felt than ever.

He had loved celebrations and parties, and excelled at making magic of the small details of the festival. The choosing of a tree, for instance, was an activity steeped in elaborate ceremony, with Nina perched on her father's shoulders whilst Helena and Michael discussed the merits of various shapes and heights until at last Helena exclaimed: 'This is the perfect one for us.' And then on Christmas morning Michael and Nina crept downstairs, switched on the fairy lights and checked the hearth for the empty whisky glass and half-eaten carrot. Nina was already at an age when Christmas had become a shining pearl of wonder in her memory.

Nothing could provide a substitute for the way Christmas ought to have been for Nina. She tried her best to be brave and to express proper gratitude for all that was done for her, but she was very subdued, and woke more frequently than ever crying for her daddy.

Helena was relieved when the Christmas week was over and they could set off on the train for London to see Victoria.

She was waiting for them at the ticket barrier, ready to embrace them in her angora-clad arms. Her red Honda was parked jauntily on double yellow lines – the threat of traffic wardens meant nothing to Victoria. Nina was strapped into the bucket seat at the rear, her thumb wedged in as she endured stoically Victoria's driving.

A breathtaking schedule of activities was planned for their amusement. Victoria pronounced that Helena had become too sheltered in little Shrewsbury and that Nina must be introduced to the centre of her nation's culture. So they were whisked from Oxford Street to the Tower to Tussaud's and the Science Museum. Nina's favourite trip, though, was to see *Beauty and the Beast* at a cinema in Piccadilly. Victoria exhausted Nina even more than she did Helena so that at night the poor child went to bed unprotestingly at seven while Victoria and Helena drank wine and shared the cooking, as they had when students.

Victoria abandoned any attempt to comfort and sympathize. She was just emerging from yet another stormy, short-lived relationship and her view of Helena's bereavement now was that she had been extremely fortunate to have experienced life with Michael and to have borne a child.

Helena made the mistake of confiding in Victoria the dreadful scene at Clara's party when Nina had bitten another child and Helena had collapsed in tears.

'Good for Nina! I bet the other little beast deserved it,' said Victoria.

'Oh yes, I could forgive Nina, but I felt dreadful weeping so publicly, especially with all those Mayricks watching.'

'Why feel dreadful? How are you expected to behave? As normal?'

'Well, it's so weak.'

'My God, why are you ashamed to show any feeling? You're like a bloody pressure cooker. Well get that lid off and leave it off. It's totally boring, all this "I'm a suffering martyr" stuff. Have a good bawl, and then perhaps you can climb down off your crucifix and show a bit of interest in the rest of the world.'

Accustomed though she was to Victoria's ruthless tongue, Helena retreated to bed that night considerably chastened by this unflattering portrait of herself. But she fell asleep smiling. I am allowed to grieve, she thought, but loudly and publicly. And I'm permitted to expect happiness from life again, according to Victoria.

## 2

Before travelling to London Helena had rung Nicholas Broadbent who, infuriatingly, appeared to have forgotten that he had asked her to see him. However, he roused himself sufficiently to arrange a meeting place in Deptford on her last morning.

'Nina will be with me,' she told him curtly. 'So I won't be able to hang around.'

'Don't worry, there won't be any hanging around. See you then.'

But as the Friday of her appointment drew near, Helena found herself unexpectedly nervous. She had thought about Nicholas often since receiving his photographs, and reflected at length upon his scrawled message: *You're the only person I know who calls me Nicholas*. It meant nothing at all, perhaps, but somehow it had pushed their relationship forward, she thought. And although there was nothing of conventional beauty about the man in the way he looked, spoke or dressed, he was definitely interesting. His expertise, his moods and his illness all intrigued Helena. She discovered that she wanted him to like her.

Victoria supplied her with a map, and after a series of cold waits at bus stops they reached the agreed meeting point, a huge, neglected Victorian church. They were five minutes early and Nicholas was late, so they sheltered in the porch out of the wind. By the time he turned up after twenty minutes, Helena had read all the dog-eared notices giving times of services, telephone numbers of local ministers and rotas for the offertory collection.

Nicholas was insufficiently dressed for so cold a day. Helena had the impression that he had fallen out of bed and into a crumpled grey tracksuit within the last half-hour. The wind made his nose an unattractively dark puce colour. His ears, exposed by his radical hair-cut, were also bright red. He did not greet them or apologize. 'We'll go straight there,' he told them. 'It's a bit of a way but this was the easiest place to meet.'

'Where exactly are we heading?' Helena asked frostily. She had been anticipating some gesture of pleasure at seeing her and was in any case irritated by her cold feet and hands.

'The house where Alan Styles died. It's in Donaldson's photograph. I thought you'd be interested.'

'Is that all?' she snapped. 'I would have taken your word that you'd found it.'

'I thought you were a researcher,' he said with unruffled good humour. 'Come on, Nina, you're not stroppy with me, are you?' He reached down for her hand, which she took without protest. 'He's buried in a place called Ladywell Cemetery,' he called over his shoulder, setting such a pace that Helena was treated to the sight of the back of his shorn head and tall, thin frame, and Nina's short legs trotting up and down. 'I could show you his grave if you like, but you probably wouldn't appreciate it, as you seem disinclined for major expeditions into your relations' past. I found the records. And I traced his last address to this one we're going to. The house belonged to a woman who lived here from 1915 until 1942 and then after she died it was inherited by a niece. But the original deed of purchase was in the name of Styles. So it would seem that Alan Styles bought the house for the lady, who must have been some kind of mistress.'

'Well, that's quite an assumption to make,' Helena said, confused by this sudden onslaught on the virtue of her ancestors. 'And even if it's true I don't see why you've gone to all this trouble, just to find out a rather sordid bit of my family's history.' The wind lashed her cheeks. She had to walk so fast that she was practically running.

'Anything to do with Donaldson is surely interesting to both of us. I wanted to know why he'd been here. Anyway, if you think Alan Styles having a mistress is sordid, you wait until I tell you what else I've found out.'

'I'm not sure I want to know.'

He stopped at last outside a modest and decidedly run-down Victorian terraced villa. The curtains hung limply at the windows and the paint-work was dull and chipped. A row of four doorbells bore witness to the number of tenants within.

'Well, that's certainly the house in Donaldson's picture,' Helena said reluctantly.

'Styles died in the spring of 1922, three years before his wife. It seems that most of the time Julia Styles was languishing in Westwich, her husband had a kept woman here in Deptford.'

'No wonder the family was so short of money after the war if he was keeping up two establishments.'

'Poor bloke. With a mad wife banged up in Westwich he probably needed a few creature comforts. This must have been quite a snug little house at one time.'

'I wonder if the family in Westwich knew about it? And I wonder what she was like, this woman?'

Nina was tugging at her hand, hopping from one leg to the other to keep warm. 'Can we go now, Mummy?'

'Yes, we'll go now. Where next?' she asked Nicholas.

'This is where it gets interesting. We'll fetch the car. I left it round the corner.' He and Nina set off again at his scorching pace to where his car, this time a battered white Cavalier, was parked about half a mile away, next to a pillar box.

Nina sat in the back with her thumb in. Hot air wafting from the heater made her so sleepy that her head lolled against the window. 'Helena,' said Nicholas, glancing back to make sure Nina was not listening, 'we're going to the London home of your esteemed – what is it – great-great-grandfather, Philip Shaw, husband of the mad Margaret who walked into the sea.'

'Goodness, you have been busy.'

'Yep, but no busier than Donaldson, who took it into his head to go raking about in the past too and find out exactly what happened to Shaw after his wife's suicide.'

'I know he came to London and set up a practice here. That's how his daughter, Julia, came to meet Alan Styles at a party in town.'

'Yes, but what you didn't know was that I don't think he voluntarily packed his bags and left Westwich. I rather think he had to decamp.'

'Of course he did it voluntarily. Don't you think you'd want to escape the place where your wife went mad and walked into the sea?'

'Yes, but why do you think she went off her head? If she really did, which I doubt.'

'What are you suggesting?'

They crossed the river and drove into Kensington. There he stopped outside a very modern, three-storey block of flats and produced a battered print of another Donaldson photograph. 'Look, this is where the house in the photo was. It must have been bombed.'

'Then how on earth do you know it was this address?'

'I followed another line of enquiry, via the General Medical Council and their records. And what do I find? That our friend Philip Shaw was struck off in 1875.'

Helena looked at the unpromisingly modern flats. A young woman was leaving through the central glass door, pausing to check her shoulder-bag for something. 'Why?'

'Professional misconduct. Our modern tabloids would have had a field-day. He had been abusing his women patients.'

The woman withdrew a set of keys, closed her bag and hooked it over one shoulder. Nina, in the back seat, exhaled softly.

'So, what has this to do with Margaret Shaw?'

'A great deal, I should imagine. At the hearing he was given by the Medical Council there was a lot of very nasty evidence from one patient after another, including a couple from near Westwich. And if he treated his patients like that, how do you suppose he behaved towards his wife?'

Helena found that her initial reaction was one of rage with this relative stranger who had been burrowing about in ancient records to demolish the fragile, rather romantic picture she had of her family history. 'I suppose it had not occurred to you that Margaret's suicide might have made him perhaps seek solace elsewhere?'

'But why did she commit suicide in the first place, do you think?'

'My mother always said it was because she couldn't stand the way the village was disappearing into the sea. It unhinged her.'

'Do you think that would be enough for an otherwise sane woman? And then there's his daughter Julia's odd behaviour. She confined herself to bed, didn't she, opted out of her marriage? Don't you think it's likely that she had seen such unpleasant things happening to her own mother that she was damaged for life?'

'A parent's suicide would be enough to destroy anyone's well-being.'

'Yes. Yes, perhaps so.'

'If you're right, what about Julia? Do you think she was safe from him?'

'Who can say? Perhaps Margaret relied on him having the decency not to touch his own child. But I keep coming back to Donaldson. It all went horribly wrong for him, didn't it – his relationship with Ruth, and your mother? My guess is he saw the roots of all the trouble here. With Philip Shaw.'

'But it must be possible to break free of such a blight in the end. What about my own mother? And me?'

'You tell me,' he said, his hand on the ignition.

Sex. Never speak of it, never watch it on the television, had been Joanna's credo. And yes, Helena, if she was honest, had inherited a little of this squeamishness. She had not often shared Michael's abandon.

She folded her hands in her lap.

Nicholas said: 'I followed the trail left by the little group of photographs which linked Philip Shaw's London practice and Margaret's route to the sea. I think Donaldson, who loved Ruth, was looking for a lot of answers.'

Helena stared at the unpromising red brick of the flats and thought again of the short village street at Westwich, the high bank of pebbles and the cold breaking of the waves on shingle. After all, what mother would kiss her daughter goodbye and walk out into the morning to drown herself unless she was at the end of her endurance?

Nicholas was watching her. 'I hope you're not right,' she said.

'I hope I'm not. But I think I am.'

'My poor mother. I'm sure she doesn't know all this. She can't bear any form of sexual scandal. She's never got over being illegitimate. I think that's why she would never forgive Donaldson for not marrying her mother.'

The engine was still running as Nicholas reached across and touched Helena on the cheek. 'Look at me,' he told her. 'Look me in the eye.'

His eyes were beautifully shaped, of a very clear grey, their expression questioning, perhaps sympathetic.

'No,' he said, 'you really don't get it, do you?'

'Get what?'

'Never mind.' He gave her a nudge. 'I'll buy you lunch. Would you like that?'

'Oh no, I couldn't … It's far too early. But what did you mean? What is it I don't get?'

He ignored her. 'All right. Well, come and have coffee at my place. I went out and bought a whole new pack of the freshly ground stuff, specially for you. Don't go yet, I want to show you my selection of Donaldson photographs for the book. Or have you got loads of other things to do?'

'No. Nothing. No.' And remembering Victoria's terse injunction to enjoy herself if she could, Helena said that she would love to have coffee with him.

Nicholas lived on the second floor of a tall house in Putney. His flat was reached by long flights of stairs which he leapt up two at a time, waiting for them on each half-landing. 'However did you get all your furniture up here when you moved in?' Helena asked breathlessly.

'Paid some other poor sod to do it.' He watched Nina as she climbed beside Helena, her little knees enthusiastically tackling each flight. Helena sensed a cheerful absence of restraint between the two of them.

The main living area of the flat covered the entire front of the house and had huge, floor-length windows and ornate cornices

– it had presumably once been a master bedroom. Helena expected objets d'art and souvenirs of foreign travel of the kind which filled Victoria's enticing rooms but instead the flat impressed only by its complete lack of character. Nicholas might have moved in one week before and been still waiting for the arrival of his belongings. And the room's bareness was not structured or planned or elegant. It was simply unloved, inhabited by someone who had no interest in it.

'How long have you lived here?' she asked, gazing at the walls which were devoid of any pictures.

'Three years now. I like the view.'

'Yes. I can see why.' Certainly the view afforded the sole prospect of life and colour in the room, but on that early January day even the trees in the park opposite could not lift the bleakness. All that could be said for the place was that it was clean and blissfully warm.

Nicholas did not offer to take their coats so Helena helped Nina out of her anorak and put it across the back of one of the three brown corduroy armchairs. Nina perched on the edge of another seat and stared expectantly across at Nicholas. Rather touchingly he produced a plate of chocolate animal biscuits which he must have bought especially for her.

He did not sit down but roamed about the room, coffee mug in hand. He seemed restless and ill at ease. Had he not been so insistent on them returning with him, Helena would have felt that he wished them away. At last she said: 'I don't think I've ever seen a room as tidy as this. What do you do with all your clutter? You should see our living room at home.'

'This place used to be crammed with stuff. I took it all to a charity shop down the road.'

'Whatever for?'

'I got rid of all the things that weren't essential: pictures, plants, cushions, rugs, knick-knacks, books – piles and piles of books – clothes, fancy kitchen stuff. The lot.'

'That was very generous.'

'I had a breakdown. Afterwards I didn't want anything that would remind me of what I felt in those days after the hospital.

And most things were relics of the time before when we were just living frantically, filling up hours and space to keep dejection at bay.'

'How do you mean, "we"?' Helena asked, though she had remembered that Victoria had spoken of a girlfriend.

'I lived here with a woman called Lucy. She left.'

'I'm sorry.'

'No. I was a monster to live with on the rare occasions that I was here. She stuck it out as long as she could though I made her miserable. I used to come home and find her crying. She was in a deeply frustrating job at ITN, working on her own a lot. I couldn't find the strength to help her move on. She's happier now.'

'I just hope you gave everything to a worthwhile charity,' Helena said. 'And are you completely better now?' She watched Nina who was arranging the biscuits round the rim of the plate so that she might make a selection.

'I wonder if you ever recover. I don't know. I'm not as stable. I'm aware that I walk on thin ice. But yes, I take pleasure in things again.' And suddenly he smiled at Helena. She had never been smiled at in such a way before. His eyes changed so that there seemed to be a smile within a smile. 'I expect you were the same after your husband's death. You adopt strategies, mechanisms for getting from one hour to the next, and then gradually you find that they aren't just mechanisms and you become fully part of what you're doing again. Our book's helped me. But I'm sorry if you didn't like what I found out.'

'That's all right. Though I'm not sure what I'll tell my mother.'

Nina, who had swallowed the last crumb of a hippopotamus, gave a deep sigh.

Nicholas said: 'There's not much for Nina to do here.'

'I brought some drawing things and a book.'

But Nicholas jumped to his feet. 'I tell you what I have got. Move the plate off that table, Nina.'

He disappeared for a moment to return with a square wooden box from which he lifted first a lacquered chess board,

227

then, wrapped in tissue paper, a porcelain pawn with a bulbous head and slender neck.

'Good grief, you can't let her play with that,' Helena said. 'She might break something.'

'It doesn't matter. I never use it. I brought the set back from Malaysia for Lucy and she left it behind. I keep meaning to send it back to her. Nina won't break anything. She's very careful.'

'I won't break them,' Nina said firmly. She crouched down to peer in the box, one index finger extended to stroke the glossy head of the pawn.

Between them, Nicholas and Nina made Helena feel ashamed, as if her objections were unworthy of his offering and her daughter's care. She subsided in her chair and watched Nina unwrap a white knight.

'Right,' said Nicholas, 'Donaldson. Now, here's my definitive selection of photographs. I've made a pile of prints, numbered in chronological order. I hope they go with your wording.'

'You could have done this book completely single-handed, couldn't you?' she asked him as he produced a thick folder bulging with photographs.

'No. There was a lot I couldn't work out until I met you. I would never have fully understood the whole Westwich thing, or his obsession with Ruth Styles.'

Carefully Helena turned over one familiar print after another. His selection had been made in part on the quality of particular photographs but also to reflect different phases in Donaldson's career. Finally she straightened her back and lifted her head. He was watching her again. She thought now that he seemed sad. 'Thank you,' she said. 'You've saved me a huge amount of work. These fit in perfectly with what I want to say. But there's one missing which I think ought to be included.' She was remembering the photograph of the grave which hung in the Donaldson Gallery, and which had become increasingly significant to her.

'You can put in any extra photographs you like.'

Nina had set out all the white chess pieces in order of size, each carefully in the centre of a square. She was now unwrapping the black king.

'What are the black ones made of?' Helena asked.

'Black marble, I think. I'm very ignorant about these things.' Helena had the distinct impression that he was slipping away from her. That air of bleakness which had so consumed him on their visit to Cheltenham was returning. She wished she could make him smile again, to thank him for buying Nina the animal biscuits.

'Could I see some of your other work? Or would you like us to go after all?' she asked.

He ignored this last question and said: 'I don't keep much here. You can see my portfolio if you like.'

He produced a tattered canvas bag in which a multitude of prints had been stuffed in a careless heap, very different to the careful presentation of the Donaldson photographs. There were many shots of the kind Helena had seen frequently in Sunday newspapers with captions such as, *War-torn Bosnia – a personal tragedy*, *A widow's tears*, *Another victim lies at the side of the road*.

'I'm good at anguish,' said Nicholas. 'Anguish makes news. It doesn't matter where or who the photograph is of. You take a grieving face and it tells a story that you hope the reader will identify with.'

'Or will sell the paper.'

'Or will sell the paper.'

'And do you think the pictures do have any effect on the reader?'

'They have an effect on me. I was there, not several stages removed like the reader of the paper. I looked at the woman crying over her dead infant and I decided where best to take her from, in what light. I didn't try to comfort her or even nourish her. I placed her in my photograph. And one day that same woman's photo is a page of a Sunday mag – next to an advertisement for sofa-beds or barbecues, and the reader sits in his back garden with a cup of coffee in one hand and studies the advert and flips past my photo, barely giving it a glance. Or perhaps he thinks: How terrible, I wish these magazines weren't full of doom and gloom. Meanwhile the woman lives on, maybe, her lot not improved one jot by the number of newspapers sold, and there is another scar on my memory. I have smelt her sorrow, touched her elbow, felt the fabric of her dress against my leg. And I moved on.'

'But at least people know about her,' Helena said. 'You've done that for her. You've been a witness.'

'A sort of silent witness. I may look. But I may not touch. It's as if you're trapped. You can't walk round the camera, get past the lens and alter what you see. Oh, of course you can trick, you can abuse your camera so that you give a dishonest view, or one that suits a particular interpretation of what's going on. You can set up whatever you like. But ultimately what you're good at is observing. Not changing. And it got to me. The temptation was either to leap out from behind the camera and scream: "Stop all this," or to take the woman by the hand and lead her God knows where out of danger. Or else to look away. I looked away.'

Helena stared at a black and white picture of a pale flower growing beside the shell of a bombed-out car. She was reminded of Donaldson's photograph of the war grave at Arras. 'Do you think Donaldson felt any of this?'

'I'm bloody sure he did. I think that's why I've always felt such sympathy for him. But you see Donaldson was a really tough guy. He didn't let it grind him down. Nothing seemed to make him bitter. Ruth rejected him but he went on and on photographing her, more and more lovingly, whilst quietly getting straight her family's past for her. And after the war, which must have been worse to witness than anything I've ever seen, he carried on with his work and invested all the money he made from it in various trusts and charities.'

'You don't think he died lonely and sad, then, because of Ruth? And I'm afraid my mother never wanted much to do with him once she had grown up.'

'No. I think he worked it all out. I think he saw a whole lot of shit, one way and another, on a personal and a more global level. And somehow he stayed good. He just went on doing his own thing, looking after Ruth, and then your mother, and his own family, and his town. Doing his bit. Taking wonderful photographs.'

Nina said: 'There.'

She had unwrapped all the pieces and now they were clustered together on her side of the board in neat rows.

Nick went to her at once. 'This is my favourite,' she told him, picking up a black knight.

'Yes, he's beautiful.'

'It's a she.'

'I never thought it might be a she, but of course. Look, I'll show you how she moves. Each one of these has a different way of getting about the board.'

He demonstrated the double jump of the knight and the zooming diagonal of the bishop.

Then, becoming totally absorbed, he helped her place all the pieces in their proper squares and taught her how the castles ran straight and the king had to hop.

'Why can't the king move a long way?' she asked.

'He's too important. He has to let his servants do all the work for him.'

Helena lay back in her chair and watched them. He was settled on the carpet with his back against Nina's chair, his legs stretched before him. His hands beside her little pink fingers looked long and knobbly. He invented a game where he set up his king in the middle of the board and an obstacle course for one of her pieces to negotiate until the king was knocked off. Nina found it hilarious to watch her pawn move helplessly past the target on a parallel line. Helena had not seen her daughter's face so alight for months. Nina had a magical smile, wicked, with white teeth gleaming between widened lips, eyes aglow.

Meanwhile her companion bent his clever, tortured mind to inventing yet another game for her. This time each had to shut their eyes, pick out a piece at random and race it with their opponent's across the board. Nicholas's brow was furrowed with concentration, his glance waggish as he teased Nina.

And suddenly Helena gripped the arms of her chair and thought: It has happened. Is this how it happens?

She was conscious of the stripped room. She visualized Nicholas carrying the carelessly packed box-loads of expensive possessions down four flights of stairs to escape his pain and his past. She imagined him, shrouded in sorrow and apathy, seated for hours by the white telephone, or his long legs pacing from wall to wall. She saw him exposed to cruelty and despair as he adjusted his camera and tried to invest his pictures with a little of his passionate sympathy.

She had to resist the impulse which would have carried her across the room to his side and made her kiss his forehead or his forefinger. She wanted to touch him. She knew that her caress on his cheek would start the blood racing in his uncared-for body.

But she sat still and thought: Is this how it happens? The room changes and your blood quickens. You see only goodness, only possibilities.

Nina, tiring of the game at last, had tucked her king into the gap at the back of her seat. Nicholas took it gently from her and asked if she would help put the pieces away.

'I'll do it myself,' she insisted.

Nicholas, looking up, caught Helena's eye and smiled again. This time she understood him. He has been so sad, she thought, that the tiniest clumsy move could blow him away.


He took them out for a pizza at lunch-time. Nina was in heaven as she consumed a plate of chips and a mound of ketchup.

Helena told Nicholas that she had decided to go back to Overstrands to finish the book on Donaldson. 'Nina likes it there, so it will be a holiday for her, and I think I could get the words just right in that place. Westwich is so full of Donaldson. And then I will put the whole thing behind me. You see, I feel I have dwelt too much in the past because of my mother's background and because of the book. As a result I've been missing out on the present.'

'The past is important. I think of us all fighting our lonely little passages through life. And all that holds us to the planet are the people we have touched, some dead now, some alive. The historical chain. It makes us human.' He grinned at her, and she smiled a little shakily in response.

The moment passed. He beckoned to a waiter for the bill.

Outside the restaurant he directed them to the nearest Tube and said goodbye so abruptly that Helena wondered whether she had said something wrong. She watched him disappear. His lanky figure quickly became remote.

They had never touched.

The next morning Helena and Nina went back to Shrewsbury. They found a seat opposite an elderly couple who smiled a little discouragingly, as if wary of having a small child fidgeting at the table all the way.

Nina tucked herself under Helena's arm and slept while Helena caressed her daughter's soft hair and thought dreamily of all that had been said and all that she had felt. But it was Michael who intruded most on her consciousness. She still took that letter with her everywhere, and the words chanted through her mind: *I envy the mountains your footsteps*...

But now, knowledge of the letter's existence brought her comfort. She was glad for Michael that he had that letter in the pocket of his rucksack. She was glad that he had climbed the mountain knowing he was so loved. What right had she to bemoan the love in the letter, when she had given him so little? It was a sort of gentle neglect, a taking of him for granted that had overcome her relationship with him. She was glad that he died with the letter as a token of love.

The elderly woman sitting opposite Nina changed places with her husband, reached across the table and touched Helena's hand. 'Are you all right, dear? What's upsetting you? Bill, go and get us a cup of tea.'

The kindness of strangers. Helena told her about Michael's death. The woman nodded and clasped her hand.

When her husband came back they talked about their grand-children and Bill's work as a church-warden. They were interested in Helena's book and said they would buy it as soon as it was published.

'Borrow it from the library,' Helena told them, 'it'll be expensive. But you might like it. You might like Donaldson.'

# Chapter Fourteen

*Past*

I

It soon became apparent that Julia was far from unaffected by the news of her husband's death.

Despite her mother's self-imposed seclusion from the world and her rigid refusal to take part in any activity or normal conversation, Ruth was convinced that she was always fully conscious of what went on. Indeed, there were times when Ruth believed that Julia had developed a heightened sensitivity to every mood and movement of those about her. There could be no secrets from Julia. It was simply that she never offered any acknowledgement, comment or comfort.

Ruth held countless silent conversations with her. Outwardly the routine of the day barely altered as the years progressed. The pair enacted unwaveringly the roles of dependent, sick mother and healthy, energetic daughter. Sometimes, as she helped Julia wash and dress in the mornings, made her bed, settled her in the chair at the window or watched her retreat again beneath the quilt, Ruth was completely silent, so accustomed to the routine that she could perform the most intimate task without detaching her mind from its persistent, internal dialogue. On other occasions she chatted to her mother, commenting on the weather, on Mrs Millerchip's latest aberration, or on Maud Waterford's likely arrival at tea-time. And then she would go to the door and say loudly: 'Is there anything else, Mother, or shall I be off on my walk now?'

There was never an audible response. Julia lay in the bed with her thinning hair brushed smooth on either side of her wan cheeks, her mouth a rigid line, her eyes, still beautifully shaped, large and thickly lashed, gazing at a spot a few inches from her daughter's face.

And then would begin a furious, silent conversation.

'Speak to me,' said Ruth. 'Give me a word. I'm lonely this morning.'

'I can't help you. Don't look to me. I have enough to think about.'

'Why have you gone back to bed? You're not ill. You're as strong as I am.'

'I have made my choice. I don't wish to make a pretence of having a point to my day as you do.'

'I enjoy my days. I make something of my life. These glorious walks. My reading. My housework. My God, I love my days. How can you waste your time like this?'

'You can't fool me. I hear you. I hear you arguing with Mrs Millerchip. I hear you moving restlessly about in your room. I know what you are thinking of. Well you're a fool, and a coward. At least I stick to my course. At least I don't fight my destiny. I no longer hold onto foolish dreams.'

'They're not foolish. I do have power still. One day...'

'It'll be too late. Don't stay here on my account. I'm biding my time. But it's not for me to release or keep you. You're here of your own free will.'

Ruth would hurry to her room, arrange her hat neatly over her unruly hair, pick up her coat and walk away from The Rush House, closing the front door on her mother's insistent, mocking silence.

But although Julia made no gesture when she received news of her husband's death, Ruth could detect a change. The electric charge between herself and Julia seemed to weaken. Julia went away, perhaps to reflect on the days when she was first married.

It had occurred to Ruth that ever since her father had planned the ill-fated attempt to force his wife back to London, Julia had been punishing him. She had not spoken one word to him that day, and on the rare occasions that he had appeared at The Rush House since, she had lain flat and rigid in her bed until he left her room. Or possibly, thought Ruth, he was being punished for some other crime. She remembered her own unease at being alone with him at the house in Primrose Hill.

When Styles died, this need of Julia's to hold out against him was gone.

In the months that followed it seemed that the death of her husband had inspired a great change for the better in Julia. When the weather was fine she allowed herself to be coaxed out of bed and down the stairs more often, even once or twice into a chair by the kitchen door from where she could look at the garden and feel the sun on her face. Occasionally, after Ruth had been absent for a few hours, she came back to find that her mother had actually got herself out of bed, and was seated in the drawing room or by a window elsewhere in the house. And in the colder months Julia lay peacefully in her bed, watching the leaves spin from the branches and the bare twigs sway. And she grew weaker. On stormy nights she was no longer a trouble to Ruth because she lacked the strength to raise herself from the bed.

Nevertheless, each autumn when the winds changed direction, Ruth sealed the windows against the draughts and rolled rugs along the bottoms of the doors.

Then one year, October marked the beginning of an Indian summer. Abruptly the skies cleared and autumn retreated. In the morning a heavy dew shone on the lawn and the sky was a flawless blue. The cattle at Upstones peered through a delicate mist. For an hour Julia sat in a pool of sunlight at the drawing room window, watching the motionless, curled leaves on the apple tree.

That night at bed-time she was particularly trying and refused to lift a finger to help herself into a nightdress or heave herself into bed. At the end of an hour Ruth's back was aching and she was wild with annoyance and disappointment at this regression.

'Very well,' she said, whisking away to the door, 'I'll say goodnight then, Mother. I hope you sleep well.'

Normally she gave Julia a kiss on the cheek.

As she turned to go she felt again the strong tug of her mother's will at her shoulders. When she looked back she found that Julia was gazing at her. Her eyes are warm, Ruth realized with a start, she has not looked at me like that, with love, for years. Still Ruth hesitated, but then ran to the bed and gave Julia a quick kiss on her cheek-bone, her senses as usual assaulted by the fragrance of warm hair, female flesh and rosewater.

Julia sighed.

'Goodnight then, Mother.'

The night, being clear, was very cold. Ruth lay shivering in her bed for a while as milky light from a half moon glimmered across her familiar furniture. As usual her thoughts, as she fell asleep, were far from The Rush House.

She woke only when she heard Mrs Millerchip let herself into the kitchen and open the front of the boiler to rekindle the fire. Outside there was a perfect golden morning. Ruth washed, dressed and went down to collect her mother's tea and toast.

Julia's room was still. The occupant of the bed lay on her side, one hand tucked under her chin, the curled thrust of her shoulder and hip outlined by the quilt. Harry Two was a fat black bundle in the concave hollow of her knees.

A post mortem showed that Julia Styles had died of heart failure, probably induced by years of inactivity.

So Ruth was alone at The Rush House.

On the morning after Julia's death Maud Waterford walked up the lane to the house. The warm weather persisted and the air was pungent with the perfume of old leaves and fruit.

Maud was sustained in her own sorrow by the need to help Ruth through the business of Julia's funeral. She had been almost constantly at The Rush House the previous day and was impressed by Ruth's composure, but she could not help anticipating some kind of collapse.

Mrs Millerchip, wearing an awesome pre-war black frock and an expression laden with disapproval and self-pity, answered the door with the curt words: 'She's up with the corpse.'

'Thank you, Mrs Millerchip.'

'She's telephoned her solicitor this morning. The house is already for sale. That's where loyalty gets you.'

Maud did not show her surprise. 'Thank you, Mrs Millerchip.'

On entering the house Maud was instantly aware of the great change brought about by Julia's death. Every window was flung open so that the rooms smelt of autumnal vegetation and very faintly of the sea. Maud stood for a moment surveying the drawing room with its faded chairs and empty fireplace and then mounted the stairs to Julia's bedroom. There she found that Ruth was packing away in suitcases all her mother's things while Julia's carefully prepared body lay disregarded on the bed.

Maud, shocked, saw that the Ruth who moved briskly about the room was as altered as the house. She had not troubled to put up her hair but had tied it carelessly at the nape with a blue ribbon. Nor had she yet gone into mourning but wore a cream blouse and light skirt covered by an overall. She looked no more than eighteen years old.

When she came forward to kiss Maud her cheek was as cool and fragrant as the morning.

Maud placed a little posy of a late pink rose and a few Michaelmas daisies on Julia's hand. 'My dear. I see they have laid her out.'

'Yes. They offered to take the body away but I said she'd rather stay here until tomorrow. She looks well now, doesn't she?' Ruth paused for a moment to look with satisfaction at her mother's tranquil features. 'I hope we've made all the proper arrangements and notified all the right people. There aren't many, I'm afraid. I sent a note to Miss Lily but I hope to goodness she doesn't come. Of course the Mayricks will be here.'

'The village will all turn out.'

'Will people understand if I only provide tea afterwards? I want to take up Esther's invitation to stay with them for a while.'

Maud was dumbfounded. How could Ruth, who had not left the village for years, speak so serenely of such a plan?

For a moment the two women stared at each other. Maud, shrinking beneath the steely determination of Ruth's regard, became aware of her own old-fashioned wool coat, heavy figure and stout shoes. Her purpose in coming up to the house had been to embrace Ruth and say: 'I'll look after you, dear. Come to me. We have both lost the mainstay of our lives and we'll support each other.' But she saw now that this disconcertingly robust Ruth would have none of such sentimentality.

'It will be all right,' Ruth said at last, more gently. 'But will you manage, Maud, if I'm gone for a while? You have done so much for us. I don't want you to be lonely.'

Maud found herself escorted down the stairs, guided to a chair in the drawing room and urged to drink tea. But even her desire to console Maud could not suppress Ruth's new buoyancy.

'I hear you're to sell the house,' Maud said shakily.

'Yes. Yes. I think I'm right, don't you? I shall move away. Besides, I have to sell. I have a few debts to settle and no money except the value of the house.'

'Do nothing in haste, Ruth, in the heat of the moment.'

'Oh, Maud. I can't rejoice in my mother's death. Of course I can't. But it feels as if all my life I have been preparing myself for the time when I could be free. And now I am. Believe me, I am not acting impulsively.'

That afternoon Ruth dressed in her favourite blue skirt and jacket, ignored her hat and gloves, and set out from The Rush House. She walked with her eyes uplifted, her shoulders straight and firm and her arms swinging at her sides. Two women standing on the step of Mrs Spendmore's shop gaped at her extraordinary choice of mourning clothes. They were favoured with a smile and a brief wave.

On the beach Ruth slowed her pace. Underfoot the pebbles ground against each other and her soles slid on the uneven surface. She followed the long line of the shore to where she had been met by Alec and Harry on the day they came to say goodbye. The sea was blue and meek and the waves shushed gently on the stones. She looked at the bright sky and water with love. 'Goodbye, goodbye,' sang her heart to the rhythm of the waves. 'This is the last time I shall see you. I'm going away. I'm going away.'

At the end of the shore she began the trek inland to make her way across the reed-beds and fields in a great semi-circular sweep behind the village so that she would pass Overstrands and come to the cliff-top a couple of miles below Westwich. Every step was significant for her. Here I stood for a while after I had news of Father's death, she remembered. This was where I came to get away from Miss Lily. She knew the hedgerows intimately, and noted that the hips were losing their plumpness and the nettles becoming faded and limp. She was familiar with each mark on the stile and every rut in the lanes.

Overstrands was soon to be restored by the Mayricks as an investment for Clara, but for the moment the house looked its usual oversized, neglected self. For once Ruth felt no nostalgic longing at sight of the place. I'm going to become part of life again, she told Overstrands. I'm going away into life, just as they left you each summer and went back to the city.

Overstrands gazed at her blankly from its impractical, naked windows.

And finally she took the field-path back to the cliff-top, on past the place where the church had been, and to Westwich. By now the sky had hazed over. The sun dipped to the horizon so that the cliff cast a deep shadow.

Donaldson.

He would be at the funeral tomorrow. Donaldson was everywhere. At the stile, among the dunes, by the few remaining stones of the old church. But at last Ruth could push him aside, and in future all the guilt and longing and confusion would be gone. Her body pulsed in memory of that hour among the dunes, but her mind was repulsed by it. She was stifled by the knowledge that he, like Maud, probably still loved her, even the old, trapped, futile Ruth. Well, goodbye, Donaldson. Goodbye.

2

The funeral of Julia Styles, was, according to Mrs Spendmore who shut up shop for two hours to attend, a very poor show.

She didn't realize how very tight money was at The Rush House. Mrs Spendmore, who loved nothing better than to extract her thick black frock from its mothbally shroud, polish her Sunday shoes until they gleamed, pin the mourning brooch containing a twist of her mother's wiry grey hair to her bosom and sigh heavily over the loss of earnings necessitated by closing the shop, had expected better from the folks at The Rush House.

Julia's coffin was carried on foot along the lane to the church, shouldered by four men from Upstones. And the brief service, during which Ruth sat bolt upright and solitary in the front pew, hardly gave Mrs Spendmore time to whisk her starched lace handkerchief from her sleeve and flourish its spotless folds before the sluttish face of old Mrs Tate from the farm cottage.

After the service Julia was buried in a corner of the church-yard next to her mother, Margaret Shaw, who, according to some, should never have been allocated space on hallowed ground given the way she died. During the ceremony Mrs Spendmore was busy planning how she would greet Donaldson. She was still affronted by his defection, but could not suppress her desire to be shown as his favourite before the rest of the village. He was dressed very soberly in a suit that must have cost a fortune, with only his wild shock of hair at odds with his respectable appearance.

When Donaldson actually approached Mrs Spendmore and kissed her cheek she could not resist smiling at him. 'You're looking thin,' she said.

'My mother always used to tell me that,' he told her affectionately, but his eyes strayed towards Ruth. She had been cornered by the vicar who had his hand on her elbow and was addressing her in low, solicitous tones. Somehow Ruth had conjured herself a neat black two-piece suit, beneath which she wore a plain white blouse. The calf-length skirt revealed trim ankles and shoes. Her wayward hair was concealed by a heavy cloche hat against which were etched the fine lines of her cheek and jaw. She was very beautiful, and remote.

'You can help me along the lane to the house for a bite of tea,' Mrs Spendmore instructed Donaldson. He took her arm obediently, though he had to stoop to reach her elbow, and escorted her to The Rush House.

If Mrs Spendmore had expected drama or sustenance from the funeral meal she was disappointed. The rooms already looked bare and anonymous. Anything that might be auctioned with the house had been left but all personal articles were packed away ready for sale. The village people clustered uneasily in the drawing room and were served tea and cake by Mrs Millerchip who was in high dudgeon at being left to the mercy of the solicitor, and certainly didn't see why she should wait on the likes of Mrs Spendmore. Fortunately, Esther Mayrick, gracious and queenly in her elegant black coat and veiled hat, with her quiet, kind husband at her side, took it upon herself to speak a few words of welcome to the guests. Ruth sat beside Maud Waterford, sipped tea distractedly and looked frequently and longingly towards the window.

One of the first to leave was Donaldson to whom Ruth had not spoken one word all afternoon. He embraced Mrs Spendmore, and promised to call on her again soon. Then he kissed Maud Waterford's cheek before turning to Ruth. She looked up at him with a coldly polite smile. But perhaps she was struck by a belated acknowledgement of all he had been to her, for a fleeting look of pain came to her eyes.

'I'll walk with you to the gate,' she offered.

Together they left the room and the house. They could be seen from the window standing in the lane where they had met so often in the past, his head inclined earnestly to hers, her hand clasped in his.

For once, Ruth thought, as she stood at the gate with Donaldson, it is I who will be leaving you behind. He was, she knew, rigid with emotion. She longed only for this moment to be over. In him alone rested the residue of her commitment to Westwich.

When he took her hand she felt a nerve ache in her wrist. She would not look into his eyes.

'Please be careful, Ruth,' he said.

'Oh, I shall, Mr Donaldson, never you worry.'

He refused to be teased. 'Ruth. Remember I will always be on your side.'

At last she looked fully at him. I love you. I love you, his eyes told her, so I acknowledge your desire to be free.

She understood all that she was casting away. When she could speak she said: 'Aren't you going to take my photo this time?'

'If you wish.'

She half nodded, and prepared a smile for him.

After it was done he walked away from her, down the lane. She pressed her fingers into the cold stone of the gate-post and closed her eyes. Then she returned slowly to the house. Esther Mayrick told her they might leave at any time.

At once there was a great flurry as Ruth's two large trunks were stowed in the Mayrick's motor car. Maud had offered to keep an eye on the house, oversee the sale and be responsible for Julia's cat, the aged Harry Two who was decidedly discomfited by the loss of his home among the blankets. Twice Ruth ran back, first to embrace a sullen Mrs Millerchip, and then Maud again.

Once Ruth had gone, there was no reason for anyone to linger at The Rush House.

The following day a note arrived from Miss Lily, hand-decorated with a drawing of a chalice and a wreath.

> *The Bower*
> *23rd October 1925*
>
> *My dear Ruth,*
>
> *What a relief for dearest Mrs Styles. You must forgive me for not attending the funeral. I know it's odd of me but I hate anything to do with death. I shall be thinking of you, dear.*
>
> *Your affectionate,*
> *Florence Lily*

Maud Waterford did not see fit to forward this missive to Ruth in Oxford.

A month later Maud received a letter from Ruth who was still with the Mayricks, saying that she was extending her stay, and asking her to check that the Millerchips were keeping The Rush House well aired so that it might look its best for the sale.

*I hope you will understand my reluctance to return to Westwich,* Ruth wrote. *Esther is so kind and I begin to see the prospect of a new life. This house is full of people. Clara is a little dear, very bright and knowing, and brave about her poor sight. And the boys are in and out with their friends and family, filling the house with young people. The difference, Maud! I do not forget you, dear Maud, and hope to see you before too long. But for now I want there to be miles between me and that place. Don't think to come yourself. I enclose money for the Millerchips. I can't wait for the sale to be complete and then I shall at last have a proper income.*

The next day Maud walked up to The Rush House, which was now bereft of all life. The Millerchips continued in the small stable cottage but for now had no cause to go in the house.

With her own key Maud let herself into the chill little hall. Mrs Millerchip had been efficient in her work. Each item of furniture was polished and arranged at an unnaturally precise angle. The windows gleamed. Not a speck of dust floated in the still air.

Maud walked slowly up the stairs to Julia's room. The bed was stripped and covered with an ugly green satin quilt formerly used in the spare room. The drawers and cupboards had been emptied and left slightly ajar. But on the dressing table, as if even Mrs Millerchip had been moved to alleviate the room's starkness, there was a little china box with a decorated lid. Maud knew it well.

She stood at Julia's window and looked out over the untidy garden, remembering summer days spent among those trees with Julia who had, as a child, such a brilliant imagination. 'I'll be the princess and you shall be the poor soldier who comes to the palace with the hope of making me smile...' 'This bush shall be a cave in which you are the damsel about to be fed to the dragon. I shall be St George...' In that garden she and Julia, with tumbled hair and torn skirts, had beaten their way through treacherous rain forests, attended each other's death beds having been attacked by poisonous snakes or fearsome lions, forded mighty rivers and camped out in freezing deserts.

Maud took the little china box. Then, for the last time, she stepped out into the front porch and locked the door behind her.

When she arrived back in her own kitchen she sat for many minutes staring at the box with its pattern of blue flowers. Julia had once kept hair pins in it. Now it contained only dust.

Ruth never wrote again though Donaldson saw her once when he called at the Mayricks on Christmas Eve. He reported to Maud that she had seemed happy and well. After Christmas, in response to Maud's enquiry, Esther Mayrick said that Ruth had left some days ago and given no forwarding address.

Donaldson came occasionally to the village, sat in Maud's parlour, ate her scones and showed her his work. Afterwards he walked up to the shop, then along the lane to The Rush House or the beach.

Ruth's disappearance was accepted by her friends. She had been confined to Westwich throughout her adult life and all acknowledged that she was right to make herself free. If, in the course of this change, she felt she must also cease communication with her closest acquaintances then so be it. Thus did Maud explain Ruth's silence in the village shop and thus did Esther and Maud write in explanation to each other.

Donaldson said nothing. No word of blame or criticism ever crossed his lips.

3

Thirteen months after Ruth's departure from Westwich, on a bitterly cold November night when a thick, freezing fog blanketed shore and village, Maud heard a loud knocking. It was ten o'clock and her front and back doors were bolted. She had prepared her hot-water bottle and cup of hot milk and was seated in the warm kitchen with Harry Two, reluctant to go up to her icy bedroom. For a moment she stood listening.

When the knock came again she walked briskly along the short passage to the front door.

A woman stood on the little step, cloaked in fog, carrying a large bundle.

Ruth's face, in the feeble light cast along the passage from the kitchen, was pallid and much thinner than before. By comparison the baby she held was rosy, tucked up snugly in swathes of shawls.

Ruth gave Maud no opportunity to speak. Her own voice was low and scarcely controlled. 'I'm sorry, Maud. I have no one else. She is called Joanna. I know that you'll take care of her.'

Before Maud could say a word the baby was thrust into her arms and Ruth was gone. Seconds later Maud heard the sound of an automobile driving away into the night.

Maud gazed down at the sleeping child.

Instinctively she brought her face close to the baby's and listened for her soft, calm breathing. Then she retreated from the cold night air into her kitchen. As she turned she saw that by the step were a large suitcase and a canvas bag.

Once more seated on her chair, trembling with fear, excitement and shock, Maud looked first to the hot-water bottle, then to the cup of steaming milk, then to the peaceful face of the baby. Her mind could form no rational thought. Instead the words 'Oh my poor Ruth' fluttered through her brain followed by the assurance that Ruth must return very soon. And then came a hundred questions.

But the babe stirred in her arms and more pressing affairs began to take a hold of her practical nature.

With difficulty, as she still held the child, indeed was afraid to put her down, she dressed in a thick shawl and stepped out into the silent village street. She had decided to ask help from Josephine MaClaren, formerly Josephine Tate, who, as a mother of eight, two illegitimate, would be the most able to assist.

Mrs MaClaren, to whom Maud had been unfailingly generous, wasted little time on questions but took the child, changed her with competent hands, warmed her some milk and found her a bottle. She then emptied the capacious bottom drawer in which all the MaClaren children had slept when infants and roused her oldest daughter. The girl, Anne, appeared in her nightgown, her eyes huge with surprise.

Maud returned home carrying the child and followed by Anne who held the drawer and a bundle of bedding. Together they tucked the baby up beside Maud's bed. Pausing only to drag the child's belongings off the step Maud again locked the door, made up a bed for Anne in the tiny box room, and lay down beside the baby.

Not for years had Maud slept in the same room as another human being. Her body was tense to the gentle breathing and occasional snuffles of the child. Every few minutes she leaned over to touch the baby's soft cheek and feel her breath flutter across her fingertips. After a couple of hours the baby awoke, startling Maud with her persistent, harsh cries. Anne came, sleepy but practised, changed the baby again and told Maud to heat more milk. And so passed the first night.

It took Maud several weeks to comprehend the extent of her new responsibility. Being at that time in her late fifties she found the early days with the child exhausting and alarming.

But the bags which had arrived with the baby were full of clothes, shawls and bottles, and a fat envelope containing enough money for Maud to pay Anne MaClaren to stay and help for a while. Meanwhile, the news of Joanna's arrival flew about the village, so that Maud had a stream of visitors, a few malicious, most kindly and eager to help.

Esther Mayrick, to whom Maud wrote with the news, volunteered to foster the child until Ruth's return. But although Maud asked Esther to make strenuous efforts to find Ruth, she would not give up the baby. That last morning in The Rush House when she had picked up Julia's china box had seemed to her like the end of her life. Now, gazing into the bright eyes of Ruth's baby, Maud discovered a new beginning.

The baby, who was, estimated the local doctor, about six weeks old when she arrived, seemed to know that she was in elderly, inexperienced hands and would lie quiet and patient while Maud fumbled with baths and feeds. She had inherited her mother's wide-set, slightly uptilted eyes and rare, transforming smile. She clutched the sleeve of Maud's blouse as if to say: I have been abandoned by one mother, I shall hold you tight. And as the cottage became strewn with small clothes airing and improvised playthings, Maud felt as if for the first time her home had come alive. Her constant hope – or fear – was that Ruth would reappear to claim her baby.

Joanna's greatest admirer was Donaldson.

A normal man, thought Maud, when confronted with the abandoned infant of the woman he had loved so single-mindedly, might have shown bitterness or resentment. But Donaldson, though tentative and fearful at first, seemed to feel nothing but affection for the baby. He dandled her on his knee, insisted on feeding her, oblivious to the damage inflicted on his clothes, bought her extravagant presents and took her for walks when the weather allowed.

Almost weekly he arrived in his ill-fitting working suit and his eyes at once sought out Joanna. He could not hide his disappointment if she happened to be sleeping. And then he would hold her on his knee in a manner at which most children would have protested. But Joanna was not many months old when she began to recognize Donaldson and would tolerate any amount of awkwardness from him. She loved his hair and clutched at it unmercifully, then pulled off his spectacles and hung on to his tie. When the warmer weather came he carried her down to the beach and sat with her on the pebbles or swooped her about in his arms as if she were flying into the sea.

There was no word from Ruth though every conceivable avenue was used to find her. Reluctantly, Maud even wrote to Miss Lily with news of Ruth's disappearance, but she did not mention the baby.

*Dear Miss Waterford,*

*Thank you for your letter. I receive any news of my dear adopted family, my dear, lost, tragic adopted family as I always think of them, with such gratitude. So few remember me and my suffering. They all forget that I must grieve too — for dear Julia and young Harry and Mr Styles who I always thought so gentlemanly and so misunderstood.*

*No, I have not seen Ruth but I am not surprised by her behaviour. I'm afraid I've always thought her a difficult little person. I usually get on so well with everybody. I think most people would say that I was a tolerant soul — perhaps too tolerant. I sit in a train and before I know it everyone is pouring out their troubles to me. I come home and I say to dear Cirrus: 'I am weighed down, Cirrus, by all these problems. What a good job I have broad shoulders!' I know the dear girl made a great sacrifice but I have always found her brisk to the point of rudeness. Not delicate. Indiscreet. Unkind. One knew, you see, from letters, what she thought and said. It is a pity she did not keep on with her painting and her piano. I could have done such a lot for her. But no. She didn't have the time to listen. Some young people do have this contempt for older folk, I've found. But I think, my dear Miss Waterford, you can see why I would not expect her to come to me. Nor why I'm not surprised she should leave you so suddenly. I'm afraid it is like her to be a little selfish. And I need not tell you that there is strangeness in her family.*

*For my own part I get by. I scratch about, though how I would manage without my dear papa's little house and tiny legacy I do not know. Of course I never expected anything from the Styleses despite my years of servitude to the family. Women like me ought never to anticipate gratitude. I have begun to sell my miniatures which bring in a little bread and butter. I never thought to see the day that I would have to sell my Art but there's so little good stuff around these days. I'm unamazed that people say: 'Oh, Miss Lily, we love your little pictures. We understand them.'*

*Well I must away now. The days when I could afford to spend time on correspondence are long gone.*

*With all best wishes,*

*Florence Lily*

4

In the summer of that year Donaldson called to say that he would be travelling abroad for some months but would be back by Christmas. He took an affectionate leave of Maud and the baby and disappeared from Westwich. After he had been gone three months it was said in the shop that he would be seen no more.

But in late November he arrived one afternoon, laden with exotic playthings for Joanna and a hamper for Maud. At first she thought that it was his long journey that had made him so sad and weary. He sat in the large chair by the table and held Joanna on his lap almost as if he were unconscious of who or what she was, though she fumbled with his buttons and pulled at his chin and then began to moan, afraid of the solemn, unmoving stranger. Maud lifted her from his arms.

As she made him tea and pushed the cup against his elbow, Maud noted that his shock of hair was peppered with grey and his pale, broad forehead more severely lined. Without his affectionate smile and the alert, kindly gleam in his eye, he seemed awesomely formal and beyond her reach.

'I found Ruth,' he said at last.

Maud's heart leapt.

'I took a photograph of where she's buried,' he added, reaching into his inside pocket. He handed Maud a picture of a bare cross and a grave strewn with white flowers.

'So she won't be coming back for Joanna?' Maud's voice was unsteady.

He understood. He lifted his eyes to hers and at last smiled. 'No.'

'Tell me. Where did she die? What happened? Did you discover about the father?'

There was a long pause. 'No. I discovered nothing.'

'Donaldson!'

'She is dead. That's enough.'

'But what shall I say in the village? What shall I tell Joanna when she grows up? Donaldson?'

'Say Ruth died abroad. Under circumstances too tragic to discuss.'

He was formidable. When he stood Maud thought that he had never seemed so tall or so much a man who could not be crossed. He reached out for the baby.

'You know it's said in the village that you are her father, Donaldson.'

Joanna was feeling safe again. She popped her lips together and waved. He kissed her hand and rubbed it across his rough chin, making her squeal with delight. 'Yes. I like that,' he said.

# Chapter Fifteen

*Present*

I

Nothing upset Joanna any more. The hunted, thin-lipped expression which often clouded her face was gone. Instead of being taboo, the subject of Donaldson seemed to be of considerable interest to her and she appeared to relish Helena's questions, though there were some that still went unanswered. It was almost as if she had decided to play a game of hide and seek with her childhood and could await with equanimity Helena's slow unravelling of the past.

Helena chose her time carefully to reveal what Nicholas Broadbent had discovered. Nina was to begin primary school after Easter and they were shopping in Telford for her new uniform.

'Oh yes,' Joanna exclaimed, examining the label of a grey pinafore, 'of course I knew all that about Philip Shaw. Look, Nina, you'll have a smart tunic like this next term. Or are you going to wear one of these lovely checked frocks?'

'My dress will be red and white,' Nina informed her, 'like those over there. But Mummy says we must see what the weather's like before we buy anything.'

'You will be a grown-up girl.'

'But Mother,' interrupted Helena, 'why didn't you tell me the truth about Margaret Shaw?'

'Goodness me. It was all so long ago I didn't think you could possibly be interested. But your friend Nicholas is quite right. Philip Shaw had to leave Westwich because of the terrible rumours about him. People knew that he had beaten his wife –

and worse. You couldn't keep that kind of thing secret in a tiny place like Westwich, though nobody understood how badly she must have suffered until she drowned herself. Maud didn't want to tell me about it but she thought I should know because the suicide was still being discussed in the village even though it was years and years since it had happened. She didn't want me to discover it through nasty gossip. Anyway, we won't speak about it any more here.' She looked anxiously about as if the store were crammed with eavesdroppers intent on hearing why Margaret Shaw had walked into the sea.

When they were at a table in the restaurant and Nina had been supplied with a milk-shake, the conversation continued in the low-voiced murmur Joanna adopted when forced to talk about sordid events.

'What about Alan Styles?' Helena asked. 'Did you know he had a mistress?'

'What's a mistress?' demanded Nina, blowing bubbles in her glass.

'The opposite of master,' Joanna said hastily. 'No, Helena, that's new to me. Maud never said anything about that. Though I've no doubt she was aware of it. There was nothing about my family she didn't know. Perhaps they'd managed to keep it quiet from the village so she thought I need not be told either. Nina, do be careful, you're getting chocolate all down your front.'

'Mother,' Helena persisted, 'is there anything else I should know for the Donaldson book?'

Joanna would not look her in the eye. 'I hardly think Margaret Shaw's suicide is relevant. I trust it's not going in the book. If there is anything else, I've no doubt you or your clever friend will find it out in the end. But Helena, you can see what I mean about our family being unlucky. We have a whole history of disastrous relationships behind us.'

'Until you met Dad,' Helena reminded her.

Joanna actually laughed. 'Yes, the great attraction of your father was that he was completely trustworthy. Nobody could ask for a more honest or dependable husband. Or a kinder.'

'You've still never said why you disliked Donaldson so.

Everything we've found out about him suggests that he was immensely kind and loyal.'

Joanna had been searching through her handbag for a tissue. She snapped the clasp shut and dabbed at her nose. 'Helena. I adored Donaldson. We were devoted to each other. No father could have been more loving or generous or reliable in his visits. But one day I was sent a letter that convinced me that I had been completely deceived in him. As a matter of fact it was from Florence Lily. I think her motive was malice. She felt, I think, slighted by the family, and by my mother in particular. By then Maud was dead, and I had no one to confide in. I believed what Miss Lily told me – that I had been deceived in Donaldson. He was not what I thought. When I confronted him he would not deny it. And I could never forgive him. Bear in mind that I had already been abandoned by my mother. But of course I now regret terribly the way I treated him. He loved me so. And I him. Pride, Helena. Wicked pride.'

2

Helena had told Nicholas that she would return to Westwich to complete the text for the Donaldson book. She resolved to go at half-term, but was thwarted in her plans because Overstrands had been let to a large family party for the week. When Clara learned of Helena's disappointment she offered them the house for a fortnight of the Easter holidays. Myra Finny would make sure the house was ready for them and the key could be collected from the village shop.

But as she packed their bags with piles of warm clothing, Helena had misgivings about returning to Westwich. She was sustained only by the sense that a visit to Overstrands would perhaps draw a line under the entire Donaldson episode, and at the same time put at an end the first, most brutal period of her mourning for Michael.

Suffolk was awash with rain. By the time she had parked outside the shop in Westwich Helena was heartily sick of the insistent swipe of the windscreen wipers and Nina's

255

monotonous chant of 'When will we be there? When shall I see the sea?'

Clutching Michael's old black umbrella, Helena lunged across the uneven paving stones to the dimness of the interior which had been uneasily fitted out as a self-service store, though the shelves were pitifully bereft of produce. There was no sign of another customer or of an assistant. She plucked a sliced loaf and some eggs from the shelves, approached the counter and coughed hopefully.

At length the unexpected and unpromising figure of Nigel, the vendor of drinks and sundries on the beach the previous year, appeared from among the plastic strands of a fringe curtain separating the back of the shop from the front. Neither the eggs nor the bread were priced, so he turned them fruitlessly in his long, limp fingers and then raised mournful eyes to Helena. 'Did you see how much they were?'

Conscious of Nina's solitary confinement in the car, Helena gave a tut of irritation and went back to the shelves. She called out the prices while his wavering finger hovered over the buttons on the till as he found the appropriate numbers.

'I believe you keep the key to Overstrands. Might I have it?' Helena asked, as he dropped her pound coins into the correct compartment and scrabbled about for change.

He ceased all activity and gazed at her from bemused eyes. 'Mum!' His voice was a high, bored wail.

'Now what?' His mother flung aside pink and yellow strands and stood peering at Helena from bulbous eyes. She had improbably black, glossy hair tonged back from a heavily powdered face. A top lip propelled forward by near-horizontal front teeth overhung her chin. When Helena repeated her query the woman's prominent adam's apple bulged with curiosity.

'Of course you may have the key, if you can tell me who you are. I have to take precautions.'

'Oh, it's all right. My name's Helena Mayrick.'

'Oh, Mrs Mayrick. I'm so pleased to meet you. You were down last year. I remember people saying. We were all so sorry to hear about your husband.' She pressed her hand to the neck of her acrylic coral-pink sweater and leaned forward, as if in preparation for a more lengthy conversation.

'Look, I've left my little girl in the car. I'm sorry to rush you but might I have the key?'

As she left the shop Helena picked up a couple of sweets to pacify Nina who must be frantic by now. Payment was refused. 'Let us know if you want anything,' she was urged 'Nigel will deliver, and he's actually quite useful when things go wrong in the house. Would you like me to order a paper or milk for you?'

'No. No. That's fine. I'm not sure how long I'll be staying.' But as she reached the door Helena knew that she had been unnecessarily curt with Nigel's mother. 'Thank you very much,' she added. 'Thank you for being so helpful. You've cheered me up, made me feel welcome.'

Heavy splashes of rain fell from a leaking gutter above the porch at Overstrands as Helena and Nina stood side by side on the step while Helena fumbled to fit the key in the lock. Already the lowering clouds had darkened with the approach of evening. But once inside Helena had cause to be grateful to Myra Finny for her conscientious care of the house. The refrigerator hummed reassuringly and the boiler had been lit so that hot water flowed from the taps.

The kitchen was the most attractive room in the house. Unlike the rest of the rooms it had not been denuded of its old furnishings, so that its centre was still a cook's table surrounded by a hotchpotch of substantial high-backed chairs. Nina had a happy time rooting through an assortment of cupboards and drawers for plates and cutlery. After supper they ran to and fro from house to car, unloading their luggage. This made them so wet that they had to sit in a steaming bath, their damp clothes heaped by the door. Finally, snuggled beneath Nina's duvet, Helena read aloud the entire story of Rumpelstiltskin.

But once Nina was settled for the night, the silence and strangeness of the big house began to intimidate Helena. She was determined not to become downcast, either by memories of Michael which inevitably pervaded Overstrands, or by her solitude, but went in search of a suitable room for her work on Donaldson. There was plenty of choice. The ground floor rooms at Overstrands were almost grandiose in their proportions, but the architect seemed to have lost his nerve when designing the rest of the house, for nowhere else matched the graciousness of the reception rooms. The main staircase was not elegantly angled to form a gallery, as might have been expected in a house of this size, but was straight and plain, and had an ungainly little twist at the top. A snobbish desire to segregate had presumably inspired the installation of the narrow back staircase which ran directly behind the main one, giving access to the attic and a couple of box rooms.

Nina slept in the dressing room between the two airy front bedrooms with their views to front and side. Four other smaller bedrooms opened from long, narrow passages. All contained cheap, functional furniture and as many beds as possible, for the chief attraction of the house to holiday-makers was that it could take large parties. At last Helena chose a squarish room at the back of the house. It had the advantage of new, sprigged wallpaper and a relatively small window. She pushed aside twin beds, hauled a table in from the adjacent room, and went downstairs in search of an electric fire. Even with her notes spread out and her word processor plugged in she had the sinking feeling that the book would make no progress at all here.

She was right. There was no peace to be found at Overstrands. Without the reassuring presence of her mother-in-law Helena found the house an echoing vault and was not at ease. The heating was inadequate, as she had been warned, and the curtains were thin. Outside, the rain thrummed monotonously against the glass. On the first night, having spent half an hour checking the fastenings on each window and door, Helena lay in her bed in the room next to Nina listening to the rain, alert to every creak of the floorboards. But after a while she acknowledged that although Overstrands was oversized and now institutional in its furnishings, it was not an entirely unfriendly house and was used to accommodating strangers.

*

When Nina got up next morning she was completely at a loose end. She could not go out into the saturated garden, which was so bare of shrubs or trees that it held no charm, and there was nothing for her to do in the house except rummage through a pile of ancient comics and play with the few toys Helena had brought with them from home.

In the afternoon they put on their wellingtons and set off for Westwich. Helena hoped that the fresh air and the sight of the sea might cheer Nina and cause poetic phrases to sing through her own mind suitable for the re-creation of Donaldson's relationship with Ruth Styles. But Westwich was still shrouded defiantly in its wintry gloom, buttoned up and lifeless. Nina's feet slid on wet pebbles on the beach and she grazed her knee. A few small boats had been dragged up to the shelter of Nigel's hut and there was a strong stench of old fish, but otherwise no sign of life.

They called at the village shop for plasters but they were out of stock. Nigel's mother, who introduced herself as Vera, leaned on the counter and offered Nina a toffee. She smiled toothily at the little girl and exclaimed: 'Aren't you like your daddy! But I can also see something of your gran, Joanna.'

Helena, completely taken aback, asked: 'You knew my husband then?'

'Of course. We all knew him. He was a great favourite in the village. I remember him when he was a boy and used to come down with his sister to buy gobstoppers. And then of course my older sister, Anne, looked after your mother when she was a baby. We thought it lovely when you and Michael met.'

'I'm sorry. I had no idea you knew so much about me. I would have said something.'

The woman tapped the counter with her nail and smiled. 'You're not used to village life. That's what it is. Families stay around for years. Things don't get forgotten so easily. Or people.'

'Does your sister live locally? I'd love to meet her.'

'Good Lord, she died more than twenty years ago. We were a huge family, you see, and I was the last. Anne was herself a mother of two when I was born.'

'I see.'

Vera beamed down at Nina. 'How would you like to come and help me out here one day? I get so busy I need an assistant, especially when Nigel's not about.'

Nina glowed at the prospect, her eyes fixed longingly on the buttons of the till.

Myra Finny was waiting for them in her car outside Overstrands. Helena was so fed up with the continuing rain that she was even pleased to see Myra and offered to make tea. Furthermore she had been unable to manage the lock on the back door, and one of the radiators in the drawing room didn't work. Myra said nothing as she revealed the secrets of both. She wore jeans and a fisherman's sweater, and had, Helena thought, the air of being completely and effortlessly at home in her clothes. Her face was as unexpressive as ever.

She did not seem inclined to hurry away. She had brought a large carrier bag containing games for Nina. 'My boys have finished with these. You can borrow them if you like.'

'How kind. What do you say, Nina?'

An examination of the contents of the bag filled a quarter of an hour, but afterwards Myra still lingered.

To cover the silence, Helena said, 'Isn't the weather appalling? Do you know the forecast?'

'It'll be like this for the next few days, I think.'

'Isn't it typical for the weather to be so grim just when it's the school holidays. I expect you find your boys a bit of a handful when it's raining. I always think boys must be much harder to amuse than girls.'

Myra grunted. She did not take her eyes from Nina's bent head.

'Mind you, Nina will get pretty fed up if it stays like this,' continued Helena. 'We'd hoped for lots of walks on the beach and nice drives down the coast. It's hopeless in this weather. Perhaps you could suggest a few places we might visit. Preferably rainproof!'

But Myra was scarcely listening. She reached out, as if with an entirely involuntary movement, and ran her index finger across the knuckles of Nina's hand. Nina, absorbed in her game, moved her arm impatiently, as if a fly had landed briefly.

'She has his hands,' Myra murmured.

'Yes, everyone says she's terribly like Michael. They've just commented about it in the shop. I hadn't realized Michael was so well known locally.'

Suddenly Myra stood. She was trembling. 'You could not help liking him. He was so generous and light-hearted. I miss him. I miss him.' She gathered her old rain jacket from the back of her chair. 'I'll call again in a couple of days. Check you're OK.'

Helena did not reply. She could not find the words.

The kitchen door banged behind Myra. It was as if the room was filled suddenly with light of breathtaking clarity. A stone rolled from Helena's heart. At last she understood.

## 3

After three days she resolved to return home. The rain was not continuous, but the weather was showery and blustery. Nina was bored and there were arguments because she refused to play alone whilst Helena worked on the book. What am I doing here? Helena thought at last. At home Nina would have her videos, her play-mates and her grandparents. I'd be warm. It's only pride that makes me stick it out. We'll leave tomorrow.

But as if in direct mockery of her decision the pay phone in the hall rang for the first time since their arrival. Nina was so excited that she nearly fell down the stairs in her hurry to answer it. She sobered completely, however, and thrust the receiver unceremoniously into her mother's hand when she heard an unfamiliar male voice on the end of the line.

'Helena? This is James Mayrick speaking.' It was the older James, Clara's nephew. 'I hope you're enjoying your holiday at Overstrands.'

Helena was so surprised to hear from him that she could only reply feebly: 'It's a bit wet here.'

He laughed. 'They say that part of the coast is one of the

driest places in England. I've never believed it. Now, we understand from Caroline that you're alone at Overstrands. The thing is, Helena, Clara has got it into her head that she would like to join you. What do you think?'

Helena was so horrified that she couldn't speak.

'You may feel you can't manage Clara, though she's surprisingly independent and is of course completely at home in Overstrands. Just say if you'd rather she didn't come.'

'But how would she get here?' Helena asked.

'I would bring her tomorrow. If we leave early we could be there by early afternoon.'

'She seems so terribly frail. I'm not sure I'd know how to look after her.'

'She's as tough as old boots. But if you don't feel able…'

Helena could do nothing but say how pleased she and Nina would be to see Clara, who after all was the owner of Overstrands. She had thought that nothing could make her stay in the house worse; the thought of having to amuse Nina and entertain Clara was almost too much to bear.

At two-thirty the following afternoon James Mayrick and Clara arrived in his maroon Jaguar. James did not waste time. His greeting to Helena was perhaps a little warmer than usual and he had brought wine and a box of food because he said he knew how limited the local stores were. When he had helped Clara from the car and carried her cases upstairs he actually took Helena aside and kissed her cheek. 'I know this is probably very awkward for you but she was determined to come. I think she thought you and Nina might be lonely here. I've been in touch with Mrs Finny who said she'd help you out, so that's something. We tried to tell Clara that she was perhaps not the ideal companion for you, but it is difficult, as you can imagine, not to offend her.'

'No, no. I'm glad you brought her.'

He looked down at her from handsome, quizzical eyes and touched her arm. 'Poor Helena. This has been a tough year for you. But it looks to me as if you're coming round.' This unwonted sympathy from James Mayrick did much to lift Helena's spirits.

James was the apple of Clara's eye. She stood in the porch with Nina, waving goodbye to him, and then exclaimed fondly: 'He's so good to me!' Sight of the stark hall of Overstrands made her smile. 'It's so kind of you to let me come, Helena. I know I'm a great nuisance. But I can never resist the chance to be here.'

But Helena could not really understand Clara's desire to come to Overstrands. The old lady was obviously desperately cold and felt every draught that whistled under the ill-fitting doors. She spent most of her time huddled in a chair by the gas fire in the drawing room, her thin little calves so close to the flames that her flesh must have been scorched. But she did keep Nina amused. A great friendship sprang up between the pair, though Clara could hear little of what Nina said and could not see the games which she offered to play with her. But they managed several rounds of Snakes and Ladders, with Nina throwing the dice for both of them and moving Clara's counter. And Clara had brought Nina a number of deliciously inappropriate presents: a lace handkerchief attached with pins to a flat box with a transparent lid, a couple of bath cubes and, most wonderful of all, an oval locket on a gold chain. 'Now that,' Clara told Nina, 'used to be my mother's. There's a photograph of her inside.'

'Clara!' Helena exclaimed, peering with interest at the obscure, tiny face of Esther Mayrick. 'You can't give it to Nina.'

Clara didn't hear.

At first Helena was terrified of Clara's age. She listened to her slow descent of the stairs or her fumbling preparations for bed and thought that at any minute she might fall or collapse. In fact there were only three full days to fill because James was to collect his aunt on the Saturday morning. Gradually Helena began to relax for she discovered Clara to be very robust, and very grateful. She ate with relish all that was put before her and seemed quite happy to sit with Radio 4 blaring in her ear, her handbag pressed against her feet. Helena, looking in from time to time, was touched by her obvious pleasure at being in the house. The old lady's tiny hands clasped the arms of her chair and the light from the long windows reflected in the lenses of her glasses.

On the evening before James was due to return Helena cooked a more ambitious dinner than usual. Nina, hungry and tired, was unusually irritable and made a huge fuss when Helena insisted on bathing her whilst the meal was cooking. She screamed when her hair was shampooed and yelled that Helena had burnt her scalp with the rinse water. At supper Helena had to endure Clara's prolonged account of her afternoon's conversation with Myra who had visited that afternoon. They had talked about Michael and of his boyhood holidays in Westwich. 'Myra and Michael were great buddies,' declared Clara. 'She's always had a bit of a soft spot for him.'

Nina insisted on a long story before she would consent to lie down, and when Helena returned to the kitchen at last she was confronted by an array of greasy pans. Clara, who had managed to clear the table, came shuffling out to help with the drying up. Helena found her assistance a mixed blessing as she was painstakingly slow but surprisingly thorough, and never broke anything.

That night, however, Helena had difficulty keeping her temper. She longed above all to rest.

When the last pan had been hung on its hook above the cooker, Clara shook out her tea towel and folded it carefully. 'Of course,' she said, smoothing the cloth over a chair-back, 'I was actually rather pleased to find you alone here. I have something to give you. I'm afraid I've put it off until tonight but I'll get it now.'

Helena was too weary to ask questions but wiped surfaces and collected the milk bottles whilst Clara climbed the stairs to her room, and at last returned with an ancient envelope.

'This came to our house in Oxford in July 1927. You see, I remember the date very well.' Clara was kneading the package with her nervous, bent fingers. 'It was addressed to my mother but she was away. In India, as it happens, visiting my brother

264

Giles. When you see the contents you will understand the irony of that. I had been instructed to open all my parents' mail in their absence. I did not give them this on their return. I have not shown it to anyone before. But I think you should have it.'

Helena had never seen Clara so uncertain. Still the old lady clutched the package, as if extremely reluctant to release it.

'You see, I couldn't read the letter inside. The writing is so small and muddled. But I knew the signature. Ruth Styles.'

Helena became fully alert to what Clara was saying.

'There is a covering note which I could read, from a woman called Florence Lily. Now I had never met her, but I had heard her spoken of. She had been at one time a companion to Ruth Styles. I knew the name very well because I always remember my mother and Ruth laughing about her. Ruth couldn't stand her, but could mimic her mannerisms beautifully. When Ruth disappeared so dramatically after her mother died nobody heard from her again. Florence Lily was written to, I think, but denied any knowledge of Ruth's whereabouts. Certainly nobody expected her to confide in Florence Lily. But she must have been so desperate that in the end she did trust this woman with her papers on the understanding that should anything happen to her they were to be sent to Maud Waterford, who of course was your mother's guardian. But Florence Lily had other ideas. She obviously read what Ruth had written in confidence and decided maliciously that my mother should see it.

'Why? If Ruth was dead what harm could there be?'

'As I say, I've never been able to read what Ruth had written. But I knew in any case. You see, I had seen Ruth in the dining room at Christmas. I thought she was with Donaldson. It was dark and I could make out nothing about the man except that he moved his hand and his ring flashed. I sat beside Donaldson at dinner. He never wore a ring. So I knew the harm Ruth's letter could do.'

'Clara. This was intended for Maud and my mother. Why didn't you send it to my mother long ago?'

This question had to be repeated several times before Clara made any response. She still had not released the envelope. 'I

# Chapter Sixteen

*Past*

It was as if Ruth were on a prolonged holiday.

At first she felt limp and sick with the sudden slackening of tension caused by Julia's death and her own departure from Westwich. In the motor car, driving away from The Rush House with Esther's arm tucked through her own, she began to shake. She was terrified lest the crippling sensation of displacement and panic which had vanquished her when she last left Westwich should swamp her again. But the motion of the car and the exhaustion induced by a week of sleepless nights and emotionally charged days overwhelmed her so completely that by the time they arrived in Oxford she was fast asleep.

For a few days she was treated as an invalid, cosseted and confined to her bed, reeling from the abruptness of her release. And then she began to recover.

She awoke amidst the blue and white draperies of her room at the Mayricks' home in Oxford and let the soft noises of the household sink into her consciousness. Water ran in the pipes. There were hurried footsteps across the hall below and the reassuring clink of cutlery. Beyond was the occasional hum of a motor car in the street.

Ruth stretched and smiled into the blue gloom of the bedroom, contemplating the day ahead. There would be shopping, callers, substantial meals, conversation and more plans. Clara might take her on an exploration of yet another college. Simon's mousy little wife, Daisy, might call round with the children. Or, if she wished, Ruth could lie upstairs here on the bed, dozing and reading.

She felt, as yet, no anxiety about the future and could safely put off any decision until after the sale of The Rush House when the reality of her financial situation would be clear. For the time being she could allow herself to be enfolded in the comfortable embrace of the Mayricks.

After she had bathed and dressed she stood in front of the long mirror by the bedroom door and peered at her reflection. At first she had wished to have her hair cut like Clara's in a dainty bob, but Esther urged her to wait. 'Don't do anything in a hurry. In a few weeks you will know better what you want.' Instead Ruth contrived a new style by brushing her hair gently back from her face and twisting it into loose coils along her collar. Everyone told her that she looked well and she could tell that her cheeks had filled out a little and her brow begun to lose its strain. Her reflected eyes smiled. 'Watch out the world. Here comes the liberated Ruth Styles,' she told herself.

## 2

Three weeks after her arrival the easy rhythm of the Mayrick household was disturbed by the news that the youngest son, Giles, and his new wife had decided to drive down for the weekend.

'Do you remember he came to Westwich after my father died?' Ruth asked Esther. 'That was three years ago. Had he met his wife then? If he had, he made no mention of her.'

They were in the dining room addressing envelopes to members of the local Liberal party. Esther had lost none of her desire to make an impact on the world. She had gained weight but retained her serene countenance and airy manner. She spoke lightly of Giles's marriage but it was clear she had some misgivings about her new daughter-in-law.

'He's known Alicia for years and they were engaged for quite a while. We all told them to wait because they were so young. Giles is such a lunatic he probably didn't think to mention Alicia when he saw you.' She threw down her pen and flexed her fingers. 'Ruth, I must have written about the wedding to

268

you, surely. Alicia's father is very wealthy and a knight, and I'm afraid that we humble Mayricks were quite outclassed all day. Not Giles, of course, he can hold his own in any situation. Alicia is absolutely delightful – a dear little thing. I'm afraid I still think of them both as children but they're certainly not. You know Giles is waiting for a foreign posting, and wherever they're sent they'll have to grow up a little. I worry that Alicia might not quite be strong enough for Giles. She actually dominates him in some ways, but I wonder if there's enough depth. Do you understand? Of course I wouldn't dream of saying this to anyone else. I rather think it was partly due to Alicia that Giles was appointed to his wonderful job at the Foreign Office. It helps to have the right connections. Trust Giles.'

Though Esther hotly denied to the family that she was intimidated by Alicia's background, it was clear that the prospect of the forthcoming visit flustered her considerably. A number of the Mayricks' friends were invited to dine on the Saturday evening, and Esther spent some time arguing with Robert about what outing they should plan for Alicia's entertainment.

'Giles is desperately busy at work you know,' said Robert. 'He'll probably just want a weekend off.'

'But we must take Alicia for a drive. She certainly won't be a bit interested in the shops. What a pity the weather's so dreadful.'

'Look, she'll love nothing so much as a good gossip with you and the girls.' By 'the girls' Robert meant Ruth and Clara. 'And if you're having all those people to dinner you'll be in the kitchen most of the day with Mrs Last. Don't take on too much, Esther.'

Ruth could not help feeling a little put out by the advent of Alicia Mayrick. For the last few weeks she had been the pampered darling of the household but now she too must participate in the preparations for Alicia.

Clara, who had become a self-assured, determined little woman, took one look at the notebook brandished by Esther and locked herself away in her room to study. She was now fluent in Braille and was working her way through every available work of literature. Ruth could not so easily avoid Esther and her list of tasks. As she helped make up the double bed in the guest room with immaculately starched linen sheets, she felt for the first time that she must soon move on from the Mayricks' house. Their concerns, after all, were not hers.

Giles and his wife were so late that the meticulously prepared Saturday lunch had to be kept back two hours. Simon, the oldest son, who was now a doctor like his father, had driven over for the occasion with his family. The children were taken upstairs to the old nursery and fed separately, while the adults sat about hungrily and demanded: 'When will they be here?'

Simon, tall and thin with long, sardonic features, blamed Giles. 'It's typically thoughtless of him. He probably didn't get up until eleven.'

But at last there was a great clamour on the doorbell, followed by the maid's quick step and the sound of voices. In bounded Giles, still wearing his voluminous driving coat. His mother was scooped into a forceful hug.

'Giles!' she exclaimed when he released her. 'What have you done with Alicia?'

'Oh my Lord, I left her in the hall. She was fussing about with her hair.' He darted away and returned clasping the hand of a delicate girl with startlingly clear white skin and a shining cap of dark hair. Alicia smiled at her mother-in-law and lifted her face to be kissed, but her presence imposed an abnormal reserve on the family.

Robert shook her hand much too heartily and offered sherry, which was refused.

'Giles, you haven't said hello to Ruth!' his mother urged reproachfully.

'Of course. Ruth! My God, it's good to see you here. You're looking wonderful.'

Her hand was taken in his warm clasp and she smiled up into his blue eyes.

'Well, that's a little more complimentary than last time,' she told him. 'You said then how old I looked.'

'Yes, well, you're still ancient, but you're wearing your years better now. Come and meet Alicia. Ali, I told you about Ruth. Here she is. My childhood idol.'

Alicia placed her tapering fingers in Ruth's for a moment, then retreated to a chair by the fire and responded to Esther's enquiries about her journey.

At lunch the presence of Alicia became less intimidating to the Mayricks, who reverted to their usual verbal skirmishes. Of the women, only Esther participated. The two daughters-in-law seemed ill at ease amidst the teasing Mayrick clan, though Simon's wife smiled shyly and giggled occasionally. Alicia gave her attention at first to Clara, and was heard to exclaim in amazement that she should wish to become a student at the university. Meanwhile Ruth, from her corner between Robert and Clara, watched them all with affectionate interest.

Giles dominated the conversation, cutting mercilessly into his brother's arguments, poking fun at his sister and teasing the maid who went pink to her ears. Occasionally his wife would lean across the table and touch his arm, murmuring something which caused him to quieten and attend solely to her. But then the familiar surroundings and faces became too much for his self-control and he would once again relapse into his old boyish behaviour.

Esther need not have worried about how to amuse Alicia because after lunch the new daughter-in-law announced that she had a headache and would lie down. When Giles escorted his wife upstairs, Esther breathed a sigh of relief and escaped to the kitchen.

Ruth spent the afternoon in the nursery with Daisy and the children. She had discovered that beneath her unprepossessing exterior, Daisy had an endearing sense of the ridiculous. 'At lunch,' confided Daisy, 'I suddenly thought: Thank God Alicia can't see my underwear. I mean, I can just imagine her in gorgeous white silk and lace, can't you? Mine's clean but that's all that can be said for it!'

Simon bounded up after a while to announce that he and

Giles were off to visit a friend on the other side of the city. Neither was seen again until half an hour before dinner.

That evening Ruth dressed to impress. She was aware that she would be an object of curiosity among the Mayricks' friends, who could not be ignorant of her peculiar history. If they expect to find a half-mad country bumpkin I hope they will be disappointed, she thought, gazing rather fearfully at her reflection.

Esther had insisted on treating Ruth to a new gown. 'Something really frivolous, for best. My poor love, you've not had much occasion for party dresses, have you?' They had chosen a dark green silk frock in which Ruth felt painfully exposed. 'My shoulders are so bony!' she cried. Both Esther and the shop assistant insisted that the dress was perfect.

Ruth rotated slowly before the glass. The flesh of her arms and neck shone very white, and her hands seemed coarse and brown by comparison. When she leaned forward the scooped neck-line exposed the top of her breasts, and the skirt came to just below her knee, revealing strong calves. Deliberately she wore no jewellery, aware that her best feature was her neck with its heavy coil of hair at the nape.

But when she went down to the drawing room she lost all sense of pleasure in her appearance. Clara was there, neat and dainty in deep red. She peered approvingly at Ruth and told her the green frock was splendid, but Clara was so tiny and young that beside her Ruth felt gawky and overgrown.

And then came the other women, scented and bejewelled, and the last remnants of Ruth's self-assurance evaporated. She wished fervently that she could return to her room and find a covering for her bare arms and neck.

The room seemed to be filled suddenly with a great many people who knew each other very well. They clustered about Alicia, who was wearing pearly white and who seemed much more at home in this large, mixed gathering than with the Mayricks earlier in the day. Her low chuckle could be heard frequently.

Clara was Ruth's saviour that evening. She seemed to consider her an expert on literature and history, and embarked on a long discussion on the relative merits of various writers. She was entertaining in her assessment of the academics at the university whom she had approached with a view to future admission. 'They do their best,' she told Ruth, 'but you can tell they think poor sight is inextricably linked with a stupid mind.'

'You make me feel very aimless,' Ruth said. 'I wish I knew for sure what I wanted to do.'

At dinner she sat beside one of Robert's medical friends who insisted on discussing various resorts in Suffolk he and his wife had visited. Ruth said repeatedly that in fact she knew very little of the coast beyond Westwich, and looked longingly down the table to where Giles was engaged in an animated conversation with one of his mother's old friends. Of course, she thought ruefully, nobody knows what to talk to me about. I've had no experience, been nowhere, met no one.

It was two in the morning by the time the last guest departed. Alicia and Clara went straight to bed, but Ruth lingered with the rest of the family who were exchanging snippets of news and laughing at what had been said at dinner. Esther wandered about, yawning and making a desultory attempt to restore the furniture to its usual position.

There was soon a general move towards the stairs but Giles caught Ruth by the hand. 'Stay up and have a chat with me, Ruth-o. I haven't spoken to you all evening.'

Esther turned at the door. 'Giles is incorrigible, Ruth. He would rather sit up all night and sleep all morning. Don't let him keep you too long.'

They sat in the dimly lit room, he sprawled on his mother's sofa, one long leg hooked over the arm, she in the armchair by the fire. The lateness of the hour and unaccustomed consumption of several glasses of wine made Ruth light-headed, but she had never felt more awake.

'So have you forgiven me yet for my appalling rudeness that day?' he asked, watching her affectionately.

'I shall never forgive you, Giles. How could I? I have never been so insulted in my life.' Unconsciously she stroked the neckline of her dress with her index finger.

He laughed. 'I bet your brother said worse to you many a time. You just don't remember.'

'You're right. Though Harry was so lazy even his insults emerged slowly.'

'God.' He swung forward and leaned towards the fire. In the red light cast by the embers, his skin glowed bronze, his eyes were shadowed. 'It's a pity you and I weren't in touch during the war. We could have helped each other when we both lost a brother. Do you remember Mark? He was always examining insects. He had hundreds of collections, all carefully indexed and arranged; stones, shells, leaves, the lot. Anything to do with nature. He was very patient with me, taught me such a lot. When he was killed I was heartbroken. I could not get over the thought of him and all he knew wiped away.'

'I know. I know. I don't think I can ever fully realize that about Harry. It's all right having one's parents die first. But not a brother.' She did not care to contemplate for long the day on which Donaldson had brought her news of Harry's death. 'Tell me about the war, Giles, no one ever speaks of it. I would like to know how it was.'

'No. We don't speak of it. It was unspeakable. I guess I was lucky, going in right at the very end. I didn't see so much. But you bury the memories, Ruth. You don't dare look at them.'

'I'm sorry. I'm sorry to have upset you.'

She touched his hand. He clasped her fingers and did not release them but began to play with them, as if absent-mindedly, stroking her thumb and gently flexing the joints. 'I keep thinking I've got over it. You know what I'm like. Good old Giles. Well that is me most of the time. And then when I remember what I did and saw, I think how can I ever laugh again? I haven't talked about this for years. It's the effect of seeing you that's done it. I can't hide from you. I always used to feel you understood me. When I was a boy you made me feel safe. As if only you knew how I frightened myself sometimes because I laughed so much and had such energy and was so wild.'

Ruth could scarcely breathe, though she sat outwardly quite calm with her hand in his.

'My goodness,' she said, and her voice sounded low, controlled, dry. 'I had no idea I had any influence on a living soul. Let alone you, you madcap.'

'You must realize what an impression a beautiful young girl, who also happens to be the most enormous fun, can have on a young lad.'

She withdrew her hand and put it to the coil of hair at her neck, looking away from him into the fire. 'I must have been a great disappointment to you, Giles, when I became so timid, confined to Westwich.'

'We understood. Of course we did.'

There was silence. She was afraid lest she might break their intimacy by some ill-judged word. 'What now, Giles?' she asked. 'I hear you have made a brilliant impression on the Foreign Office.'

At once he jolted upright and grinned at her with pretended arrogance. 'Of course. I have the world at my feet. No. They need young, energetic pups like me. The trouble is, I could end up anywhere on earth. I'm expecting my first foreign posting in the spring. Alicia's poised to kit herself out either in Eskimo furs or jungle wear. Do you like Alicia?'

'Goodness, I've hardly spoken to her. But yes, she looks lovely.'

'She is. Yes.'

Another silence.

'I wonder where I shall be in a year's time?' Ruth said softly.

'The world's your oyster too, Ruth-o.'

'It's harder for a woman. On my own. I think I must study. Clara makes me feel ashamed. She's so determined.'

'Oh, Clara. She's a frantic blue-stocking. But she's got plenty of determination, I'll give her that.'

The clock chimed 3 a.m. Giles yawned hugely. 'Come on, little owl. Bed-time. Alicia wants to be away by ten tomorrow. She's got a tea party in town, God help us.' He put out a hand and hauled Ruth to her feet.

At the bottom of the stairs he touched her upper arm and kissed her cheek, near her left ear. 'Good night, dear old lady.

Sleep tight. And listen, if you want to come up to town give me a call and I'll buy you lunch.'

She ran up the stairs ahead of him. Inside the door of her room she turned to gaze unseeingly at the face in the mirror with its pale cheeks and glittering eyes.

3

That dinner party put an end to her peace of mind. She told herself that she had been too much under the shadow of the Mayricks and that her attendance at dinner, amidst their friends and family, had served to underline that she had no real place in the house and must find a life of her own. And if she stayed in Oxford, she argued, she would be for ever in their shadow. She was aware that Esther was ever watchful, afraid that she might show signs of her former reclusiveness and inability to face a world beyond Westwich. In order to find true independence, Ruth now thought that she must break free of all her old connections.

London was the place. She would take a room, perhaps in familiar territory, near Primrose Hill. Once installed, she would study the prospectuses of the London colleges or find work. She expected The Rush House to be sold by Christmas. Money from the sale would enable her to afford a low rent, and college fees.

With these plans in mind, she told Esther that she intended to take the train to London for a day's sightseeing. In order to avoid awkward questions she made no mention of more ambitious plans.

Esther was instantly concerned. 'Let me come with you. You'll find London terribly changed. It's ten times as noisy as Oxford, and quite intimidating. Don't go alone. Or take Clara. She'd love that.'

'No. No. I'd rather be alone. I must begin sometime, Esther.'

'Well, let me telephone Giles, then, and see if he's free to give you lunch. I think Alicia is with her parents at present so he might be glad of the company.'

At first Ruth expressed reluctance to put Giles to so much trouble but Esther insisted. 'He's not so important that he can't afford an hour or two away from the office.'

In the train, on her first journey alone since before the war, Ruth sat at the window with her hands clasped in her lap, as if afraid to move. She felt as tiny as a mote of dust blown from one destination to another. And at the same time she was aware of an immense excitement. She told herself that she was glad simply to be going to the capital. And it would be lovely to see Giles again. He was so friendly and amusing, and would be going far away very soon. Perhaps he would help her by suggesting a possible career or course of study.

But as the journey progressed, so her confidence ebbed. Perhaps Giles would be terribly bored at having to meet her again so soon. He had probably only agreed to lunch with her because Esther had begged him to make the effort. To him, after all, Ruth was just a friend of his parents to whom he must be polite and tolerant.

He had agreed to meet her at twelve-thirty near Westminster Bridge. All morning Ruth walked, being too impatient and over-wrought to enter a church or monument. She marched from Primrose Hill to Regent's Park, her stride as determined and rapid as when she had covered miles each day along the beaches and paths surrounding Westwich. The bustle of Regent Street and Trafalgar Square confused and exhausted her, however. Her feet were unaccustomed to walking so far on paving stones.

With immense relief she reached the relative openness of the Embankment. London was in the grip of a hard frost but sunlight glinted on the river and gilded the ornate stone-work of Westminster. She was suddenly overwhelmed by the memory of an afternoon on the Thames with her father and brother. Hadn't they taken a boat from Greenwich to this very bridge? The reawakening of her own girlish excitement and her father clasping little Harry by the hand was so powerful that she peered into the glimmering water as if expecting at any moment to see them emerge beneath her.

Giles was five minutes early. She stepped back in affected awe at sight of his dark City suit and hat. 'My goodness, you do look different in that get-up!'

'I could say the same for you. What a hat!'

She smiled from under its low brim. 'This was considered to be the most daring hat ever to hit Westwich when I ordered it two years ago.'

'It would be more at home on a teapot.'

'Thank you, Giles.'

He blotted out the river, the elaborate sky-line and the teeming city. They were quite alone. She could not tear her gaze away from his bright eyes and what she read in them. He said nothing but took her hand and drew her arm through his.

'Where are we going?' she asked.

'I know a place. It's quite a walk. Are you up to it?'

She did not tell him she had walked all morning.

'I don't suppose you've got very long,' she said.

'An hour. I have an hour.'

'Your parents send their love. And Clara.'

'How are they? I hope poor Mother didn't wear herself out with all that entertaining at the weekend.'

Ruth could breathe a little more easily. Giles was family after all. Just a boy. This talk of Esther and Robert made all safe.

They came to a dark little restaurant where Giles was obviously well known. He greeted a waiter and one or two friends, and for a moment Ruth was afraid that they would not eat alone. But they were led to a table so small that his knee touched hers.

She was handed a menu. 'It's no use pretending,' she said. 'I won't be able to eat. I'm not hungry.'

'Of course you must eat.'

'I can't. I'm sorry. I feel a little unwell. I had a huge breakfast. I'm not used to all this gadding about.' Although an hour ago she had been hollow with hunger, now she felt unable to swallow a mouthful.

'Well, you can't sit and watch me.'

'Yes, I can.'

'Mother will never forgive me if she finds out you've eaten nothing.'

'Then don't tell her.'

'You need fattening up, Ruth-o.'

'Now don't start on my appearance again. I know. I'm a scraggy old thing. You've told me.'

'You are. That sums you up. Well, I'll order for you.'

Ruth resented the waiter and the time Giles spent talking to him. And when a colleague of Giles' approached the table she could scarcely hide her dismay. The stranger seemed likely to spend the entire lunch-hour hovering above Giles and discussing business to do with the Far East. Giles introduced Ruth as 'an old friend of my parents'.

'Well, thank you Giles, for your repeated use of the word "old",' she said, when the man had at last gone.

'It's worth repeating, your reaction is so predictably delicious.'

He ate his own lunch and most of hers at a great rate, pausing in between mouthfuls to inform her that he and Alicia would be leaving for India in March. 'It's a brilliant posting,' he said. 'Really brilliant. Quite a plum. Alicia is absolutely thrilled.'

'And shall you be able to return to England often?'

'I don't know. Every couple of years. I hope perhaps to persuade Pa and Ma to come out to me. It's time they saw a bit of the world.'

'It seems an awfully long way away.'

'The world is shrinking, Ruth-o. You'll have to emerge from your little cocoon and find that out.'

She sat with her wine glass cupped in her hand, watching the dark liquid swill from side to side. Giles threw down his napkin and pushed back his chair, watching her with eyes as blue and promising as a summer sky. 'What happened to you Ruth-o? You disappeared. Why did you shut yourself away? Tell me. Why can't you be free?'

'I don't think you could understand. I can't. It was partly my mother. I felt I had to protect her. She was not just ordinarily ill. I had loved her so much you see, when I was a little girl. She was bright and funny and then it all went out like a candle. I wanted to bring it back. I thought I could save her. She was so haunted. And I came to London but it didn't work. I don't know.'

He leaned towards her. 'You're like an enchanted princess, all locked up. You're like snow that hasn't been walked on. My God.' The expression in his eyes intensified as he gazed at her, mouth, hair, neck and breast. Then, pushing back his chair abruptly, he beckoned to the waiter. 'I have to go, Ruth-o. I'm sorry. I hadn't noticed the time.'

'Shall I walk back with you to your office?'

'No. No, I must dash. Listen, can you find your way all right? I'll be off then. Goodbye, Ruth-o. Take care.'

His departure was so sudden that he left Ruth bewildered and frightened. What had she said? How had she failed?

She was so confused that she stood for half an hour by the river, shivering and reliving every word he had spoken, every gesture he had made. Then she began walking again, in any direction, until she at last consulted her map and began the long trek back to the station.

On the train she sat bolt upright all the way to Oxford where she was met by Esther Mayrick who took one look at her rigid posture and white face and exclaimed: 'I knew I shouldn't have let you go alone.'

4

By Christmas The Rush House was sold and Ruth was an independent woman. She insisted that she would stay with Esther only until after the festival, when she would move to a boarding house in town. Her mind was made up, she said. She had relied for too long on the Mayricks' kindness.

Giles and Alicia came on Christmas Eve. They were to spend the next day with Alicia's parents. Ruth overheard Esther say to Robert with unaccustomed malice that it would not do to interfere with the wishes of the cherished daughter of a knight. 'Of course, I said nothing to Giles,' she added, 'but I thought as they had spent Christmas for the last two years with them, it must be our turn now.'

For Ruth those last days at the Mayricks were electrically charged. She floated from hour to hour, only half present, in a dream-like state, waiting. She had packed her bags.

She helped in the house and was unfailingly cheerful. 'How shall we manage without you?' Esther exclaimed again and again. Giles's imminent departure for India weighed heavily on her mind. 'The family will be so fragmented. First Mark. Now Giles. This is what comes of having sons.' And Clara was completely impractical and no help at all with the baking and the decorations. 'If she had been a normal girl I could have had a companion in her,' Esther confided in Ruth.

'But surely,' Ruth said, 'you of all people must be glad to see Clara so determined and clever.'

'Oh, of course. But other girls manage to study and be beautiful and want to marry. Clara will never marry, will she?'

On another occasion Esther reminded Ruth of that Christmas long ago when she had been so miserably homesick for Westwich. Ruth said, 'It is as if then I lived in a dense fog. I was conscious of a thick cord that tugged at my heart like a physical pain and drew me back to the sea and my mother. Nothing else made sense to me. But now I see clearly. I am fully alive.'

Each time the phone rang her heart beat faster. She was terrified lest Giles might not be coming. I shan't see him again after this, she told herself by way of excuse. He will be in India. I must say goodbye.

But at one o'clock on Christmas Eve they arrived, filling the elaborately decorated hall with parcels and Alicia's fragrance. Ruth waited on the landing until the family had greeted one another. Even from that height she knew he was waiting for her, seeking her out. When she went slowly down she sensed that he was conscious of her presence though his back was turned. He seemed to stiffen.

He sprang to her side. 'Ruth-o. Happy Christmas.'

By the time lunch was over it was almost dark. The day had

been dank and surprisingly mild, completely unseasonal, Esther said crossly. Traditionally the Mayricks kept open house in the afternoon and every few minutes the doorbell rang. Ruth sat by the window in the drawing room, sometimes pressing her hot forehead to the cool glass, sometimes smiling vaguely across the room or talking quietly to anyone who approached. She was only aware of Giles, who was boisterous and over-loud in his conversation. She knew that he was to leave after tea. Two hours passed. Still he did not come near her.

At last she made a quick excuse, left the room and hurried upstairs. In her room she paced back and forth, pausing at the mirror and the window. She even took up a book, telling herself that nobody would miss her and she would do better to spend her time in useful study.

But after a few minutes she tiptoed down again. She could not be far from him, even though to watch him at a distance was so painful.

The doors of the downstairs rooms stood open. In the dining room the table had already been laid for dinner. Silver and glassware glinted in the light cast by the lamps in the hall. Ruth wandered along the row of chairs, touching a napkin here, a fork there, and then lingered at the window to stare out over the dark, wet garden. She could just make out the shapes of shrubs and trees.

For the first time she wished passionately that she was back in Westwich where it had been familiar and safe. On Christmas Eve she had always eaten a cosy tea at Maud's cottage and then returned to The Rush House to drink a glass of wine in Julia's room.

'Ruth.' He came into the room and closed the door behind him. 'Ruth.'

She did not attempt to speak or hold back the tears.

'Ruth.' He was at her side. With warm, sure fingers he raised her chin and turned her face towards the garden so that he might see her more clearly in the pale reflection thrown across the lawn by the light on the landing above.

She jolted her face away.

'I could not be in that room any longer without you,' he said. 'All those mouths opening and closing. That senseless conversation. Why did you go away? Answer me, Ruth. Are you homesick again? What is it?'

She could not speak.

'Were you thinking of your home? Your mother? What was it?'

'Yes. I was thinking of The Rush House.'

His voice lost its edge of urgent eagerness. When he spoke again he sounded distant. 'You must find us very overwhelming as a family. Perhaps insensitive.'

'You have all been kindness itself.' But she could not keep the bitterness from her voice, nor the harshness of restrained tears.

'Mother tells me you are moving away. You must let me know where you will be living.'

Again she was silent.

'Will you, Ruth?'

'No. No, I won't do that, Giles.'

'You're afraid, aren't you? Is that it? Are you disappearing again? Do you know what I think? That you will retreat to your little house by the sea.'

'I can never do that. It has been sold. I am a woman of means now. Quite independent. I can go where I like, do what I like. I could travel to India if I wished.'

'Ruth.'

'Giles, please understand that I have a desire for self-preservation.' The doorbell rang in the hall. Ruth gave a great, shuddering intake of breath. 'They'll be missing you, Giles.'

He placed both hands on her head and pressed her face to his chest. She felt the heat of his breath in her hair. 'You used to be so beautiful. Light and carefree, and full of laughter. Like a bird. Like the sea, I always thought. I associated you with the sea. And then the light went out in you and I found this old woman. But the other girl is still there, waiting to break out. Ruth. I have thought about you night and day, every minute of every hour since we last met. I have never felt for anyone as I have felt for you these past days.'

She shook from head to toe, her body quivering as it struck against his. He released her head and took her in his arms. 'Ruth.' He was kissing her wildly, her hair, cheek, neck and eyelids. She raised her face as if she were parched with thirst and his kisses falling on her skin and lips were clear-running water.

There was a fumbling at the door handle. They sprang apart in the sudden blaze of light from the hall.

'Ruth! I've been looking for you everywhere. Oh. He found you then. I'm so sorry to disturb you. I've told Mother there'll be an extra for dinner.' Hurriedly Clara moved away and Ruth stumbled after her as far as the drawing room door. But there she halted. She had noticed a figure lurking in the little recess by the front door.

'Donaldson.'

He looked pale and chilled. She stared at him for a moment, unable to compose her thoughts. 'Donaldson.' And then she ran forward and reached out her hand. 'Let me take your coat.'

Tea was brought to the drawing room. Donaldson sat on the sofa, the pet of Esther Mayrick and her friends, for his reputation as a photographer was known to many. He was quite at ease in this social setting and replied to their questions with polite nods and modest jokes. Ruth, seated at a distance, watched him with dispassionate eyes and thought how strange it was to see his familiar figure so formally dressed and seated with such dignity in Esther Mayrick's elegant drawing room, his long, artistic fingers holding a delicate cup, his singular features, topped by their extraordinarily vigorous crop of hair, inclined towards Mrs Mayrick. Though he never glanced in Ruth's direction, she read him like a book. His outer composure could not conceal from her his anguish at her appearance as she had come to him from the dining room. Donaldson had missed nothing.

Giles stood by the door. Ruth knew that he willed her to look at him, but she would not.

As soon as tea was over Alicia began her dainty farewells. She was charming to Donaldson and begged him to call next time he was in town. While Giles was bidding his family goodbye Ruth hung back. But she caught his eye as he cast one long searching look in her direction. Her flesh was burning.

Afterwards Donaldson tried to strike up a conversation but her false brightness must have been too wounding because after a while he moved away. But at dinner she was placed beside him. She had begun to recover a little from the scene with Giles, though she glanced often to where they had stood, and the sensation of his kisses flamed through her again. But she was able to be kinder to Donaldson and even expressed pleasure in seeing him. He told her that he was spending Christmas with his brother in Enfield, but had wanted to reassure himself that Ruth was well.

'Goodness,' she said laughing. 'I always forget you have family. I tend to think of you simply emerging in Westwich.'

'Esther tells me you are moving away after Christmas.' He watched the movement of her glass from the table to her lips.

'Yes. Yes. At last I feel grown up enough to manage alone.'

'Don't forget to let us know where you'll be.' She smiled at him blithely, and her eyes told him quite clearly that she had no intention of disclosing her whereabouts to him. 'Well then, please be careful, Ruth.'

5

She took a room in a boarding house in Fulham. For a week she went through the motions of establishing her future. She consulted one or two agencies and was told that she might be eligible for work as a clerk or a governess, although such posts these days required some training. And she approached the University of London for prospectuses. But most of the time was spent walking.

She held out for six days of solitude and then she addressed a note to Giles at his work, giving no name or message, simply her address. There could be no harm in this, she argued, the sending of an address could hardly be construed as an invitation. It was up to him now. If he, as an old friend, wished to look her up, then so be it.

At five past six the next evening she heard the doorbell ring downstairs. Her landlady trod slowly up the long, narrow flight of stairs to her room. 'There's a gentleman to see you, Miss Styles.' Mrs Peters had a florid complexion and spoke in a high-pitched, over-loud voice, but she was well meaning and not too inquisitive. 'There's no one in the drawing room, if you want a private word.'

The high ceiling lamp in the vestibule burnished his hair a rich, dark gold. He had obviously charmed Mrs Peters who lingered beside him as Ruth walked down, commenting on the freezing fog outside and asking tenderly if he had come far.

Ruth shook his hand and led him into the drawing room where a feeble fire burned and the ill-assorted furniture was cluttered with cheap ornaments. She stood by the hearth and he, decorously, folded his long body into a distant chair.

'Whatever are you doing in this delectable abode, Miss Styles?' he enquired.

He was the fraternal Giles, teasing her. She responded in kind. 'These are very respectable lodgings I'll have you know, Mr Mayrick.'

'Oh, we will soon sort that out.'

She could not help smiling at him though the lift of her chin was a little defiant as she told him of her recent activities. The expression in her eyes tried to warn him that she would not be overturned by him again.

They carried on the charade of friendly, disinterested conversation for a couple of minutes, either in deference to their own sense of decency or to Mrs Peters, for the door had been left ajar. Then he got up, crossed the room to her side and said, 'We mustn't pretend any longer, must we? I want to be honest with you, Ruth.'

To steady herself she put her hand on the cast iron of the mantel.

'There is no escape. I thought I understood what it meant to desire someone. I was a child then. I can scarcely breathe I long for you so much. Ruth.'

She put her finger to his lips, as if to quieten him. He closed

286

his eyes and was quite still as she stroked his mouth, her finger-tip as fearful and tentative as a butterfly.

At last she dropped her hand to her side. A tear glistened on his eyelash. 'I know where we can go, Ruth-o. To be away from everyone. We can't escape who and what we are. But will you come with me? Next weekend. I love you. I love you.'

Ruth's mouth slackened.

'Please. Please.'

She half shook her head. 'How can I? Oh God, what are we doing?'

'Don't let me down, Ruth. I'll come for you on Friday at five-thirty. I trust you to be here.' He kissed her forehead and then her mouth. Her lips parted but he had already moved away. She heard the front door slam.

6

It was the longest week of her life. Every minute of every hour she conducted the same internal argument, which had in fact been won even as he kissed her. You must go back to Oxford, she told herself, or you must return to Maud at Westwich, or travel abroad and spend some of your money. Get away. Move out of danger. But a fiercer, more compelling voice, above all a voice to which her whole being wished to attend, argued that for as long as she could remember she had been lonely and unhappy. Never before had she been in love. Giles was married. His parents were dear and loyal friends. But she could not help any of that. This was her only chance.

And then for many hours she would repeat the fiction to herself that of course it was quite inconceivable either that he would actually come for her on Friday or that she would go with him.

She told a surprised Mrs Peters that she would be leaving for good and packed her bags. All Friday she sat in the stark, clean little room and waited.

Giles was very prompt. Once more he waited for her under

the light in the hall, his face unusually strained. Though her legs were shaking Ruth spoke to him quite calmly. 'There's a great deal to be packed away in the motor. I hope you've space. I have given in my notice here.'

He asked no questions as he stowed her cases and few boxes in the boot. Mrs Peters stood on the step and watched them go, torn between anger at Ruth's brief stay in the house and a vicarious excitement. The tension between them had been almost tangible.

Ruth did not know where he was taking her at first. She was conscious only that their time was restricted to one weekend so was determined to waste none of it on questions, forebodings or regrets. She watched his face, with its faultless, clear-cut profile, as he negotiated the London traffic. Aware of her gaze, he took his left hand from the wheel and gently touched her thigh.

'What have you told Alicia?' she asked.

'She is spending the weekend with friends in Dorset. We go away most weekends. I told her I had too much on my mind to go with her. Which is the truth.'

Ruth pressed her shoulders into the leather seat and closed her eyes. She had scarcely slept since his last visit.

'I was afraid you would not come with me. All week I've been terrified that today you would be gone,' he said.

'You do not know me, then, or you would have some idea of the strength of my feelings. I could not give you up.'

Suddenly, violently, he swung the motor towards the kerb. It jerked to a halt, though the engine was running.

He twisted his cramped frame so that he might see her face. 'What do you feel for me, Ruth? You've not said one word. I need one word.'

'I sent you my address, Giles. I am here. Isn't that enough?'

He leaned forward to kiss her mouth. His fingertip stroked her breast. 'Tell me you love me. Say it, Ruth.'

'I would die for you.'

He drove to Overstrands and they were within a couple of miles of the house before she realized where she was. Then she sat bolt upright and cried, 'Giles! Where are we going? What are you doing?'

'I have the key to Clara's house. It's empty.'

'We can't go there. Giles, for goodness sake. It's the very last place I would ever want to go. People will see us.'

'No, they won't. The house is isolated. We'll be quite safe. And if anyone comes you can hide and I'll say I needed a quiet retreat.'

She was furious with him. 'But can't you understand? I spent most of my life in Westwich. It's taken me all these years to get away and now you have brought me back. How could you, Giles?'

'It's so perfect. The perfect place, Ruth. We met there. I remember you at Overstrands. It's perfect.'

'No. No. Please. Not there.'

But he laughed at her and seemed unable to understand the urgency of her wish not to be at Overstrands. The wheels of the motor car scrunched on gravel as he drove to the rear of the house and switched off the engine. At once the complete silence of the wintry countryside closed about them. He withdrew a key from the flat pocket of his waistcoat and she watched him fumble with the latch of the door leading to the scullery, and then tread softly back to where she still sat, tense in every muscle. 'Come on, silly girl. You'll be frozen out here. Come in and I'll make you warm.'

'Take me somewhere else,' she pleaded.

'Foolish old lady. I'm not wasting another minute in this car. Listen. Nobody will find us out, if that's what you're afraid of. We're totally safe. And there is nowhere else we can be so alone.'

She pushed him aside and hurried through icy, salt darkness into the house. At once she was struck by the intense chill of the unheated, uninhabited rooms. Giles was unloading bags from the back of his motor but she would not help him. Instead she stood rigidly by the table in the kitchen, her heart beating wildly, her hand pressed for reassurance on its worn surface. If I run, she told herself, I could be across the fields and in Maud's cottage in no time.

What a fool she had been to trust herself to Giles, who had

always been wild and audacious. How like him to bring her to within a mile of the one place in the world where she was known.

But then she heard him lock the door behind her and move along the passage. He was by her side. The kitchen was so cold that she could feel a throb of warmth from the proximity of his body.

His breath was hot and moist in her ear. 'Don't be angry with me, Ruth. Forgive me.'

He took her gloved hand, pressed it to his lips and began to undo the three little buttons at her wrist, kissing the skin as it became exposed. The glove was peeled slowly away and tiny, ardent kisses dropped along her palm. Her cold hand was cradled against his warm throat. She could feel a strong pulse beating and the roughness of his skin.

'You're so cold, ice maiden, so cold,' he murmured, wrapping her in his heavy overcoat and enveloping her in his broad embrace. She did not resist when he urged her along the corridor and up the wide, shallow stairs to a room at the back of the first floor.

For two days they camped beneath piles of blankets. In the morning a pale grey light appeared in the uncurtained window, revealing faded trellis wallpaper and cumbersome furniture. Ruth lay in her warm nest while Giles waited on her, bringing her sandwiches and fruit. When he returned to her side his feet were icy. She was on an enchanted island, she thought, in the midst of a silent, wintry ocean. She hardly dared peep out of the window for fear of being seen, but when she did she saw the wide, flat landscape she knew so well. She never ventured to a room at the front, knowing that from a window there she would see a grey line on the horizon, the sea, and closer still, the squat tower of Westwich Church and the sturdy roofs and chimney pots of the village.

Now I am walled up in the house I used to regard as a symbol of the free, she thought. And nobody but Giles knows I am here.

She began to speak at last of the nights she had spent

pursuing her mother through the dark rooms of The Rush House, sharing her dread of the storms. Giles listened quietly, lying on his back, his arms behind his head. She was not surprised or even hurt when she realized that he had fallen asleep. He was a boy. His glorious, young body was stretched before her and his tranquil, slumbering features were unmarked by pain or age. She had confided in him because she understood his ability to blot out the unpleasant or the incomprehensible.

In turn he talked of his marriage. Ruth noted with fleeting amusement that in his wife's absence Giles could be quite dispassionate about Alicia. 'She's terribly young and pretty but a bit shallow. Don't you think? She's the kind of girl everyone thinks I ought to be attracted to. And I am. They don't realize I have this other side to me. A deeper side, which loves a woman with a wonderful abundance of silk-like hair, and a trembling, untouched body that I have discovered and brought to life.'

He began to make love to her again, pouring endearments into her ear, calling her his wanton, his darling, his adored one. Day merged into evening, and evening into night.

At lunch-time on Sunday they dressed. Ruth folded blankets and tidied the bed. Downstairs in a cupboard she found a broom and a cloth and with these she erased from the room even invisible signs that they had slept there. Meanwhile Giles packed away the sheets and the remains of the food he had brought with him.

The magic was gone and they passed each other on the stairs with intent, preoccupied expressions, as if too busy to smile. Then he escorted her from the house and into the biting wind, stowed her away safely in the front seat of the motor car and returned to lock the door with painstaking deliberation. She sank low as the gravel of the drive spat under the wheels and they turned out of the gates. She did not look back at Overstrands.

She spent the long drive back to town in a kind of drowsy state that forbade conversation. And Giles was not disposed to speak much. His face wore a frown of concentration, as if he were pondering a problem quite unrelated to his present circumstances.

'Where shall I take you?' he asked at last.

'I don't know.' Until this moment she had assumed that he would have arranged her future, as he had organized her weekend.

'By the way, why did you leave the other place? It seemed all right, as these things go.'

'Oh, you know, a whim.' She did not tell him that the prospect of returning to that room had been unbearable. Quite clinically she had thought ahead and understood the desolation of waking in the same room, after her weekend with Giles, as if nothing had changed.

His voice was brusque. 'There's a hotel for women where Clara sometimes stays. Perhaps you could go there.'

The words 'a hotel for women' and the pronoun 'you' brought home to her at last that they were to separate.

'And you will go back to Alicia?'

'Of course. You knew that.'

'Yes. I knew that.'

He touched her thigh, as he had on the journey out, but this time the gesture was of empty reassurance. 'Trust me, Ruth-o. It will be all right. Nobody will know.'

She kept her voice very quiet, her expression casual. 'When will I see you again?'

'Soon, of course. Very soon. We'll find a way of meeting.'

They came to the entrance of a shabbily respectable hotel. Giles deposited her possessions and kissed her cheek. After he had gone she was escorted to a quiet, austere room which seemed instantly dwarfed by her pile of boxes and cases, and by the profundity of her despair.

7

For two weeks she waited for him. When she thought she must have made herself conspicuous by remaining too long in her room she tucked a book under her arm and went down to the muffled lounge, where she sat hour after hour, grateful for a cheerful fire. While in her bedroom she stayed very still, her hands and feet numb, watching her face in the small mirror on the chest of drawers. It seemed to her the face of a stranger with its eyes deep-set smudges, its mouth a tense line.

What are you waiting for, Ruth-o? she asked herself, over and over again.

I am waiting for Giles.

You know that he has another life. He will be preparing for India.

No. He won't go to India. He won't leave me. He will be tying up his affairs. And then he will come to me.

You know him, Ruth-o. He made you no promises. When he does come, if he does come, he will bring you no hope.

He will come.

And what will you do after the meeting?

I'll wait and see.

Ruth. You must begin planning now. Have you no pride? You must prepare yourself for what he will undoubtedly have to say to you. Be ready.

I have no future beyond him. I have given him everything.

You know that is nonsense. You have money, you have your independence.

I have given it all away. I have chained myself body and soul to this man, as once I was chained to my mother.

But this time you can break free.

No. I see now. It is not in my nature to be free again.

Then find someone who wants you.

It is too late.

On the Tuesday after a fortnight had gone by he came into the lounge at five o'clock and took her to tea in the dining room. She had watched for him so long in her imagination that she scarcely recognized the real Giles in his heavy coat and with his hair dusted by a slight fall of snow. His cheeks were ruddy with cold.

He laughed as he shook out his coat and watched her pour tea from the genteel pot. 'So Ruth-o, how have you survived in this nunnery? What have you been up to?'

'I have been waiting for you.'

'That's very flattering. I hope you told nobody about what we'd done. Most of the women I see here would fall into palpitations at the very thought.'

'I dare say.'

'Well, we have been thrown into a terrible fluster. Would you believe they've brought our departure date to the end of February? Four weeks away. You can imagine the state Alicia's in. And my mother. They keep talking about you, by the way, wondering where you are. Do you want me to let them know?'

'Certainly not.'

'Very well.' He leaned forward and clasped her hands. His own were much warmer now. 'Listen, I'm sorry, Ruth, it means I shall be even more pressed for time.'

'I hope you will be able to see me.'

'Of course, though when, I'm not sure.'

'Have you thought about that weekend? Have you missed me?'

'God. Of course. Of course. But we both knew the score, didn't we? That's what I tell myself. I say to myself, Giles, it's given to us only once in a life-time to love like that, and we made the best of it we could.'

'I have thought of nothing else.'

The absoluteness of her misery at last touched him. His hold on her hands tightened. 'Ruth-o. Don't look like that. I can't bear to see you so strained. Try and do as I do. We must move on. Don't you see? We always knew it would be like this but we dared to take the chance. We must never regret it. And now we must look ahead.'

She loathed her own self-pity. 'You have a future, change, a new country, for heaven's sake. It is easy for you to put what has happened behind you. But I have returned to the same solitude so a longing for you fills every thought.'

He withdrew his hands. 'It's no use talking like that, Ruth-o. You're strong. You have money. Come on now, this isn't a bit like you. Where's the spirit? When I think of how you were ...' He leaned back in his chair and smiled. 'We were reckless, weren't we? Love. Oh God, Ruth-o, did you suffer too those first days afterwards? I woke every morning and longed for you. It was almost like the days after we got the telegram that Mark had been killed. That same sense of bewilderment, knowing that you were torn away from me.'

'Yes, yes, I know.'

'But after a few days, with Alicia fussing about, thinking I was dying or something, I pulled myself together. In the office they think I've been metamorphosed into some improbably efficient automaton. I have worked so hard. At least some good has come of it.'

'Yes.'

She noticed him glance at his watch. 'Well, I must be away, Ruth-o. So listen, you know where I am if you need me. Will you be all right?'

'Yes, Giles. I shall be all right. Of course.'

She no longer waited for him in the hotel but went walking. Instead of going north or west where she might have come to fields and hills she chose the dusty streets of the city, where dirt chased about her ankles in the chill wind which blew all through those weeks. One day she found lodgings in a tall dark villa in Islington. It was arranged between herself and the landlady, a tiny, frightened woman, who, Ruth judged, would not trouble herself with her tenant's affairs, that Ruth would take a room from 1st March.

As she had expected, Giles came back one more time. He was pacing the street outside her hotel and was irritated with her for not being there.

'I had so little time to spare,' he exclaimed, 'and now it is all gone. I have to be back for dinner. We are seeing Alicia's parents.'

'Nevertheless, I must speak to you, Giles, I have something to tell you.'

He softened. 'And I you. Let's not go inside. We'll walk.'

Her feet ached and she was very hungry after her day in the city but she allowed him to take her hand. Overhead, across the yellow street lamp, a mist of drizzle danced.

'Well. We have done it. We are all packed. All we have to do is endure the goodbyes. That is why I am here now. I wanted our farewell to be private, although you can come to the ship if you like. Mother would like to see you.'

'I don't think so, Giles.'

'And we have an added complication. I must tell you. You are almost the first to know. I don't know how you'll feel, but I want you to be glad in the end. Alicia is expecting a child. Poor love, she's dreading the passage more than ever and is afraid of giving birth in India, but from what I gather it's as civilized there as anywhere. I'm amazed and terrified, needless to say, and a bit inclined to laugh. Giles Mayrick a father. Of course it's what I'd hoped, but not so soon.'

Ruth made no reply except to remove her hand from his arm. He halted and put his hands on her shoulders. 'Be pleased for me, Ruth-o. I want you to be pleased. I thought it best to tell you, was I right to tell you?'

'Oh yes, of course.'

After a moment she asked to be taken back to the hotel.

His attempt at cheerfulness was quite crushed. 'I understand how you must feel. I'm sorry. I know it's rough for you.'

Still she said nothing and even he was quietened by the finality of those few minutes and perhaps, a little, of what he had done to her.

'I'll write,' he assured her as they turned into her street.

She actually smiled. 'No. You won't write. Don't make promises you can't keep, Giles. I know you. In a few weeks I shall be dropped from your consciousness.'

'No. No.'

'Trust me, Giles, I know.'

He was pleased at what he interpreted as an attempt at levity. 'No, in this, wise woman, you shall be proved wrong.'

Under the high wall of the hotel he dragged her into deeper shadow and kissed her. 'I never want to forget you, or the smell of you, or the way you kiss me.'

For a moment she clasped the damp fabric of his sleeve but then felt him withdraw.

'Goodbye, Ruth-o.'

'Giles. Please. Don't turn away until I am inside. Please.'

'Of course. Silly woman. I'll be the last to walk away. I'm brave. Don't worry.'

She moved from his side and stumbled up the three steps to the heavy, panelled doors, conscious that he stood watching her but that he was impatient to be gone.

# Chapter Seventeen

*Present*

The package presented to Helena by Clara contained two letters. The first was addressed *Maud Waterford, to be read by her after my death.* The second was inscribed simply *For Donaldson.*

In her letter to Maud, Ruth explained the circumstances of a brief love affair with Giles Mayrick.

> *I never told him I had a daughter. You must not think, Maud, that the father wanted nothing to do with his child. He did not know she existed. You see, he went away to India and by then his wife, Alicia, was also expecting a baby. I thought he'd hate me if he knew about our child. He would have disliked the complication of that.*
>
> *So for nine months I stayed at the boarding house, walking, reading, waiting for the baby. It seemed very little different after all to my Westwich life, except that I did not have you to keep me company. I made some friends. My landlady was very kind. She thought I was a widow. I wrote to Giles every month. He never replied. I decided that he could not have received my letters. I did not tell him about the baby.*
>
> *You see, I thought I had a choice, Maud. I thought the choice was between Giles and the baby. I thought at least if I had been free, I might have gone to India, and stayed close to him. It was not that I any longer had any illusions about him or that he loved me. It was that I had to see the thing through, do you understand? I had given myself to him and to make that whole, to make it complete as an experience, I could not simply let him cut the bond. You know me, Maud, I have to be there at the bitter end.*

*And then, a fortnight before Joanna was born, I received a letter from him. In it he said that Alicia had returned to England to have their child because she hated the Indian climate so much. He said he thought that I would like India and he might be able to find me a teaching position with a family he knew. Don't forget, Maud, he did not know about the baby.*

*Yes. He is married. I know you will think that all I did was wrong. I know the patterns of your judgements, Maud, but I also know you are kind, and that you understand what it is to be solitary. What future did I have in England? The baby's dependency, and I so lonely. No. No. I remembered The Rush House, and all those years with my mother, and I thought, no. I cannot. I cannot bear that burden again, this time with a baby.*

*Joanna was born. I brought her to you. I had not known how terrible it would be to feel her pass from my arms.*

*I had a passage booked. But already I was ill. There was something wrong after her birth.*

*I am writing this because I think I will not get better after all.*

*Giles met me from the boat. He was very shocked at my condition. I had been sick throughout the journey. How many years had I spent in The Rush House dreaming of such a boat, and me sailing away on it? He found me a room but I have seen him only once since. It has been very hot, very strange. All strange.*

*Donaldson found me, of course. Of course I sent him away.*

*Maud. I have been asked to pay and pay and pay for what I did with Giles. It seems a heavy price.*

> *Tell Joanna I did love her.*
> *Thank you, Maud.*

The curtains at the bedroom window were too thin to blot out the night sky made luminous by a full moon. Helena lay awake in the grey light, occasionally opening her eyes to stare at the now familiar furnishings. The house was so quiet that it seemed she could hear the peaceful exhalations of Clara and Nina, both deep sleepers.

There were no ghosts.

Parading through her mind were several faces. Michael, his eyes grey and tender, his smile broad and dare-devil. Ruth Styles, young and untried, standing with her hand on the gate, her skirts blowing.

Giles Mayrick.

There was a photograph of him as a boy in a family album Caroline had once shown Helena. It was a wooden and probably uncharacteristic family portrait, with Esther and Robert seated amidst their children; Esther heavy-bosomed and bedecked in the froth and frills so beloved of the Edwardians, the boys scrubbed and suited, Clara a tiny doll in ruffles and lace. Giles was the smallest boy. Of the three, he alone looked as if he were in the photograph under sufferance for his body was turned aside as if poised for flight. On his face was a cheeky, challenging grin.

So Joanna was his child. Joanna, repressed, over-anxious, respectable, carrying the weight of her past, the confusion and bewilderment of having been betrayed by both parents carefully buried beneath her polyester-clad composure. How much did she know?

Perhaps she knew all but, understanding little, could forgive nothing.

Helena now thought of her mother as a candle, its steady, luminous flame suppressed beneath a confining shade. No wonder she had been dismayed by her daughter's marriage to Michael Mayrick. Helena had attached herself to the one family who had known Ruth Styles and the scandal of her disappearance. How ironic that the self-assured, carefree Michael Mayrick should have the same blood in his veins as the cautious Joanna.

Michael, you shared Giles's recklessness, his headlong attitude to life. But I don't believe you were cruel or disloyal.

And Donaldson. The only constant. He had known all, understood all, forgiven all. Was it wishful thinking, Helena wondered, that has made me go on convincing myself that I was his grandchild all these months?

At five Helena got up, wrapped her quilt about her shoulders and went to the window to watch the light filter from beneath the horizon. Her room faced the wide flat fields between Overstrands and Westwich. As the dawn advanced the sea seemed to climb from the land in a metallic sliver.

Secrets.

The past threw long shadows. How would they ever be free? How odd it was that if Florence Lily had sent the letter to Maud, or if Esther Mayrick had been in Oxford to receive it, family history would have been jolted out of its pattern so much that Michael Mayrick and Helena would have met under very different circumstances or perhaps not at all.

And still, thought Helena, tiptoeing down the long flight of stairs to the kitchen, Overstrands floats calmly amidst its green fields, untouched by all that happened here. You would think some of the passion would register.

But the house seemed completely Clara's, self-possessed, obstinate, prosaic.

Clara was in hiding. She was at her most obtuse at breakfast, locked behind her twin shields of poor hearing and myopia, shouting pleasantries to Helena and Nina, crunching her way through three noisy pieces of toast and then announcing that her favourite radio programme was about to begin and she would listen to that in the drawing room until James arrived to collect her. Outside there was a flawless spring morning and long rectangles of sunlight fell across the faded carpet to Clara's chair. Helena switched on the fire and kissed her cheek.

'Are you sure you'll be warm enough, Clara?'

'Oh yes. I'm always comfortable in this room.'

Helena went to the long window and watched Nina, who was out on the drive riding a little bike borrowed from Myra Finny's youngest son. The drawing room at Overstrands had a sweeping view of the lawn, and beyond, the gate and the fields leading to Westwich. Had she the eyesight, Helena thought,

Clara might have seen me over there on the stile, watching Michael that afternoon when we first met. Nina scooted over the gravel on the shabby bike and seeing her mother at the window, waved.

Myra came to say goodbye to Clara. Afterwards, Helena waited for her in the hall and walked with her down the gravel drive to the lane. They stood by the open gate, not looking at each other.

'Thank you for helping with Clara,' Helena said.

'That's all right. It was a pleasure.'

'Myra. I have something for you.' Helena reached in her pocket for the tired, folded sheet of paper that she had found in Michael's rucksack. 'I wanted you to know that he always carried this with him. It was in his bag when he died.'

Myra did not take it. She looked over Helena's shoulder towards the house. 'I could not keep away from you after he died. I wanted to see Nina, what she was like. He was never unfaithful to you. I hope you know that. When he met you we were together, I mean, we had been out a few times, slept together, but I think he loved me out of pity. My husband had started to drink. I was very lonely and confused. Michael and I had known each other off and on all our lives. I always loved Michael but knew he would never want me. And then he came down for the summer to help Clara. I was miserable, he was very sympathetic, and that was it. But the day he met you I knew that was the end. He was looking away from me. In any case, I couldn't leave my husband then, with a young child. I wrote to Michael, endlessly. I knew where he taught. But he never replied, except with a Christmas card a couple of times. In the end I didn't mind that he didn't answer. It was enough that I had someone to love. And then he was killed and I saw you at the funeral. For the first time I understood why he had fallen in love with you. And there was all that I knew of your family. I saw it written in your hair and your features. Ruth Styles, Margaret Shaw. I knew why you were irresistible to Michael.'

'He should not have abandoned you so completely if you were lovers. That was very cruel.'

'Michael wasn't cruel. It isn't in his nature to be cruel. I know the Mayricks, you see, all of them. I remember Michael's father, Simon, and Clara's other nephews. They were the same. They dip into life and take deep swallows, but they don't connect one action with another, they don't see that what they do may have repercussions on what may come after. So once he had met you, the door simply closed on me for Michael. It would not occur to him that I would go on and on waiting for a sign from him.'

'Yes. Yes. I understand.' They stood for a moment with a light, heady sea-breeze ruffling the new leaves in the hedgerow. 'Myra. Please understand why I am giving you back this letter. I think when someone has died so suddenly and so young, you have to be pleased for any lovely thing that has happened to them.'

James Mayrick arrived an hour later.

My God, Helena thought, watching James unfold his long, elegantly clad legs from his expensive car. This is my mother's half-brother. Yes. Yes, there was a likeness. In the jaw perhaps, and the angle of the head. But Joanna lacked the lazy, self-confident Mayrick smile.

At what price your respectability, James, son of Giles Mayrick? Helena asked silently as he trod from hall to car with Clara's little suitcases. No wonder you regard me with mistrust and unease if you have the slightest inkling of the truth. No wonder you were appalled by my marriage to Michael. But don't worry. I won't explode my grenade into your smug world. I will do as Donaldson would have wished and keep quiet.

At lunch-time Nina said: 'I like Aunty Clara, but it is nice to be just you and me again. You go all sort of posh when she's around.'

Afterwards they bundled into wellingtons and outdoor clothes and set off across the fields towards Westwich.

Nina pranced ahead, excited by the prospect of her spell as shopkeeper. Helena hoped that a few customers would oblige by making purchases in the shop that afternoon.

Their pace was brisk. The hedgerows were perfumed by the sappy scent of budding leaves, warmed by the sun. By the time they reached the lane which led past the church to Westwich Nina had a pocket bulging with treasures: a long, grubby feather, two hefty, misshapen stones and a soggy pine cone.

Helena made wordless greetings to the blunt Victorian church, snug in its graveyard well away from the encroaching sea, and to The Rush House, from which Ruth Styles must have stepped with such high hopes after her mother's funeral.

They came to the shop where Nigel's mother, Vera, was waiting gleefully for Nina who climbed with superb assurance onto the high stool and regarded Helena with dismissive detachment.

'Could I be your first customer?' Helena asked, after she'd watched Nina being swathed in a huge, striped apron.

'If you like.' Nina's glasses flashed as she surveyed her new kingdom and smiled delightedly at Vera, who was showing her the contents of a set of drawers behind the counter.

'Well, perhaps I'll buy something when I come back in an hour's time,' Helena said. 'I shan't be long, Nina.' But Nina didn't hear, and taking a last look at her daughter's tumbled hair and absorbed little features, Helena departed.

She walked down to the beach and sat on the pebbles, watching the sea make benign, regular little surges onto the shore. Gulls floated abreast of the waves, swaying up and down with placid ease as they made a calm survey of their domain. She tilted her face to the afternoon sun and thought of how almost a year ago she was here, seething with resentment and grief, beside Caroline Mayrick. Time, on the whole, is kind, she thought.

After a while she took the cliff path leading past the ruins of an old friary to where the church had once stood. The turf underfoot was damp and springy. To her left the sea was losing its brilliance. She climbed on and on.

There was a man with a camera on the path ahead of her, his tall frame silhouetted by an intense blue sky. Helena's pace did not alter, though her breath caught in her throat.

'Just the person I need,' he said.

'Oh yes?'

'I want to take your photograph. For the book. You know. Where your grandmother once posed for Donaldson's picture.'

'Thank you very much but I can't oblige. The path where Ruth stood with Maud is now deep under the sea.'

'All right. Here will do.'

'It won't be very interesting. Just me and a lot of sky. Donaldson had the ruined church to give drama.'

'I can make even the least promising subject fascinating. It's why I'm paid such extortionate fees.'

She had another objection. 'I don't want to be like Ruth. I'm superstitious. I don't want to turn out as she did.'

'Why, what was the matter with Ruth?'

'She could never look forwards, or about her. It seems to me that she carried the past with her like a ball and chain. She could not shake free.'

'Can any of us?'

'Perhaps not. But we can learn. We can try. Oh, I've felt today as if I might be able to breathe clean, fresh air at last.'

He held the camera to his eye. 'I think you need have no fear of looking like Ruth. Especially if you glare at me head-on as you're doing now with one eye shut, arms crossed and your mouth screwed up.'

She obliged him by laughing into the lens.

They began to walk back towards Westwich. 'Why have you come?' she asked.

'Oh, you know, for the sake of the book. To find out what it's like here. I wanted to discover why Donaldson was so keen.'

'I see.'

Again he gave her the smile that made her heart turn over. It was his usual, cheeky grin, matching so well his gelled shock of hair and impish features, but in his eyes was a clear, boyish tenderness which made her so afraid of shattering his present joy.

She told him about Ruth's love affair and death in India, and took from her pocket the letter to Donaldson.

They had reached the gate which led to the friary. He leant against its old wooden bars to read.

*Donaldson.*

*You were here. You thought I was too weak and did not know you, or was not aware that you sat for an hour by my bed. You went away. I knew you were here. You could not save me, Donaldson.*

*What is this trick you have of finding me out? This time you were too slow. This time when I really wanted you to find me, you left it too late.*

*What I want to say, Donaldson, is that I wish with all my heart the child had been yours. I told you once that I loved you. I do. When I lay with you it was like becoming my true self. I spent a lifetime pushing you away because you were too familiar and too loving. I wanted excitement and novelty and the pain of passion. I thought I knew you so well, but only now do I understand that I would have found all I wanted with you.*

*With him at Overstrands I realized. You see, he understood nothing about me. And then I knew what I had lost. And that I could never let you, who are all goodness, reach me again, after the terrible things I had done.*

*Oh Donaldson, this longing I have to walk with you one last time by the sea at Westwich will be the death of me.*

Nicholas turned to rest his elbows on the gate. 'Bitch,' he said.

'Why? Nicholas, she was dying.'

'That's as may be. But what a lot of grief to load onto his shoulders.'

Helena, who had found the letter tragically sad, was hurt by his reaction. 'I thought you'd be interested. I thought you'd be pleased to be proved right.' She took the sheet of paper from him, folded it protectively and tucked it back in her pocket. But as she did so she remembered the other letter she had carried with her like a gaping wound since Michael's death. 'You knew, didn't you, about Donaldson not being my grandfather? I've worked it all out. You knew, because there's nothing of him in me, is there? And because in his self-portrait in the gallery he looks so solitary.'

When she began to retrace her steps along the path towards Westwich and Nina, he did not follow. She felt the gap between them widening, like a taut elastic band. The conflicting emotions of pride and longing tussled within her.

Turning back, she saw that he was still leaning on the gate. His head was bent and too shadowed for her to see his face.

'Do you know what I'd like?' she shouted.

He did not move. 'What?'

'I'd like to take your photograph. Can I borrow your camera?'

'No. Oh no.'

'Go on, I won't hurt it. You set it up for me and I'll press the button.' She was advancing towards him.

'No. I never have my photograph taken.'

She started to laugh. 'Why ever not?'

He held the gate now as if poised for flight. He was smiling but still she could not see the expression in his eyes. 'You know me. I hate commitment. Can't stand it. A photograph is a commitment. You can't escape the fact you were there, once you're in a photograph. I should know. I've spent my life pinning people onto film.'

'Oh my goodness. All I want is a little snap-shot. Please.' Her tone was light-hearted but she was beginning to panic. The photograph had taken on a profound significance. They stood confronting each other, she with her face to the long, orange rays of the sun. But she could detect a gleam returning to his eyes, a softening of his mouth.

He reached out, put his hand on her arm and pushed her back a metre or so almost to the edge of the cliff. 'Stand there.'

Heaving the gate ajar he perched the camera on the rough post, peered through it at her, pressed a button and pranced back to her side.

'Now then, Mrs Mayrick.'

He was in the act of kneeling and kissing her hand when the little click came. She was laughing down at the top of his head.

After the photograph had been taken there was a sudden moment of stillness. Helena turned her head back to the sea, though her hand remained in his. The evening sky was draining light from the water, which was now a darkly glimmering sheet.

'You're right about Ruth. She was a cruel woman, as well as a sad one,' she said quietly.

'No more than most.'

'No, our family has a cruel streak. I see that. We try to mould and reshape till the world is how we think we want it. And then, if it won't change, and maybe if it does, we begin to despise it. I think that's how Ruth was with Donaldson. And I'm a bit like that.'

He used her hand as a lever to pull himself to his feet and stood so close to her that her shoulder was pressed to his upper arm.

'Your problem, one of many,' he told her, half teasing, 'is that you dislike yourself so.'

'Michael used to say that. And I know it is an excuse for not fully participating, being too fearful of inflicting damage. Whereas you, you get out of it all by looking on and giving the odd kick, is that right?'

'Maybe.'

'But it isn't all bad. People have been so kind since Michael's death. At first I mistrusted their kindness and thought it put me too much in their debt. But I think that for Donaldson the giving of love was the purpose of his life, and his generosity glowed through everything he did, like you said. I should like to be more generous, more unconditional.'

'Unconditional love. A tall order.'

She had, for a moment, forgotten who he was and why he was there. But a consciousness of his proximity and their solitude on the quiet cliff-top returned to her.

The sea made its slow shushing fall against the shore and the air was stirred by the call of a late bird. She felt his fingers tighten a little around hers as they walked to the gate. He fastened the latch with his free hand and lifted the camera round his neck.

They set off towards the village.

'You'll have to buy something in the shop,' she told him, 'or Nina will be mortified.'

'What do they stock?'

'Oh, I don't know. Most things. Nothing useful.'

He smiled at her and then looked ahead to the beach and the village.

'I'll buy a postcard then, shall I? For the record.'

# FOOTSTEPS

*Reading Group Notes*

# IN BRIEF

**Present**

It began like any other day for Helena, apart from the letter that arrived in the morning; a rather abrupt request to work on a book about her grandfather, Donaldson, the photographer. She tossed the letter aside, aware that if she accepted the commission it would cause trouble in the family. Later she took her daughter, Nina, swimming. Her husband, Michael, a schoolteacher, was in Snowdonia with a group of pupils – he was expected back the next day. Afterwards Helena was to wonder why she had felt no jolt, no premonition, at the moment of his accident.

One of Michael's pupils had slipped whilst fooling about on the mountain. Michael had rescued him, but fallen himself. He was dead when they reached him. Later, the police returned Michael's rucksack. When she could bear to sort through it, Helena discovered, along with his clothes and scuffed boots, a letter from another woman – a love letter.

Michael's mother asked Helena if she'd like to bring Nina to the seaside at Westwich for a holiday. For Helena, Westwich was full of memories; it was

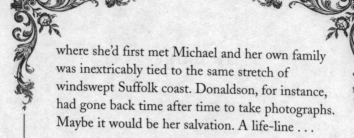

where she'd first met Michael and her own family
was inextricably tied to the same stretch of
windswept Suffolk coast. Donaldson, for instance,
had gone back time after time to take photographs.
Maybe it would be her salvation. A life-line . . .


**Past**


Aunt Maud dragged Ruth out on a stormy day to
be the foreground interest in one of the young
Donaldson's photographs. After much standing
about in bad weather, Maud invited Donaldson to
tea, and then she and Ruth hurried on ahead, as he
gathered up his heavy plate camera and tripod and
struggled after them.

Ruth's brother, Harry, soon escaped Westwich
and went back to school leaving Ruth to care for
her mother, Julia, who suffered from a nervous condition and spent more and more time in bed. In the
long periods while her mother rested, Ruth was left
to wander the coast alone. Sometimes she met
Donaldson, who seemed to lie in wait. It soon
became clear that he had fallen in love with her –
but how did she feel about him?

**Present**

Helena's mother, Joanna, shut up like a clam. At first she would tell Helena nothing about Donaldson, and even suggested that the box of family papers might have been destroyed. But Helena was drawn to the task of finding out more about him. As Helena researched the life of Donaldson, she visited the same stretch of coastline that her grandmother Ruth had haunted years before. The lives of the two women are separated by decades, and yet both are inextricably tied to their environment, and to their tragic family history.

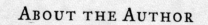

# ABOUT THE AUTHOR

Katharine McMahon was born in north-west London, and studied English and Drama at Bristol University. She wrote her first novel in a gap year, before spending two years teaching. Finding teaching incompatible with writing, she then began a balancing act of writing, part-time jobs and bringing up her children.

As well as writing six novels, she has taught writing skills with the Royal Literary Fund at the universities of Hertfordshire and Warwick, performed with the Abbey Theatre in St Albans, and serves as a magistrate.

She lives in Hertfordshire.

# THE STORY BEHIND *FOOTSTEPS*

*Katharine McMahon, April 2008*

This book began with a postcard, bought in Dunwich Museum – Dunwich being a tiny village on the Suffolk coast. Dunwich's history is a haunting one: it was once a major port but is now a handful of cottages, the rest of the town having been eaten away by the sea; churches, houses, civic buildings, shops, all gone. The church depicted in the photograph (taken 1903) has now completely disappeared but there are stories of bones from the old graveyard dropping out of the eroding cliff. But what intrigued me most about the postcard were the two women in the foreground who in the novel become Ruth Styles and Maud Waterford.

I'm fascinated by photographs, although I rarely take pictures myself for the very reason that I find them so compelling – I think the act of taking a photograph distorts the moment, makes it self-conscious. *Footsteps* has a lot of photographs in it and at least one of the photographers, Nick Broadbent, is aware of the bitter irony of taking pictures, especially of suffering, whilst not being able to intervene in any other way. But of course photographs are also mysterious; they are a snapshot of a long-lost moment and open to misinterpretation. They can be unbearably poignant – there's a photo of Michael a few minutes before he fell to his death.

Although this combination of disappearing landscapes and photography gave me the seeds of a novel, what I really wanted to write about was family history, to test how much we all have a foot in the past. *Footsteps* is about women in particular for whom the past is a burden. They can't break free of it. But what strikes me most strongly on re-reading the book is how much it is also about women who are afraid of the opportunities that are open to them. They use the past as an excuse not to engage fully with the present. The point is that Ruth doesn't need to stay in Westwich with her mother, she chooses to sacrifice herself because the alternative is too frightening. At school she had been apprehensive 'not because she had been unable to flourish in such an environment, but because she succeeded too well. So much was expected of her.' And in the book the alternative to domesticity does often prove very dangerous: people fall off mountains or get killed in battle or fall in love unexpectedly and sometimes with the wrong person. But on the other hand, indoors is unsafe too. Julia can't escape the storms that batter her bedroom, Ruth can't evade the men who come calling, and houses are full of secrets.

In some ways it was unnerving to re-read this book some time after writing it as so much has changed. In *Footsteps* there's not a mention of mobile phones, Nina draws on perforated computer paper and plays cassettes in the car. Nature is unpredictable and sometimes dangerous but there's no mention of global warming. And yet *Footsteps* has themes that I have since returned to again and again, not least, women confined by their sex and historical context. Above all, I have gone on writing about love and death, in all their many shades, because those two inescapable facets of being human are eternal and never lose their fascination.

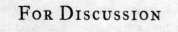

# FOR DISCUSSION

- 'Today there were little smooth shinings of sand left by the retreating tide, kinder to the feet than the pebbles. Ruth ran along these and turned to see that her footprints had disappeared instantly. For some reason this intensified her despair and she began to sob.' Why is the novel called *Footsteps*?

- 'And yet she was also conscious that his perfect absorption in his task, the self-possession which had at once attracted her, had been marred by her arrival.' What does this tell us about Helena and Michael's relationship?

- 'I think it is hard to be a girl in a family of boys.' Esther feels this, but would she still feel it today?

- Why is erosion so important in the novel?

- Ruth is pulled 'back to the hypnotic, insistent surge of the sea'. Why does this represent the wrong direction for Ruth?

- 'Although Joanna could not bear a display of emotion in her own family, she relished the discussion of trouble in other people's domestic worlds. Perhaps this also explained her love of television soaps. Through their characters she could explore vicariously passions which were never given expression in her own life.' Is this why most people like soaps, do you think?

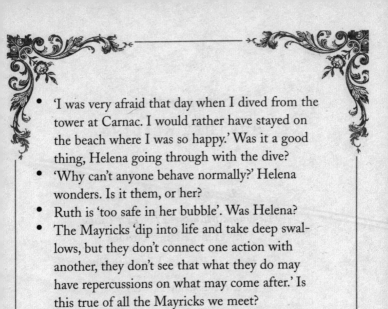

- 'I was very afraid that day when I dived from the tower at Carnac. I would rather have stayed on the beach where I was so happy.' Was it a good thing, Helena going through with the dive?
- 'Why can't anyone behave normally?' Helena wonders. Is it them, or her?
- Ruth is 'too safe in her bubble'. Was Helena?
- The Mayricks 'dip into life and take deep swallows, but they don't connect one action with another, they don't see that what they do may have repercussions on what may come after.' Is this true of all the Mayricks we meet?
- Ruth 'could never look forwards, or about her. It seems to me that she carried her past with her like a ball and chain. She could not shake free.' Why? And does Helena? Can Helena be free?
- Did Giles know Ruth at all?
- 'A photograph is a commitment.' Why is photography so important in the novel?

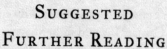

# Suggested
# Further Reading

*Atonement* Ian McEwan

*Le Grand Meaulnes (The Lost Estate)*
by Henri Alain-Fournier

*The House in Paris* by Elizabeth Bowen

*Howards End* by E. M. Forster

*Sepulchre* by Kate Mosse

*The Sea, The Sea* by Iris Murdoch

*The Thirteenth Tale* by Diane Setterfield

*Touching the Void* by Joe Simpson